'Here's a great excuse to put your feet up and escape into a world which celebrates Portsmouth's past . . . It's really well worth the read.' *Portsmouth News*

'A rich first novel conjuring up a vivid and realistic portrait of Portsmouth in the final years and aftermath of the great war . . . A pulsating and heart-warming saga peopled with human and compelling characters and with convincing dialogue.' *Yorkshire Post*

'Julia Bryant creates a vivid picture of Portsmouth in the final years and aftermath of the "Great" War of 1914–1918, weaving it into a story that pulses with the warm blood of humanity.' *Rhona Martin*

'A readable saga with a whiff of history.' *Manchester Evening News*

'Julia Bryant has clearly found her voice. She writes with growing confidence and maintains rhythm and pace throughout.' *Historical Novel Society*

'A family saga full of rich characters and intertwining stories . . . well written, real dialogue and real people.' *Huddersfield Daily Examiner*

'Packed with interesting people living what might appear to be mundane lives, but of course they are not. We get an insight into the lives of the families of sailors, their good and bad fortune, their ups and downs. Decent people who we want to win through.' *Betty Burton*

By the same author in Coronet

Waiting for the Tide
Written on the Tide
Borne on the Tide

About the author

Julia Bryant was born in Portsmouth: her stepfather and husband both served in the Navy. She trained as a nurse, then after her three children grew up earned an honours BA in English and history. She and her husband now live in Portsmouth once more.

JULIA BRYANT

The Restless Tide

CORONET BOOKS
Hodder & Stoughton

Copyright © 2002 by Julia Bryant

First published in Great Britain in 2002 by Hodder and Stoughton
First published in paperback in Great Britain in 2003
by Hodder and Stoughton
A division of Hodder Headline
A Coronet paperback

The right of Julia Bryant to be identified as the Author of the Work has been
asserted by her in accordance with the Copyright, Designs and Patents Act 1988.

2

A CIP catalogue record for this title is available from the British Library

ISBN 978-0-340-81960-9

Typeset in Plantin Light by Palimpsest Book Production Limited,
Polmont, Stirlingshire

Printed and bound in Great Britain by
Clays Ltd, St Ives plc

Hodder and Stoughton
A division of Hodder Headline
338 Euston Road
London NW1 3BH

For Sean and Barbara
my son and daughter-in-law
with much love

ACKNOWLEDGEMENTS

I should like to thank all the following people for their help.

Guests at Cakes and Tea in Portsea:
Mrs Baker, Mrs Bell, Mrs Benfield, Mrs Bevis, Mr Bing, Mr Bridle, Mr Cluett, Mr Coombes, Mr Cramer, Mrs Forder, Mrs Gamble, Mrs Goodrich, Mrs Greenwood, Mr Greer, Mrs Haines, Mr Hankers, J Hartley, Mrs Hill, Mr Knight, Mrs Mason, Mr Newton, Mr Norman, Mr Perratt, Mrs Pitman, Mr Spurrier, Mrs Smythe, Mr Stockley, Mr Tobin, Mrs Towler, Mrs Townsend, Mr Wain, Mrs and Mrs Warren, Mr Watts, Mr J White, Mr P White and Mr Young

Dancing teacher: Miss Jean Hapgood

The staff of Portsmouth Libraries and the Gosport Library especially Leila and Kieron

Submariners and Families: Molly Bastable, Gladys Dawes, Jimmy and Beryl Hamlyn, Les Hanks, Taff Harper Richard Jordan, Maurice Perrat, George Pickup, John O'Sullivan, and Maurice Walsh

Margarert Bidmead Librarian from the Royal Naval Submarine Museum.

Captain Steve White of the Salvation Army, Simon Harmer, Miss Mainstone and Mrs Florrie Padgham.

I

⚓

The ferry crossed the harbour from Portsmouth to Gosport under a grey November sky. On the bow seat, in the open, a group of women clutched their children to them, their eyes blurred with tears. Among the sailors and dockyard mateys crowding the deck, the mood was sombre.

As the boat swung past Haslar Creek, nineteen-year-old Mary Vine stared across the water at her rivals crouching at their moorings. Blunt grey shapes with numbers painted on them. Furthest away was the *L75*, Matthew's submarine.

Behind her one of the mateys said, 'Terrible about that lost submarine. Not much chance of getting those matelots out alive.'

'Bloke next door's on board, his wife's just had a baby,' said another. 'That nipper won't never see his dad, now.'

Mary swallowed down their words like gristly meat. No, she would not let them frighten her. This was their day, hers and Matthew's. The fourteenth of November 1925, a date they'd remember forever. Over in Gosport a new life awaited her. No longer the snot-nosed nipper from Lemon Street, she would become Mrs Matthew Miller.

Turning from the sea she looked at the crying women then snapped her eyes shut. Drowned sailors had no place in the mind of a girl that was getting engaged.

A crewman flung the rope to his oppo on the Gosport jetty and the passengers surged off the ferry. Dodging the mateys' bicycles Mary thundered up the pontoon past the paper seller and his grim placard.

'*Little hope for the crew of the M1 submarine.*'

There in the Ferry Gardens was Matthew, grinning from ear to ear. Ooh! She could never get enough of that gladness. Mary cannoned into him, burying her face in his coat, sniffing the familiar diesel fumes that clung to his clothes. He was alive and she could touch him.

'Hello, love,' he said, bending to kiss her, his hands icy against her face. 'You're shaking. We best get you in out of the cold.'

'Hello yourself,' she said grinning up at him.

'Let's go and get some Bovril before we're perished.'

The windows in the café were all steamed up and the air ponged of hot lard and gravy. Matthew held out the chair for her as if they were in a swanky restaurant and took off his cap. 'Like some bread with it?' he asked.

Mary nodded. While he was at the counter she fiddled with the ribbon on his cap. The golden letters spelled out 'HM Submarine L75'. Everything conspired to remind her of what she was trying to forget. Impatiently she drummed her fingers on the table, wanting him to hurry up. Then he turned and grinned at her. She smiled back at her tall red-haired fiancé. Dad called him the racing snake. Nobody thought him handsome but he made her so happy. They were laughing all the time. It was a wonder that he had taken to her at all – she was so vinegar-tongued and hard to like. Of course, getting to know one another by letter had helped. By the time they were face to face she felt safe with him. Matthew could always coax her out from behind her fortress. For the first time in her life she felt loved.

'Here, wrap your hands round the mug, that'll warm you through,' he said, setting the steaming Bovril in front of her.

'Ooh,' he teased, looking at her fingernails, 'still got your long talons. Just like a fashion plate.'

'All the better to scratch you with,' she said, making claw marks on his sleeve. Love had stopped her biting her nails.

'What's the programme? I'm sure you've got today mapped out to the second.'

'Get the ring first, then something to eat and back over to the market to cash up and store away.'

He grinned at her. 'Forgot you were a business lady, proper old money-bags. Couldn't your dad pack up for you?'

Mary laughed. 'He's got no idea of trade. Gives the stuff away if he takes a liking to someone. Besides, his hands ain't as quick as they used to be, before the fire.' The stall had been a godsend to the family after Dad lost his job. Mary had worked with Nelly Moyes since she was sixteen, and, good as her word, the old woman had left the stall to her when she died. It was in Dad's name until she was twenty-one. The year 1927 would be an important one: marriage, stall-holding and moving to Gosport. Mary sighed – only fourteen months to go.

'I was glad to get out of *Dolphin*,' Matthew said, as he handed her the plate of bread. 'Those poor blokes on the *M1*. No one expects them to make it. Knew some of them, I did; decent lads with families. When I left there was wives and mothers at the gate – really brought it home to you.'

HMS *Dolphin*, the submarine base, was housed in Fort Blockhouse, a great slab of a building on the Gosport side of the harbour. Would she be waiting at the gate for news, one day? she wondered. She swallowed down another gristly lump of fear. 'Don't want to know about the *M1*,' she snapped. Anyone but Matthew would have called her a heartless bitch.

He held her hands between his. 'Being an ostrich won't make it go away, love,' he said.

'This is our day and nothing's going to spoil it,' she insisted.

'I just want you to know what you're getting into, marrying a submariner. We don't get the extra money for fun. Being in boats is a risky business.'

'Thinking about it don't make them any safer,' she said. 'All the women in Portsea was prayin' their heads off, after Jutland in 1916, but it didn't make no difference. Blokes still got drowned. We were just kids out playing in the street when the telegram came about Dad being killed. Mum locked herself in the lavatory and screamed her head off. The twins and me was wetting ourselfs with fright. Even when he came back safe she couldn't believe it.' Mary stared at the tablecloth. It was never the same after Jutland. There was Ma going mental and Dad as much help as a paper bucket. All the time, she had been trying to keep her little brother, Blyth, and the twins together and out of the workhouse. She grabbed Matthew's hands, wanting to impress on him the importance of her words. 'You gotta live for today, for what you can see and touch this minute. Tomorrow's anyone's guess.'

He kissed her fingers. 'Calm down, love, no need to lose your rag. It's just you and me today. *Dolphin* can go hang till Sunday. I've been looking forward to this for weeks.'

'What? The Bovril?'

Matthew laughed and so did she. 'No, you daft ha'p'orth! Getting engaged.'

Later, they walked up the High Street and stared into the window of Dukes, Jewellers and Watchmakers. On the middle shelf was a tray of engagement rings. Her eyes were drawn to one with a blue stone surrounded by a circle of diamond chippings. The ticket attached to it said five guineas. That would be a whole month of Matthew's pay. Trust her to like the dearest. Trouble was that the one for two pounds looked so much meaner than the one she wanted. There was a notice saying that hire purchase terms could be arranged. Right at the bottom of the window, in the corner, was another collection of rings advertised as second-hand. No! She wouldn't entertain them. All her life had been hand-me-down clothes, broken biscuits, stale bread. Mrs Matthew Miller's engagement ring was going to be new and sparkling: she would flaunt it to the neighbours in Lemon Street. Them that had called her a guttersnipe would have to sit up and take notice.

'What's your fancy?' asked Matthew. 'Bound to be others inside.'

'I've seen one, but . . .'

'You have what you like, love,' he said, 'you only get one engagement ring in a lifetime. What's the damage?'

'Five guineas, but they do terms. So much down and half a crown a week.' Mary watched his face for any sign of doubt. The ring was so lovely and nothing else in the window quite came up to its shiny splendour.

'Won't be able to have such a posh dinner as I'd planned, but that won't matter so long as you have what you want.'

'Why can't you put so much down and pay it off like they say?'

'I pay as I go, Mary. Can't abide debt.'

'But Matthew . . .'

'We'll have the ring today and a slap-up meal later on, that way we parcel out the treats.'

Mary almost bit her nails. She wanted the lot: the ring, the meal and Matthew holding her tight. For a second or two she thought of going into a sulk but knew that he wouldn't wear it. If she tried that on he'd just walk away. She wasn't used to giving in.

'Let's go in and try it on,' he said. 'It's arctic out here. Come on, love.'

He'd calmed down. She swallowed with relief. Only when he was mad with her did he call her Mary.

The bell on the door tinkled. There was a carpet on the floor and the counter had a glass top with all the jewellery set out on little velvet trays. Mary was used to seeing rings heaped together on a stall in the market or in the pawnbroker's window. Standing in the shop was like being in church.

A man in a black jacket and striped trousers came out from a curtain behind the counter. He had a moustache like a Shredded Wheat biscuit and peered at them through the thick lenses of his glasses. 'Madam, Sir, how may I be of assistance?' he said.

'We are getting engaged and my fiancée would like to try on a ring from the window, please.'

'Certainly, Sir, I won't be a moment. I need to fetch the window key.'

Mary giggled. 'Fiancée,' she whispered, 'makes me sound like Cinderella.'

He laughed. 'Sit down on that chair over there. You can pretend it's a throne.'

'OK, Prince Charming,' she said.

'Which particular ring is it, Madam?' The little man had the doors open and was poised to lift out whichever tray she pointed to.

'It's the tray on the middle shelf. The blue stone with the diamond cluster,' said Mary, springing off the chair. Oh, she had never wanted anything so much in her life.

'Ah, yes! The sapphire.' The tray was set on the counter and the jeweller placed the ring on a little satin mat with 'Duke and Son' written on it in gold letters. He had starched cuffs, gold links, and nails that looked as if they'd been polished. Deftly he slid the ticket from the ring and stood waiting like a courtier.

'I want you to put it on for me,' she whispered.

Matthew blushed. 'I've got engine oil under my fingers,' he said.

'Think nothing of it, young man, honest toil, honest toil.'

Old Shredded Wheat looked down, discreetly, at the tray of jewellery.

She held out her hand and Matthew picked up the ring and slid it on her finger. Mary gasped. 'It fits perfect. It's so beautiful.' She wanted to cry.

'Are you sure that's the one? You're certain?'

She nodded, unable to speak.

'Five guineas, Sir, if you please. I will get the box for it.' The little man turned his back and busied himself at a row of wooden drawers.

'Happy?' whispered Matthew.

She stood on tiptoe and kissed him quickly, before the little man turn round. 'I love you,' she whispered.

'Me too,' Matthew whispered back. He took out a ten-shilling note and a fiver from the back of his pay book and placed them on the counter.

'Thank you, Sir; now, if you will kindly sign your name and address on the back of the five-pound note, I will make out a receipt for you and get your change.' He turned and smiled at Mary. 'Do you wish to wear your ring, Madam, or shall you put it in the box?'

'I wants to wear it, please,' she said, unable to tear her eyes away from her ring.

'The receipt for you, Sir, and the box for you, Madam.' He coughed. 'As it's for cash, I would like to give you a small token with my compliments.' He gave Matthew his five shillings change, and then an extra two-shilling piece.

'That's good of you, Sir,' he said. 'My fiancée and I appreciate that very much.'

'I'm so excited I needs to run,' said Mary, grabbing his arm as soon as they were in the street. 'Come on! Let's dash all the way back down to the gardens.' Laughing, they raced down the High Street past the grim placards and onto the ferry.

*   *   *

Breathless and in a daze, Matthew sat with Mary cuddled up beside him. They had done it, they were promised to each other. Never had he seen her so lit up. Her brown eyes shone and she kept squeezing his hand and looking up at him. In that red cloche hat, she reminded him of a robin: bright and brave. With the loss of his father in Gallipoli and death of his mother the year before, Mary had become his whole world. There was no one like her. He so wanted to make her happy and yet there were moments when there was no pleasing her. She could flare up one moment and the next break out in tears. Her intensity frightened him sometimes. Still, once he'd got her across the water and away from her rackety family, she'd be sure to calm down.

The wind tugged at his collar as Matthew looked out over the harbour. Every crossing was different: the sky sometimes a glowing sunset over Gosport or a lowering grey, the sea ranging from blue to stormy pewter. On the horizon the Isle of Wight could be a distant blur or a sharply defined pattern of fields and hedges. Old Portsmouth was a jigsaw of brick pubs and stone walls fringed by shingle and shell. Guarding the entrance of the harbour like open jaws were Fort Blockhouse and the Round Tower.

Today the talk around him of the lost submarine distracted him from the view. It gnawed at him. What did civilians know of his world? A submarine crew, all volunteers, were there because they had chosen the life, and were trained to deal with danger. The officers were mostly high calibre men who could respond to any emergency. It was early days yet for the lost *M1*, and there was always a chance.

Matthew liked the snugness of submarines, and the sense of family among the crew. Although shy by nature, he had become used to the coarse humour among the men and began to retaliate in kind. He loved being at sea with the noise of the engines throbbing in his ears and the familiar fug of diesel fumes, mildewed bread and boiled cabbage. It was better still when they dived and the big electric motors took over with their low hum accompanied by the plop, plop of the propellers driving the submarine forward. He would stand on watch checking the dials in the control room, in the gloom of the low-wattage bulbs. As his knowledge of mechanics increased so did his confidence. He would be twenty-two soon and was ambitious to become a Leading Hand.

Of course, there were bad times too: the squalor of living and sleeping, day in day out, in the same clothes, lack of sleep, stale food and stale monotonous jokes. After too many hours submerged your head ached and your brain got fogged. Your mouth felt as if it was full of mud. Coming up and opening the hatch, you'd be drunk on the sweetness of the air and the relief of being back on the surface.

They had crossed to Portsmouth and were walking up the jetty hand in hand when Matthew felt a tap on his shoulder.

'Dusty, got cloth ears, 'ave ya?'

Startled, Matthew turned to see his old shipmate, Mary's elder brother, arm in arm with his wife, Dora.

'Hello, Harry, where you off to?' he said, shaking him by the hand.

'Upstairs, in Driver's Café, to have a slap-up tea. We're celebrating.' He turned to Mary and kissed her on the cheek. 'Hello, our kid. What you bin up to? Thought you'd be down the market with Dad flogging the toys and making your fortune.'

Mary grinned from ear to ear. 'We just got engaged. Want to look at me ring?'

'Blimey! You Rockefeller or sommink, Dusty?' Harry laughed. 'Here, Dora, look at our Mary's ring. Got herself engaged she has.'

'What's your good news, then?' Matthew asked, while the girls pored over the ring.

Harry grinned. 'We found ourselves a place to rent. We'll be on our own.'

'No more kowtowing to my mum and dad,' laughed Dora. She looked questioningly at Mary. 'Off to Driver's we are, for a slap-up dinner. Want to come with us and make it a double celebration?'

Mary hesitated. At first she had been furiously jealous of her brother's girl, now she was wary. Everyone loved Dora. It was that sweetness that got on Mary's nerves and showed up her own mocking nature. But today, she grinned up at her fiancé. 'What ya think? Haven't never been upstairs in Driver's.'

Matthew swallowed. He had hoped to have Mary all to himself. Getting engaged was a milestone in a couple's life, there was so much to talk about and decide together. He had wanted to take her for tea to a really nice place like Handley's where there'd be bone china cups and cakes on a little stand, even linen serviettes. Driver's was all right but it wasn't what he would have chosen. He tried to think of an excuse, but Mary squeezed his hand. 'Yes, of course we'll come,' he heard himself saying. When she was all lit up like that, he could refuse her nothing, and Harry was a good bloke, always one for a laugh. He watched the girls chatting away. Once we're married we'll be in Gosport and Harry and all the rest of the Vines will be safely on the other side of the water. We shall be the new Miller family answerable only to ourselves.

Mary walked hand in hand with Matthew up from the ferry and across the bridge. She relished the thought that only she called him by his proper name. Every Miller in the navy was called Dusty. A Saturday crowd of sailors poured out of the dockyard gates, ready to invade the pubs and eating places along The Hard. Mary was skipping with excitement. Outside the café she said, 'I used to go downstairs, in here, for a bit of bread-pudding when we'd been slithering about the harbour, mud larking. Afterwards we'd share out our takings, what people had thrown us from the bridge.'

'Bet you were a fierce little nipper,' he said, grinning at her.

Mary laughed. 'I punched this boy once so hard I made his nose bleed.'

'Better keep on the right side of you then.'

'I'd need a bloomin' great ladder to reach your snitch,' she giggled. She turned round to see if Harry and Dora were catching them up – fancy having a place of their own. She felt a surge of envy. Still, she mustn't spoil their joy. Her brother was grinning like a lunatic and Dora looked ever so pretty.

As they walked up the stairs in Driver's Café she felt relieved. The thought of Handley's, with its thick carpets, snooty waitresses and posh women with plummy voices had seemed more an ordeal than a treat. Of course, growing up in a posh house Matthew knew how the toffs carried on. Although Mary had been a scullery maid once, in Lancaster Terrace, for a naval officer's family, she'd hardly got a sniff of the dining room. All her time was spent at the big brown sink. Every bloomin' crack and cranny of it was burned into her memory. For a time she had tried to get Dad and the family to lay the table properly, and use a cloth. Her enthusiasm soon fizzled out when she was left to do the extra washing up and ironing. Half the time at home they spread newspaper on the table and it was everyone for themselves – the first in, the biggest share. Oh yes, Driver's would be much more chummy and relaxed.

Matthew helped her out of her coat and hat. She shivered as his hands brushed against her shoulders, wishing they could be alone together, somewhere where he could hold her close and drown out the fear prowling in her stomach. She felt self-conscious in her new red jumper suit, until she saw the admiration in his eyes.

'Very smart', he whispered. They found a table by the window overlooking The Hard and all the bustle of sailors and passengers crossing the bridge to the ferries and trains.

'We'll wait for our friends,' he said to the girl who stood waiting for their order.

'You got enough money?' Mary whispered as the girl began clearing the plates from another table.

'I've got twenty-five shillings altogether, what with the money the chap in the jeweller's gave us. What d'you fancy?'

'Everything,' she said, reaching across the table and squeezing his hand.

'Mixed grill would be good. You get a sausage and bacon, liver and onions, fried tomatoes and a fried egg.'

'Go on, gal, fill your boots,' laughed Harry sitting down beside her.

'Plaice and chips for me,' said Dora.

Matthew and Harry settled for beef and dumplings.

'Service, please,' said Matthew and with a sniff the girl took her pencil from behind her ear and began to take down their order. 'Tea all round and bread and butter?' he asked.

Mary was so proud of him. He had such lovely manners and treated her as if she were a lady. What he saw in her she didn't know. When she was with him it was as if she were someone else – someone she could almost like. The hard, mistrustful self could be left behind in Lemon Street and the real Mary could show herself.

'Champion!' said Harry. 'All right with you, my babes?'

'I could eat a horse,' said Dora, smiling at all of them.

When the tray arrived and each of them had their tea,

Matthew said, 'Here's to a new life for the Millers and the Vines.'

Down below on the pavement a newsboy was shouting, 'All hope gone for the *M1*. Sixty-nine men lost.'

Mary looked at Matthew, willing him to smile at her. She clinked her cup against his. 'Cheers,' she said.

2

Fred Vine shivered. He was dying for a fag and a pee but something else had wakened him. What was it? Struggling into the coat he used as a bedcover he stepped barefoot across the cracked lino and twitched the curtain aside. The sky was black. He breathed on the windowpane and smudged away a patch of frost flowers illuminated by the light from the street lamp. Outside, all was still save for a paper bag bowling along the pavement. On a mattress, at his feet, nine-year-old Blyth was snoring. Before going downstairs Fred pulled the thin blanket up over his son's shoulders.

A light was glinting from under the kitchen door and there were sounds of swearing and the clash of pots. Mary was pulling the big saucepan and rusty roasting dish out of the cupboard under the sink. 'Jesus! It's only half four,' said Fred, peering at the clock. 'What you doin' clattering around in the middle of the night?'

'Lots to do,' she snapped. 'Got the stall to run, the shopping to get and you lot to organise. Christmas dinner don't arrive on a bleedin' sleigh, you know.'

Fred chewed his bottom lip. His daughter was on her high horse. They would all be in for a thin time if he didn't get her to climb down.

'We got us five, Dora, Harry and Matthew. That's eight wedged around the table. Not enough chairs and the place like a tip.'

'Why d'ya think I'm up early?' he said, giving her a coaxing smile.

'You just got up for a fag and a pee. I know you.'

'May be so, but you can't afford to turn me down. I'm cheap to run, just a cup of hot tea and a crust of toast. Come on, gal, you can still be the captain and I'll be your master-at-arms.'

'Get down the yard and stop flannelling,' she snapped, standing there in a faded cotton nightdress, her arms folded around herself, jigging up and down with the cold. 'Don't think you're slidin' off to the pub, today, 'cos I got a list of jobs for you long as yer arm.'

Fred slocked down the yard, his laces trailing. He would like to have smacked her one but he deserved her scorn. Christ, if it hadn't been for Mary and some of the neighbours they'd have fetched up in the workhouse long since. Trouble with his daughter, she didn't know how to bring out the best in people, didn't get them on her side. Refused help and then carried on top ropes when her plans didn't pan out. He smiled as he emerged later from the lavatory door and smelled the toast from the kitchen. 'Course, all this carry-on was because her chap was coming over to dinner. He seemed a nice enough lad from what he had seen of him, but he was in for a rocky ride with Mary.

'Here you are, Dad. Tea hot and strong, and the crust.'

Fred looked around the kitchen. It was the usual choas: last night's clothes flung in chairs and jammy knives on the table. Mary was sat there writing out her lists.

'Tell us the worst,' he said, biting into his toast. 'Watcha got me down for?'

'Last night's washing up, buying all the veggies and finding some chairs.'

'What's on the menu?'

'Whatever we can get, needs another quid at least to get

everythink. I'll hang around down the market tonight till about eight, see what's going cheap at the meat stall.'

'What's on for pudding? Are we getting any mince pies?'

'You just cut your cackle and finish your fag,' said Mary. 'I 'spect Granny Pragnell will give us one of her puddings. Due back today, she is.'

Fred smiled at her. She was calming down but they were not out of the woods yet. There were Faith and Mercy to deal with. 'How you gonna get the twinnies to muck in and help ya?'

'Ah!' said his daughter. 'I boxed clever, there. Know how dance mad they are? I got some taps and the nails to fix on their shoes. I swapped them with this bloke for a bag of soldiers and some comics. They don't get them till they've washed up the Christmas dinner.'

Fred laughed. 'Artful, that's what you are,' he said admiringly. 'What's Blyth in for?'

'He's your assistant and he's doing the Christmas tree.'

'Thought we couldn't run to a tree this year.'

Mary tapped her nose conspiratorially. 'Wait and see,' she said, dragging on her coat and fingerless gloves.

Fred got up from the table and hugged her before she shrugged herself out of his arms. Young Dusty would have a treasure, he thought, if he had the patience to work his way past all her prickles. If he could make her feel safe he'd be king of her castle.

'Now, d'you want me to help you set up this morning or come down later?'

'You get the kids organised with their jobs, then come up to me about eleven. Fetch us a cup of tea and a bacon buttie from the caff, then we'll see how it's going.'

Fred waved his daughter away into the morning gloom then crouched by the range with his fag and his tea. They were over the first hurdle. If the youngsters upstairs would just fall into line they might all have a halfway decent Christmas.

Blyth poked his head out from under the blanket and, just as quickly, pulled it back over his face. He'd just remembered, everything was different this year. There was no Father Christmas. His pals had told him it was all make-believe. It was really your dad what left the presents. He pretended that he knew that, all the time, but it had been a plummeting disappointment. His dad was full of stories and promises, but they were like sand castles – soon knocked over. Trouble was, Blyth could never get mad with him because Dad got as disappointed as he did when his plans fell apart. It was Mary and his big brother Harry what got the presents, stuck up for him and kept his secrets. He wished they were his mum and dad. Couldn't remember Mum, except a lot of shouting and screaming. He was glad that Harry and Dusty were coming on Christmas Day. They might play battleships or even have a kick about with him in the street.

'Here, son, I brought you up a cup of tea and sugar toast,' wheedled his dad. 'You and me gotta run the ship today and get those girls up and doing.'

In the twins' bedroom, Faith began to uncurl herself from beneath the lumpy eiderdown she shared with Mercy. There was a cold space where her sister should have been.

'Sit up! Got us some tea and bread. Catch hold while I gets back in,' demanded Mercy.

'Ooh! get yer feet off me! Like ice they are,' grumbled Faith.

'Keep still, you daft cow, you'll have the tea all over us.'

The twins sat up with the eiderdown clutched up almost to their chins. Faith warmed her hands around the jam jar full of tea while Mercy chewed her way through the thick end of a slice of bread and jam.

'D'you reckon they've bought them for us?'

'Dunno,' mumbled Mercy. 'Said last night as she'd leave a list of stuff for us to do and then she'd see about it.'

'Ooh! She don't half get me riled. Always a sprat to catch a mackerel.'

'Narky cow. That Dusty don't know what she's like. You reckon he really loves her and gets all spooney over her?'

'Hope so,' said Faith. 'Once she's married we'll be able to please ourselves. Come in when we likes and keep our own money. Next May, when we're fifteen, we'll get a pay rise from the brewery. We'll be up to ten bob each.'

'Cripes!' Faith whistled at the thought.

'What we gonna give Mary fer Christmas?' Mercy mused, hoping her twin had got something as she had spent all her money on their curling tongs.

'Got some scent what that bloke give me, at work. Ashes of Violets, don't half pong.'

They laughed.

'Dora's coming, I got her a hankie with a "D" on it,' continued Faith, 'ever so pretty and only sixpence.'

'Snap,' said Mercy, 'I got her one as well. Here, greedy guts, hand over that bread.' She licked the jam from her fingers. 'Watcha reckon they've got for us, apart from the shoes?' she asked.

'Ooh, pearl earrings, silk stockings, gallon of scent and a Rolls-Royce.'

'That was before you woke up,' yawned her sister. 'Probbly be mince pie and a new threepenny bit wrapped in paper same as last year.'

They jumped at the sound of rapping on their bedroom door.

'Right, you two,' said Fred, 'it's all hands on deck. We gotta put this place to rights before Mary gets back tonight or there'll be all hell to pay.'

'We'll fetch the shopping and give Mary a hand with the

stall,' said Mercy, sitting on the floor and buckling her shoes. 'What we gotta get?'

''Ere's the list under the spill box,' said Faith. 'There's a ten-bob note here and Mary reckons we'll need at least another one, so we'll all have to cough up. There's all the veggies and meat and bread and the tree's not bought yet.'

'Gotta have a Christmas tree,' said Blyth, licking the knife before flinging it into the sink.

Fred reached into his pockets and brought out a handful of loose change. 'What we got here?' He counted out the coins that amounted to two shillings and fivepence. 'It's a start,' he said.

'Let's go through all the pockets,' suggested Blyth. 'Yours, too,' he insisted, glaring at his sisters. 'All for one and one for all.'

'We ain't the bleedin' Musketeers,' snapped Mercy.

'You eats as much,' her brother shouted at her as she tried to slink away. 'I'll go up in your room and search your drawers,' he threatened.

'What about all them jamjars under the sink? Fetch ha'penny each from Jacksons. There are tons under there. That can be Blyth's job, washing and taking them.'

Their father rooted about in the cupboard. 'Twelve here; no, fourteen.'

'That's only seven pence,' mumbled Blyth. 'Still got to find another seven shillings.'

'What's this rattling in your handbag?' he asked, climbing on the table and holding it out of Mercy's reach.

'That's private,' she snapped, grabbing his leg.

Blyth went to open the clasp and his sisters hauled him onto the floor. He threw the bag to his father and lay there roaring at the girls.

'Blyth,' shouted Fred, 'get yourself together. I'll get the washing up done then you can start on them jars.' He looked at the clock on the mantelpiece. 'Jesus, it's gone ten. Your sister will skin us alive if we don't get down Charlotte Street in one, one, two. You gals, get yourselves in the rig of the day and I'll see what I can scrape together from upstairs. But you 'ave gotta put something in the pot.'

The twins had a whispered conference in the scullery and came back with a shilling, grudgingly given.

Fred rubbed his hands dry on his trousers then went upstairs to take off the jumper he slept in, and find some clothes. Resignedly, he pulled on a pair of odd socks and threaded his toes through the holes. After putting on a crumpled shirt he prised his tobacco tin from beneath a loose floorboard. His cache of coins amounted to half a crown. How he hated all this scratching about. Savagely he banged his shoe against the bugs stirring behind the wallpaper. Everything was stale. They were living on the leavings of others. It was Mary who kept them all going with her plotting and planning. She was the one standing in the market at all hours in all weathers. What with his burnt hands and bad chest he was a liability. Christ! He wanted a drink somewhere in the warm with a few pals, then he could hide from himself and all his failings.

'Dad, you comin' up Jackson's with us?' called Blyth. 'I just found another tanner down the side of the chair.'

Fred shivered. *Get moving, useless bastard*, he whispered to himself.

At Charlotte Street, Mary was doing a roaring trade. There were only half a dozen bags of marbles left and the fort with the tin soldiers had sold for ten bob. Her best sellers were the matchbox dolls. Little celluloid figures tucked into their snug beds complete with a pillow and blanket. She painted the top of each matchbox with different girls' names. There was even a Dora that she would give to her sister-in-law when they met on Christmas Day. She smiled to herself. Now that Matthew loved her she could afford to be generous. Yawning, she went round to the front of the stall to put out some more bundles of comics and watched Danny Sullivan sorting out his trees. Broad, blue eyed and full of nonsense, he and Mary were old sparring partners. Once she had even fancied him, but that was before ever she met Matthew. Beside him Danny was a slippery chancer as much to be relied on as the weather. Narrowing her eyes she spied the tree she wanted between two rather spindly specimens. It was small and bushy – just perfect.

'How much you want for that one over there?' she asked, trying to sound unconcerned.

'Five bob, to anyone else,' Danny teased, 'seven and a tanner to you. How much for them boxin' gloves and that football? Come on, old Shylock, give us a price.'

'Me, Shylock!' exclaimed Mary with exaggerated outrage. 'Sell your old granny you would for the right price.'

'There's not much call fer Grannys at the moment. But what would you give me for an Irish tree-seller, hardly second-hand, barely been kissed.'

'You lying toad, saw you last week with that girl from the Co-op, nearly chewing her face off you was.'

'Aahh! Well I'm nothing if not thorough.' He smiled at her. 'Thought you was too caught up with your sailor to notice what I was doing.'

Mary blushed, furious with herself. Oh, he was sneaky. He always managed to get in under her guard. 'Do you a swap. On top of what you wants I'll throw in a Pompey football rattle,' she said, avoiding his eyes, knowing there was a lace missing from the left boxing glove.

'Lets seal it with a kiss,' said Danny, taking her hand and raising it to his lips.

'Oh, bugger off back to yer trees, Father Christmas,' she snapped, unable to stop herself smiling at his cheek. 'I'll parcel your stuff up and send Dad over for the tree, soon as he gets here.'

She was soon swallowed up again by the demands of her customers. Forward and back went the trade. Toys left the stall and coins rattled in her money-bag. From time to time she looked at the rabbits swinging from the back of the meat stall, with the tins attached to their heads to collect the blood, and wondered how much the butcher would let them go for at the auction that night. The morning flashed by and when Dad appeared with two mugs of tea and some bacon sandwiches the stall was looking threadbare.

'You done well, gal,' he said. 'Want me to fill up for ya, while you takes a break?'

'Ta,' said Mary, warming her mittened fingers around the mug. 'Where's the kids?'

'Twinnies getting the veg and Blyth's round here some-where.'

Mary bit into the sandwich, suddenly ravenous.

'Here, gal,' said Dad. 'You have this other half.'

She wondered what Matthew was doing. He was on duty until Christmas Eve. What did you do on a submarine when it wasn't at sea? It was a mystery to her, something that she couldn't share with him. She thought of the other Sunday when they had walked along the sea front to the naval war memorial. The wreaths from the families of the lost submarine were still there, the flowers dead and the rain-splotched cards indecipherable. Mary pressed her hand to her neck where Matthew's ring hung safely on its chain, as if it were a talisman. Why did he love her? She knew without a moment's thought why she loved him. He saw her as she would like to be: laughing and full of hope. His love had prised her free of the imprisoning shell of hurt and mistrust. For moments at a time with him she could dare to be happy.

'Dished out the money for veg and stuff to the twinnies

and here's a ten bob what I got from Dora and she's bringing a pudding, mince pies, crackers and a cake from her mum.'

'What the bloody hell you do that for?' she shouted, her joy evaporating, and her face flaming with temper. She slammed down the tea on the stall, upsetting it over the comics. 'You always has to go on the cadge. Where's yer pride? I wanted us to do it all ourselves. Saint bloody Dora always rides to the rescue. Comes round with her presents showing us up.'

'Hold ya fire, gal. I'll pay her back next week, I got it all under control.'

Mary blew a derisive raspberry. 'You,' she snorted, 'couldn't organise a bun fight in a bakery.'

'Well, Miss-know-all,' snapped her father, 'you ain't the only one with a bit of nous and cappernosity. I'll show ya.' He flung down his mug and disappeared into the crowd.

'Anyone workin 'ere or shall we 'elp ourselves?' said a woman with a baby in a pram and two children clinging to the handle.

'What can I get you?' mumbled Mary, still red-faced and furious.

'Two bundles comics, a colouring book, one of them matchbox dolls, a box of soldiers, that little rabbit there and two Pompey football rattles.'

One of the boys took a rattle and swung it round and round. He laughed gleefully as it let out a satisfying rat-a-tat-tat.

'That's five bob,' said Mary, putting the coins in her money-bag and setting all the toys into a paper carrier. She wanted to scream with frustration. What was the good of trying to get things going when Dad always put the kibosh on everything. Now, wonderful bloody Dora would take the credit. Always helping out, she was. Blyth and the twins loved her and her brother Harry treated her as if she was blooming perfect. Mary burned at the unfairness of it all. All the things she did for them were never even noticed. Dora would swan around with her cakes and stuff and they'd all make up to her and Matthew would think she hadn't done nothing. Mary turned around to have another rant at Dad, but he had vanished into the crowd.

'Got the veg we have and brought ya some toffee,' said the twins, lugging a sack between them.

She nodded, too furious to speak.

'Dad said we was to hold the fort and ter send you home. He's going to be here till five with us. Says you're to go home and cool down.'

'You got us a tree!' said Blyth, appearing from nowhere. 'I'll carry it home for yer.'

'Over there, the short one in the corner,' said Mary, taking off her apron and handing it to Mercy.

'Here you are, young feller,' Danny said, smiling at Blyth as he wrapped the roots of the tree in newspaper. 'This little one is like your sister, the pick of the crop.' He grinned at Mary, but she was in no mood for flirting.

'Ta,' she said and turned away.

There was a queue forming around the stall and the twins were soon in the thick of it. 'We'll take the veggies as well,' she said to her brother. 'You and me can take a handle each.'

Blyth chattered on and Mary trudged along beside him. She felt tired and defeated. They passed a baby in its pram warmly wrapped and fast asleep. How she wished she could change places with the child and be so snug and cosseted. They stopped to swap hands and reposition the tree. She bit her lip and blinked away her tears. At one stroke Dad had ruined her Christmas.

3

Captain Charles Clements turned the key in the lock of number fifteen Lancaster Terrace and stepped inside, his footsteps echoing in the tiled hall. He shivered. Four years in Singapore had spoiled him for an English winter. The stillness shocked him, but what had he expected? Returning home alone to a place that had been locked and shrouded in dust-sheets was bound to feel dispiriting. He realised that never, in all the years he had lived there, had he entered his house without being greeted by someone.

'Oh, 'ello, Sir,' little Cissie the maid would say, flushing as he spoke to her. 'Madam's expectin' you. Up in the sitting room, she is. Says to hurry, you're expected at Keppels' at eight.' She had come to them at fourteen, looking no more than twelve, her pale face overwhelmed by a mass of blonde curls. Rarely had he spared her more than a moment of his time and yet, remembering Cissie, he was touched afresh by her innocence and simplicity.

What was that other girl's name – came from a large family in Lemon Street? She had been rough around the edges without an ounce of courtesy. Yet he had liked her and admired her spirit. He remembered her greeting him at the door.

''Ello, Sir, your missis is in a right rage. You'd o' bin better off staying on board.' She had a way of sniffing when corrected, that always made him smile and infuriated Lettice.

'Daddy, daddy, come quick and see, I've made a castle.' Charles could almost feel his son Miles tugging at his sleeve and jumping about impatiently while he hung up his coat and followed him to the nursery.

'You've missed the dollie's tea party and they've eaten all the cake.' He imagined Charlotte, her mouth ringed with chocolate crumbs, laughing and holding out her arms.

He sighed for all those times when he had run up the stairs to his wife's sitting room and she had turned towards him offering her cheek for him to kiss. He would be engulfed in a cloud of L'Aimant. Lettice would stroke his face and then look past him as if he were the understudy and her real husband was somewhere behind him, in the distance.

'Darling, how late you are,' she would complain. 'Hurry, hurry, we're due at the Pembroke in half an hour. No, darling, don't be silly, we haven't time, you'll spoil my make-up.'

There never was a right time for them. He would attempt lovemaking and she would lie beneath him unresisting but indifferent. Worse still were the times when he pleaded with her to show some affection.

Then she would taunt him, shrivelling his manhood. 'For God's sake, Charles, don't be so bloody reverential. Take me, take me.'

The more he thought of her and their days together the more he realised how little she had loved him. He had merely been the provider of the children and the dress allowance. All the time, she had been pretending. Like Charlotte, she had been playing house.

His posting to the admiral's staff in Singapore had provided her with plenty of opportunity to find a partner more suited to her taste. It was almost a relief when he found the letter telling him she was going away with Lawrence Davenport, a rich planter from Malaya. Lettice had not been in the least discreet, and the fact that Lawrence's wronged wife Elizabeth was the daughter of his admiral did not help matters. In the midst of all the public humiliation was the knowledge that his wife's happiness was no longer his responsibility.

Then his concern switched to the welfare of Miles and Charlotte. Thank God Lettice in the first flush of passion had fled alone to her lover. Thank God also for his sister Lavinia, recently arrived from England.

'Charles, for pity's sake show some backbone. Divorce the woman, face down the scandal and let me take the children back to England. Custody will be a mere formality, after your wife's behaviour.'

'Vinnie, I'm almost bankrupt; when she left, Lettice emptied our account. Yesterday the admiral sent for me and suggested I resign my commission. That will mean the loss of my pension and the likelihood of having to sell the house.'

'By God, that woman has done a thorough job, I'll say that for her,' Lavinia had raged. 'In that case I shall pay the children's school fees and bale you out for as long as is necessary.' She held up a silencing finger to Charles's protests. 'What else should I do with Gonville's money?'

And so it was settled.

He would never forget saying goodbye to them on the dockside before the ship sailed. Nine-year-old Miles's face was stiff with unhappiness. Charlotte, only six had clutched his hand. 'Take us home, Daddy,' she had pleaded.

'Soon, soon, my pet,' he had said. 'Daddy will see you as soon as ever he can.'

Charles began to shiver.

Lavinia had given him a perfunctory kiss. 'Charlie, brace up. You're almost over the worst. If you can survive Jutland, you can survive that woman.'

Standing there in the hall, Charles felt like a convalescent returning from hospital. But what was he recovering from –

blind stupidity? He had believed, naively as it turned out, that if he loved Lettice enough and was sufficiently patient, she would in time return his affection. He had been humiliated by her deceit and had tried to forgive her and make a fresh start. But she had not wanted his absolution and her fresh start had been with another man.

Enough of all this self-pity, he must stir himself, light a fire and make a bed for the night. It would be Christmas Day tomorrow and the prospect was depressing. Had Lavinia any idea that he was back in England she would insist on him going to Dorset. It had been a tempting thought. He could have seen Miles and Charlotte but his stubborn streak asserted itself. Charles had promised himself not to, until their home was ready and waiting. He would probably go to the service at St Thomas's, then call in to his old club on Western Parade for a meal of some sort. After surviving the festive season he would begin 1926 in better spirits. He had done with the navy, and the New Year would be a fresh start.

Charles got the coal bucket and opened the cellar door. Action was the thing. He must pull himself up by his boot-straps and carve out a fresh career for himself. Within half an hour he had managed to get the kitchen range going and filled the kettle. He was surprised the caretaker he had employed to do a monthly check had not turned off the water to prevent burst pipes. But that was the least of his worries. The steward at his London club had packed up some venison pie and a generous slice of Dundee cake. While the water boiled he went into the living room and took the dust-sheets from the sofa and armchairs. There was work to be done. A list – that was it – jot down all that he must achieve in the next few days. That would focus his mind.

Fortunately he had managed to secure a post as mathematics master in a little school in Mile End. It was some sort of crammer for boys sitting the Dockyard Apprentice's examinations. It would suit him very well for the present. What with that and the sale of his copper shares, he would be able to keep himself afloat until he had got his bearings. Mathematics had always been his salvation; there was certainty in numbers. Every problem had a solution that could be arrived at by simply moving logically from one stage to the next and the answer never altered. People were a different matter. What was certain one day was uncertain the next. Intentions changed and feelings could be veiled. You responded to what you thought was wanted, and yet, beneath the surface, another desire was at work.

Charles found that he was rather hungry. After he had the range alight he fixed a hot toddy, sat by the kitchen fire, and polished off the pie, saving the cake for later. Warming some blankets by the fire, he put the two kitchen armchairs together and settled down for the night. Just as he was drifting off to sleep the name of the scullery maid came to him. It was Mary.

The sailor tossed a shilling at her, then pulled up his trousers before buttoning his coat and setting his cap straight. Cissie was glad that it was dark in the alley and that she couldn't see his face. He had been impatient and torn her drawers but she'd had worse: mean men who made her lay on the ground, others who'd wanted her to kneel in front of them and used her like a privy. Good job it wasn't raining. Soon they'd all be back on board or down at the Home Club snoring off their beer. She looked at the night's takings – four shillings. Well, it would have to do. She was shaking with cold and wanting to lose herself in sleep. Good thing she'd kept that key to the back door of the house in Lancaster Terrace. Cissie had tied it in a hankie and thrust it deep into the bolster case along with her frock and spare drawers on the day that the Clementses left for Singapore. Nobody had asked for it and she would not willingly give it up. It had been months before she touched it again. Between the losing and the finding had been the upset with Ted Garland and his wife. When she sat on the pavement with her stuff emptied at her feet, there had been the key still knotted in the handkerchief. That key and her old pink hatbox were what amounted to her life history.

Sometimes it was possible to pretend that she still lived in Lancaster Terrace and any moment Mrs Mullins would be hauling the bedclothes off her and screaming.

'Get up, Cissie, you lazy trollop. Madam's rung already for her breakfast, she'll be boilin' if you don't get a move on.'

The best times had been Christmas with the tree all lit up and a dinner fit for royalty. Once, she had gone with the Clementses children to see Father Christmas. He had given her a red paper fan as a present. It was in the hat box along with all her other treasures.

It was Christmas Day tomorrow. One thing was certain, there'd be no turkey and no presents. Still, if she could just rest up for a couple of days, sleep in a bed and not be pestered for a while. Not much to ask. Everything was such an effort and she was tired all the time. Couldn't get back into service because she had no references and no decent clothes to wear to the Servants' Registry. All she could do was to try to avoid getting hit. If she hadn't the safety of her room Cissie wouldn't have lasted this long.

As she turned the key and stepped into the scullery she started up in fright. Even in the dark she knew someone was in the house. It was warmer. There was a faint smell of whisky and a light showing beneath the kitchen door. Cissie froze. She couldn't be found here, she'd no right to the key. Who could it be? The caretaker came on the first of the month, as she had found by almost running into him one day. Besides, he was never around at night. Perhaps it was a tramp or some old soldier who had broken in through a window. They'd got

a bit of warmth and a fire going. By now they could be asleep.
Cissie stood in the scullery swaying with tiredness. It had been
bound to happen. Having the place to herself, all this time, was
too good to be true. Most nights she would go into the kitchen
and heat up some water and find some cleaning rags in the
cupboard under the sink and wash herself all over. Couldn't
sleep with the smell of a man still on her – it made her skin
crawl. Up in the first-floor cloakroom there was a candle
stub and a box of matches on a ledge above the wash-basin.
She would light the candle and stand it on the sink while she
ran some cold water and had a strip-wash, using a corner of the
towel as a flannel and a lump of yellow household soap. She
had planned, one night, to sneak into Madam's bedroom and
snitch that tablet of gardenia soap from the bottom drawer of
her dressing table that had been forgotten when she swanned
off abroad.

Cissie was sick with disappointment. It was cold and bare
in the scullery with nothing to lie on and not a stitch of
anything to cover herself with. She dare not creep through
the kitchen for fear that whoever was in there might have a
knife or something. She lifted the latch and crept back into the
yard. Kneeling under the windowsill Cissie peered through a
gap in the kitchen curtains. Whoever was in there had pulled
the two old chairs together in front of the range and covered
themselves with a dark blanket of some sort. An empty bottle
lay on the floor. She shivered. What she would do would be
to leave the back door open then risk going into the kitchen.
If the bloke reared up and turned nasty she would leg it back
into the yard.

Holding her breath, Cissie turned the handle and inched her
way through the door. The man was turned towards the range
and the blankets were pulled up around him. On the floor
beside the bottle was a pair of black, highly polished shoes.
Whoever he was he had a cheek, pinching the blankets. The

man was snoring softly as Cissie, her heart banging against her ribs, flitted past. She crept into the hall and up the two flights of stairs to her bedroom in the attic. Familiarity with the house enabled her to make the journey without switching on the light. The attic had neither electricity nor gas fittings. Cissie felt along the mantelpiece above the fireplace for her matchbox and candle. It took her several minutes to steady her breathing and calm herself before she felt able to creep down to the first-floor bathroom. Quickly she half-filled the basin with cold water then took off her tattered drawers and used them as a flannel.

Back in her bedroom, Cissie took off her shoes and crept under the thin blanket fully dressed. She thought about Ted Garland tucked up snugly somewhere with not a thought of what he'd brought her to. Nearly died, she had.

His missis had found out about them and there had been hell to pay.

'Ted, I thought you loved me,' Cissie sobbed.

'Well, you was wrong, darling,' Sally snarled from the doorway. She'd knocked her over with the force of her slap. It was her that chucked her stuff out. 'As for you, you worthless tyke,' she screamed at Ted, 'you can sling your hook. Deserve each other, like Eve and the serpent. Just get out of my sight the pair of you.'

Cissie ended up at the Slum Post scrubbing floors. Early in the mornings she would push the cart through the streets to collect vegetables from the market. They was kind to her, the Sally Army. She had gone to Springhaven with other pregnant girls. Cissie cried at the memory of her child. She clasped her hands over her belly and tried to feel again that first fluttering movement, to pretend that there had been a happy ending.

'So sorry, my dear, your baby was just too frail,' Major Grice had said as Cissie lay in that narrow bed, her child cold in her arms. 'Will you name him?

'Charles,' she had whispered. Even now she wondered why she had used Captain Clements' name – he'd hardly known she existed. Oh, he'd been kind in that vague way that toffs had. But, if he met her now, probably wouldn't know her from Adam.

Poor little Charlie, she had buried part of herself in that little shoe-box.

Afterwards, she had had to move on. Couldn't stay at Springhaven, there were other girls needing her place. Cissie began to beg in the street. Then she fell into a more certain way of making money. The past and the future became meaningless: life was a matter of existing from moment to moment, hoping that the men would not be too rough or lice-ridden. If she were not so terrified of hell she would have topped herself ages ago. If only there really were a heaven she would go there and find her son. Cissie pulled up the blanket and closed her eyes. She hoped whoever was in the kitchen would not come up to the third floor. All she wanted was to blot out yet another Christmas.

Charles woke feeling grubby and stiff. The range had gone out and the kitchen felt like a mausoleum. Why had he come back to the empty house? Why back to Portsmouth at all? Where else? He had been born in this house, he had been happy there – it belonged to him.

Enough, enough, he berated himself. He must unpack and settle in. The first move was to get the boiler going and to have a bath and a shave. After that he must get himself to church and then to his club and have a Christmas of some sort. Later, feeling more optimistic, he was coming out of the bathroom when he heard a movement in the hall. 'Stop,' he cried, hurtling down the stairs. As he reached the bottom step the front door closed behind his visitor.

4

As Matthew turned into Lemon Street a strange procession made its way into number twenty-three. Taking the lead was Harry followed by Mary's dad, carrying a door between them, accompanied by the twins with a chair apiece, then Dora, carrying a loaded basket.

'Happy Christmas, Dusty,' they chorused.

'What are you up to?' he asked.

'Bit of a conjuring trick,' laughed Harry. 'We're turning this door into a table, then adding chairs and extra grub. Fish the key out the letterbox and stand back, mate, while we gets things sorted.'

'You're in the best place, son,' gasped their dad. 'Mary's on the rampage. Stay in the street and have a fag till things quietens down.'

As he turned the key and stepped aside a mouth-watering blend of roasted meat and fried onions tantalised him. Harry and Fred with much to-ing and fro-ing manoeuvred the improvised table into the house.

'Can't you see, we're not ready? Get out the bleeding way and take the chairs with you,' yelled Mary from the kitchen.

'Narky cow,' yelled one of the twins, thumping back down the passage. 'Oh stick them in her room. Trust her to spoil things,' said the other, slamming the front door.

Matthew's spirits fell. He stood on the pavement sorely tempted to make his getaway before getting embroiled in the Vines' Christmas. What would his mother have made of them? he wondered. How would she have coped with all the pushing, snatching and grabbing? All the talking with their mouths full, the shouting and elbowing that went on among them. He used to tease her for her insistence on all the little courtesies.

'Manners maketh man, Matthew,' she would say. 'They cost nothing and oil society's wheels.'

Each day he realised how much she had influenced him. Quiet and self-effacing though she was, Elizabeth Miller had a strong set of values and led by example. Even for the simplest of meals they always had a napkin and she insisted on him holding out her chair before she took her place at the table. How he missed her letters full of acute observations of her employers and interest in what he was doing. What would she have thought of his fiancée?

Once, when he had talked to Mary about the differences between their childhoods she had snapped at him.

'It's all right for you at home with your mummy, livin' in that big house. Always knows where the grub's comin' from and can sit there pretendin' you're one of the nobs. You ain't 'ad to go to school in your mum's old dress pinned up off the floor or searched out bugs with a candle flame. Think you're better than us, don't ya?'

Matthew struck a match and drew deeply on his cigarette. Was he really so stuck-up?

She could be so unreasonable sometimes, and then when he least expected it, quite wonderful. He would be weak with laughter from her imitations of the characters at the market and full of admiration at her inventiveness in the things she made for her stall.

'I loves it down there,' she told him, 'especially at night, with the naphtha flares hissing and glowing; the smell of fried onions from the pie stall, and all the apples shining and the nippers' faces when they sees what I've made. You got to make it by your wits, workin' longer and being tougher than the bloke on the next stall.'

There was an innocent, childlike quality to her, too, that only rarely showed itself. Once, she had asked him to comb her hair and been like a child in her delight.

'No one done me hair before,' she said, 'except Granny and the nit nurse.'

Never had Matthew felt such tenderness. He had kissed the hollows above her collarbones and stroked the shape of her breasts through her cotton blouse.

'We will be happy, won't we?' she had whispered against his neck, her fingers stroking his chest. 'Promise!' she had demanded.

'I promise,' he had said, knowing the impossibility of his words. It had been difficult to call a halt. He so wanted to explore her body and to have her touch him. Mary was neither coy nor flirty but open in her desire for him. Matthew feared where their eagerness could take them. Talk on the mess deck of babies coming too soon and their being crushed by debts put a break on his passion.

'Hey, Dusty,' said Blyth, slapping him on the back and startling him back to the present. 'You can come in, now. Shove your mack in Mary's room. Hurry up!' he yelled, his face flushed with excitement. 'Dad's just going to carve the birds.'

Matthew opened the door into the front room and left his coat amid a muddle of clothes heaped on top of the unmade bed. Going into the kitchen he was hit by a wave of sound. Everyone was talking at once: teasing, laughing, bossing about and squabbling as they sought to drown each other out. Harry's door had been converted into a table. It was covered with a sheet with one end resting on a trestle and the other wedged against the window. Heaped on the top was a random assortment of plates and cutlery. Harry shoe-horned himself into a seat between Faith and Mercy. Matthew smiled at his fiancée and was rewarded by an answering grin. Next year in Gosport, he prayed.

Mary was light – headed with relief. She had done it. There they were, eight of them, wedged around the table, mouths watering and stomachs rumbling. Sizzling, on a borrowed platter, were two bronzed chickens stuffed to the gunnels with sage and onion and surrounded by a necklace of pork sausages. Accompanying the birds were a dish of roast potatoes, golden and crisp, and two dishes of sprouts and carrots.

She had meant to wear her engagement ring, but in the hurly-burly of getting the food ready and everyone seated she had forgotten to get it from the cup on the top shelf of the dresser. Now, with everyone so jam-packed against each other, was not the moment to disturb them. She looked across at Matthew and he smiled at her, melting all her fears.

Mary looked at her family. Dad had shaved and put on the grey jersey the Sally Army woman had given him, while the twins looked merry in the red jumpers Dora had knitted. Blyth winked at her and she wanted to cry. At nine-and-a-half he was on the edge of growing up and growing away from her, although he would still give her a kiss sometimes and come to her with his secrets. His face was flushed and his blond hair fell over his eyes.

Back and forth went the plates and Dad piled them up with chicken and sausage while Mary spooned on the roast potatoes, sprouts and carrots. Her mouth was watering.

'Happy Christmas,' said Dad, after he'd poured everyone a glass of ale. 'Now before we all dive in I'd like us all to drink a toast to our Mary, whose hard work made it all possible. To our Mary,' he shouted above all the talking.

'To Mary,' said Matthew, raising his glass.

'To Mary,' they all cried. 'Happy Christmas.'

Having people all looking at her and smiling she didn't know how to be with them. Squaring up to people and back-answers were her usual ammunition. Mary felt as if they were peeling back a layer of her skin and she trembled. 'Weren't nothin',' she shrugged, staring at the tablecloth. After taking a spoonful of chicken she began to relax. 'Pass us up the gravy,' she said to Mercy.

'Ooh! That jug handle's too hot, give us that cloth. Ooh!' screeched her sister. She leapt to her feet as the boiling gravy scalded her hand.

Faith struggled to her feet and shoved past Matthew, anxious to get to Mercy, who was screeching and hopping about in pain. With all the twins pushing and shoving, the trestle began to topple. Powerless to stop it, everyone watched horror-stricken as it became dislodged from the tabletop.

'Watch out, the dinner, Jesus Christ,' yelled Dad; 'grab that plate.'

It all happened at once. What had been a flat surface was now a slope down which the Christmas dinners slid in rapid instalments. On the mat at Dad's feet was a muddle of plates and food. The cloth was awash with beer and gravy.

There was a stunned silence and then everyone moved at once.

'It's all down my dress,' said Dora, dabbing the gravy from her sleeve.

'I could bloody kill you,' raged Mary, lunging at Faith.

'Narky cow,' Faith roared back. 'Was only gonna help Merce, she's hurt herself.'

'Look out, Blyth, you're stood on that plate,' said Harry, pushing his brother out of the way. 'Calm down, everyone.'

'Trust you two to muck things up,' raged Mary, lunging at her sister.

'Was 'elping Mercy, she's hurt herself,' roared Faith, glaring at her.

'Come on, girls,' soothed Dora, taking the twins out to the scullery, 'let's get a flannel and wash the gravy off.'

'I'll put all the grub into the roasting dish and shove it back in the oven, while we sorts ourselves out,' said Harry, taking up the plates. 'Dusty and me will square up the table, then we'll share it all out again.'

'Oooh! It's all blistery,' wailed Mercy.

Dora took hold of her other arm and led her into the scullery. 'Come on, Faith, you can give us a hand,' she called over her shoulder.

'That's it, I've got the meat safe,' said Dad, passing the sausages over to Harry, kneeling on the floor, filling the roasting tin with a greasy mound of half-finished meals.

'Ooh!' yelped Mercy, from the scullery.

'It'll cool down in a tick,' said Dora, coming back from the scullery with Faith who clutched a flannel to her sister's arm.

'I'll give Harry a hand to square up the table again,' said Matthew, 'but I think the cloth's past saving.'

'We could wring it out over the plates so's we don't waste the gravy,' Dad suggested.

'Worse things happen at sea,' said Blyth.

Everyone laughed but Mary. 'They've mucked up everythink,' she snapped, close to tears. 'Friggin' twins always buggers things up.'

'That's not fair,' said Matthew, carrying the dripping cloth out to the scullery. 'It was an accident.'

Mary sat back in her chair watching them all trying to resurrect the dinner. The day was ruined. All those hours stood in the market in the perishing cold, all the bargaining for the tree and the meat had come to nothing. She'd been dog-tired when she'd got home last night to find the place like a tip and Christmas Day yet to organise. Well, it served her right for trying to make her family into something they could never be.

Mercy was grizzling while Dora fussed over her tying a hankie round her wrist. Harry and Dad held up the door while Dad picked up the trestle and set it back in place. Dora and Matthew laid out sheets of newspaper instead of a cloth.

'I'll just rinse all the eating irons under the tap and you'll have to use them wet,' said Dad. 'God knows where the tea-towels are.'

Harry carried in the roasting dish, now filled with a mess of chicken slices and congealed vegetables. 'We was lucky with the plates: only two broke,' he said. 'Me and Dora can share one and so can the twinnies. We'll just have to make the best of it.'

Mary raged down the passage to her bedroom. Slamming the door behind her she paced the room. Make the best of it! she fumed. Why must I always be pinning a smile on my face and pretending? Back in the kitchen they'd be laughing and talking together like she wasn't there. Ten minutes ago they had all been drinking her health and now she was nothing again. Who'd shopped and scrubbed and ironed and cooked the bloody thing? Me, me, me!

It had been like climbing a mountain getting them all to pitch in and help her, plus the anxiety of stretching out the money, and all for nothing. Between getting up at five and the one mouthful of food that she'd attempted at half past one, she had been on the go and eaten nothing. Her head throbbed and she was trembling with tiredness. She sank down onto the bed, amid the clutter of coats.

There was a knock on the door.

'Bugger off,' she yelled.

Matthew came into the room and sat beside her. He took her in his arms.

She couldn't speak. Tears stood behind her lashes.

'I can't have my dinner without you,' he said. 'It wouldn't be Christmas. I've dished you up all the best bits.'

'I can't,' she wailed, 'they all hates me out there.'

He held her close, letting her cry out her weariness and frustration. 'Look, you clear us a space on the bed and I'll bring us our plates in here.'

Mary set Matthew's raincoat on a hook behind the door and smoothed the blanket straight. The last thing she wanted now was Christmas dinner, but she couldn't disappoint him. He was trying so hard to make things right for her. Oh, she would make it up to him once they had a place of their own.

'What's it like out there?' she asked, when he returned with their dinners on a battered tin tray.

'Well, it looks like a battlefied, but they're so busy eating I don't think they care.' He set her plate down on the bed. 'Happy Christmas, love,' he said.

'I s'pose we shall laugh about all this later on,' she said, spearing a slice of chicken with her fork.

Matthew smiled. 'It's like Blyth said, "Worse things happen at sea."'

'Like what?' she challenged.

'The stores were flooded once and all the labels were washed off the tins. We had to sit down to a dinner of stewed greengages and pilchards.'

Mary laughed

After they had finished, Matthew set the plates back on the tray. 'Why don't you put your ring on?' he coaxed.

She smiled, not trusting herself to speak. Having it back on her finger, seeing it sparkle in the light, would soothe away the day's disappointments. 'It's in the kitchen in a cup on the dresser. Took it off 'cos I didn't want it ending up in the stuffing. Can you go and get it for me?'

'Let's go together,' he said. 'You can put it on, then we'll go out for a stroll. Leave everyone else to do the washing up.'

'Can I have a kiss, first? she asked.

Matthew put the tray on the floor and they lay down

together. He held her close. 'Mary,' he whispered. 'What am I going to do with you?'

'Marry me and take me away with you,' she said.

He kissed her face, the eyelashes still wet with tears, her little snub nose and then her lips.

Mary kissed him back. Little nibbling kisses that slowly gave way to slow, drenching, open-mouthed exchanges. Tenderness gave way to a fierce desire. Even as he matched her passion, stroking her body over her clothes, he was aware that at any moment they could be interrupted. 'Let's get the ring,' he gasped.

'We could go round to Harry's,' she whispered; 'please, Matthew.'

He nodded, too stirred up to say anything. Never had he wanted her so much.

Mary went down the passage first and he followed after with the tray, his face flushed and collar creased. Would Harry have left the key, hanging loose, behind the letterbox or would he have wound it up for safety? What if the other people from upstairs were in? When they went into the kitchen he was hit by a wave of sound. Everyone sat there, laughing and talking at once.

Harry winked at him across the table and Matthew looked away. If they could just slide off and be on their own . . . He stared down at the empty plates while Mary edged past Dora and Dad.

'That's it, my gal,' he said. 'You come and sit down with us. The panic's over. Best grub I've tasted in ages. All down to you.'

Mary swallowed. Perhaps, after all, it was going to be all right. She reached up to the top shelf and brought down the broken cup. It was empty.

'It's gone,' she gasped. 'My ring – it's not there.'

Nobody heard her.

'Someone's took my ring,' she screamed.

'You've probably forgotten where you left it,' said Matthew. His calmness infuriated her.

'Think I'm daft?' she challenged. 'Told you, I put it in this cup on the top so it wouldn't get mucky while I was seein' to the dinner.'

'Let me have a look,' he said, stretching up his hand and running it along the shelf.

Mercy giggled.

The sound ignited Mary. 'You took it,' she screamed, pushing Matthew out of the way and lunging across the table at her sister.

Matthew was talking to her, but she couldn't hear what he was saying. 'Shut up, shut up, shut up,' she shouted. 'You bloody stupid or sommink? Them girls 'as had it. I'll kill them.'

They hurtled through the house into the yard and down the cellar steps, locking the flap behind them.

'You can bloody stay there,' Mary roared, dragging the mangle across the yard and setting it on top of the flap. She would call the tune now. When they climbed out all tearful and snot-nosed she'd have them.

Wanting to continue her rampage, she turned back to the kitchen.

'You ain't coming in, till you've calmed down. I've locked the door,' shouted Harry. 'Dusty's shoved off back to *Dolphin*. He's had enough of you and I don't blame him.'

5

The cellar was cold and damp and the candles threw distorted shadows across the walls. Mooching about in the gloom, the twins kicked aside a hairless scrubbing-brush and empty paint tin.

Faith began to shiver. 'It's all your fault, what you want to take her ring for?' she moaned. 'Knew it would rile her. We ain't had no grub and I'm nearly wettin' meself.'

'Weren't going to keep it for long,' said her sister, 'but she fired up so quick I didn't have a chance to do nothing.'

'Did you see Dusty's face? He was all white and furious. Reckon he'll finish with her, and it's all your fault. She won't never give us our tap shoes now.'

'Reckon I could find them,' said Mercy. 'First we gotta get out of here. Could try and crawl up into the street through the coal hole,' she suggested.

'Don't fancy that much. What I was really looking forward to was me dinner.'

'Thought you wanted to go to the lav? Either we gets up through there, or we stays down here in the dark, and you wets yerself. Them candles won't last much longer.'

'All right,' said Faith, opening the door at the far end of the cellar. 'There ain't much coal here, but I don't think we're gonna be able to reach the lid.'

'How about this tin bath?' said Mercy. 'We turn it upside down and stand on it, I reckon we would just about reach.'

With much dragging and scraping they positioned the

upturned bath half in and half out of the coal hole. The girls began to shiver and the candles guttered. Even standing on the bath and reaching upwards their fingers were inches short of the coal-hole lid.

'Here let's take this broom handle and bash it up and force it open.'

Panting and grunting the girls repeatedly shoved the broomstick up against the cellar lid. 'Wheee!' they cried in triumph as the lid fell open. The cold air rushed in and the candle flames went out, but there was a patch of light flooding in from the street.

'Bags I go first,' said Faith, crouching on top of the wobbling bath. 'Gonna be a tight fit.'

'I'll bunk you up from the bottom,' said Mercy, 'then you can pull me up from the top.'

What with squirming and twisting, and a generous shove from her sister, Faith wriggled herself out onto the pavement. 'You ready?' she said, peering back into the cellar.

'Ooh! ooh! yer 'urtin' me 'and,' yelled Mercy.

'Hang on while I kneels down and gets you under yer arms.'

With further wrenching and grasping, Mercy emerged to join her sister.

Looking at each other they burst out laughing.

'Like a couple of Africans we are,' they giggled, coughing and brushing coal dust from their best jumpers

The street was deserted. Faith pulled the key on its string through the letterbox and turned it in the lock.

'Now you go for a wee while I looks for them taps,' said Mercy.

All he could think to do was get away – to walk and walk until he exhausted himself. Still he could not believe the change in Mary, just as they had been so happy. Tears rose in his eyes and Matthew dashed them away with his fist. In seconds she had become ugly and raucous. What was he to do? He had been sleeping on the floor at Harry's house during his leave. Now he couldn't bear the thought of their concern or answer any of their questions. Matthew wished he were under sailing orders, busy on board with no room for thoughts of Mary. Well, he'd better go round to Harry's and leave a note saying he'd returned to *Dolphin*. As he turned the key in the lock he thought of their talk barely an hour ago. She had wanted to come here with him. They would have made love. He had wanted her, throbbed with the wanting, and now he almost hated her. Quickly he got his kitbag and threw his shaving gear and a few odds and ends into it.

> *Dear Harry,*
> *I've had to go back on board. Thanks for letting me stay.*
> *Will see you some time,*
> *All the best,*
> *Dusty.*

He put his hand into the pocket of his raincoat and found the red scarf wrapped in Christmas paper that he had bought for Mary. He flung it on the kitchen table, picked up his kitbag and left the house.

Standing in the stern of the ferry he stared unseeingly into the darkening sky, his face stiff with misery. At *Dolphin* he handed back his leave chit and made his way to the accommodation block, his boots hollow on the stone floor. The bareness of the mess, with its rows of identical lockers and stand of lashed hammocks, suited the bleakness of his mood and made a welcome contrast to the shambles of the Vine household. After a few minutes the door opened behind him.

'Jesus! Dusty, what you doin' here? Thought you was on leave till the twenty-eighth.' His friend, Bob Cowley, went to his locker and got out a crib board. 'Over Pompey seeing your girl, wasn't you?'

Matthew shrugged.

'Had a set-to have ya?'

Matthew nodded.

'Least said soonest mended, mate,' Bob said, patting him on the shoulder. 'I'll get a fanny of tea going. The others will be up from the dining hall soon. We could make it a foursome. Fancy a game?'

'In a bit,' said Matthew, dully.

'If you're hungry, there's still some of me mother's cake in that tin over there.' Bob busied himself with the tea while Matthew stowed his gear.

'You know, Dusty, there's plenty more fish in the sea, but who wants to marry a kipper?'

Matthew tried to force his face into a smile. 'Reckon I'll pass on the crib game,' he said. 'I've got a bit of a headache. I'll turn in and try and sleep it off.'

Wearily he took his hammock from the rack, slung it from a hook and swung himself up into it. He pulled the blanket up over his face and closed his eyes. The little sitting room in Cranbrook sprang into his mind with its ordered calm. As if he were in a museum, Matthew walked around touching the embroidered chairbacks, the collection of farings in the glass-fronted cupboard, and the photographs on the mantelpiece. His mother's face smiled out at him from a silver frame, her grey eyes calm and her hair tidied into a bun at the nape of her neck. For once, her hands were folded in her lap and not busy at her needlework or writing letters. He wished he were a child again setting up the draughts board on a winter's evening or in the summer out talking to the hop-pickers.

The rest of his leave stretched out ahead of him, with nothing to do. From the other end of the room his mess-mates voices rose and fell as they settled over the crib board. How had it all unravelled so quickly? It was only six weeks ago that they had got engaged and now Mary had turned into a shrill foul-mouthed stranger. All the time it had taken to save up for the ring, staying on board instead of out with his messmates, denying himself little extras he would normally have bought from the canteen. What was the point of trying to build something together when they were both so different? The headache he had pretended to have a while ago was now there with a vengeance.

Swearing to herself, Mary searched about for a stone to crack the window-pane. She must get back in. The ring must be somewhere in the house, else why would Mercy be so pleased with herself? She must catch up with Matthew and say sorry. After the set-to they'd had today he would have gone back to *Dolphin*. He wouldn't want Harry and Dora feeling sorry for him. Once she'd found it Mary would run like the wind for the ferry. Of course he was mad at her, she could see that, but once everything had been explained and he'd seen the ring she knew that he would understand. *He must! He must!* She shouted down the worm of doubt writhing in her head. It was getting dark and cold and Mary began to shiver. Matthew's face, when she screamed at him and called him stupid, refused to fade from her mind. No, no it was not her fault – it was those bloody twins. Always they ganged up against her, whispering and giggling.

Even when she was little they had stood in her light, taking all the love.

'That's a good girl, Mary, you look after your sisters, Mummy's got a headache.'

'Hello, my little darlings, give Daddy a kiss.'

'Bet you can't tell them apart. Good job they've got a sister like you to look after them.'

'Hello, Twinnies, you going to give your big brother a kiss?'

Tears pricked behind her lashes. When she looked at the

kitchen someone had drawn the curtains and she could hear them all laughing together. They had shut her out. Mary wrapped her arms around herself. She was so weary of it all: trying to keep the family together, making a go of the market-stall and squeezing a life for herself between all the competing demands of everyone. Again she shivered. How badly she wanted to unwind the clock and be back to the moment just after Dad had toasted her, when they were all raising their glasses and Matthew was smiling at her. Most of all she wanted to sneak back indoors, crawl into bed, pull the covers over her head and forget Christmas. She had two choices. One was to climb over the garden wall and go through Granny Pragnell's house out to the street. Then she would pull the key through the letterbox and slide back into her own room unnoticed. The second option was to go back to the kitchen and face everyone. Both alternatives took away her pride. What would she do if she lifted the latch and found the back door still locked against her?

For a moment she thought of taking shelter in the outside lavatory, but it hadn't been cleaned for ages. She crouched, weeping, beside the privet hedge. Immersed in her unhappiness it was some time before she became aware of someone calling to her.

'Who's there? Is it you, Blyth? Mary, Faith, Mercy, who is it?'

'Mary, my dear child, step over here, whatever's the matter?'

She climbed over the wall into Granny Pragnell's arms and walked up the yard into the next door kitchen.

'Albert,' she called to her husband, 'put the kettle on. I think Mary could do with a cup of tea, good and strong.'

Shivering and crying, she was now beyond pride.

'Sit down by the fire, my duck. That's it. Mr Pragnell will go and get you a blanket, you must be perished.' Granny's dark eyes were full of concern. She tucked the blanket around Mary and set her feet on a little stool. 'Let's get those shoes off and I'll find you a pair of slippers. They're old and worn but will fit the purpose for now.'

Mary stared into the red heart of the fire, watching the spark fairies travelling up the chimney. The warmth began to seep into her and overcome the shivering. Mr Pragnell pottered about with the kettle and the tea-things. He handed her a steaming cup, making sure she had a firm hold of the saucer.

'Here you are, dear lady, drink it while it's hot, it will put fresh heart into you. Beatrice,' he said to his wife, 'I will take my cup up to the studio.'

Granny Pragnell handed her a handkerchief then settled herself in the armchair opposite.

Mary could not stop crying. She was raw with grief. Every hurt welled up in her and poured out in gasps and sobs. 'He's left me, Mercy's pinched me ring and I've mucked up Christmas fer everyone.' Then she was swamped afresh.

'There, there, my duck,' said Granny, patting her hand. 'You'll melt if you don't stop blubbing. Here, give me that cup and you blow your nose. That's it. Now, drink up this tea while it's good and hot.'

'What am I going to do?' Mary wailed.

'Do you want to tell me what happened?'

'I've said.'

'All you've said is the outcome. What went before? We can't mend anything until we know how it got broken.'

Mary didn't want to tell her, to admit afresh that it was all her fault. She wanted to sit here with Granny as she had done when she was little.

'Mary,' she said stirring her tea, 'I've known you all your life. Really known you: impatience, bad temper, jealousy and all. Nothing you can say is going to make me think badly of you. I know the good things, too, your courage and determination, and there's a loving heart under all that barnacle shell. If there wasn't, Matthew wouldn't have bothered with you in the first place.'

'It was my fault,' she whimpered.

'I'll be the judge of that,' said Granny, after she had gone over to the table and cut her a slice of Christmas cake.

Mary began to feel less desperate. Everything here was settled and familiar from the red tablecloth with its heavy fringe to the collection of shells on the dresser and the treadle sewing machine by the window. Granny Pragnell with her pillowy figure and grey hair skewered into a bun had been her lifeline in many crises in the past. Mary bit into the cake and realised that she was hungry.

Granny drank her tea and stared into the fire. She reminded Mary of a lighthouse; solid and unchanging amid all that flowed around her.

'I was so fagged out with getting everythink ready for the dinner,' she burst out. 'Eight of us, there was. Had to borrow an old door from up the road, for a table, and a trestle. Got the dinner dished up then when the twins knocked over the trestle and all the grub got messed up I wanted to kill them.'

'I think I would have wanted to do the same.'

Mary looked up in surprise.

'What did they know or care how hard you'd worked, all the planning it took, list making, and getting everyone on your side?'

'I couldn't sit there afterwards with gravy all over the tablecloth, the meat and veggie's all mixed together on the plates as if someone had sicked them up.'

'And all in front of your Matthew.'

Mary looked up at her and Granny Pragnell smiled. 'What my first husband Joseph would have called "a bugger-up in a pudding-basin".'

Mary smiled, then finished eating her cake. 'I went into my room all steamed up and spitting feathers. Then Matthew came along with a tray with our dinners sorted out nice. I was calming down and he said as I should go and put my ring back on.'

'Where had you put it?'

'It was in a cup, on the top shelf of the dresser. I went and got it down and there was nothing in there. It was gone. I was asking everyone and Mercy giggled all smug like, as if to say, I'll pay you back for shouting at me when I burnt myself.'

'You didn't tell me about that,' said Granny. 'What happened?'

'She just poured the gravy on her hand. Made such a fuss she did. It was all their carry-on that knocked over the trestle.'

'It must have been a shock. Mercy must have hurt herself and been quite frightened.'

'It didn't mean she could nick my ring.'

'There's no doubt that she took it?'

'She took it and it's thanks to her that Matthew left.'

Granny gave her one of her beady looks. 'Are you sure about that?' she said.

Mary blushed. 'Well,' she mumbled, 'he told me to calm down and he'd help me look for it.' There was a long silence and when she spoke again her voice was barely above a whisper. 'I called him stupid and then he went and got his mack and pushed off.'

Granny didn't say anything. She cut another slice of cake and put it on Mary's plate and refilled her cup.

'See, I've ruined everythink.'

'The ring is not what's important.'

'Mercy's took it and Matthew pushed off because of it.'

'Are you sure?'

'Well, it ain't turned up.'

'No,' said Granny Pragnell, pouring her another cup, 'I think it was calling him stupid that was the final straw. He'd made a lot of effort. From what you said, he's a quiet fellow, a bit overwhelmed by your family. Came over to dinner and then you lose your temper and show him up in front of everyone. You're not the only one with pride, you know.'

'He was the one what walked out,' said Mary fiercely.

'What choice did he have?'

Mary squirmed.

'It's quite simple, really,' said Granny Pragnell. 'You have to write and tell him that you're sorry. Explain that you were tired and over-wrought and didn't mean it. Tell him how much you valued the ring and what it represents for you.'

'I can't.'

'Mary, Mary,' the old woman said, shaking her head. 'Pride is a cold bedfellow. Would you swap it for a chance to mend things with Matthew?'

'What if it don't make no difference?'

'Well, you will have made every effort to mend things. The next move is down to you.'

'I'm so tired.'

'Sleep on it, my duck. This letter of yours is important. Not something to be rushed over. On the other hand don't leave it too long. Some other girl might snap him up while you're diddle-daddling.'

'Glad you're back home,' said Mary, staring at her feet.

'So am I, dear,' said Granny. 'I'm a fish out of water anywhere else. You let me know what you decide to do. Nothing comes of nothing. Only the brave deserve the fair, so screw up your courage and get that pen out.'

Granny sat with Granny talking about her Granddaughter Lily and her new baby, down in Plymouth. The clock over the mantelpiece chimed six.

'Now, my duck, Mr Pragnell will be getting cold upstairs, I must go and rescue him.'

Reluctantly Mary said goodnight and went out into the street. The house was in darkness, as she let herself into the passage. She felt for the matches on the mantelpiece in the kitchen and lit the lamp.

Mary was amazed to find all the pots, dishes and cutlery washed, dried and stacked neatly on the makeshift table. There was a plate with a bowl inverted over it. Inside she found a round of chicken and stuffing sandwiches, also a note.

> *Dear Mary,*
> *Have gone round to Harry and Dora's.*
> *Hope you enjoy the grub. Come round if you want.*
> *Love, Dad.*

Her spirits lifted. It would have been Dad, too, that thought of leaving her something. After finishing every crumb she set the plate in the sink. Passing the Christmas tree on her way to bed she saw something glinting on one of the higher branches. It was her ring.

6

Gradually, Charles Clements was settling into his new life. As he looked in his new diary he realised that it was three weeks since he had returned. Tomorrow would be the seventeenth of January. In that time he had removed the dust covers on the furniture, sent most of the bed linen to the laundry and begun to air the house. He had visited the employment exchange in an attempt to find a scullery maid and a cook.

'I would suggest daily staff would be sufficient for your needs, Sir, and be more suitable for a gentleman on his own,' said the woman behind the desk at the Employment Exchange.

'Quite so,' said Charles. 'There will be little for them to do while the children are at school. Of course, in the holidays they will be kept quite busy.'

Charles had led the woman to believe that he was a widower. Admitting divorce was still shaming to him. Mercifully, Malaya was a world away from England and the possibility of bumping into Lettice or Lawrence again was a distant and unlikely possibility. By the time either of them came back to England he would have his life and that of his children running smoothly, of that he was determined.

After a disastrous week with a slatternly mother and daughter who made off with half the cutlery and left behind slimy dishcloths and burnt pans, he decided to manage for himself. He used only his bedroom, bathroom and the kitchen, eating mainly at his club or at the homes of a few old naval companions.

His sister Lavinia had visited the children at Cerne Magna and expected them soon for a week-end stay in her cottage nearby. He drew her letter out of his pocket and tried to read between the lines.

I think Miles was a little overawed when he first arrived at Chantry House but he now appears more settled. The news that he would be seeing you for Easter has cheered him enormously. Little Charlotte has now stopped wetting the bed and speaks of a little friend she has made recently. The child is equally delighted at the thought of seeing her daddy again.

I will bring them down on Maundy Thursday as arranged. They will both be writing to you themselves now that they know you are settled in Portsmouth.

Each day Charles waited for their letters. He had written to them himself and promised all sorts of treats, and today he had been rewarded.

Dear Daddy,

I will see you soon. My Friend Kate has a rabbit and I would like one, too. Please Daddy. Aunt Vinnie will buy one if you say yes. Is the picture of Mummy and me still in my bedroom?

Love from Lottie.

When had she become Lottie? he wondered.

Dear Pa,

Only 8 more weeks and I will be home. It is all right here but I miss you and the sea. Rugby is a struggle but I am getting better slowly. Mr Wallis is a decent man and says I have a first class brain. I would rather be good at rugby.

From Miles

Charles sighed. His son seemed to be following in his own unhappy footsteps at school. He resolved to talk with him. If he was really unhappy Miles could go to school in Portsmouth. Lettice could think what she liked.

He had settled well into his job at the school in Mile End. The boys were a mixed bunch: some natural mathematicians, others having to cram for all they were worth. He found that his quiet encouraging manner yielded results. On Thursday evenings he returned to give extra coaching for the slower pupils and was glad to see some improvement in their work. Activity, that was the cure.

He realised that he must get the house into better order for when the children came. But in the meantime he had another problem to solve – an unknown visitor. Days would go by and he would convince himself that he had imagined the back door closing in the early hours of the morning, or the piece of pie that went missing from the pantry. Obviously the intruder was not a serious thief, for there had been ample opportunity to make off with several valuable items, but nothing was misplaced. The only evidence of their presence was a damp towel in the upstairs cloakroom and the diminishing bar of soap. What could they want? Perhaps it was just a warm billet away from the winter streets. Certainly Portsea had its fill of poor wretches down on their luck. He felt ashamed of his country when he passed old soldiers with medals pinned to their jackets, selling matchboxes or bootlaces. Once, he had seen a lad, not much older than Miles, pushing a handcart with all his family's possessions on top and a pregnant mother and toddler following behind.

Perhaps if he could meet up with the mysterious night-visitor he might be able to help him. Charles sighed. He would have to do something before the children arrived or they would be badly frightened. Just in case the intruder had a more sinister purpose, he had taken to sleeping with his service revolver beside his bed and he was determined to use it should the need arise.

Cissie crouched over the cup of cocoa in the Slum Post at Lemon Street. Major Grice had sorted her out some new drawers and a winter frock. She hoped to sneak up to her room in Lancaster Terrace later, if the coast was clear, and change into them. Her present jacket and skirt were too thin and hung on her skinny frame. First she had to scrub the floor for the major but that was no hardship. It was warm inside, and she liked hymn singing. In the afternoon the women would come with their children. She would go then. The sight of their babies made her sad.

Sometimes she would go with a sailor in the afternoon. Thursdays was good because they had free time. A make-and-mend it was called. They were less trouble then, not being so drunk. She had had a scare the other night when one of them had followed her home. Hours she'd had to wait hidden behind a dustbin until he grew tired and went back to Queen Street, swearing to himself. More frightening was the man back at Lancaster Terrace. Cissie had had some narrow escapes. He seemed to be making himself at home, opening all the windows and moving around the furniture. The biggest worry was if he changed the locks. She couldn't bear to be exiled from the house and the memories locked inside: Christmases with good grub inside her and a present from the tree, sharing nursery tea sometimes with Miles and Charlotte and listening to Nanny reading stories to them. Best of all was larking about in the kitchen with Mary when cook was out. Cissie had thought about her today when she was at the Slum Post. It was on the corner of Lemon Street where Mary lived. She'd been there once, a long time ago, and seen her family. Pride had kept her from calling, not wanting her friend to see her looking so down-at-heel.

'Here you are, Cissie, a little parcel of sandwiches for later. Come back tomorrow and we might be able to find you somewhere to live. They could do with someone at Springhaven for the rough work, might even be able to find you a space in one of the dormitories.'

No, she couldn't do it. Couldn't watch those girls with their babies – not after Charlie. Besides, she had somewhere to live as long as she sneaked in and out and kept quiet.

'That's kind of you, Major, but I think I might find something myself. Ta for the sandwiches.'

'God bless you, my dear. Come round on Monday when the doctor's here. He should listen to your chest. That cough of yours sounds really bronchial.'

''Bye, Major, God bless,' Cissie said, hurrying down the street. Today was Saturday and mostly she had to wait for clients until the pubs closed. When she'd had her room to herself, before the strange bloke moved in, she would have gone back now and had a bit of a sleep to keep up her strength. Now it was getting more dangerous by the day, as the bloke kept rummaging about the house. Any moment they would bump into each other and the game would be up.

She wandered down Queen Street and rested on a shop window ledge while she looked about her. It was seething with sailors roistering from one pub to another. Cissie sniffed the air laced with beer, fried fish, vinegar and hot meat pies. Her mouth watered and she took her packet of sandwiches and cake from her pocket and bit into a piece of gingerbread. What she wouldn't give for a bag of chips, piping hot and covered with a snowstorm of salt – piping hot.

Cissie yawned and thought of her little room, warmer now that the bloke had started lighting fires. As she hurried down one of the side streets she saw a sailor approaching, his rolling gait testament to a beery dinner-time.

Anticipating a likely client, she hid her new clothes and

sandwiches in a hedge outside a house with no curtains. When she looked up again the sailor was getting closer.

'Give ya two bob, lying down,' he said. 'Where can ya take us?'

Cissie had dealt with him before and tried to shrink away. He had been rough with her and bruised her breasts.

'Ain't got nowhere,' she muttered, still struggling with him.

'Won't get no better offer,' he snarled. 'It's blank week, don't get paid till next Thursday. 'Side's, you're a skinny little bitch, should be bloody grateful.' He shoved her towards an old shed, kicked the door in, then dragged her after him.

It was cold and dark and smelt of cats. He made her lie on the floor and dragged down her drawers his nails scraping her thighs. While he was thrusting at her a rat ran over her foot. She screamed and pushed him away with all her strength, leaving him unsatisfied. He grabbed her leg as she tried to escape.

'Back here, you poxy bitch, you don't short-change Taffy Jenkins.' As she fell over he smacked her in the eye.

Cissie flinched. 'It were a rat,' she whimpered.

'Come back here or I'll give you such a wallop,' he roared, catching hold of her hair and dragging her back onto the ground. Later, her torturer thrust her aside and buttoned his trousers. He flung some coins on the ground. 'There's ninepence! About all yer worth.'

The shed door slammed behind him and Cissie was alone. Shamed and weary she scrabbled up the money into her pocket. If she had not been so frightened of the rats she would have stayed in the shed till it was dark. Only the thought of her bundle, hidden in a hedge down the street, gave her the impetus to move.

Looking about her Cissie turned the key and slid inside the back door of Lancaster Terrace. The kitchen was empty and the house shadowy and still. She took a glass tankard from the cupboard and filled it with tap water. With thumping heart she turned the door handle and crept into the hall – still no sound came from the house. After setting the glass on the mantelpiece in her room, Cissie crept down to the linen cupboard and found a clean towel, pillowcase and sheet. She looked longingly at the bathroom. How she would have revelled in a long hot bath, but it was too dangerous. Instead, she made do with the washbasin in the lavatory and a bar of carbolic soap. Cissie stripped off her clothes, stood on the bath mat and washed herself all over, then towelled dry before creeping back up the stairs.

In the cupboard at the bottom had been a nightdress of Madam's, pink silk with lace edging. After putting it on Cissie used the last shred of energy to strip and remake her bed. The crisp freshness of the sheets settled around her like a blessing and she fell into sleep. Later in the night she awoke in a sweat with a pain in her chest. Peering out of the window Cissie saw that it was still dark. After eating one of the fish paste sandwiches she gulped down the remains of the water in the tankard. It took her a while to settle again because of her cough. She hoped the man downstairs couldn't hear it. Sometime in the night she awoke with a raging thirst and the need for the lavatory. As she crept down the attic stairs, towards the family bedrooms, Cissie stepped on to the landing and a creaking floorboard froze her in her tracks.

The door of the bedroom nearest her burst open.

There was shouting, a great flash and then a bang filled her head, knocking her off her feet. Falling . . . she was falling into the darkness. A crack jolted her, as she hit the tiled floor. 'Aahhh!!' Cissie screamed as pain bit into her shoulder. 'Aahh! Aahh!'

7

It was January the seventeenth, her twentieth birthday, and Mary paced up and down outside the post box with the letter to Matthew in her hand. Dad had promised a fry-up for breakfast and the whole family was going round to Harry and Dora's for tea. Thank goodness it was a Sunday and she could please herself what she did.

A birthday was a time to take stock. She had come to a decision – it was time to move on. Regardless of what had happened between her and Matthew she was leaving Lemon Street. Dad and the kids would just have to muddle through. Tomorrow she would get the paper and see what jobs were going in Gosport. Mary had no illusions about her employability. Probably she'd end up scrubbing floors or waiting at tables. Might have to take on more than one job to pay for food and lodgings. If she could, she would still go over to the market on Saturdays. Anything was possible, anything but hanging around the house doing nothing. Life had got to be more than just waiting for a letter. There was her whole future ahead of her with or without Matthew.

The postman shoved some envelopes through the Vine door then walked on towards her. Mary stuffed Matthew's letter back in her pocket. She'd see if he sent her a birthday card before doing any posting.

'Happy birthday, my gal,' said Dad, as she went into the kitchen and sat herself at the table. 'Want to look at yer cards 'fore I dishes up?'

'Have me grub, first,' she said, already having seen that there was nothing for her from Matthew. 'Ta.' She smiled at Dad as he set a sizzling plate in front of her.

For the first time in ages she was hungry. As she dipped the sausage into a blob of brown sauce Blyth came thumping down the stairs.

'Happy birthday,' he said, laying cards and a lumpy parcel down in front of her. In spite of his protests she hugged him and planted a kiss on his cheek.

'Blaahh!' he cried, scrubbing at his face with his fist.

Mary laughed. 'What's this?' she asked.

'Made it for you meself,' he said proudly.

Slowly, teasingly, she untied the string and removed the paper from her present. It was a hoopla game. On a large square of wood a scene from *Jack and the Beanstalk* was painted. Set at intervals, across the picture, were cup hooks with numbers painted underneath. Hanging from the hooks were hoops made from coiled rope. The scene was lively with a fearsome giant, a flourishing beanstalk and a plump brown and white cow.

'It's wonderful, love,' said Mary, threatening Blyth with another hug. 'Ain't you the clever one? We'll take this round to Harry's tonight and try it out.'

'Could do some for down the market,' said her brother, blushing with pride.

'That'd be champion,' said Dad, slapping Blyth on the back. 'Watcha reckon Mary?'

'Could be a real money-spinner,' she said, smiling at him.

Blyth wandered down the yard and Mary poured herself more tea before opening her cards. There was one from Granny Pragnell with a green chiffon scarf folded inside and another from the twins with 'To Our Dear Sister' on the front. She chuckled. They probably got it cheap from the penny bazaar. Turning it over she saw a footprint on the back. Likely they'd found it in the street. Well, it served her right for nagging them.

'Happy birthday', they chorused, coming through the kitchen door together, yawning and rubbing their eyes. 'Gotcha this.'

It was a black tube with the words Crème Simone Vanishing Cream picked out in gold. She always laughed at the name, it sounded like something from a conjuror's box of tricks.

Mary smiled at them. 'Ta,' she said.

The last card was one from Harry and Dora with a ten-shilling note attached. She looked up and saw Dad watching her.

'Nothink from my fiancé,' she snapped. 'Just as well I didn't post me letter to him.'

'By rights you should have,' he said, setting some fried bread on plates for the twins. 'You was in the wrong whatever way you looks at it.'

'If he really loved me . . .'

'Ain't got nothink to do with it, gal. You've boxed yerself into a corner with that pride of yours. How long you gonna wait? Till you've got artheritis and bunions. Life's too short. All this bunkum about love! If you really cared about him, who was right wouldn't come into it.'

'Waahh! Listen to this,' said Faith, who had just come back from the outside lavatory with a square of newspaper in her hand.

'What you got there?' asked Dad, blinking behind the smoke from his cigarette.

'This is our chance.'

'Watcher on about?' said Mercy, drizzling brown sauce on her bread.

'Auditions will be held at the Hippodrome Theatre, Wednesday January 20th, at 11.00 a.m., for dancers.

Debonnaires Touring Company.
Under 16 years need parents' written consent.'

Faith chuckled. 'Lucky I didn't wipe my bum with it, was just going to, our fortunes would've gone down the pan!'

They all laughed.

'Good job your sister give you them taps and yer old Dad fixed them on for you,' said Fred, sitting down to a bacon sandwich.

'How you gonna look sixteen?' asked Mary, gathering up her cards.

'We can dress up and put lipstick on,' said Faith, butting in. 'We got time to practise. Stop pickin' holes. We don't want ter spend our life in the brewery washin' bottles what matelots have peed in and stickin' on labels, day after day.'

Mercy was startled at her sister's sudden confidence. Again she read the notice in the paper. 'All we gotta do is practise like mad,' she said, catching Faith's excitement. 'We'll wear them jumpers what Dora give us, our black skirts and put red bows on our tap shoes. Call ourselves the Scarlets, watcha think?'

'What if all the others is better than us?' asked Faith.

'Don't matter what the others is like. We got the edge.'

'How come?'

'We're twins, you cloth-head. People likes identicals and we're both good lookers.'

'I ain't seen your dancin' fer ages,' said Fred. 'If you gals washes up and makes the place look shipshape, your old dad might fetch down the gramophone.'

Mary smiled. Dad's gramophone, won in a card came, was his only bargaining counter with the twins and he used it shamelessly. There were two records, one of them patriotic songs and the other ragtime favourites. Fred wound up the gramophone and the twins clattered across the kitchen in their tap shoes. As soon as the music began they waved their arms and stretched their mouths into the exaggerated smiles of the chorus girls they'd seen in variety shows. When the gramophone began to run down they danced more and more slowly, matching their voices to the lugubrious tones of the record. Fred began to turn the handle once more and they giggled as the voices sang with frantic speed.

'When the red red robin goes bob bob bobbin' along, along . . .'

Fred and Blyth laughed, too.

Dad wound the gramophone up again, then sat there watching them, a dreamy expression on his face.

He's thinking about Mum, thought Mary. Dolly Vine had been at her best when dancing and singing. Everyone had been caught up in her enjoyment. The twins had the same red curls and impish faces. Wouldn't Mum have been proud of them? she thought. Wouldn't she have laughed and kicked up her heels? It was rarely that Mary thought of her and when she did it was always the girls that reminded her. She wondered what Mum would have done in her position. Live now, pay later, was her motto.

'Just going out a minute,' she said. 'Won't be a tick.'

'Wind it up again, Dad, go on,' pleaded the twins.

Matthew was relieved when the Christmas leave was over and the *L75* was under sailing orders. At least at sea his troubles had practical solutions.

From his position below in the engine room, he could visualise the leaving-harbour-routine taking place above. The Captain would be on the conning tower issuing a succession of orders while, on the casing, able seamen in white jerseys and bellbottoms would be coiling down cables and other deck paraphernalia. The diesel engines would kick into life, creating a creamy wake astern, and the sea would roll along the curves of the ballast tanks. On passing Fort Blockhouse the White Ensign on the Jack staff would be raised and lowered and all the problems ashore would be left behind.

Matthew and Bob were like automatons: reading gauges, turning wheels and shutting off valves. In the confined space of the boat the noise of the diesel engine was magnified into a crescendo of sound. Later they would dive and the clamour of the engine would give way to the steady hum of the electric motors.

After the Officer of the Watch had called, 'Diving stations, diving stations,' everything happened in a rapid succession of barked orders and responses. Water flooded into the ballast tanks and the boat sank, guided by the hydroplanes. The bridge watchmen dropped down the conning tower into the control room, followed by the Captain who shut the hatch just as the sea surged over the boat.

'Thirty-two feet, Number One,' he said and the needles on the depth gauges began to fall.

Matthew and the duty stokers proceeded to shut down and de-clutch the engines from the propeller shafts while the electricians at the main motor panel followed orders on the telegraphs. He never ceased to marvel at the smoothness of the complex manoeuvres required to submerge the submarine, and the ensuing silence after the surface clamour.

'Hold her at thirty-two feet,' ordered the First Lieutenant from the control room to the diving team. 'Flood forward, stop flooding. Pump from aft, stop pumping.'

Water was pumped fore and aft until the submarine was at a state of equilibrium or trim. It required some mathematical skill in balancing inner and outer pressures to arrive at this happy state.

'Up periscope,' the Captain said. 'Hold her steady now, Number One.'

'Aye, aye, Sir.'

'Down periscope. Take her down to sixty feet. Finish with diving station.'

'Aye, aye, Sir,' said the First Lieutenant. He then ordered, 'Blue watch, patrol routine. Up spirits, hands to dinner.'

Matthew and Bob were relieved and they left the engine room to take their daily tot of rum in their mess, poured into their glasses by the senior leading stoker from a pussers' measure.

Matthew smiled to himself. He had once got very involved in explaining the word 'pusser' to his mother.

'It's the essence of the navy, the absolute correct thing. If you're pusser navy, you're a real spit-and-polish merchant.'

'It sounds like a horrible infection,' she had said, not in the least impressed.

Poor Mother, always so precise, she wouldn't last five minutes in a stoker's mess.

Bob's laughed pulled him back to the present. 'Old chef's looking green,' he said. 'Been throwing up into one bucket while he peels spuds into the other.'

'That don't sound promising,' said Bob Cowley. 'Still, as long as he doesn't get the buckets mixed up we're laughing.'

'What's on the menu?' asked Matthew, his appetite diminishing.

'Cottage pie.'

They downed their tots and went back to their stations to be relieved later by Blue watch who had eaten and washed up.

'What's the date?' Matthew asked as he forked up a mouthful of mashed potato.

'Twenty of January, I think. Why d'you want to know?' asked Bob.

'I've missed Mary's birthday,' he said.

'Thought you'd finished with that party,' said Boggy Marsh, another stoker. 'Came back Christmas with a face like a bloody kite. Ain't heard nothing about her since.'

'Dunnow,' said Matthew. 'I was just thinking.' The last thing he wanted was to have his private life subjected to the scrutiny of Boggy.

'Lethal, that is,' laughed Marsh. 'My missis is always thinking. We gets on champion the first week I'm home. Can't get enough of me, afternoons, mornings and nights. Bleedin' insatiable she is.'

Someone blew a derisive raspberry.

'Second week she gets to look at me different. Starts talking about all the little jobs round the place what needs doing. Christ! By the time the leave's up we're getting on each other's nerves something chronic.'

Matthew nodded, knowing that Boggy was a man of urgent appetites and little imagination. He was right; since Christmas he had hardly mentioned Mary. At first he had fumed about her, regretting all the money he had spent on the ring and smarting at her showing him up in front of her family. But he missed her. All the chaos and fury of that afternoon seemed harmless now. He had known her for nearly three years, more if he counted the time they had written to each other while he'd been out in the Far East. Mary was not all sound and fury. Beneath her toughness was a frightened little girl. She trusted him and sometimes she could be so tender. There were things they had told one another that he would not dream of breathing to another soul. What did being called stupid matter in comparison with all the loving moments they had shared? Before they had sailed Matthew had looked for a letter but none had come. He had hoped to hear from Mary yet not really expected her to write. Saying sorry would be such a hard thing for her to do, she would be so fearful of exposing herself to his rejection. Perhaps it was up to him. When he got a minute he'd try and get his thoughts together, put his side of the day – all the hope and disappointment.

*   *   *

After they had washed up and squared away the plates Matthew and the rest of Red watch climbed into their bunks. This was the time when Mary flooded his mind, when he played and replayed their every meeting. He tried to remember how it felt when they were lying together on her bed and he was stroking her. She had been so warm and defenceless. It had started with him wanting to soothe away her distress, and then another feeling overtook him. He had wanted to lose himself in her without that cautionary voice nagging in his ear. To be skin against skin, led only by their need of each other. *Mary, Mary, Mary*, he breathed against the blanket, his body taut with frustration. Matthew sighed. Whatever he thought or did it would be another six weeks or so until she'd get his letter. Sometimes he hated the navy.

8

The flash and crack of the shot, the thud as the body hit the stairs and then the scream terrified him. Charles fumbled for the light switch. 'Oh, my God!' He hurtled down the stairs to the figure lying face down at the bottom. It looked to be a child, partly clothed, with blood pouring from a wound in the shoulder.

'Aahh, aahh! Don't shoot me no more.'

'Sweet Jesus!' he gasped as he recognised her. 'Cissie!' Horrified, he put the revolver down on the hall table. Oh the blood! He must stop the bleeding. Snatching up a towel from the cloakroom he bunched it into a pad, rushed back to Cissie and pressed it to her wound. She screamed in pain.

Charles was sweating with fear. My God! He had shot her. She could die. Right in front of him she could bleed to death. He tore into the sitting room and grabbed up a cushion and tried to make Cissie more comfortable.

'Aaahh!' She ground out the sound between clenched teeth.

It was impossible to get her into a sitting position. She was still lying face down on the cold tiled floor. All he could do was slide the cushion under the side of her face. Cissie's nightdress was now soaked in blood.

'Aaahh,' she gasped. 'Me back.'

Charles continued to press the pad against the wound, his fingers slippery with blood. If he let go the pressure in order to ring the ambulance the bleeding would increase; if he didn't ring she could die.

He stared at her as he dialled the number for the police station, willing the blood to stop. She seemed to be shrinking before his eyes. Her whole body was shaking and there was a dark pool forming on tiles. Before he had a chance to speak to the voice at the other end of the telephone, he was distracted by a thundering on the front door. Leaving the receiver trailing from the hook he went to answer it.

Standing outside were two policemen.

Charles stared at them.

'What's been going on?' asked the older of the two men, looking past Charles and into the hall. 'We heard a gunshot coming from this house and someone screamed.'

'It was me,' he gabbled, 'I shot her. It's all a most ghastly mistake. Cissie, it's Cissie Nugent. I was her employer but I didn't realise she was, she was . . .'

'I'm Constable Hammond and this is Constable Perks,' said the older of the two policemen hurrying to Cissie's side. 'Call the station. Get them to send an ambulance at once and we'll need a detective sergeant. You, Sir, get a cloth and a blanket, quickly now.'

Ignoring Charles, Perks went to the telephone. 'Who's that?' he said into the mouthpiece. 'Yes, we needs an ambulance at 15 Lancaster Terrace, urgent. Girl hurt bad. Send Stanton down here. It's Perks speaking.'

'Don't be frightened, Miss,' said Constable Hammond to Cissie. 'We'll have you in hospital in no time.'

'Please God, please God, please God,' Charles implored, unable even to form the words of a prayer, as he rushed up then down the stairs with the blanket and a shirt.

'Give me that,' said the constable, folding the shirt into a square and pressing it over the sodden material already on the wound.

'Cissie, this is going to hurt but we must stem the bleeding.'

'Aaaaahh!'

Her screams echoed round the hall.

Charles knelt beside her holding her hand. 'Cissie, I'm so, so sorry. I never dreamt it was you. I had no idea.'

'Do you know this man?'

'Captain Clements. Aahh!' gasped Cissie, eyes wild with fright, her hair plastered to her face with sweat.

'Is that correct, Sir?'

'Yes,' mumbled Charles.

'Are you the only occupant of this house?'

'Yes, Constable.'

'What were you doing here last night, Cissie? Had he invited you to stay?'

'Aahh!'

'How did you get in?'

'A key,' Cissie was shivering and chalk-faced.

Charles couldn't believe he had done it. Never had he had cause to shoot anyone. Threatened yes, but shot, no. Poor, harmless little Cissie! He remembered how she would stand with her back to the wall like a shadow when Lettice used to shout at her, trying to melt into the brickwork.

'Ambulance is here,' said the other constable. 'I'll let them in.'

'You go with her, Perks, and stay till you're relieved. Note down anything she says.'

'Can I go with her, I'll fetch my coat.'

'You must remain here for questioning, Captain Clements,' said Hammond, sternly.

The driver of the police ambulance and Perks lifted Cissie onto a stretcher and the other constable held open the front door.

It was then that he realised the implications of what he had done. He could be sent to prison, he could be hanged. He might never see his children again. Cissie could die.

'May I telephone my sister and ask her to come here?'

Lavinia – the thought of his sister was like a life-belt. Always, in childhood, she had rescued him, but now he doubted that even her remarkable powers would be equal to the task.

'This is a very serious matter, Captain. But I think you'd best wait till the detective sergeant arrives.'

'May I change out of my pyjamas?'

'When he gets here you can. I shall have to come with you.'

Charles felt cold and his skin was clammy from his blood-soaked jacket. 'May I make us some tea, Constable?' he asked

Hammond handed him the blanket left behind by Perks. 'Why don't you sit down, Sir? He'll be here any minute.'

Thou shalt cleanse me with hyssop, and I shall be clean: thou shalt wash me, and I shall be whiter than snow.

Would that it were that easy, thought Charles as the verse from Psalm 51 sprang into his mind. Bathing and washing his pyjamas would be a simple matter, but freeing himself from the guilt of harming Cissie was another matter entirely. She had screamed like a fox in a trap. Never would he forget that sound. Poor Cissie, such a frail, inoffensive creature, the last person in the world he would willingly have injured.

Charles leapt with fright at the sudden rapping of the door-knocker.

Hammond answered the summons and stood in hushed conversation with a gaunt man swamped by a large overcoat.

'This is Captain Clements,' said the constable.

'Good morning, Sir,' said the sergeant, staring at him. 'The name's Stanton. I believe there has been a shooting and a young woman badly injured?'

Charles nodded. He felt seedy and wretched. The idea that he could coherently give an account of the events of the last hour or so seemed fantastical.

'The Captain wanted to wash and change before making a statement,' said Hammond.

'Where is the revolver, Sir?' asked the sergeant, appearing not to have heard.

'Oh, umm, oh, it's there, on the hall table,' muttered Charles.

'It's an 0.5 Webley and Scott, Sir,' said Hammond. 'One bullet fired and five left in the chamber.'

'Does the gun belong to you?' asked the sergeant, picking up the revolver in his gloved hand. He pushed a catch, which freed the chamber, and the bullets and spent cartridge fell into a glass ashtray. Taking a newspaper from the table he parcelled up the gun and the contents of the ashtray and handed it to the constable.

'Right, Hammond,' he said, turning towards them. 'Go with Captain Clements while he gets himself ready. Wrap up his pyjamas, they will need to be taken with us. You will have to accompany us to the station, Sir, for questioning and to make a statement.'

'My sister,' muttered Charles.

'All in good time.'

Charles washed and changed into a clean shirt and his grey civilian suit. He did not trust himself to shave, his hands were too unsteady. Strangely the presence of the stolid grey-haired constable was comforting. He couldn't bear being alone with his thoughts. If only he could find out if Cissie was still alive.

'You had better get your coat and hat, Captain Clements.'

The ride to the station was like a sequence from a nightmare. Charles sat in the back seat with Constable Hammond, praying to wake up at any moment. He was led through the station entrance into a room with mustard coloured walls and a desk with three rickety chairs.

Sergeant Stanton hung up his coat and hat on a hook behind

the door and indicated that Charles should sit down with Constable Hammond on the opposite side of the desk.

'May I phone my sister?' he asked. Lavinia, the thought of her no-nonsense common sense and rough kindness was like the grasp of a life belt.

'Write down her name and address,' said the sergeant. 'There's a phone over there on the desk. Have you the number?'

'No,' said Charles, feeling inept and disorganised.

Stanton took the piece of paper, took up the telephone and read the name, into the receiver. 'That's it operator, Dorset, Cerne Magna. The name is Mrs L. Mowbray, Simla Cottage.' He held out the phone to Charles, 'It's ringing now, Sir.'

'Vinnie, is that you? It's me – Charles. Yes, something is wrong, something terrible. I'm at the police station in Park Road. I've been arrested. I've done something terrible.'

'Charles, listen to me,' barked his sister. 'Calm down, now. Say nothing, admit to nothing until I arrive.'

'Oh Vinnie!' To his horror, Charles burst into tears.

'Charles,' Vinnie roared, 'you're a naval officer, take command of yourself.'

'I'm sorry, so sorry,' he wailed.

'Blow your nose, for God's sake, and get them to give you a cup of tea. I shall be down by lunchtime. Remember, Charles, silence until I get there.'

Charles sat staring at a poster on the wall, describing the perils of swine vesicular disease. The constable and the sergeant stood at the desk in whispered confab. Above them the second hand on a large clock swept ceaselessly round the dial. It was ten minutes to eight, less than two hours since Cissie had gone hurtling down the stairs. How was she? He was afraid to ask. 'May I go to the lavatory?'

'Of course, Captain.'

Charles left the room accompanied by the constable. He

was taken downstairs into a small cloakroom that smelt of vomit overlaid with Jeye's Fluid. Fear pulsed through him; the sound of his heartbeat seemed to fill the room. As he stood at the sink washing his hands Hammond began whistling through his teeth. Charles flinched at the sound. Every sense was heightened. His throat felt as if it were closing up through lack of moisture. 'May I possibly have a cup of tea,' he asked, 'or even a glass of water?'

'I'll just see you back to the room then I'll fetch one for you, Captain.'

He took the cup, when it was offered later. The hot liquid revived him. As he put it down the cup rattled in the saucer.

'Captain,' said Sergeant Stanton, taking a pen from his pocket, 'do you feel ready to answer some questions? I shall first caution you that anything you do say may be taken down and used in evidence against you.'

Charles nodded, gripping his hands together to stop them shaking. How very long ago it seemed that he had been in control of his life. Captain Clements, the man who had been responsible for the lives of hundreds of sailors, was now a criminal, awaiting sentence. If only he were awakening from sleep to find it all a nightmare. Lavinia would be furious with him for not waiting for her arrival, but he couldn't help it. It was the waiting that unnerved him.

After giving his name, age and address Charles took another gulp of tea.

The sergeant looked up from his writing and said, 'Constable Hammond tells me that the young woman, Cissie Nugent, was known to you?'

'Ah yes,' he answered. 'My wife employed her as a maid to assist my children's nanny.'

'When was that, Sir?'

'About five years ago and then a year later I was posted to

Singapore. The house was then closed and Cissie and the other staff went to other positions.'

'When did you last see Miss Nugent?'

'I suppose it must have been before going abroad.'

'Did you ever wonder what employment your maid found for herself after she left you?'

Charles flushed. He hadn't given it a thought. He had been caught up with settling his family in naval quarters in Singapore and taking command of his new ship. 'I believe my wife said something about Cissie working as a domestic for a firm of undertakers.'

'Where is your wife, Captain?'

'In Malaya,' he said, staring at the desk. 'We are divorced. She has since remarried.' When he looked up again Stanton was watching him.

'Would it surprise you to learn that Miss Nugent is known to the police as a common prostitute?'

'Dear God!' Charles leant on the table his head in his hands. Poor little Cissie! He could not imagine how she had survived in such a harsh environment. The same girl, who trembled between the tantrums of his wife and the swearing of the cook, having to withstand drunken men mauling her in back alleys.

'Why do you think that Miss Nugent was wearing a night-dress in your house, Captain?'

Charles could see that the policeman would be making a connection between his divorced state and Cissie's line of work.

'I believe she had been sleeping in the house for some time. It seems she had a key to the back door.'

'When did you return to your home, from abroad, Captain?'

'Christmas Eve.'

'You say that Cissie had been living at your house for some time. Why do you think that?'

He thought of that morning when someone flitted down the stairs and out of the door, before he had a chance to catch them. 'I heard movements from time to time, there were things taken from the linen cupboard. I just thought I had mislaid things. Once I heard someone coughing.'

'Didn't it occur to you to search the attic bedrooms? Or to call the police?'

'No,' said Charles. 'Since they took nothing of value I turned a blind eye. That is until I thought about my children coming to me for their holidays. Then I took to sleeping with my service revolver at my bedside.'

'This revolver was fully loaded, was it, Captain?'

As Detective Stanton's pen scratched on, Charles saw the pit opening up beneath his feet. What a fool he had been – letting things drift. If he had caught Cissie she would not be lying in hospital now, facing God knows what danger.

Stanton laid down his pen.

'Captain Clements, I must warn you of the seriousness of your position. If Miss Nugent dies you could be looking at a manslaughter charge and a term in prison.'

Charles gulped. It was so unjust. If he had to shoot anyone, why could it not have been Lettice's lover or even his worthless wife? 'Poor little Cissie,' he sighed, 'so innocent and defenceless.'

'In my experience, Captain,' said Stanton, 'most prostitutes are far from that.'

'If we had not gone away she would still have been in my employ. I am in some way responsible for what has happened to her.'

The detective coughed. 'Let's not speculate on that, Sir. What I want to do is to go back over the events of last night. Tell me what happened. What time did you go to bed?'

It all seemed a lifetime ago, that he had sat in his study with a glass of port preparing his lessons for the next week. 'It must have been about eleven or so. By the time I had finished reading and put out the light it would have been nearer to midnight.'

'What woke you up?'

'I had had a nightmare and was lying in bed trying to calm myself when I heard someone coughing and then the creak of a floorboard on the landing near my bedroom door.'

'What did you do?'

'I grabbed my revolver and rushed out of the door calling, "Who's there?" Someone ran past and I fired into the darkness.'

'Can you tell me exactly where you were at the time of firing, Captain?'

'At the head of the stairs.'

'On your way from the bedroom to the landing, would you have passed a light switch?'

'Yes.'

'It didn't occur to you to put on the light?'

'I think I was still in the grip of the nightmare, fearing for my life.'

'And so you fired into the dark?'

Charles nodded. How could this man, quietly going about his questioning, know about the dream? The ship had gone down and he was in the water alight with oil and surrounded by men screaming from their burns. He was swimming towards the lifeboat trying to keep a young sailor afloat at the same time. It always finished as he hauled the boy on board and found that he was dead, his face burned beyond recognition.

'What happened next?'

'I heard this scream and someone fell down the stairs and there was a crack as they hit the floor.'

'What did you do?'

'I put on the light and rushed down after them. It was Cissie.' He sat with his head in his hands unable to continue.

'Were you surprised to find that you knew the intruder?'

'Could, could I have a glass of water, please?' he gasped.

'Certainly, Captain. Hammond, fetch some water.'

Charles gulped the water down then tried to gather his thoughts into some coherence. 'I seem to have forgotten your last question,' he said, setting the glass back on the table.

'Were you surprised to find that Miss Nugent was your intruder?'

'Surprised! I was horrified.'

'What did you do?'

'I tried to staunch the bleeding and to make her comfortable. I was on the point of calling the police when they came knocking on my door.'

Stanton looked at Hammond and the constable gave a nod in corroboration.

'Were you surprised to see your ex-maid in a nightdress, in your house?'

'What? Oh I don't know that I noticed what she was wearing, I was so concerned about the bleeding.'

Stanton put the top on his pen and rose to his feet. 'Captain Clements, we shall want to detain you while the statement is written out. You will then be required to read it. If you are satisfied that it is a true account of what you have said you will sign it and will then be released to your own home.'

'Where am I to go?'

'You may stay in this room and the constable will remain with you.'

'Thank you,' said Charles, relieved to be done with the questioning. His release was unimportant, he didn't care where he was. What mattered was Cissie.

9

She had been falling through the air, forced off her feet by an explosion that drove the air from her body. Crack! Cissie hit the floor. Captain Clements leant over her with a gun in his hand. She wet herself. It wasn't just the gun that frightened her but his face crumpled and nearly crying. Then the pain bit into her back and she clenched her fists. When she opened her eyes Cissie saw blood spreading over the tiles and her hands red and slippery. She screamed as he pressed something against her shoulder and then he stopped and ran across the hall. Cissie clamped her eyes tight shut as she saw the pool of blood spreading further and further across the floor. Banging! Someone was banging at the front door like they wanted to break it down. Voices, lots of them, swirled about her and she felt that she would die of the cold. Faces; Captain Clements', a policeman's then another one swam before her. She screamed as they lifted her onto a board and carried her away to be lurched and jolted off to somewhere else.

'Cissie, we will have to operate to remove the bullet,' said a man in a white coat with a face like John Gilbert, the film star. 'Before we give you an injection to send you to sleep, is there anyone you would like us to contact for you?'

It was too cold to think and the face was so far away. She had to force her mouth to make the words. 'Slum Post, Lemon Street.'

There was a prick in her arm, the nurse in her starched cap smiled down at her. Everything began to spin. It was all happening so fast. What was real and what was dreaming? Cissie floated away.

She awoke to a nauseous stink in her nostrils of ether and her own sick. Her shoulder was swathed in bandages. The pain skewered through her and she could not stop shaking. If she could just change her position it might be possible to find a cool patch on the pillow and a way of stopping her arm hurting.

'Hello, Miss Nugent, we're going to give you a wash and make you comfortable.'

One of the two nurses removed the vomit bowl. The flannel was cool on her face and they dipped her left hand into the water. Later she swished a beaker of pink liquid around her mouth and savoured its freshness. Blood had leaked from her dressing and Cissie cried out as one of the nurses peeled her away from the pillows. She slumped into the other nurse's arms while her hair was brushed and tied back from her face. Exhausted and tearful she was set to rest on a nest of cool pillows on the bed table in front of her and submitted to another injection. Cissie slipped away into a world of soft voices and clean sheets.

Every time she opened her eyes there was a policeman at the end of her bed. He got up and moved towards her but she closed her eyes and retreated back into sleep. It was dark when the pain awakened her again. She could see a star between the gap in the curtains. Cissie realised she was not alone. On either side of her were beds, with people asleep in them, with the white counterpanes pulled high around their shoulders. Someone was moaning – she wished they would stop.

A nurse in a blue dress and a man in a white coat stood looking down at her. 'How are you, Cissie?' asked the man she took to be a doctor.

'Hurts,' she gasped. 'Drink – I wants a drink, so hot in here. What you done to me?'

The doctor drew up a chair beside the bed. From behind him she could see the policeman being waved away by the nurse.

'Do you remember being shot, Cissie?'

She nodded.

'You are a very lucky girl. The bullet passed through your arm and no vital organs were damaged. However, your fall has damaged your shoulder, tearing the muscles and fracturing the top of the ulna. It will take some time to heal. You will need rest and skilful nursing. Do you understand what I've said to you?'

'Hurts,' she gasped.

'A drink of water and give her a quarter grain of morphine every six hours. The registrar will see her in the morning. Good night, Miss Nugent.'

'Ta,' was all she managed to say to the doctor before he nodded to her and walked back down the room.

Lavinia Mowbray poured herself a brandy, and knocked it back in one gulp. Her intention had been to spend the day catching up on her correspondence and reading through the seed catalogues, prior to planning her spring garden. Now, all these activities would have to be abandoned. Instead, she flung her luggage in the boot and drew on her driving gloves.

Lavinia thanked God she had to concentrate on the road. It took her mind off Charles's disturbing news. Her brother had been arrested and had broken down in tears. It was like the plot from a woman's magazine, not something involving her family. Of course all this instability could be laid at Lettice's door. Flaunting her affair, humiliating Charles and then swanning off to Malaya and abandoning her children. Oh, Geminis were always so unstable.

'Vinnie, I've done something terrible,' he had sobbed at her. But what did that mean? Her mind skittered from one dastardly crime to another: treason, arson, embezzlement, buggery. Lavinia blushed and reached for her matches and the packet of Craven A in the handbag on the passenger seat beside her. Her inattention caused her to drift towards the centre of the road. A motorist seeking to overtake hooted loudly. Shaken, she pushed Charles to the back of her mind and concentrated on getting the Bentley safely to Portsmouth.

It was mid-afternoon when she came to a halt, at last, in Lancaster Terrace. Barely had she turned off the ignition when Charles rushed down the steps towards her.

'Vinnie, thank God you've come,' he said, opening the door and hustling her onto the pavement.

Lavinia was thoroughly alarmed. Her brother was in a crumpled suit and needed a shave. How had he let himself get in such a state? 'Charles, please, I beg of you, make me some tea, at once. I will see to my unpacking.' She followed him into the house, her stomach clenching at what she might find.

She looked around her. How drab and neglected everything was – no wonder, with the house shut up for three years. At the sight of a dark red patch covering the floor tiles, her hand flew to her mouth. My God! It was blood – she was certain of it. Throughout her journey she had been able to convince herself that Charles had exaggerated his problems – but now? Never had she seen her brother in such a wretched condition. He was jittery and on the verge of collapse.

She drew in her breath and squared her shoulders. Long years of being an army wife had taught her the futility of hand-wringing. Sizing up, making lists and apportioning tasks – that was the ticket.

Charles appeared from the kitchen with a tray of tea. Thankfully, Lavinia sank down into an armchair opposite her brother, in the sitting room. 'Where are your staff?' she asked.

'They weren't satisfactory,' he muttered.

'Very well, I will attend to that tomorrow. This house must be cleaned from top to bottom.' She sighed. 'It looks positively seedy. Such a tragedy, for a fine town house like this, I could weep.' As she began to pour the tea Charles burst forth in a torrent of words.

'Oh, Vinnie, do shut up about the house. It can fall in rubble around my feet for all I care. It's Cissie that matters. Poor, poor soul, she could die, you know. If that happens I'm for the gallows. I may never see my children again.'

Lavinia was aghast. 'Charles, whatever do you mean? Who in God's name is Cissie and what is she to you? Tell me, tell me at once.' It was all beyond belief. As she listened she tried to build a coherent picture of the events of the last few hours. For some unaccountable reason Charles had shot the little maid who had once worked for him and he had then been arrested. That was the nub of it. The hows, whys, and wherefores could be gone into later. Lavinia tried to bring her to mind. Small, and whey-faced with frizzy blonde hair – that was it. What colour her eyes were was a mystery to her, probably because she always seemed to be creeping around looking at the floor. Poor little wretch!

'If you could have seen her, Vinnie, she was like a wild animal in her pain and distress. I don't think I shall ever get the picture from my mind. And the blood!'

'Charles, for pity's sake stop pacing. It has all been a terrible mistake. The child, Cissie, has been taken to hospital, I presume?'

He nodded.

'Well, we must put her life into the hands of the Almighty. In the meantime, sit down, please, I beg of you.'

Lavinia took off her hat and coat. She could see that it would take some doing to put the fight back into her brother. Well, there was not a moment to lose. In six weeks Miles and Charlotte would be down for their Easter holidays. As for

Cissie, the least she could do for the child was to send her some flowers and a bowl of fruit. Would that be too much? Would she be overwhelmed? Lavinia pursed her lips. It was important to strike the right note.

The sky was streaked in pink when Cissie heard a trolley being pushed down the room and the rattle of cups and saucers.

''Allo, babes. You looks' zif you bin in the wars, what's up with ya?' The woman lumbered towards her in a vast flowered nightdress. 'Fancy a cuppa?' she asked.

'Wants a wee,' said Cissie.

'Right you are, babes. I'll get a nurse for ya and a bedpan.'

The nurse dragged some screens towards her and a strangely shaped metal bowl.

'Can I go to the lav?'

'Put your good arm around my shoulders, Miss Nugent,' she said, folding back the sheet and sliding her onto a cold metal pan.

Cissie felt dizzy and shamed by the nurse lifting up her nightgown and expecting her to pee in front of her.

'Best stay in bed for a day or two, my dear,' she said. 'When you're stronger you'll be pushed out to the lavatory in a chair.' She turned to the big woman with the trolley of tea. 'Not yet, Mrs Buggins, Miss Nugent will be on sips of water only for the next few hours.'

'There's a copper outside waiting to arst you loads of questions,' said Mrs Buggins, leaning over her directly the nurse had removed the screens and taken the pan away. 'Ooh! you've had them all running around like scalded cats.'

'I'd be obliged if you would take the teas around to the other patients,' snapped the nurse gliding up behind the voluble ward-maid.

'Right ho, Matron.' The big woman winked at Cissie and shuffled away.

What was going to happen to her? Would she ever get back to her little attic bedroom? Where was Captain Clements? The questions buzzed about in her head. She lay back against her pillows, too tired to worry about the answers. People were looking after her. That was enough for the moment. Cissie sighed. She was cool and clean and cared for and in no rush to get better.

10

There were two hours before they must present themselves at the Hippodrome and the twins were having one last rehearsal. They laughed and sang while clicking and clacking a path around the kitchen table. Yes, we're good, thought Mercy, but are we good enough?

Dad sat in the one battered armchair and bobbed his feet in time to the hundredth repetition of 'The red red robin', a cigarette dangling from his lips.

'You will write the letter for us, won't you, Dad, saying as you give permission?' She wheedled, standing behind his chair and winding her arms around his neck.

Fred drew in a deep, considering breath. 'Takes a bit of thinkin' about,' he said, between coughs. 'Leavin' home and goin' on the road be a sight tougher than you gals have bargained for. What'll you do if some old ponce wants ter interfere with ya?'

'I don't know,' said Faith, twisting a curl of hair round her finger.

Mercy frowned. She was not very sure what being interfered with amounted to. The Sunday papers were full of it. It seemed to happen most often with vicars what got unfrocked or something. It sounded more daft than dangerous. 'If we stays together all the time we'll be all right. They can't interfere with two of us at once.'

'You just brings up yer knee and give him one in the testimonials.' He rubbed his chin. ''Spose if you sticks together should be all right. I'll 'ave a think about it.' After a fit of coughing he said, ''Course, if one of you gals was to iron my shirt and the other was to polish me shoes,' he shrugged, 'it might help me to pull me thoughts together.'

While Mercy ran upstairs for the shoes and Faith stuck the iron on the range to warm, Fred drew a piece of paper and a crumpled envelope from between the old newspapers under the chair cushion.

> *Dear Sir,*
>   *My gals, Faith and Mercy has my permishion to go off dancin. I hopes they will be taken care of and learn their trade. If they comes to any harm I shall want to know the reason why.*
>   *Respekfully Fred Vine (Father).*

After kneeling on the floor and pressing his one and only shirt over the ironing blanket Faith held it out while Fred struggled into the sleeves.

'Champion, gal,' he said. 'Likes it fresh ironed, nice and warm.' While he tied his shoelaces the girls put their tap shoes in a carrier bag and dragged on their coats. Snatching up the envelope they hugged their dad and hurried up the street.

'Good luck, my babes,' he called from the doorway.

The twins joined the queue outside the theatre and their spirits sank. They raised their eyebrows at each other, signalling their misgivings. All of the other girls were better dressed and better prepared, holding music sheets and little cases containing their shoes and costumes.

'I've auditioned for Max Lemco before,' said one of them, holding a cigarette holder and blowing smoke rings. 'Harmless, he is.'

'Where you worked before?'

'Brighton and Bournemouth, the Isle of Wight and along at Torquay,' boasted another with an air of weary sophistication.

'I was in London; dying to get back there.'

'Where have you been?' asked a girl with bleached hair in tight pin curls around her face and hardly any eyebrows. 'Never seen you before.'

'We've been out of the country,' said Mercy. 'Just come back from Paris.'

'Oh yes,' Faith said, backing up her sister. 'We was in the Follies.'

Mercy could feel the other girls laughing at them, but she was determined not to let them see her discomfort.

'Dressing room twelve and look lively,' said a fierce woman with blue rinsed hair. 'Madame Lapin's the name and don't you forget it.'

'She's the chaperone, or busybody,' said the girl with the pin curls. 'Got to make sure we're on stage on time and don't get put in the family way by no one.'

'Or interfered with?' suggested Faith.

'Well, not where she can see you,' laughed the girl. 'The name's Jeanette. What's yours?'

'Mercy and Faith,' said the twins, shaking her outstretched hand.

'We'd best stick together,' she said. 'The others are a right toffee-nosed lot.'

Encouraged by her friendliness, they followed Jeanette along a corridor and into a bare echoing room, along the whole length of which was a mirror framed with light bulbs. Underneath was a shelf littered with stubs of greasepaint, an overflowing ashtray and a vase with stagnant water and two wilting roses. Below the shelf was a collection of rickety chairs. Mercy sniffed. The room stank of gin, old clothes and cheap scent.

The other girls began to change into their stage clothes, standing about half naked, smoking and chatting with one another. Some of them stared into the mirror while they did their hair or drew their mouths into an exaggerated Cupid's bow with bright red lipstick.

'Where's your togs?' asked the curly blonde, smoothing the wrinkles on her silk tights.

'Lost them when the boat sunk,' blustered Mercy.

Faith bent down and took their tap shoes out of the brown paper parcel and handed Mercy her pair. They were wearing the short-sleeved scarlet jumpers that Dora had given them at Christmas and two heavy Scotch kilts that they had bought from the old clothes stall at the dockyard walls. They were heavy and much too long. It was all a mad idea. They'd be better off back at the brewery. At least they'd be having a laugh. Among these girls they were fish out of water and they were drowning by the minute. She pinched Mercy's arm.

'Watcha do that for?' whispered her sister, fiercely.

'Let's get out of here. We don't stand a chance. Just be making fools of ourselfs.'

'I ain't lettin' them toffee-nosed cows get the better of us,' snapped Mercy. 'Got as much chance as they have. You want to go home, I'll do it on me own.'

Faith admitted defeat. She couldn't go home without her sister. They were in this together, sink or swim.

'Would you take a bit of advice?' asked Jeanette as she set a sequinned cap on top of her blonde curls.

Mercy scowled but Faith nodded.

'Those skirts will be hopeless to dance in. Haven't you got something shorter and lighter? Old Max will want to see your legs.'

'I told you we might as well shove off home,' said Faith near to tears.

'Don't give up, now, when you've got so close,' said Jeanette. 'There might be something behind that curtain in the corner.'

The three of them pulled back the long dusty length of cloth to reveal a tired collection of costumes hanging from a rail. To the twins' eyes there was nothing there of any promise. But Jeanette took down two pairs of short trousers with bib and braces such as a small boy would wear.

'Try them on,' she demanded. 'Take off your jumpers and slip the shorts on underneath. For God's sake hurry. Ain't no time to be shy; whatever you got I seen it all before.'

'Who d'you reckon they b'longs to?' asked Mercy, slipping the braces over her shoulders.

'Who cares? They ain't here, now,' said Jeanette, smoothing the twins' jumpers down over the shorts. 'Not wonderful,' she said, 'but they'll pass muster. Don't forget, when you're out there, eyes and teeth. Flash them for all you're worth.'

Faith would like to have asked her what she meant, but there was no time.

The woman with the blue hair clapped her hands together. 'Hurry up. Max'll be petulant if you keep him waiting. Up to the wings and no shoving.'

'The side of the stage,' interpreted Jeanette, following behind them.

As always in a crisis, the sisters held hands and shrank themselves against the wall. They were relieved to be last in the queue, which gave them a chance to size up the opposition. Each performer stepped confidently onto the stage as their name was called. Before beginning their act they went over to a woman at the piano, and gave her their pieces of music.

At a small table in the centre aisle of the auditorium sat Max Lemco.

'Now, darlings, give me some brio. Lightness, joy and above all brio.'

'Ain't he posh,' whispered Faith fascinated by Mr Lemco's fluty voice and the carnation in his striped blazer.

As the girls leapt into their performance, grinning madly

into the stalls and screeching out their songs, what little confidence the twins had mustered leaked away.

Max Lemco smoked a cigar and had a thin cane stick on a table along with a jug and a glass. At the end of each act he would assess their performance in one sentence or less. ''Bye, darling,' or, 'Ten o'clock, town station on Sunday.'

In between acts the pianist, a mouse of a woman with large tortoiseshell glasses, rummaged in her bag and brought out a half-finished sock that she was knitting and proceeded to turn the heel.

'Out,' Max snapped to a rather hefty girl with a husky voice. She stormed away, red faced and weeping.

'The Scarlets. Come along, ladies, knock me dead,' he demanded.

'Music,' called the pianist as the twins walked onto the stage.

'We ain't got none,' whispered Mercy hurrying across the stage. 'Can you do, "The red, red, robin"?'

'Right ho,' said the pianist, putting her sock away.

'Smile your heads off,' said Jeanette, holding up her thumbs.

Faith and Mercy blinked as they walked across the enormous empty space, their footfalls echoing behind them.

The pianist started playing.

The twins raised their arms and began to dance.

'Wait for your intro,' said the voice from behind the piano.

The pianist started again, this time nodding to them to begin and they once more raised their arms. After a few stumbling steps they began to keep time with the music. Faith began to get the giggles and soon Mercy was infected by her mood. They smiled and cavorted round and round the stage their feet tapping and hands waving.

'Very charming,' called Max. 'Anything else?'

It was then that Mercy remembered seeing this dance at the pictures. She and Faith had been mesmerised. They'd stayed through the whole programme twice and gone back the next day. 'Charleston,' she shouted to the pianist.

They threw themselves into the performance, going through all the moves that they'd seen at the Queen's Cinema. They waved their hands, crossed them back and forth over their knees and smiled for all they were worth. The audition was forgotten, they were just having the most glorious fun.

'The Scarlets, come down here, if you will,' called Max Lemco.

'Waah!' gasped Faith. 'D'you reckon he's taking us on?'

'Fingers crossed,' said her sister, following her off the stage.

'Pleased to make your acquaintance, my dears,' said Max Lemco, holding out his hand and blinking at them like a startled owl.

The twins shook hands and stared at him, never having seen such a man before. Their experience of men was limited to those they met at the brewery, larky working lads or those they chanced on in Portsea, sailors, dockyard mateys and the down-at-heel unemployed. Max Lemco was a bird of a very different feather. He would have been quite splendid if his striped blazer and plum-coloured cravat were not encrusted with cigarette ash and spilt food.

'Young ladies,' he said, 'I think you could be turned into a spirited pair of performers. Initially you will have to help behind the scenes, but it will all be rich experience.' He disappeared behind a cloud of cigar smoke. 'You look to be maids of very tender years. Have you your parents' written consent? I cannot devote hours of time to your improvement only to have you snatched away by an irate Mama.'

Mercy handed him the letter she'd forced from Dad.

He took up a pair of glasses hanging from a string on his

waistcoat and set them on his nose before peering at the crumpled scrap of paper.

'Faith and Mercy, what virtuous names. Very well, my poppets. Be at the harbour station at ten on Sunday morning with your luggage. We're off to Bournemouth.'

'Waah!' Faith gasped. 'Ta ever so, Mr Lemco.'

'What we get paid?' asked Mercy, trying to appear unimpressed.

'Five shillings each and all found. A most generous start to two such absolute beginners.'

'What's that mean, all found?'

'Your food and lodging and instruction. Quite a generous offer, I feel.'

'You will be lodging with me,' said Madame Lapin, 'so I shall put you straight. Have a good breakfast beforehand and bring plenty of sandwiches. It'll be a long day and there's no telling what we'll find in Bournemouth.'

'See you on Sunday,' grinned Jeanette.

'Can't hardly believe it,' laughed Faith, as they hurried home. 'No more piddly bottles, no more labelling. We'll be theatricals.'

'Watcha think of that Max Lemco? asked Mercy. 'He had scent on and nail varnish. When he shook me hand it was liking holding a wet fish. Didn't have no grip at all.'

'Dad would say he don't know whether he's Arthur or Martha.'

After hugs from all the family and two days of ironing their own clothes and making off with half of Mary's it was the night before the great adventure.

They lay curved like commas around each other on their lumpy mattress. Back and forth the 'What ifs' were batted from one to the other.

'What if one of us breaks a leg?'

'What if we gets diffeeria?'

'What if we're drugged and taken off by white slavers to Marrakesh?'

'Gotta get some sleep or we'll look all baggy-eyed.'

'Got to give it a go,' said Faith, doubtfully. 'Look a right pair of nannas if we chucks in the towel before we've even started.'

'We ain't never had a train ride,' said Mercy, trying to recapture her early excitement.

Half-past nine chimed on the kitchen clock as the Vines filed out into the street to see the twins off to Bournemouth. They headed the procession carrying Dad's old kitbag between them. Mary and Dad followed behind. Blyth skipped along at the rear with a bag of jam sandwiches and a bottle of lemonade for the girls to take on their journey.

At the railway station they found the Debonnaires with no difficulty on account of their flamboyant attire. Max Lemco had a black fedora and matching coat with a red silk handkerchief trailing from the pocket. There was a girl in a man's suit with a long cigarette holder. The pianist in her woolly hat and scarf looked a dull bird among all the extravagant plumage of the others. Madame Lapin, complete with feather boa, swooped down on them.

'Ah, the Scarlets. Down here with the others, you can help load the skips,' she said, indicating some large wicker boxes.

'Hang on, Missis, give us a chance to say goodbye,' Dad demanded. 'You keep this safe,' he said, handing them a small package. 'It's writin' paper and envelopes and stamps. Any trouble, you let us know. There's a quid in there for your fares if you needs it.' He gave them both a hug. ''Bye, my babes, and just you stick together.'

''Bye, Dad,' they muttered, flinging their arms around him.

''Bye,' said Mary. 'Look after yerselfs.' She surprised herself by wanting to cry.

Blyth squealed in protest as the girls hugged and kissed him.

They all waited as the carriage doors slammed, the whistle blew and the train steamed out of the station.

Dad sank down on one of the seats and drew out a grubby rag from his pocket and mopped his eyes. 'My gals is grown up,' he sighed.

Mary looked at him. When had he got so thin? she wondered. He was shivering and seemed dwarfed by his overcoat. In her growing up she had loved and hated him in equal measure as he wheedled money out of her for drink, entertained her with his stories and failed all her expectations of a father. Now she felt pity. This would be Dad's future, sitting at the station while his children steamed past to their new lives.

'Half me riches gone,' he mumbled to himself.

'Come on,' she coaxed, 'treat you to a rum over at the Ship Anson.'

Fred nodded and got to his feet.

'Give us a bag of crisps?' asked Blyth. 'I'm off to see Harry.'

'You got hollow legs,' laughed Mary,' after all that bread and jam you put away.'

They left the station either side of Dad, with their arms linked through his. In one morning their family had been halved. How she had wanted to be rid of her sisters, how jealous she had been of their closed little world. And yet, now they were gone she didn't feel at all as she expected.

She was in the kitchen making a scratch meal of leftovers when Dad burst in.

'There's a bit of excitement up in Lancaster Terrace, the pub was full of it – bin a shootin'. That Captain Clements what you worked for have shot that gal Cissie.'

'Jesus!' Mary stood with an onion in one hand, a knife in the other. 'You sure it was him? Never have put him down for a shooter. Christ! She ain't dead, is she?' Mary felt a surge of anger. 'What call had he too shoot her?'

'Here, I got the paper,' said Dad. 'Wonder we didn't see it last week, was on your birthday it happened.'

Chewing her lip she studied the report.

'Naval Officer shoots Scullery Maid in tragic Accident.

In the early hours of January the 17th Captain Clements, lately returned from a posting in Singapore, shot Miss Cissie Nugent, a past employee, mistaking her for an intruder. Miss Nugent was taken to the Royal Portsmouth Hospital where she underwent a lengthy operation to remove a bullet from her shoulder. Her condition remains critical.

Captain Clements was taken for questioning to the Portsea Police Station and released on bail of £500, awaiting trial at the Quarter Sessions.'

'Gotta go, Dad,' she gabbled, dragging her coat from the chair. 'Have me dinner later. I gotta go.'

11

Cissie stared at the vase of chrysanthemums on the locker beside her bed. Bold, bossy flowers they were and so yellow they made her eyes hurt. Their smell always reminded her of grapefruit and set her teeth on edge. Beside them was a bunch of purple grapes threatening to escape over the side of the bowl. Who could have sent them? Her only visitors, so far, were the policeman and Major Grice from the Slum Post. She wished she'd kept up with her reading and then she would be able to make out the writing on the card.

From the corner of her eye Cissie could see the policeman nattering to the ward sister. As he approached her bed she once more feigned sleep.

'Good morning, Miss Nugent, my name's Perks. Sister says you're well enough to answer my questions.'

'All right,' she said, feeling cornered.

He pulled up a chair beside her bed and took out a notebook and pencil.

Cissied studied him. A bit on the skinny side, he was, but then, so was she. It was his eyes she liked, dark like treacle and lashes like a girl. He had become a part of the place. Each time she awoke there he was sat in the corner – almost part of the furniture.

'Can you give me your full name and date of birth?' he asked.

'Cissie Nugent, born fifth of November nineteen hundred and six.'

'So you'll be twenty this year?'

She nodded.

'Tell me what happened on Saturday, January the six-teenth?'

Cissie looked blank. 'Dunnow.'

'It was the day before you got shot, Miss Nugent.'

'Be better if you could call me Cissie,' she said. 'No one never calls me that. Almost forgot I got a second name.'

'Right-ho, Cissie,' said Constable Perks, licking his pencil.

'Went to the Slum Post and had me dinner and scrubbed out the office and kitchen for Major Grice. She give me some clothes and a packet of sammidges.'

'What did you do then?'

Furious with herself, Cissie blushed. 'A bit of this and a bit of that.'

'Who d'you do it with?' asked the constable, helping himself to her grapes.

'Dunnow,' she mumbled, not wanting to think about, let alone say, what her business could have been.

'Where was this?' he persisted.

'Back of Bishop Street,' she said, feeling shamed and angry. Here she was being stripped bare by his questions and there he was eating her grapes.

'Why did you go to fifteen, Lancaster Terrace?'

''Cos I lives there.'

'I thought the house had been shut up three years ago when the Clements family went off to Singapore.'

'Still me home,' she persisted. 'Got the key to the back door. Ain't took nothing, just washes me things and kips in me bed.'

'What time did you get there on the night of the six-teenth?'

'Can't remember. I hung about in the back alley for a while, just in case there was anyone in the kitchen. 'Ventually

I sneaked in and went up to the lav on the first floor. Was tired, washed me clothes and settled down about six.'

'Why did you get up later?'

'Was thirsty. I'd eaten the sammidges. They was fish paste, salty they was, and made me thirsty. Got up to get a drink of water.'

'Why did you go all the way down to the kitchen? Couldn't you have got some water from the tap in the bathroom.'

'Tastes furry from there, besides I knew someone was sleeping in the bedroom next door. Didn't want to wake them up.'

'Why?'

''Cos they might have gone for me.'

'Well, they did, didn't they?' said Perks, reaching for another grape.

'It was that bloomin' squeaky board what done it?'

'When you trod on the board, what happened next?'

'Door busts open and I makes for the stairs then there was this roarin' and I was fallin' through the air. Bang! Something exploded in me head, thought I'd bin blown to bits.'

'What happened next?'

'I was screamin' with the pain and someone was rushing down the stairs crying out.'

'Who was it, do you think?'

'Was Captain Clements, stood there with a gun. Frightened he was, and then, when he saw it was me, he looked like he wanted to cry. It's all mixed up in me head, him looking like death warmed up, the pain and the blood, then someone crashing on the front door.'

'Why was that? Why was he frightened?'

''Cos he never meant to hurt me. S'pose he thought I was going to snuff it.'

'How d'you know he never meant to hurt you?'

'First off, he didn't know it was me,' said Cissie, ticking the reasons off on her fingers. 'Second, Captain wouldn't hurt a fly. He just meant to scare what he thought was a burglar. Bad luck it was me.'

Perks wrote down what she had said, then cleared his throat. 'Why were you wearing a nightdress?' he asked.

'Was night-time,' she said, irritated by the question.

'Did Captain Clements ask you to wear a nightdress for him?' he asked before taking some more of her grapes.

'What you getting at?' asked Cissie, feeling the blood rush to her face. 'Told ya I didn't even know he was in England. Sides, why would he care what I had on me? You're trying to make sommink dirty out of this,' she snapped, feeling a rare burst of temper. 'I ain't saying nothink else and stop eating me grapes.' She had the satisfaction of seeing Perks blush.

'Constable, I think you will have to come back later. My patient must have her dressing changed and then she will need to rest.'

Having her bandages removed made the pain come roaring back. She leant over her bed table while the sister and another nurse swabbed the wound. Tears of weakness trickled down her face.

'You have been very brave, Cissie. In a few days we will be able to take out the stitches and then you will feel much more comfortable. I will give you an injection and then you can have another sleep.'

Captain Clements and Perks the policeman whirled around in her head like figures skating on a pond, and then she was gone.

Mary hurried down the road towards the Royal Hospital clutching a bag of treacle toffee – Cissie's favourite. It was ages since she had given her a thought. When they'd both worked at Lancaster Terrace for the Clementses, they had been quite pally. She had been tiny, like a fairy, with fluffy blonde hair. Used to flit about like a shadow, specially when old Lettice was on the rampage or Mrs Mullins, the cook, was getting stroppy. Often Mary would shout back at old Mullins, and then Cissie would run out into the yard. Poor kid, she hadn't had anyone behind her, what with her dad dying in the war and her mum took with the flu soon after. Even with her own daft Dolly and boozy Fred for parents, she was tons better off than Cissie. Besides, she had Harry, the twins and Blyth; for all their aggravating ways she wouldn't have been without them. Might even yet have Matthew, there was still a splinter of hope. No, she wouldn't think about him now, it was Cissie she had to bother about.

It was strange, Mary thought, as she entered the hospital, there had been no mention in the paper of old Lettice Clements. Perhaps she had been eaten by a snake, out in Singapore, or savaged by a tiger; Mary did hope so.

Still, she couldn't believe all this stuff about the shooting. It was like something out of the pictures. She knew toffs were capable of anything, but Captain Clements! And what was Cissie doing there, in her nightdress, in his house in the middle of the night? Cripes! They couldn't be carrying on together, could they?

Mary tried to remember what he had looked like. Tall, with blue eyes and wispy brown hair, with his head always stuck in a notebook. They were full of curves and numbers. Pale hands he had, with a big gold ring on his little finger. Nice voice, though – rich and deep. It always reminded her of the taste of Bourneville chocolate. She supposed he had been quite kind in that distant way that toffs had.

Going to hospital always reminded her of that long walk up Asylum Road to visit Mum with the twins dragging behind her. Dolly sat there looking like the light was turned off behind her eyes, gibbering and tearing up bits of paper into tiny strips.

Worst of all was that sickly, sweet smell that clung to her from the medicine they made her take.

Mary stood with the other visitors outside the women's surgical ward waiting for two o'clock to come, when the doors would be opened. Her stomach churned with alarm. God, she hoped Cissie wouldn't look too bad and wasn't hurting too much. The doors opened and she was swept in with the others into an overwhelming world of white bedclothes, sick people and everything cleaned to death. Mary looked about her determined to scarper if she didn't find Cissie among the next few patients.

Then, between two old dears was this face peering at her from under a muddle of blonde hair.

'Mary!' The voice was hoarse as if it hadn't been used for a while.

'Hello, Cis, whatcha bin up to?' she asked, pulling up a chair beside the bed, and swallowing down her shock. The figure in the bed was all blankets and bandages with only the tiny face to tell her it was Cissie. She looked diluted, as if the colour had been washed from her by all the nurses' energetic hygiene. Her hair was a dull straw and her eyes barely blue.

'Had an accident,' she said.

'D'you mean he didn't know it was you?'

Cissie nodded.

'What was he doing going around shooting people? Must reckon he's Al Capone or somethink.' Mary rattled on then looked up and saw Cissie blink, like she used to when she wanted to change the subject.

'Brought you some toffees,' she said, putting them on the locker; 'treacle, your favourite.'

'Ta,' Cissie breathed.

'Fancy one?'

She shook her head.

'How long you gonna be here?'

'Dunnow.'

'Likes yer flowers,' Mary said, casting about for something else to say.

'Can you read the card, for me, Mary, I can't make out the writing?'

Dear Cissie,
  Rest and get well. I will be in to see you soon.
  Kind regards.
  Lavinia Mowbray.

'Blimey! Mrs Mowbray give you them grapes; treatin' you like royalty she is.'

Cissie raised her eyebrows.

'You remember old Clements' sister – yes, you do. Used to bring stuff up from Dorset – plants and things. The kids used to go out on treats with her. Only person old Lettice was scared of. You was there when she had hysterics over me spilling the wine on her dress. Mrs Mowbray smacked her face. Cor! It was better'n being at the pantomime.'

Her friend smiled and Mary knew she was on the right track. For the next few minutes she ransacked her brain for more goings-on at Lancaster Terrace. She was between tales when Cissie touched her arm.

'Watcha doin' now?' she asked.

'Running a stall down Charlotte Street. Got engaged but it might be off now. All 'cos of me temper.'

Cissie shook her head. 'Why would you fall out with someone what loved you?' she asked. Mary blushed and looked away. 'How's Blyth?' she asked, sensing she should change the subject.

'He's a big boy, now, nearly ten. Ever so clever.'

'Twins?'

'Off dancing all over the place; Brighton, Bournemouth, Littlehampton.'

Cissie smiled. Her face looked pinker and her eyes were shining. Always she seemed to live through other people, taking nourishment from their lives, seeming unable to take anything for herself. Again she touched her arm. 'Lost a baby,' she whispered, her eyes filling with tears.

Mary took her hand, looking down at the tiny wrist. She couldn't believe it. Poor, poor Cissie!

'Wanted to die.'

'Oh, Cis, I'm ever so sorry. What d'you have?'

'Little boy, Charlie – only lived a little while.'

Mary wished she could say something that would make a difference, anything to take the pain away. She raged at the unfairness. Some gentle bloody Jesus He was that would take away that little boy before ever she'd known him. She wanted to kiss her friend but could not make herself do it. Even stood up as if she were going to and then she saw the policeman looking at her and the moment slipped away. Instead she took the brush from the locker and said, 'Do yer hair like before?'

Cissie leaned forward clasping hold of the bed table and Mary began to draw the brush through the thin pale strands. Once she had got rid of the tangles she divided the hair into two bunches which she secured with elastic bands from her coat pocket. 'That better?' she asked.

Cissie nodded.

'Where you going, after you're better?'

'Dunnow.'

'You a friend of Miss Nugent?'

Mary turned round, startled to find a policeman behind her.

'What's it to you?' she snapped.

Cissie grinned. 'Worked with me for the Clements,' she said.

'Must be Mary Vine?' he said.

'No,' said Mary,' 'hi am Lettice Clements. 'Goin' now,'
blurted Mary. 'Lives at 23 Lemon Street,' she said to the
policeman. 'Any questions you can arst me round there. See
you later, Cis,' and then she was gone.

Cissie felt hot and thirsty. 'Get us some water, will ya?'
she asked Mrs Buggins, who was lumbering about with the
tea trolley.

'You looks rosy,' she said, pouring her a glass, 'must be yer
visitors perked you up a bit.'

'Hello, Cissie, how are you, my dear? I have been so worried
about you?'

She smiled at the plump lady in the hat with its bobbing
cherries. Yes, she did know her, but not as Mrs Mowbray.
She was Miles and Charlotte's Auntie Vinny.

'Thirsty,' she said.

'You look a little feverish. Here, let me pour you some
more water.'

Cissie sank back against her pillows. She was bursting for
a wee but didn't like to tell Mrs Mowbray, not when she'd
come all this way to see her.

'Cissie, Captain Clements is most distressed at what has
happened. He would like you to know that.'

'I knows that, he said when it 'appened. Thought he was
gonna cry.'

'Fortunately there is unlikely to be a trial. Until we know
whether or not that is going to happen he is advised not to contact you. It would prejudice the case for the prosecution.'

'Will they send him to prison?' Cissie blinked. She didn't
think she could stand the worry of it all. Already a man had
sneaked in and asked her all sorts of questions, trying to make
out that Captain Clements was some gangster and that she
was his floozie.

'I told the policeman he didn't mean me no harm.' She

began to cough and the pain in her chest made her gasp. 'All my fault.'

'Why were you there, Cissie?' asked Mrs Mowbray, handing her a handkerchief.

'Didn't have nowhere else to go,' she gasped. 'It was my home.'

'You cannot go back there now. The police would not allow it. Is there anywhere else you could stay? Have you any relatives?'

Cissie shook her head. 'Could go to Springhaven, the Sally Army home. Only for girls what's havin' babies.' She blinked. 'Don't want to,' she whispered, 'makes me sad.'

'It's as I thought,' said Mrs Mowbray.

Cissie looked at her. 'Sorry for being a trouble,' she gasped, her eyes once more filling with tears.

Mrs Mowbray smiled at her and the cherries quivered on her hat. She patted her hand. 'You just put all your energy into getting better, my dear. Captain Clements is relying on you. If you make a full recovery they will very likely drop the charges, especially as you spoke up so bravely for him. I shall go and have a word with Sister and see what can be arranged for your convalescence.'

While she was away, Cissie managed to get one of the nurses to bring her a bedpan. She sponged her face with a wet flannel after making her cough into a horrible chipped metal mug called a sputum pot.

'You need to rest and drink more water, Miss Nugent, if you want to get rid of that bronchitis.' The nurse reached into her pocket and handed her an envelope. 'This came for you with the second post.'

Cissie recognised the envelope from tidying Mrs Clements' sitting room. Her stationery, as she called it, used to be stacked in a carved wooden box. Kenilworth Cambric, that was it. She studied the handwriting, the thick down and thin up loops. It was from the Captain, she knew it. Cissie closed her eyes. Oh, she was glad, so glad to hear from him. 'It's private,' she said, as the nurse stood waiting to know who had written to her.

'I'm not one to pry, I'm sure,' she said, sniffily, clattering the screens away.

Cissie smiled to herself. It didn't matter that she couldn't read it. Just having it, there under her pillow, was joy enough. It was a letter from home, as if she were part of a proper family, with a dad or a brother. Later, someone would tell her what he had said.

Looking down the ward she saw Mrs Mowbray walking towards her and sighed. Everything had been so peaceful before she arrived with her posh voice and fussy hat. She had been safe. Now it was all her responsibility what happened to the Captain.

'Well, Cissie,' said Mrs Mowbray. 'I have good news for you. Sister says, as soon as you are fit to travel, I may take you home with me to Dorset, to convalesce.'

Cissie smiled and nodded, anything to make her go away. In her mind she travelled up the stairs, to her room, with the hatbox beneath the bed, climbed beneath the sheets and got back to the moment before she took a bite from the fish-paste sandwich.

12

Matthew stepped out onto the submarine casing, the air pure and chill after the stink of diesel. They were back at *Dolphin* after six weeks away. His eyes felt gritty and his mouth sour. The stubble on his chin itched and his whole body craved hot water. Woven into all the watchkeeping and torpedo exercises, the eating and sleeping, were thoughts of Mary. There were moments when he simmered with the unfairness of her anger and wanted to roar out his frustration, to hit out with his fists, to throw spanners across the engine room. Other times he didn't care who was at fault, he just wanted to hold her. The seesawing between hope and disappointment, when they called in to port and waited for the mail, wearied him. He kept his thoughts bolted within him. The mess-deck was not the place for confidences. Advice when offered was salty and harsh.

'Treat her rough and tell her nothing.'

'If she won't give you a bit try old Ruby at The Red Flag; she's a right old bike.'

'First few weeks she'll want to eat you, Mate, then when she's got a kid in her belly she'll bloody wish she had.'

Ashore he might have spoken with Bob Cowley, but on board the rough philosophy of the lower deck held sway. Being so long on the boat, and in each others' pockets day and night, had exhausted all the jokes and stories. Everyone was ready for fresh company. They carried their gear in their steaming bags over to the accommodation block eager to clean themselves, scrub their kit and get into fresh clothes.

Matthew stared at himself in the mirror. It was cloudy with steam, making shaving a hazardous business. Voices echoed around the washroom and the air was thick with the smell of grey green soap known as pusser's hard. With his towel tucked round his waist, he carried his wet clothes over to the drying room and hung them on the racks.

'Going over to Pompey?' asked Bob, collecting up his toothbrush and razor.

'Don't know yet,' Matthew said.

'See you over the mess. Might be a letter for you, never know your luck.'

'Pigs might fly,' he answered, trying to sound indifferent. Had she written, and if she had, how would he answer? Matthew felt sick. It would be a relief to have the waiting over. If there were no letter he would go up to Kent on his next leave and sort out his mother's things. That way he would be done with his past and could concentrate on getting his Leading Seaman's rating and making some headway in the navy.

Later, when he had changed into clean clothes and stowed his gear in the locker room, Matthew joined the others in the canteen. There were loud cheers, backslapping and laughter as he went up to the table to get his tot.

George Kendall, their petty officer stoker, was surrounded by a group of well-wishers. 'Missis has had the nipper,' he said waving a letter at Matthew. 'It's a boy.'

'Sippers all round,' someone said, passing their glass to the jubilant George.

'Congratulations!' said Matthew, genuinely pleased. He went across to him and shook him by the hand before offering up his rum.

'No, thanks, mate, I got to keep a clear head. I'm going off to borrow a bike; we only live down the road, I want to see the lad and make sure Vi is all right.'

So the post had come. Matthew gulped down his disappointment. He thought he had prepared himself. Perhaps she was right not to contact him. They were too different, much too different to make a go of things.

'Dusty! Over here,' called Bob.

Setting his face in neutral Matthew went over to his oppo, who was busy rolling a cigarette.

'In me top pocket,' Bob said quietly.

Matthew took the white envelope and slid it into his hand. Looking around to ensure that he was unobserved, he walked across to the window and turned his back on his mess-mates before dealing with his post. Inside was a letter addressed to him in Mary's swirling copperplate. The sight of her writing winded him like a punch in the stomach. He held the envelope between his fingers trying to regain his breath. Matthew began to tear open the flap, a storm of conflicting feelings battling inside him. Taking in a breath he let it out in a ragged sigh as he smoothed out the page. Now, now he would know what she felt.

> *Dear Matthew,*
>
> *I am sorry for what happened on Christmas Day. It is me that is the stupid one; stupid to bite off more than I could chew. Me and my temper have ruined everythink. For a bit, when you was all drinking a toast to me, and the dinner was set out so fine, I thought I had carried it off. All the waiting and hoping, the shopping and the scrubbing had ended in a triumph. But it all ran away with us. And then, your loving kindness to me smoothed everything down.*

Matthew closed his eyes and saw them all wedged in around the table with glasses raised and Mary smiling at him. She had looked almost beautiful in her sudden unexpected joy.

Not able to believe that they were all saluting her. His Mary! All Matthew's pressed down emotions welled up in him. He combed his fingers through his hair. *Mary, Mary, Mary*, he whispered to himself. It was some moments before he could steady himself and begin reading again.

> *If only we had delayed looking for the ring and gone to Harry and Dora's instead. Then we would have memories of such loving between us. The sad thing is that all the time the ring was hanging on a branch of the Christmas tree not a yard away from us. If I had not flared up so quick, Mercy would have told us. I wear it still but I don't know yet if you still want me to. I don't know where you are and I'm afraid to come looking in case you no longer want me. If everythink is finished between us please let me know and I will send you back your ring.*
>
> *Since I don't know where you are you must come and find me and tell me what you think about everythink.*
>
> *I love you like always,*
> *Mary.*

Matthew slid the letter back in his pocket. Yes! He would be through the gates of *Dolphin* and over on the ferry the moment night leave started.

Mary hurried home with a bowl of faggots and roast potatoes from the shop in Bishop Street. The saucepan lid rattled on top and the savoury steam made her mouth water. She would like to have eaten them there and then but Blyth and Dad were waiting. It was the end of February and the twins had been away for over a month. There had been a postcard from Bournemouth in the first week, full of excitement about being fitted out with costumes and indignation at having to share a kipper between them for breakfast – since then, not a word.

'No news is good news,' Dad had said, ''sides I thought you was pleased to see the back of them.'

Mary had been surprised at how much she missed the chaos and clatter of her sisters. The place had never been so quiet. They were a strange trio now. Blyth was rarely home. He raced up and down the street with his pals, Charlie and Norman, with their soap cart, or they went mud-larking: slithering over the harbour mud for the few coins tossed by the passengers passing along the bridge to the trains and ferries. Other times he was sat at the kitchen table poring over his drawings of ships or doing complicated sums way beyond Mary's understanding.

'We're just a feeding station,' Dad had laughed. 'Good to see the lad out with his pals.'

Most evenings it was just her and Dad, like they were an old married couple. Mary sighed. Her life was leaking away like water through a colander. Even working the market failed to hold her enthusiasm. She was living in a fog, not looking forward or back just moving through the greyness. Ages and ages ago she had dropped the envelope through the letterbox to Matthew. Might as well have stuck it in a beer bottle and lobbed it into the harbour for all the response she got. In it she had opened her heart to him and taken all the blame. Why hadn't he written back?

'Thought you'd lost your memory,' said Blyth when she got back with the supper.

'Fat one to talk you are,' she snapped. 'Last time we sent you for them you ate half the spuds on the way home.' She set a saucepan of water on the stove and sat the basin on the top to warm through.

'Can't we eat them straight off?' moaned her brother. 'Don't care if they're cold.'

'When you buys the grub you can make the rules. Where's Dad, thought he was hungry.'

'Gone to get a paper from Granny Pragnell see the jobs.'

'Some hopes,' said Mary. 'There's blokes much younger than Dad walkin' the streets. Even the market's dead lately.'

'P'raps he'll win the pools,' said Blyth, watching the plate steaming over the saucepan as if his life depended on it. 'We could have a car and a party with iced cakes like them in Campions' window at Christmas.'

'Reckon your brains is in your belly,' she laughed. 'Get the plates out, we'll have ours and Dad can see to himself.'

'How's that Cissie?' he asked as she loaded two faggots onto his plate. 'That girl what was shot?'

'Pretty rough,' said Mary, her stomach jolting at the memory of the last visit when Cissie had lain there flushed and breathless. 'Got bronchitis. Nurse said it was a complication. That Captain's sister was there looking all worked up about it.'

''Course,' said Blyth, spearing a potato from Mary's plate and into his mouth. 'She dies he'll be done for murder.'

'Don't say that,' she said, pushing her plate away, 'don't even think it.' Almost forgotten Cissie she had for years, yet now Mary couldn't get her friend's face out of her mind.

The key rattled in the lock and Dad whistled his way down to the kitchen. He stood there beaming at them.

'You looks pleased with yerself,' she said, getting up to dish up his dinner. 'Lost a penny and found a fiver, have ya?'

'There's a surprise for ya out the street! No, Blyth,' he commanded, 'this is fer her eyes only. You just hand me the cloth so's I can get at them faggots.'

'Better not be one of your stunts,' she snapped, picking up her coat and making for the front door.

'Hello, Mary.'

She stared at him not knowing what to do. All her dreams and hopes of this moment had her rushing into his arms, laughing and crying and saying sorry. Now she felt awkward and tongue-tied. She had wanted to choose the moment.

'Fancy going up Queen Street for a drink or something?' he asked.

'All right,' Mary said, putting on her coat and fastening the buttons. Oh, she wished she looked prettier, instead of all pale and washed out with her hair needing a wash.

'How have you been?' he asked as they walked up the street together.

'Ploddin' along doing a bit of this and that,' she said. Mary kept taking sideways glances at him. He looked so smart in his uniform, his coat brushed and his shoes shining so you could see your face in them.

'How's the market?'

'Slow this time of year. Nobody got no money and it's freezin' down there. What you bin doin'?'

'Exercising down off Plymouth, away a month. Got your letter this morning.'

She felt a rush of joy. 'So you came to see me straight off?'

'Straight off,' he echoed, turning and smiling at her.

'Dunnow what to say,' Mary mumbled, looking down at her scuffed boots.

'That's good,' he said. 'It gives me a chance to get my oar in. Let's go up the Captain Hardy, nice quiet little pub, we can sit in the snug.'

Mary walked beside him all stirred up like a bottle of ginger beer: fear, hope and happiness bubbling away inside her. They'd got a second chance but she was so afraid of mucking it up. Matthew chatted away to her as they walked up Queen Street towards the pub, about his boat and his mess-mates. Something about a new baby and a football match in Plymouth.

'Here we are,' he said, holding open the saloon door of the pub.

Immediately she was wrapped in a warm fug of beer and tobacco fumes. A group of sailors were playing darts and by the fire were three old chief petty officers smoking their pipes and laying down the law to one another.

'What'll you have?' Matthew asked.

'Shandy, please.'

'Shandy it shall be.' Matthew went up to the bar and she stood behind him conscious of being looked over by two women in black with peaked caps skewered in place by ferocious looking hat pins.

'A shandy and a boilermaker, please,' he said to the barmaid, 'and can we take it into the snug?'

'Haven't lit the fire. You can please yourselves,' she sniffed.

'I'll wait for you there,' said Mary, locating the door. The little room was cold and frowsty. There were two tables, their surfaces ringed with beer stains. She sat on the edge of the least rickety of the chairs and stared at a picture on the wall opposite of 'The Wreck of the Hesperus'. It was not an encouraging atmosphere. She studied her fingernails, bitten down to the quick, and her spirit wavered.

Matthew came towards her carrying their drinks. He kicked the door shut behind him. 'Blimey,' he said, looking around him, 'bit gloomy in here; no wonder we've got the place to ourselves. Cheers.'

Mary nodded, raising her glass. 'I'm sorry about . . .'

'I got your letter.'

'About what happened.'

They laughed nervously as their words fell over one another.

'Ladies first,' said Matthew, smiling at her.

'You know what I wants ter say. It was in the letter,' she whispered.

He reached across the table and took her hands in his, kissing her bitten nails. 'Let's make a fresh start,' he said. 'I haven't come over here to keep raking over the past. I need to know if we've got something worth going on with.'

Mary looked up at him, feeling the warmth stealing into her fingers. 'I wants us to be together.' She paused, near to tears. 'Just scared of getting it wrong again.'

'It's simple really,' said Matthew; 'boils down to one question. Do you want to marry me?'

'Yes, yes, more than anythink,' she gasped, watching the smile crinkle the corners of his mouth. He was her Matthew again, just when she had given up all hope of him. Oh, she'd be different this time, she'd batten down her temper and be whatever he wanted her to be.

'I want that, too,' he said.

'I'm so frightened.'

Matthew laughed, 'So am I.' He took a long draught of his beer then brushed the froth from his lips. 'We need to decide what we both really want – not what your family wants or what my shipmates think or even the bloomin' king of England, but you and me together.'

'I was thinking about moving over to Gosport. Taking a room and getting a job, cleaning or in a shop or something. The twins is off with their dancing. Blyth and Dad can sort themselves out.' Mary looked questioningly at him. 'We could meet up over there, with no family sticking their oar in.'

'I'd like that. It's not that I don't get on with your dad and everyone but things get muddled. You get stuck in the middle and I get moved off to the edge of things. We got to feel that it's the two of us first and foremost.'

'The two of us,' she said, raising her glass.

He leant across the table and kissed her. 'I've missed you so badly,' he whispered.

'Me too,' she sighed, kissing him back, tasting the beer on his lips.

'Let's get out of this place. It's like a blooming undertaker's.

They left their drinks half finished and hurried out into the street. Matthew pulled her into a shop doorway, took her in his arms and kissed her. She stood on tiptoes, her hands on his shoulders, as his leaned down to her. All the weight of her misery floated away. She stepped up onto his boots to get closer to his face. He turned himself around with his back to the street to shield her from the cold. 'Mmhh!! I've missed you,' he breathed against her neck.

'How much?' she asked.

Matthew held her face between his hands and kissed her eyebrows and then her eyelids. He pressed his lips to her forehead and then her cheeks and lastly, teasingly, her mouth. Mary clung to him, feeling the knot of distrust unravelling beneath his touch. They held each other close, button to button, their passion separated by layers of winter clothing.

'I wish we were married already,' he whispered. 'I hate this sneaking into doorways and having to hold back all the time.'

'What's stopping us?' she asked.

'Have to live like beggars, we will. Be lucky to have a quid a week until I make up me Leading Hand's rate.'

'I can get something over in Gosport, like I said. Waiting at tables or laundry – whatever it was we'd be together. Not as if I'm used to much anyway,' she laughed. ''Sides, fortune favours the brave.'

'Where did you get that from?'

She could tell from his voice that he was smiling. 'Probbly a Christmas cracker.'

'I'd better be going. If I don't get back to *Vernon* I'll miss the last ferry across. Don't want to get stoppage of leave for being late. Last thing I want is being cooped up in *Dolphin* when I could be seeing you.'

'Why don't we meet next Thursday over in Gosport?' said Mary, loath to let him go. 'I could go over in the morning and have a good look round, see what's about in the way of work and places to live.'

'Don't like thinking of you having to work,' he said. 'I wanted to take care of everything.'

'Matthew,' she said, gripping the lapels of his coat, 'you was saying about that bloke on your boat – wife's just had the baby. He was the only one not lost on the *M1*. Bet she feels the luckiest woman in the world. We gotta make the most of every minute together. You could be sent out to Hong Kong for ages and ages, could even be sunk.'

'Proper little lionheart, you are,' he said. 'Just give me another kiss and we'll have to get back to Lemon Street at the double.'

Linking hands they ran back home and took a breathless leave of one another.

'Thursday at the Black Cat Café,' he called.

'Thursday,' she whispered to herself, sitting on the edge of her bed looking at her engagement ring glinting in the light.

13

—◦~~◦—

'Captain Clements, come in, please, and be seated,' boomed the detective inspector, rising from behind his desk. 'I have some news for you.'

It was a fortnight now since the shooting and Charles had barely slept. If it had not been for his sister's bracing company and his pupils' forthcoming examinations he would have fallen to pieces. At night Cissie's face, pale and terrified, swam before him and when he dropped into an exhausted sleep her screams awakened him. He would lay there with his pulse racing and pyjamas drenched in sweat. For the first few days a small sharp-featured man in a raincoat dogged his footsteps. He said he was a journalist. Charles thanked God that he had not found out that Cissie had been a prostitute, so simply described her as a lady's maid. The articles had been salacious enough with titbits like 'Miss Nugent was found to be wearing Mrs Clements's nightdress', without the slavering there would have been over her being a common tart. Fortunately the hacks' interest had now cooled.

'Captain Clements, are you with me?' said the inspector, looking at him over the top of his glasses.

'I'm sorry, I am rather tired and anxious.'

'In that case my news will set your mind at rest.'

'Miss Nugent, in the opinion of her doctors at the hospital, will make a slow but steady recovery. The bullet passed through the muscle in her arm and did little damage. It was the fall down the stairs that caused the fracture to her shoulder. It will take some time to mend, and coupled with the loss of blood and the onset of bronchitis, Miss Nugent will need a long convalescence. In her statement, she absolves you of all blame and acknowledges that she acted unlawfully in entering your home. I have also spoken with your sister, Mrs Mowbray, an excellent woman, who has most generously undertaken to make a home for Miss Nugent in Dorset.

The inspector looked up from his report and smiled at him. His face reminded Charles of the granite features he had seen of the Presidents of the United States hewn into the side of Mount Rushmore. 'After careful consideration, therefore, we have decided there is no case to answer. However, we want to stress to you the seriousness of the incident and advise you that we shall impound your revolver.' The inspector smiled. 'I would advise you, Captain, to change the locks on your house. You don't want the criminal element to see you as easy prey. Miss Nugent may still have your key. Don't want her taking any further advantage.'

'Thank you,' he managed to gasp. Anger bubbled up inside him. How quickly we spring to judgement, he thought. Shaking the inspector's hand he left the station. Why wasn't he filled with relief? He had failed her. As his servant, Cissie's safety had been entrusted to him and he had broken faith with her. She must believe that, too, for there had been no reply to his letter.

Cissie stared at herself in the ward mirror. A pale, washed-out figure, kitted out in a tweed coat, a beret and clumpy brogues stared back. She felt weighed down by it all like a deep-sea diver.

'Ah, Cissie.' Mrs Mowbray swooped down on her. 'Ready, at last. Have you got everything?'

She nodded. Nothing had been forgotten. Tucked beneath her vest was the letter Captain Clements had sent her, still in its envelope. In the month that she had been in hospital, there had been no one that she quite trusted enough to read it to her.

'You look after yourself, gal,' said Mrs Buggins, clasping her to her winceyette covered bosom.

'What a lucky girl you are, Cissie,' said Sister Washborne; 'a holiday in the country. Don't forget your breathing exercises and use your arm as much as possible. You must build up the muscles again.'

'Thanks for looking after me,' she said, wishing that she could turn right round and be back in her bed in the corner.

'Off we go,' said Mrs Mowbray, turning the key in the ignition. The engine purred into life and they swept out under the hospital's memorial arch and into Commercial Road. 'Have you ever been in a motor car before?' she asked.

'No,' said Cissie, not anxious to relive an incident in the back of a taxi with a midshipman.

'You are fortunate that your first experience is in a Bentley. Gonville would have a fit if he knew. Bought it six months after he died. The happiest day of my life when I set out in her on my first solo trip.'

'Who was Gonville?' Cissie asked.

'My husband, Brigadier Gonville Mowbray – a great six-foot blustering bully of a man, but I adored him. So thankful that he passed away promptly. I have found widowhood a liberation.'

It was like a foreign language this talk of adoring someone and then being happy they were dead. As Mrs Mowbray rattled on Cissie looked around her. She felt unhitched from all that was familiar to her as the Bentley purred past bare trees, ploughed fields and towns full of strangers. She saw primroses in clusters in gardens and on roadside verges.

'Likes them flowers,' she said, as they sped past.

'Oh, there are masses of them in Cerne Magna. Your

bedroom overlooks the back of the cottage and so you will be able to see them from your window.'

Cissie saw sheep and tiny lambs close to their mothers. In another field were pigs, wallowing in mud. What struck her were the long empty stretches between houses and how few people she saw.

'We'll soon be up the hill in Shaftesbury and we'll stop for lunch.'

In the Golden Lion she felt better with all the noise and the jostling as they walked through the public bar. In the lounge they sat at a heavy wooden table and Mrs Mowbray ordered them steak and kidney pie, mashed potatoes and peas. The silver knives and forks weighed a ton and were slippery in her anxious fingers. Quickly Mrs Mowbray sized up the problem and simply cut up all the food on her plate and then swapped plates with her. She showed her into the Ladies' and waited outside for her. As she washed her hands Cissie looked up at herself in the mirror above the basin. What a sketch she looked, with nothing fitting right, and the dark brown clothes seeming to steal the colour from her face. She bit her lip and tried not to cry.

'Here we are at Cerne Magna, my dear. Your holiday home,' Mrs Mowbray said, when Cissie had given up hope of ever getting out of the car.

She looked about her. It was like a village she had seen once on a jigsaw box in a toy shop window, with thatched roofs and windows criss-crossed with black. Mrs Mowbray climbed down from the car and tossed her gloves onto the seat. She opened the car door for Cissie then hurried over to a wooden gate and disappeared up a path bordered by a thick hedge.

'Ah, Mrs Willow, how good to see you. Is Ted about?'

'Yes 'm, he be filling the coal scuttle. I'll send him out directly for your bags.'

'Cissie, this is Mrs Willow, my housekeeper.'

'Hello,' said Cissie, shyly taking the woman's outstretched hand.

'My, what a little scrap you be. Soon feed you up, us will. Come you along in.'

Her voice was rough and the words cobbled strangely together yet Cissie felt reassured. She was ordinary like herself and would understand how strange everything was for her.

'Here, let me take that coat and hat. If you wants the lav it be up them stairs,' said Mrs Willow, her smalled body dwarfed by a flowered apron.

Cissie climbed up a steep set of stairs with the aid of a rope banister. Every square inch of the cottage that wasn't dark oak beams was whitewashed and hung with pictures of a big, beefy man in army uniform. There were photographs of Mrs Mowbray with an Indian behind her, waving a fan, even one of elephants. Each picture had some writing beneath it but she couldn't make it out. It was strange, thought Cissie, that of all her reading and writing the only words she could be confident of reading were 'God' and 'Cissie Nugent' The smell of baking lured her downstairs to the sitting room.

'Sit down, Cissie,' said Mrs Mowbray, who was settled into a plump armchair with her feet on a matching stool. 'I'm sure you could do with a cup of tea and some scones.'

She was surprised to see Mrs Willow settle herself in a chair at the table after having served them all.

'How be your brother, Ma'am, he settling to the land, after all his seafarings? Must be famished for the sight of his young'us. Still, Easter be only a few weeks away.'

'Charles is in very good spirits,' said his sister, spreading jam on her scone. 'As you say, he's counting the days.'

There was a tap on the door and a fresh-faced lad lumbered into the room.

'Ah, Ted! Good afternoon. Would you be so kind as to take the cases out of the car. Oh this is Cissie, she will be staying with me for a while. Hers is the smallest case, please put it up in the spare room; the others can go in my bedroom.'

'Yes'm' seemed all that he could manage before lumbering out again.

After the sound of much thumping and banging, followed by the slamming of the front door from Ted, Mrs Willow got to her feet. 'Well, Ma'am, I shall wash they tea things then'll be off home to get Willow's supper. Laid you a few sandwiches and put the bottles in the beds. Be in tomorrow at seven as per usual.'

Mrs Willow smiled at Cissie. 'I hope you will take to the countryside – a bit of walking, in God's good air, that'll set you right. Soon have roses in yer cheeks.'

From the talk between them Cissie did not think that Mrs Willow knew anything about her having been shot by Captain Clements. So there would be no awkward questions.

'Thank you most kindly, my dear,' said Mrs Mowbray, smiling at her. 'I must say, it is good to be home again.'

''Bye, young maid, you sleep soundly, mind.'

Cissie smiled at her. ''Bye, Mrs Willow,' she said shyly.

By the time eight o'clock chimed on the gold clock on the mantelpiece, Cissie felt exhausted. She stifled a yawn.

'You must be worn out, Cissie,' said Mrs Mowbray, getting to her feet. 'Let me get you a bedtime drink and settle you down for the night.'

Wearily, Cissie climbed the stairs with her hostess following behind her carrying up a cup of cocoa and a plate of biscuits on a tray. The bedroom smelled of lavender, and the dark floorboards were covered with red and blue striped rugs. On the bed were large plumped-up pillows, a patchwork quilt and a very worn-looking rag doll in sailor's clothing.

Looking at it, Mrs Mowbray smiled. 'That's Jolly Jack,' she

said. 'Poor soul, he is over fifty years old. Do you know he
belonged to Gonville? Took him away to boarding school
when he was seven years old. Told me he used to tell Jack
here all his troubles. Poor lamb, his parents were miles away
in India. My niece, Charlotte, wanted to take Jack with her
to school, but I couldn't be parted from him. I don't think
he could cope with a move, at his age.' She perched him on
the dressing table beside a photograph of Gonville in army
uniform, sporting a fierce moustache.

'Thank you for looking after me,' said Cissie, desperate to
be alone.

'Not at all, my dear,' said Mrs Mowbray, getting to her
feet, 'it is naught but my Christian duty. You tuck yourself
up in bed now. God bless you, and sweet dreams.'

Cissie was glad to be alone at last. She felt weak and
tearful. It had been a long, confusing day and she found Mrs
Mowbray exhausting company. Perhaps, tomorrow, everything would seem less frightening.

Cissie opened her case wondering what could possibly be
in it. She had left Lancaster Terrace with nothing. Whoever
had packed it had put in two new winceyette nightdresses
and a new brush and a comb and some new knickers and
vests. In one side of the case was an elasticised pocket in
which she found what looked like a prayer book. Inside, on
the front page, was Captain Clement's writing. It reminded
her of the letter hidden beneath her blouse. For the hundredth
time, she wondered what it said. Instinct told her to hide it
from his sister. She thought about the Clements family and
the time she'd spent with them, especially the Christmases.
There was the last one, when they had gone to the Landport
Drapery Bazaar to see Father Christmas. He had given her a
little red paper fan. Mrs Clements had wanted her to give it to
Charlotte but the Captain had insisted she keep it. 'Poor girl,
she has little enough,' he had said. Just his skivvy, she'd been,

yet he'd wanted her to be happy. The paper fan was still in her hat box, in the cupboard up in her bedroom at Lancaster Terrace. Cissie prayed it would be there still, waiting for her when she went home again to Portsmouth.

Her mind switched back to Captain Clements. What was going to happen to him? she wondered. He had never meant to harm her. She couldn't bear it if he got took to prison. Cissie wished she could ask Mrs Mowbray what had happened, but she sensed her disapproval. It was as if she were not entitled even to use his name. If only she could speak to him and know that he was all right. Unbuttoning her blouse, she took out the Captain's letter and hid it under the mattress. Perhaps here, someone could be found to read it to her.

She was too anxious to say any prayers. Besides, God seemed always to be looking the other way when she needed Him. Instead, she nodded towards Jolly Jack. 'Night,' she whispered.

14

The twins joined the other girls forming a long line across the rehearsal room as Bunny Beaumont, the dance master, tapped his cane on the floor for attention.

'We're off to Aldershot soon to entertain all those handsome soldiers!' He rolled his eyes and the chorus line giggled. 'So, my dears, it's marching, marching, marching.'

The rehearsal room was cold and smelt of sweat and gas fumes from the spluttering fire. Faith and Mercy yawned. In their Brighton digs they were sleeping three to a bed, with Jeanette hogging the blanket. Sleep had become a luxury.

Once more Bunny banged his cane. 'Into a line, chop-chop! We have not a second to waste. By the time we get to Aldershot you'll be stepping out as if born on a parade ground.' He glared at the yawning chorus line. 'What a bunch of useless tarts you are – legs like tree trunks and the timing of a superannuated snail.'

'Vinegary old dwarf,' hissed Jeanette.

The twins giggled.

'Precision, precision, precision,' Bunny snapped and then he noticed the pianist busy at her needles. 'Madame Défarge,' he said with icy politeness, 'could we trouble you to relinquish your knitting and do us the honour of playing the pianoforte.'

Mildred sniffed and the chorus giggled.

'"There's Something About a Soldier," if you please.'

Mildred set aside her half-finished sock and rifled the contents of the piano stool.

'Acid drop, he is this morning,' muttered Jeanette, 'must be disappointed in love.'

'Why did he call old Milly Mrs Défarge?' asked Mercy, 'She ain't married.'

'It's the woman what was knitting at the foot of the guillotine, while all the nobs was having their heads cut off. Out of some book by Charlie Dickens what Bunny was reading – reckons 'e should be made into a saint.'

'Who?'

'Dickens, you deaf cow.'

Noticing the silence around them, they turned to find the dance master walking soundlessly up the line towards them.

Mercy stared at his eyelashes, thick with mascara, and his mouth pleated in displeasure, like a drawstring purse.

'Are you sure that you have finished, ladies?' he hissed. 'No more little gobbets to exchange?'

Red-faced Mercy shook her head.

'Then for Christ's sake let's get marching.'

Back and forth they went until their bones ached and their feet burned. Bunny tirelessly beat time with his cane while the hands of the clock dragged on.

'Stop,' he called, at half past twelve. 'Twenty-minute break. Jeanette, I want to see your can-can this afternoon, and the Scarlets, I've something for you.'

The chorus piled into the café across the road from the stage door.

'One Bovril and two rounds liver sausage,' said Faith, handing over one and sixpence to a greasy-haired boy. She sat on the bench next to her sister, and began eating.

'Here,' said Mercy, cheeks bulging, 'end of April we're back in Pompey. Saw it on the notice board. Be able to sleep at home.'

'If I does that I won't want to go back,' said Faith, stabbed with homesickness.

'We're just getting the hang of it,' protested Mercy.

'It's all the other stuff,' whispered Faith. 'Not enough grub and paying for every bath we have. I know it's only fourpence each when we shares with Jeanette, but she's always first and we gets left with the scum. I reckon she peed in the water last time. And, what about them Scotch eggs landlady left us last night, they was hard as cannonballs. Then there's the chorus, right lot of spiteful cats they are. Least at the brewery we had some proper friends.'

'Here, you two,' said Jeanette, passing round a plate of Swiss roll. 'I reckon old Bunny's going to give you a routine of your own. Max must have put in a word for you. Been giving him a bit of what he fancies?'

'We ain't that green,' snapped Mercy.

'Only wants to feel yer fanny and pinch yer tits. He can't rise to nothing else.'

Everyone laughed except Faith. For two pins she would pick up her case and run. For her, the world behind the curtain was a shimmering, sequinned lie. She wanted to go home to see Dad and Blyth and find a plate of faggots waiting in the oven. Even Mary's temper was better than Bunny's rages.

'It's ten to one,' gasped Jeanette, cramming the last of the Swiss roll into her mouth. 'The old queen'll be boiling over.'

The chorus swigged down their tea and rushed back across the road.

The twins sat on the floor watching their friend leap through her can-can number. It looked so easy. They were all caught up in the magic of her performance, clapping in time to the music. Jeanette was a star. She high kicked around the room with such energy, rising and falling, never losing the beat. Faith sighed. Compared to her, she and Mercy were a pair of cart-horses. It didn't matter how much they let old Max pinch their tits they were never going to see their names in lights.

Mildred stopped playing and reached up on top of the piano for her glass of stout.

Bunny picked up a large picture frame and got two of the other girls to hold each side. 'Now, Scarlets' he beckoned, 'listen to me, as if your life depended on it. This number is called, "Through the Looking Glass." For its success, both of you must mimic the other, in perfect synchronicity. The audience must believe that there is only one girl sat at her mirror adorning her face. If you do as I say, at the end of your performance they will be enchanted to discover that it was a very clever illusion.'

The twins stood facing each other, either side of the frame. Bunny got them to mime his movements: powdering their noses, brushing their hair and puckering up their faces as they put on their lipstick. Painstakingly he took them through each movement again and again. When they thought their torture was at an end, he called to Mildred to accompany them with a tinkling tune full of trills and arpeggios. Now they had to suit the gestures to the music. They repeated and repeated each move, desperate for the music to stop and to go back to their digs and loll on their mattress.

As they left the rehearsal room Max Lemco appeared and drew Faith towards him.

'What lucky girls you are,' he drawled. 'A spot of your own.'

'Ta, Mr Lemco,' she muttered, trying to squeeze past him and catch her sister.

He pressed her up against the wall. 'Thank me nicely, duckie,' he breathed at her.

Faith recoiled from the stench of rotting teeth and old trousers.

'Nicely, now,' he insisted, putting his arm against the wall to cut off her retreat before gripping her chin with his other hand and forcing her mouth open.

Faith gagged as he thrust his tongue into her mouth. She shook her head from side to side. He pressed himself against her. Was this being interfered with? If so, she didn't have room to knee him in the testimonials. If she didn't do something quick she was going to choke. Closing her eyes she brought her teeth together and bit his tongue.

'You viper,' he choked, blood dribbling from his mouth. 'By God you'll be sorry.'

Scrubbing her hand against her mouth, Faith broke free and hurtled down the stairs. Dirty old bugger! she seethed. He'd be sorry for that she was determined.

The next week in Aldershot Mercy studied the programme. They were in the fifth spot after Jeanette's can-can: 'Mademoiselle at Her Mirror, a beguiling illusion performed by The Scarlets.' This was their chance.

'You'll wear out them words with looking at them,' snapped Faith. 'We ain't given one performance yet and you're seeing us in the West End.'

'Right misery guts you are,' said Mercy in surprise. 'What's up with ya? We're just getting the hang of it. Even the digs is better – a bed each and the grub's good.'

'You ain't got old Lemco breathing down yer neck.'

'No, I got that sweaty fire-eater pinchin' me knees under the table. His missis keeps glaring at me fit to kill.' Mercy reached in her coat and found two fruit pastilles. She picked off the pocket-fluff and handed the green one to her sister.

'So what's the bright side?' snapped Faith. 'Cerise borrowed me stockings and give them back all sweaty. Old Madame Lapin's got the hump cos I forgot to fetch her mints and I've lost Dad's envelope with the pound in.'

'Five minutes, beginners, please,' called someone.

They clattered down the steps and into the wings.

The orchestra struck up and the chorus marched onto the

stage with arms swinging. Jeanette swaggered in front of them with a cane, which at the end of the number sprouted a Union Jack. Everyone saluted and the audience roared their approval. It was a mad rush back up the stairs to the dressing room to change while the jugglers kept the audience entertained, throwing Indian clubs across the stage followed by flaming torches. It would then be the turn of a little French woman and her performing poodles. Following them would be Jeanette and her can-can. While the audience were still clapping her the twins had to step through the looking glass.

In spite of herself Faith had been excited when they slipped the satin dresses over their heads and smoothed down the frilly skirts.

'Looks a treat, the pair of you. That green sets off yer eyes,' said Madame Lapin, really smiling at both of them.

'I wants to be sick,' muttered Mercy, her face the colour of putty.

'You ain't got time,' said Faith, looking equally pasty.

'Off you go, quick, now,' said Madame Lapin, giving them a shove.

They arrived at the wings as Jeanette's number ended in a roar of applause. The curtains closed and the picture frame was lowered from the scenery loft. Mercy stood facing through it and Faith stood in front of her with her back to the audience. To the side was a table with hairbrushes, lipsticks and powder puffs.

'Timing,' hissed Bunny, signalling the stagehands to raise the curtain.

Mildred began her trilling notes on the piano, and the twins picked up their brushes.

Mercy smiled as if in to her mirror and Faith smiled back. Each copied the other's every move: tilting her head to one side, pinching colour into her cheeks then outlining her lips with lipstick. Both girls reached for a strip of green ribbon hanging through the frame and tied a bow around their curls. At the last tinkle from Mildred, Mercy slid her hand under the frame and held onto Faith while the table and frame were winched up out of sight and the one figure at the mirror was revealed as two.

The audience 'Ooh'd' and 'Aah'd' with pleasure, then burst into wild clapping.

The twins, trembling with relief, curtsied then hurtled off the stage.

'Still wanna be sick?' asked Faith, as they climbed the stairs to the dressing room.

'Na, I feels great, wants to do it all over again. They loved us, didn't they?' she babbled. 'We could be stars.'

Faith could see Mercy was enthralled. Any talk of going home would now fall on deaf ears. The clapping had been good, exciting even, but it only lasted for seconds. They paid for it shivering beneath one blanket, being shouted at and dragged from one seedy digs to another – then there was Max. When she'd told her sister about his slimy ways she had just laughed.

'Keep out of his way. 'Member what Dad said, knee him in the testimonials.'

That had been a fat lot of good last time, Faith thought sourly. Mercy hadn't been there while he was pawing at her. She felt dirty and cheap as if there were something in her that invited such attentions. A wave of homesickness washed over her. Even standing in Charlotte Street on a rainy Saturday flogging comics was better than this life of pretending all the time. But going home on her own, Faith chewed her fingers. They had never ever been apart. The Scarlets were taken on as a pair. Individually they had little talent, couldn't even keep in step. Alone, Mercy would be hard put to survive.

Later when they reached their lodgings, Faith left her twin chatting over her stale cheese sandwiches with the other girls.

Half asleep, in the early hours, she stretched out her arm and found a cold space. Dragging on her coat she crept downstairs to find the sitting room empty. Perhaps Mercy was in the outside lavatory. When she found the door swinging open Faith's stomach knotted with fright. She rushed back upstairs and knocked on Jeanette's door.

'It's the middle of the bleeding night, 'course I ain't seen her. Left her downstairs about half twelve,' muttered her friend.

Faith panicked. Wild images of Mercy in the fire-eater's clutches or wandering the streets penniless tore through her mind. She rushed out of the house. Where, where could she be at this time of night in a strange town? Mercy had been so lit up by their performance earlier on, what could have happened to make her run away?

She had never lost her enthusiasm for the Debonnaires. It was Faith that was homesick. But what if Mercy had been pretending, not letting on how she really felt. She had a fierce pride and hated being shown up. Faith would cry when Mary hit her, but Mercy would bite her lip and say nothing.

Faith stopped her pacing and made her way down a long, dark street. At the end was the railway station with a notice board, lit by one solitary lamp. The two platforms appeared to be deserted but as she walked past one of the benches a figure reared up at her.

'Hello, darlin', what you doin' out this late? Come over 'ere and keep me warm, why don't ya?'

'Bugger off!' Faith shouted. 'No, get your hands off. I'll give you such a kicking.' She was angry rather than afraid and the drunken soldier was no match for her speed and determination.

'Tight-assed bitch,' he yelled after her, as Faith ran towards the footbridge.

By the time she had raced up one side and down the other

she had the stitch and was almost out of breath. Trembling, she sank down on the nearest bench and looked about her. Where was Mercy? She knew, in her bones, that she was on the station. Digging her hands into the depths of her pockets for warmth, she walked to the end of the platform. As she turned to retrace her steps a figure leapt at her from the bushes. Faith screamed and thrashed about with her fists.

'It's me, it's me, no, stop, you daft cow. It's me – Mercy.'

'I could kill you!' screamed Faith. 'Frightened the life out of me you did, selfish mare. Thought you bin raped or run over. All sorts I bin thinking. She clutched her side as the stitch stabbed at her. 'What was you gonna do, push off home and leave me to face the music?'

'Knew you'd find me,' said Mercy, smugly. 'There's a milk train to Fareham at half past four. I got two tickets.'

'Bloody hours away, that is. We'll be froze to death by then. Where'd you get the money? Told me you was skint dinner time, in the caff.'

'I got ten bob off Fernando and I found Dad's letter.'

Faith's eye's narrowed. 'How come you found it, now? We've searched the place, over and over. Unless, of course, it was you that had it all the time. Was it you?'

Mercy said nothing.

Faith boiled over. 'You're a twister,' she screamed, pummelling her sister with her fists. 'You lying toad. All these weeks I bin desperate to go back home and you've sat there smug as you like with the fare tucked up the leg of your drawers.'

'Stop it. Ow! No, don't.

'I could kill you,' gasped Faith, running out of steam. 'And how come you're pally with the fire-eater? Thought you couldn't stand him. What you done for him that's worth ten bob?'

'I ain't done it yet, I said as how you fancied him. Promised to keep his missis busy while you and him went up to our room.' She shielded her head as Faith set about her in earnest. 'Listen . . . ow! No – stop, stop. We was gonna be home before anythink happened.'

'Prove it,' snarled her sister clutching her hair.

'Just let go, and I'll show ya,' urged Mercy prizing her sister's fingers from her head. She reached into her coat pocket and drew out two crumpled tickets.

'You could've told me,' panted Faith, ''stead of worrying me guts out.'

'Sorry,' she mumbled. 'I got them this afternoon when you was asleep. Kept trying to tell you but old Jeanette kept shoving her oar in. Then when you went out to the lav old Fernando's missis dragged me in her room and went for me. Soon as I could get away, I grabbed me coat off the hallstand and legged it down the street.' Mercy put her arm around her sister and they sat on the bench, together, their teeth chattering. 'I wanted to go home just as much as you,' she said, 'but I wanted to do that one performance with the mirror first, so we went home with a bit of success behind us.'

'Ain't never going anywhere else,' said Faith. 'Even working at the brewery'll be a luxury after this.'

'Tell ya what, why don't we go back to bed? It's frigging cold out here and the train ain't coming for ages. We could go home tomorrer.'

'What about the tickets?' asked Faith, not wanting to let her off the hook too easily.

'Well, that was Fernando's money. I still got Dad's letter with the pound note in it.'

'And what you gonna say to Fernando and his missis?'

'That's easy,' said Mercy. 'I'll say it's you what's keen on him and you'll say it's me. Any trouble, we'll give him one in the testimonials.' After all,' she said, 'it was being identicals what got us the job in the first place.'

'Race you back over the bridge,' said Faith with a sudden burst of energy.

15

Belching steam from its tall brick chimney the Gosport Steam Laundry faced her at the end of Nelson Lane. Mary bit her lip. Her plan to meet Matthew at four o'clock with both a job and some lodgings under her belt was looking shaky. She had crossed on the half past eight ferry and traipsed up and down the High Street from shop to shop, but even the pubs weren't interested. It was now almost twelve and she'd not even begun to look at rooms.

A gold finger painted on the wall directed her to the office. Inside, a woman in a starched overall presided over a room composed almost entirely of parcels.

'Got yer receipt?' she asked, tucking a wisp of grey hair behind her ear.

'I've come for a job?' said Mary, beginning to swelter in the heat.

'Bit old to be starting on this line of work, ain't ya?' said the woman, seeming to sum up her unsuitability at a glance.

'Washed and ironed for my family since I was ten and I've run a market stall. Anythink you show me I'll pick up in five minutes,' she boasted.

'You'll need to be quick, I'm telling you. Don't like taking older girls. We favour the youngsters.'

'Cheaper, aren't they?' burst out Mary. 'Chuck 'em out when they're sixteen and get in another lot of green young kids.'

'You want a job or just to argue the toss?' the woman snapped, turning away from her to string up a parcel.

'Yes, I wants one.' She couldn't make herself apologise but she hoped her tone was suitably meek.

'Stay there.' The woman, wearing an ugly caliper and surgical boot, limped through a door at the other side of the counter.

Mary tried to stoke up her spirits. All this was for Matthew so they could be together. If he could work beneath the sea in all that danger she could face whatever the laundry threw at her. She was starting at the bottom. Washing other peoples' dirty drawers, you couldn't get nearer the bottom than that.

'Right, Miss,' the woman said, 'job going for a sorter. Monday to Friday seven till four, eight till twelve on Saturday – the pay is nine and six.'

Mary swallowed. She would have to find cheap lodgings if she was to exist on that pittance.

'That would be a week in hand, of course. Means we keeps yer first week's money and gives it back when you leaves. When can you start?'

'Monday,' said Mary, trying not to let the disappointment show. A whole seven days to keep herself with no money. It would probably be the same arrangement for the lodgings.

'Be here sharp ten to seven. If you're late we docks yer money. Go round the back and ask for Miss Chapman.'

Once more out on the street, she shivered. Her day had not panned out as she had expected. It had been disappointing to find that there was no market in Gosport. Her intention had been to bring the stall over on the chain ferry and set it up with the help of Dad and Blyth. Mary shrugged – that was plans for you. The alternative of leaving the two of them to keep it going back in Charlotte Street was no longer possible. With the twins to help they might have survived. Without them things were falling apart. Blyth pushed off round to Harry and Dora's at the least excuse or next door to Granny Pragnell's. As for Dad – Mary shrugged. At least he wasn't drinking now, but he didn't seem to be doing much of anything else. Oh, he went and stood in job queues but who would employ a man in his forties with a hacking cough when there were young lads almost two-a-penny? Mary bit her lip. If she wasn't careful she'd be feeling sorry for him. The stall would just have to stay in the lock-up until she could figure out something else.

Wandering around the warren of little streets near the laundry she looked for cards in windows advertising rooms to let. Her new job would be exhausting and she wanted something close at hand. Besides, it wasn't too far away from the Haslar Bridge and the gates of HMS *Dolphin*. That, after all, was her reason for coming – to be near Matthew.

Around her were the trades associated with the sea: caulkers, watermen and ropemakers. Behind her was the huge sail loft of Ratsey and Lapthorne, and in front the yard of Camper and Nicholson, boat builders to royalty. In Shore Street the prows of great ocean going yachts, laid up until spring, loomed over the roofs of the cottages. In the window of number nine, was a card advertising 'Room to let, three shillings a week. Jabez Churt.' The whole street could do with being sent to the laundry, she thought, imagining the giant washtub and scrubbing brush required for the task. It was down-at-heel and not at all what Matthew would want for her, but it had the virtue of being cheap.

A whistle blew and hordes of workers came out of the yards and lofts and made their way to The Vixen, a pub nearby. A crowd of girls came from the direction of the laundry down the street with arms linked, laughing together. Mary followed them inside. She was thirsty and needed to weigh up her alternatives. Wedging herself in a corner by the fire, she sipped her shandy and looked around.

The laundry girls sat with their pints of beer, laughing and swearing together. They seemed to be a regular feature of the pub and there was much teasing between them and the workmen from the yards. There were a couple of women near the door with heavy make-up and raucous voices. One of them had artificial flowers pinned in her hair. Their eyes were flickering around the room from one man to another and whenever the pub door opened they studied the newcomer closely.

Mary went up to the counter and bought another half-pint of shandy and a bag of crisps. This would be her local, the laundry girls would be her pals, across the street would be her home. She undid the blue paper twist of salt and shook it over her crisps. It was an adventure, her adventure.

A hooter sounded and the pub emptied. Mary went back to the cottage with the card in the window and knocked on the door. A dog barked, a great booming sound, and someone swore at him. Just as she was turning away the door opened.

'Watcha want?' A bewhiskered man in a navy jersey and bellbottoms stared at her. He rubbed his eyes and yawned, displaying a mouthful of crooked brown teeth. Waking him up from a beer-laced sleep was not going to get her off to a good start.

'Come after the room.'

'You daft or sommat? Wants a waterman not some young floozie.'

'I'll be working in the laundry and I can pay in advance,' said Mary, keeping a grip on her temper.

'Don't want no dame with all her knick-knacks hanging about the place.'

'I ain't no dame,' she snapped. 'I'm Miss Vine and I'm engaged to be married. I shall keep my things in my room.'

'Don't want you.'

Mary pushed the door open and the man pushed it closed.

In between their struggles the sound of barking intensified.

'You bloody deaf or sommink. Bugger off.'

The dog joined the struggle and the man fell back into the room. Leaping up at Mary the mongrel licked her enthusiastically on the face. He rested his front paws on her shoulders and managed to push her hat to the ground.

'Gerroff, gerroff,' she shouted, hitting the animal with her handbag.

'I'll fetch you such a wallop,' screamed the man, advancing out of the house with his stick in his hand, while the animal bounded off down the street.

While the waterman's back was turned, Mary seized her chance and thrust her way into the cottage. It was gloomy inside and smelt of ale and old dinners. She had her foot on the bottom step leading upstairs and her hand on the rope banister when the owner returned.

'Jesus Christ, girl, you doolally or sommat? I don't wantcha.' He flung the stick on the floor then sank down into a chair.

While Jabez sat there, gasping at her like a stranded cod, Mary studied him. He was, she supposed, about sixty years old. His grey hair and beard formed a tarnished halo around his face which, had it been washed, might well have placed him ten years younger. Tobacco and spilt food stained his clothes. Barefoot, with big toes that pointed away from each other at a quarter to three, Jabez Churt glared at her.

Mary glared back. Why did she want a room in this dirt-box of a cottage? Was it simply because he had refused to let it to her? Nothing made her more determined to have something than outright denial. In the pub she had begun to doubt the suitability of Shore Cottage but the cussed waterman had lit the fire of battle in her and she would not be thwarted. Mary took a ten-shilling note out of her purse and stuck it on the mantelpiece under a tobacco pouch. 'That's one week in hand

and two in advance,' she said. 'I'm just going to look upstairs. If it ain't what I wants I'll be down for my money.'

Leaving Churt to stare at the money she climbed up the stairs. It was clear from her struggle with the latch that the bedroom had not been used or even opened for months. Mary pressed down the latch again and thrust her shoulder against the door. It shuddered and juddered then swung back on its hinges. She fell into the room, landing on what she took to be an old mattress. The acrid smell of urine burned in her nostrils and Mary struggled not to vomit. Set into the wall opposite was a curved window like an eyebrow. Taking off her scarf she spat on it and rubbed a clean patch on the grimy pane. Peering out she could see between the yachts in Nicholsons' yard way out across the harbour. In the distance was the ferry chugging over from Portsmouth and near at hand a waterman, similar to Jabez, standing on his boat tamping tobacco into his pipe. In spite of the grey sea and the scudding clouds the scene excited her. She could see beyond this first glimpse to other times when she would have her bed pulled against the window and be able to see the ships lit up at night. From here she would see the yachts setting off for Cowes Week on the Isle of Wight. Better still, if she could open the window and twist her head around she might even be able to wave to Matthew's submarine at Haslar Creek.

I'll take it, she thought. Turning away from the window she studied her surroundings. The room was completely bare save for the mattress. Not even a shred of curtain clung to the nails above the window or a thread of matting lay on the floor. Still she wanted it. As she closed the door, and went downstairs, Mary's brain was listing all that would be needed to set her seal on the place.

'Be back tomorrow to clean up. Need you to turf out that mattress and get us a key cut,' she informed Jabez.

'I don't know as I'll have yer,' he muttered.

'Well, you've took me money. Bound to have me now.'

'Got a mouth on you, for a wench, I'll say that for ya,' he conceded. 'If you wants to do up me room it's to come out of your pocket. Never arst yer to stay.'

'Where's the lav?' she asked.

'Through the scullery.'

'Bloody mad, you are' Mary said to herself, after a visit to the noisome privy. When she walked back through the cottage she was leapt on and had her face licked by Jabez's lively hound.

'What's his name,' she asked, 'since we're gonna be neighbours?'

'Just Dog,' said the waterman. 'Don't need no name. Won him at dominoes, workin' dog he is. Don't want you feedin' or petting him.'

'No chance of that,' Mary snapped. 'I'll be here tomorrow, eight o'clock sharp,' she reminded Jabez Churt before slamming out of the cottage.

There was an hour to kill before meeting Matthew at the café but she went there early and sat over a mug of Bovril, busy list-making. Washing soda, green soap, clean rags, vinegar for cleaning the windows, a mattress, sheets, a pillow and blanket, her head buzzed with all that she needed to do. Perhaps Harry would help her bring her stuff over on a handcart on the chain ferry on Sunday. Mary twisted her engagement ring round her finger to give her courage. There was fifteen shillings in her purse. They'd have to have a good day down the market on Saturday to keep her going to her first pay day.

'Mary, Mary, you deaf or something?'

'Oh, Matthew! Is that the time?' She blushed in confusion. 'I was making plans.'

'I'll get us some tea and you can tell me.' He leaned down and kissed her cheek. 'What shall it be, beans on toast or poached egg?'

'Do you reckon we could have both?' she asked, grinning at him.

As he stood at the counter she rehearsed how she would tell him about the laundry and Shore Cottage. Would he think the view from the window worth the accompanying grime?

'Is it that serious?' he teased, settling himself beside her.

'Will you just listen to me and not say anything till I've finished?' she asked, taking hold of his hand.

'Of course,' he said, smiling at her.

Mary watched him closely. She could feel the protest bubbling up in him when she spoke about the pub, and even more in her telling of the meeting with Jabez Churt.

'Wouldn't you be better staying at home and just coming over to work each day?' he asked when she'd finished. 'Sounds as if you've rushed things and gone off at half-cock.'

'Knew you'd say that,' she flared. 'Got no faith in me, none of you. Don't you want me in Gosport? It's you I'm doing it for.'

The arrival of their beans and poached eggs interrupted them on the verge of a row.

'Why do you always do that?' he asked.

'What?'

'Flare up the minute anyone disagrees with you.'

'I don't,' she mumbled, looking at her plate.

'You know how miserable we were after the row at Christmas?' He reached across the table for her hand. 'If we are going to be married we've got to be able to talk things out between us, without always falling out.'

'That was the twins' fault and Dad,' she muttered. It wasn't fair! Matthew was putting her in the wrong.

'Why do you think I'm not happy at you staying in this cottage?'

''Cos people will think I'm a tart.'

He shook his head and then took up another forkful of beans.

Mary wanted to hit him. She'd looked forward to telling him all that she'd done and to see the pride in his face.

Matthew put down his fork. 'Because I love you and want you to be safe. This old man, in his run-down place, could fall asleep with the baccy-pipe in his mouth and set the cottage alight. If I'm away and you're ill, who will look after you? Who will even know that you're lying up there in the dark with no one to care for you?'

Mary wanted to cry. 'I'm not used to it,' she whispered.

'To what?' Again he held her hand.

'Someone looking out for me. Always bin me keeping everyone else together.'

'I'm proud of you,' he said, 'that you kept your family together, but now you've got me. We've to make our plans and take decisions together. We need to be extra sure of each other.'

'Why?'

'I shall be away on the boat and you'll have to manage on your own. Perhaps even with a baby.'

'Thought we was doing things together,' she said, not wanting to think of him being away from her. In all her calculations Mary had somehow buried the fact of Matthew's likely foreign drafts. Being alone in Gosport for months on end was not something she wanted to dwell on.

'That's why it's important for us to know what we both want and to be used to working as a team,' Matthew said. 'Then when I'm away you'll know what to do as if I was here.'

'Dunnow if I can do that,' Mary said, before swallowing a mouthful of egg. She had forgotten to put salt on it and also, with all the talk between them it had grown cold and rubbery.

He smiled at her. 'We shall have to help each other.'

The danger was past. She rubbed the tears from her eyes with the back of her hand. They both finished their tea and Matthew went back to the counter and fetched them each an Eccles cake.

'When do I get to see this new place of yours?' he asked when they left the café.

'Sunday night,' she said, praying to herself that she could work a miracle by then.

'You're out of luck,' he said. 'I'm off tomorrow down to Portland for exercises. I won't be back till Saturday.'

'You're a mind reader,' Mary said, feeling a mixture of relief and panic at his going away. 'Knew I needed extra time.'

'By then you'll be able to tell me all about the laundry, too.' He looked at his watch. 'What you want to do now? Only half past five, we've got bags of time till I have to be back on board. Do you want to go back home now and tell your dad your news?' he asked, as they walked down the High Street arm in arm. 'Or do you want to go to the pictures?'

'Pictures,' Mary said, squeezing his arm. Telling Dad was something that could be put off until tomorrow. It would be like a rat deserting a sinking ship. That would be how he would see it. If only he had a job. One moment she felt impatient with him holding her back and the next she was filled with pity, remembering the lively fun-loving dad of her childhood. It was all the twinnies' fault, buggering off like that.

'It's Greta Garbo and John Gilbert,' said Matthew, reading the poster outside the Rex Cinema.

Mary didn't care if it was the Kaiser and Marie Lloyd going six rounds in a boxing match. Sitting close to Matthew in the dark, that was what she wanted. She waited impatiently while he fished some money out of his pocket and the woman in the kiosk tore off the tickets. The usherette shone her torch and Mary pulled Matthew towards the back row. They sat in the smothering dark, oblivious of the film playing out in front of them. He put his arm around her and drew her close. She tried to put everything into those kisses – all her love and fear and gratitude that he had chosen her. Soon she'd have that room in Shore Cottage like a new pin. Then she would really show him the depth of her passion.

16

Fred Vine looked at the queue at the back of the insurance offices for the night watchman's job. It stretched halfway down the road – hardly worth his while standing there, behind young men half his age. He got out his tickler tin and rolled himself a cigarette. As he drew in the first gasp he could feel the eyes of the two fellows beside him fasten on his fag. Fred knew the feeling. Nothing seemed so desperate if you could just light up a tickler and draw in that first breath. It bought you a few seconds' space to face up to the day. As he was about to speak with them someone from the office came out and waved the queue away.

The two men with him stood there gaunt and threadbare. Poor buggers thought Fred, fumbling in his pocket for the sixpense he'd saved for beer money. Looking at the older fellow was like a reflection of himself. Nodding to them he said, 'Fancy a tea at Driver's? Ain't in a hurry, are you?'

'Got all the time in the world,' the young lad said.

'Much obliged,' said the man, following Fred towards Edinburgh Road.

The three of them settled at the counter waiting for their mug of tea each and plate of bread between them.

'Didn't stand a chance,' said the man, 'back there at the Prudential. Still gotta go through the pantomime ain't ya? Else ya can't go back and face the missis.'

Fred nodded. In his case it was Mary. The market stall was going through a lean patch with most of Portsea out of work.

Buying toys was out of the question. At least with Dusty back in the picture she was giving him a rest from her nagging. Once she'd married and gone over to Gosport it would be just him and Blyth. Fred dreaded the prospect. It had been bad enough losing the girls. Christ, he missed them! All the noise and the leg-pulling, all the gossip from the brewery. They were like looking at Dolly, only twice over. Since they'd gone he had difficulty picturing his wife as she had been when he first met her. With the twinnies about she was constantly before him.

Since Christmas he had not been able to rid himself of a persistent cough and a feeling of exhaustion after the slightest bit of exertion. Dragging the market stall out of the lock-up and wheeling it down to Charlotte Street was beyond him, on his own. Without Mary they might as well sell up. Although it was difficult to see who might risk their savings on a stall the way things were. What with the miners, the railwaymen and the transport workers threatening to strike, and the dockyard on short time, things were the bleakest they had been since the war. Thank God Harry was in the navy still, and Dusty. At least Dora and Mary could count on their money. Without his own naval pension of twelve and six a week, and what Mary chipped in, he and Blyth would be on Queer Street. His lad would be reduced to going to school in charity boots and having farthing breakfasts.

'Here, mate,' he said, passing the bread towards him.

'Ta,' said the man, taking a slice. 'My son,' he said, turning to the lad. 'I'm Frank.'

'Fred Vine. Pleased to know ya.'

They sat huddled over the tea in silence until Fred asked, 'Where you living?'

Frank stared down at his tea. 'Missis and daughter-in-law in a room in North End. We bin kipping at the Sally Army in Queen Street. They're getting assistance. If we're seen round there as two able-bodied blokes they'll cut their money.'

Fred looked at the father and son. Able-bodied was not a term he would have used to describe them. The pride had been filleted from them. Unshaven, with frayed cuffs and sour breath they slumped over their food, chewing slowly as if to make that one slice last the day.

'My Lizzie's having a nipper any day now,' said the son, looking sheepish.

Fred smiled, trying to look as if the prospect of an extra mouth to feed was cause for celebration.

The lad clenched his jaw and blinked.

Fred touched him on the arm. 'This calls for one all round,' he said, reaching in his pocket for his tickler tin. Clumsily he made up the cigarette. Since the fire his fingers had never recovered their nimbleness. But it was more than clumsiness. The destitution of the father and son frightened him. If he didn't make a better fist of things he could be joining them. Anxiety burned in his belly as he passed the fag over to Frank. 'Better times,' he said.

'Better times,' said the father, inhaling deeply before passing the fag to his son.

'Better times,' said the lad returning it to Fred.

In silence they passed the tickler from one to the other until it was spent. When their tea and bread was finished they got up to leave. Out on the pavement they shook hands and went their separate ways.

Blyth finished the fish-paste sandwiches and the crisps that Dad had left for him and slung the plate in the sink. He was off next door to see Mr Pragnell. The old man had promised to teach him how to play chess. He had taken him his last school report showing his top marks in arithmetic and drawing.

'You have the makings of an engineer or draughtsman,

young man,' he'd said. 'You obviously enjoy figuring things out. Your father must be very proud of you.'

Was Dad proud? He didn't know. Most times he was either sleeping or coughing. Blyth always came home to something on the table and he had clean clothes to wear, but that was mostly down to Mary. It wasn't any fun indoors now, with the twinnies gone. His sister rushed around doing most things and nagging the pair of them. Sometimes Dad tried to take an interest and even played cards with him or asked him about school. When he joked with him, Blyth felt his stomach churn. It was as if he really wanted to cry but tried to plaster over his sadness with a shaky smile. There were tons of times when the twins used to drive him wild with their teasing, but now he would give anything for them to be back home and Dad laughing again.

'Chess is the game for you,' Mr Pragnell said. 'It will teach you strategy. Come over on Thursday at six and we will make a start.'

It wasn't just talking to Uncle Albert, as he called him, but seeing Granny that lured Blyth to the Pragnells' house. He had been going there ever since he could crawl. First she had been called Granny Forrest and then she married Uncle Albert. It wasn't just her cakes and stories neither. You could talk to her about anything and she always made things better. Even Mary listened to her and stopped her raging.

Before leaving, Blyth put the guard around the fire and left a note for Dad, to say where he was going.

The smell of baking wafted towards him as he knocked at the back door. Jam tarts, Blyth's mouth watered.

'Hello, Blyth, sit yourself down. I expect you can make room for a couple of these,' said Granny, passing him a bowl in which nestled two strawberry tarts. She poured some milk from a tiny jug with a picture of a cow on it.

'Ta,' he said, settling his legs under the table and reaching for a spoon. Everything was familiar and unchanging. Even his body felt different at Granny's, less cramped, and his breathing filled all of his chest and his brain stretched out.

'Heard from your sisters, have you?' she asked pouring his tea.

'Not for ages and ages,' said Blyth, stirring a second spoonful of sugar into his cup.

'Have you written to them?'

'Dunno where to write.'

'I think if you went to the stage door of the Hippodrome, they'd give you an address. These theatricals travel on a circuit from one place to another. Likely they'll be back in Portsmouth soon.'

'Probbly be so puffed up with all their travelling about, won't want to come home.'

Granny chuckled. 'You'd be surprised, Blyth. Those girls could be stuck in some gloomy place missing you, just as hard as you and your Dad are missing them.'

'D'you reckon so?'

'Certain of it. Could be that they're worked so hard they haven't time to write. You go and find out where they're staying and I'll give you a stamp. Put a smile back on your dad's face to hear from them.'

'Do it tomorrow,' said Blyth, smiling at Uncle Albert as he came into the room.

'You give me a hand to wash up and clear the table then you'll be set for the evening,' said Granny.

Blyth swirled the wire soap-saver through the water, eager to be out of the scullery. He was relieved that there were only cups, saucers and tea plates.

'How's Mary?' asked Granny as she stood beside him with her tea-towel at the ready.

'Ever so crabby. Been out all day don't know where she's been.'

'I remember her as a little girl, not more than nine or ten, packing up the sandwiches and taking you all down the beach for the day. Got the courage of a lion has your sister.'

'Don't have to be so narky all the time.'

Granny chuckled. 'With families, you have to take the rough with the smooth. Is that the last spoon? Right, off you go, I'll square away out here.'

Uncle Albert had laid out the chessboard and opened the box of pieces. 'Sit down, sit down,' he said, 'there's much to learn. We will start with the names of all the pieces and their moves.'

Blyth picked up the chessmen, repeating their names to himself: bishop, knight, rook, king, queen, pawn and castle. He liked the hardness of the ivory and the different shapes and purposes of each piece.

'This is a game for life, Blyth, a game of strategy and patience. It will sharpen your mind and set you challenges at every turn.'

Blyth smiled at Uncle Albert. He hunched over the board eager for whatever the old man could teach him.

Her spirits sank at the sight of the unwashed plates and Dad sat there coughing by the fire. All her carefully rehearsed words withered on her lips. 'Some bloody welcome,' she snapped.

'Sorry, gal,' he wheezed. 'Been out half the day chasing a job at the Prudential.'

'Where's Blyth?'

'Gone next door to play chess with old man Pragnell.'

'Could have got him to clear up first. Christ, Dad, he ain't helpless. He should be pulling his weight.'

'Leave the lad alone. He does his best.'

'Well,' Mary said, stamping out to the scullery to fill the kettle, 'you're both gonna have to do a sight more than that in future.' Sod breaking her news gently, she thought, he could have it now with both barrels. 'I'm moving out on Saturday, over to Gosport. Got a job and a place to live. You two will have to buck your ideas up.'

'What d'you mean, you're moving out?' demanded Fred. The girl had come in and dropped the bombshell before even taking off her coat. 'What does Dusty reckon to all this, or ain't he taken into account, like the rest of us?'

Mary's courage faltered. 'He don't mind,' she blustered. 'Means we'll have more time together. 'Sides, I was going to move over there anyway when we gets married. Just going a bit sooner.'

'What about the stall in the market? How d'ya reckon me and Blyth is going to manage?'

'P'r'aps Harry'll give you a hand,' she said.

'What, from the bleedin' West Indies? Due out there next week, he is. Saw him in the pub.'

'Always manages to get to the pub,' she sneered.

Fred swallowed down his temper. 'You always gotta go the whole hog. Why can't ya sort something out so's you can help us of a Saturday? It's your stall, when all's said and done. Nelly left it to ya. Without us, you'd have had to sell up long since.'

'Hardly worth the trouble of getting it set up lately. Only made five quid last week standing there all day. Paid off the arrears of the rent to Mr Pragnell and we was left with thirty bob. Down to five bob now what with Blyth's new shoes and getting the coal.'

'Paying for a lock-up with nothing coming in don't make much sense.'

'P'r'aps we could sort something out with Danny Sullivan. Maybe he could help set up and clear up with you.'

'Thought you never wanted to be beholden to him. That's what you said last time he offered. Can't work in Gosport and keep things going over here, gal, ain't a magician.'

'I thought my family would muck in. Not much chance of that.'

'Mary,' he said wearily, 'I does me best with the market, but I just ain't got the strength and Blyth's a good lad but he's only nine.'

She looked at him and felt a stab of pity. Dad was only forty-six yet he looked sixty. He was thin and bent, his blue eyes faded and his hair curling round the back of his collar in grey strands.

'There's no call for you to be in such a rush. Just see us through the next few months, gal, please,' he said. 'What's six months out of your life? Reckon you owe us that, me and Blyth.'

The words ignited her rage. 'You gotta bleedin' cheek,' she flared. 'Who was it kept you all together when Mum died and you was on the booze? Me, me, me,' she screamed. 'Talk about owing. It's me what's owed.'

'Christ, we ain't going over all that again,' shouted Fred, stung at her throwing his failings in his face.

'I gotta a right to a life of me own instead of always slaving over you lot,' she roared. 'Never told the twins they gotta stay.'

'Mary,' he pleaded, close to tears, 'don't get on yer high horse. Can't we sit down and talk it over.' Fred got up and went to her and touched her arm. She flung him aside. He couldn't blame her. What sort of parent had he been? Worse than useless. If he wasn't at sea he was in the boozer, and poor old Dolly hadn't been much better. 'It's Blyth I'm thinking of,' he said. 'The lad's clever and needs books and stuff.'

'Don't you use him to get round me,' she snarled. 'If it wasn't for me he wouldn't be here, still.'

'Watcha mean, still?' he asked, feeling his temper rising.

'You know, that Christmas when I come back from the

Clements and he was missing. Where was you? Sat there drunk out of yer head.'

'I went in after him,' he raged at her, waving his hands in her face. 'How d'ya think I got them burns.' The sounds of the flames roaring in that little house, the smoke stinging his eyes and the fear were still with him. Fred sank back down in the chair, his heart thumping. He had been afraid to go back into the street without Blyth and even more afraid to climb up those stairs in the heat and the dark.

'But who made ya do it?' she screamed. 'You wouldn't 'ave gone in there if I hadn't made ya.'

There was a shocked silence.

Truth or no truth Mary knew she had gone too far.

'You are one cruel bitch,' he gasped. 'D'you think I don't know that? That I haven't dreamed about it night after night after night, crucifying meself with guilt? Why don't you get the whole bloody catalogue of me failings out while you're about it? Reckon they're etched in yer head like letters on a tombstone.' He sank back into the armchair covering his face with his hands. The agony of waiting, burnt and exhausted, for the firemen to search that house for his son was as fresh as yesterday.

Mary chewed her hand in frustration. She had made a muck of it. The only thing to do was say that she was sorry. If he would just look up at her and give her an opening instead of sitting there all defeated . . . Why did he always crumble? Where was his spirit?

She flung out of the house and went to the chip shop in Queen Street. Mary loved the noise and bustle there with the sailors carousing outside the pubs, the smell of beer, fried onions and meat pies. Tonight it failed to rouse her. The 'sorry' she should have said still stuck in her throat. Even the chips had no flavour. Why was it so hard for her ever to be in the wrong?

Letting herself back into the house she was all set to offer to warm up the chips for Dad and make him a fresh pot of tea. The kitchen was empty. Mary flung the chips on the fire and slammed off to bed. She was glad to be leaving. Once she was over in Gosport he and Blyth would miss her. They'd realise all that she'd done for them. Furiously she scrabbled about under her pillow for a rag to blow her nose. It didn't make sense. If she was so pleased to be leaving, why was she crying her eyes out?

17

Cissie stood in the poky little flower vestry, cleaning the vases, and holding her breath against the green stink of rotting stems. Mrs Mowbray was in the church waiting for the vases. Cissie had been at Simla Cottage three weeks now and it felt like forever. When she thought about it, she knew she was in clover, here in the country, being waited on hand, foot and finger. She should be grateful, yet she longed for the clamour of Portsea. It was all so quiet. Well not quiet exactly, what with the screech owl in the tree at the end of the garden, or the lowing of the cows in the field nearby. Then there were all the little twitterings and rustlings in the thatched roof over her bedroom. She missed the red-brick houses – it was all grey stone in Dorset.

At least in Pompey she knew her place. Tarts was at the bottom of the heap, abused by customers and police alike. Here she didn't know whether she was supposed to be Mrs Mowbray's friend or servant. Getting dressed up and sitting about all the time was such a pretend life. There was no flavour to anything, like someone had pinched the salt. Madam organised her to death. There were trips round the village to her old biddies. After dinner, or luncheon as she called it, they had a nap, then sewing and visits to church, morning, noon and night.

Cissie liked breakfast best, which she took in the kitchen while Mrs Mowbray had her tray upstairs. She understood Mrs Willow and felt comfortable with her. Once when she brought up the subject of churchgoing, the little Dorset woman carried on top ropes about it.

'Powerful for the Lord is Missis, don't leave him alone five minutes,' Mrs Willow told her. 'Trying to pray her old man into heaven.'

'What was he like?' Cissie asked, spreading her toast with gooseberry jam.

'He was a bit of a roistering gentleman by all accounts, in his young days. Had some trollop over near Dorchester.'

Remembering the picture of the paunchy, bewhiskered figure hanging in the sitting room, Cissie felt that the trollop must have been well paid for her labours. But she said nothing, delighting in Mrs Willow's confidences.

'Her Gonville used to be quite 'andsome, in a beefy sort of way, with a voice like a bloomin' foghorn. Zeemed to fill the room, he did, and always knocking things over. Thought the zun rose and zet on him, did Madam.'

'How did you know about his trollop?' asked Cissie, watching the brisk little woman setting about the ironing while she washed up the breakfast things.

'Come to the funeral, bold as brass, she did. Darned great hat done up with zilk flowers and her face painted like Mr Punch.' Mrs Willow paused to turn the sheet onto the other side. 'Left a wreath of lilies must have cost a fortune, and a card.' She paused to blow her nose then pressed on until the sheet was completed.

Cissie fidgeted with impatience. 'What did it say?' she urged.

'What you on about?' asked Mrs Willow, relishing her captive audience. 'Ooh, aah, the card. 'Course, rain had well nigh washed off the words when I looked at it next morning. What was it – ah, yes, I 'members what 'twas: "Zuch memries, my love, zuch memries."'

'Waahh!' gasped Cissie. 'What did Mrs Mowbray do?'

'Invited the trollop up to the house for sherry and biscuits along with all they other folks. Proper Christian woman is Madam. 'Course they all looked at her with eyes on stalks. Mind you, that card went missing off they flowers, and never again zight nor zound of that trollop.'

Cissie wondered, later, what Mrs Willow would think of her if she knew of her life in Portsea, and how she had earned *her* living. She had the strong impression that she had been talked about in Mrs Mowbray's sewing circle and at the bridge afternoons. Once when she had come in with a tray of tea and biscuits an old man had touched her arm.

'It's the little Magdalene,' he said, smiling roguishly at her.

Mrs Mowbray had blushed and the women had looked away.

'My name is Cissie,' she had said, rushing out and leaving them to pour their own tea. It wasn't just that he'd got her name wrong, there was some hidden meaning that made her feel ashamed.

She stood in the vestry filling up the big enamel jug with water to take out to Mrs Mowbray in the church. It was March the fifth already. Soon the cold weather would be gone and there would be young lambs in the field beyond the garden. It would be Easter in a few weeks perhaps, then they would let her go home.

After taking the vases into the church she refilled the enamel jug and retraced her steps. The smell of narcissi and daffodils greeted her as she walked up the aisle to where Mrs Mowbray stood swathed in a green apron, scissors in hand.

'Aren't they beautiful, Cissie? Oh! I love this time of year. Soon it will be Easter and we shall have lilies. It's my favourite festival – so full of hope. Just think of the joy of those women seeing Jesus risen from the tomb. What a happy thought.'

'Reckon as I'd a bin terrified. Seeing a man in his grave clothes and bleedin' wounds.'

'Yes, well, I was not being quite so literal,' said Mrs Mowbray snappishly.

'Used to go to the Sally Army,' said Cissie, feeling that she had spoilt something. 'Liked the singing. My favourite was, "What a friend we have in Jesus".'

'Charles, er Captain Clements, used to be in the choir at Portsmouth. Had a voice like an angel as a boy. Now, dear, go and fill the jug again. There are the flowers for the font and the porch yet to do.'

Portsmouth: the word filled her with longing for the sight of the sea, the rush of mateys pouring out of the dockyard gates on their bicycles, sailors cruising down Queen Street all beery and hopeful. She wondered if Captain Clements thought of her at all. If only it had been someone else that had shot her. Someone that deserved to be put away, like that Lettice with all her rages. He didn't deserve none of the bad things that happened to him – neither did she. Sighing, Cissie lifted the jug out of the sink. She wished she was going to one of the Sally Army services with its tambourines and trumpets, with ordinary people like herself, shabby but joyful – singing fit to bust.

In St Anselm's even the poorest wore the best that they had: suits shiny from much pressing, starched collars that cut the neck, hats with faded paper flowers and working boots shorn of their week-day mud and agleam with polish. They all sat there while the vicar dosed them with guilt, and they doffed their hats to the local toffs when they shuffled out at the end of the service.

Lately she had felt little bursts of anger at things she would never have bothered about before. Getting mad at things had never been her way. Normally she believed herself to have earned any criticism or slight, but now her mind rebelled. What was different?

Shrugging, she picked up the jug and carried it back

into the church. 'They looks lovely,' she said, watching as Mrs Mowbray placed the last stalk of greenery in the big brass vase.

'Yes, I'm rather pleased with them. Now, we'll move down to the font.'

Cissie followed Madam down the aisle. Her stomach rumbled. She knew that Mrs Willow was making one of her bacon roly-polys and there would be onion sauce and green cabbage. Since being at Simla Cottage she had put on weight.

'Miles and Charlotte will be with their Daddy now. I do hope they are enjoying themselves. He will call in on the way back from returning them to school, in a fortnight's time. I'm so looking forward to hearing how they got on with each other. They haven't seen each other for over a year. There'll be so much to catch up on.'

'When can I go home?' Cissie asked, the words out before she could stop them.

'You are home, my dear,' said Mrs Mowbray, turning towards her, scissors in hand. 'Didn't you realise that?'

Cissie was breathless. 'When did you tell me?' she gasped.

'I thought it was understood, when I talked to you in the hospital.'

'It was just till I was better. What did Captain Clements say?'

'Naturally, he thought, after the unfortunate accident you would not want to remain in Portsmouth and certainly not at Lancaster Terrace.'

Cissie stood there trying to swallow down her rage. She wanted to snatch the scissors and cut the head off all the flowers, to tip over the vases and scream her head off. 'Nobody asked me,' she gasped.

'Aren't you happy here, Cissie? I'm sure I've tried my best.'

She stared at the stone floor, gritting her teeth. Always put you in the wrong when you spoke up, did the nobs. Here she was dressed in the clothes Madam had bought and eating her food. All that she wanted was her gratitude. 'Always bin in Portsmouth from a nipper. Mum and Dad buried there.'

'But everything is entirely different, now,' said Madam, her face flushed, twisting a stalk of laurel between her fingers. 'I think it would be best for us to finish the flowers and then return home for luncheon.' Mrs Mowbray turned her back and fussed with the greenery. 'If you are unhappy we shall have to find you somewhere else.'

'I'll get the brush and dustpan and sweep up round the altar,' said Cissie. She knew Madam was waiting for her to say sorry and tell her how much she'd enjoyed her stay at Simla Cottage, but she wouldn't do it. Now she knew how the land lay she would hatch her plans. No need to rant and rave like old Lettice. I'm going home, she said to herself as she emptied the leftover leaves into the dustbin in the yard, but first I got to get Captain Clements' letter read.

18

Saturday at Shore Cottage passed in a frenzy of scrubbing. Jabez had done none of the things she had asked for.

'Ain't nursemaiding you. Got to fettle for yourself,' he snarled.

His sourness fired Mary's determination to make a go of things. The window was too small to push the mattress through. Besides, the men in the boatyard might have had something to say about it landing at their feet. Swearing to herself she lashed it up with string and hauled it down the stairs. It cost her threepence to bribe a boy to haul it off somewhere out of sight. By the time she had finished cleaning, her hands were raw and eyes stinging from the ammonia needed to scour the dirt away.

She slumped over the ferry railings in a fog of exhaustion. On the way back to Lemon Street she bought a packet of five Woodbines for Dad and some treacle toffees for her brother. The last couple of days had been wretched, with Dad silent and Blyth wary. She hoped, on their last night together, they would at least talk to one another. If only they would wish her well, be happy for her. It wasn't as if she were going off to Africa or anything, she'd only be a ha'penny ferry ride away.

Dad was in the kitchen cutting up newspaper for the lavatory as she walked in. 'Hello,' she said, putting the cigarettes on the table.

'Hello, my babes,' he said. 'How d'you get on?'

A lump came in her throat. She didn't deserve his forgiveness after what she had said. 'Brought a saveloy over from the pie shop. What we got to go with it?' she asked, avoiding his question.

'There's a bit of mousetrap-cheese what needs grating, some stale bread, and onion and two rashers out in the wall safe. Don't need to worry about Blyth, he's in next door. Albert's taught him chess.' Fred smiled. 'Mad for it he is. If I know Granny she'll have lashed him up with sammidges and cake already.'

'Reckon we can make a supper of sorts. Save you the rashers for tomorrow.'

'Blyth and me got an invite round to Dora's for Sunday dinner,' he said, 'so you don't need to worry about us.'

How quickly I'm replaced, she thought, as she fried the onion and sliced the saveloy into the pan to heat it through while she toasted the bread. Nobody's wished me well, even Harry moaned about helping. Look at all the shemozzle there was when the twins left, everyone crying. I ship out and nobody gives a toss.

Dad set out the plates and she hunted out some cutlery from the sink and ran it under the tap.

'Saw Danny Sullivan, offered to pay the rent on the stall and set up for us. Just gotta let him have half the space for his plants. What d'ya think?'

'Between you and him, now,' she said. 'Long as he knows it's my stall and don't get any funny ideas about changing the name. Seeing as your working it, the takings'll be yours.'

'You're a good girl,' said Dad, mopping up his plate with half a crust. 'Fancy going halves with me on a bottle of stout?'

'Don't mind,' she said, smiling at him. As he got up and poured the drink into two cups, Mary looked around her. The kitchen would dishearten a saint, with everything faded and second best. They were a family of heapers and slingers. Coats slung in chairs, washing heaped in a basket, pots slung in the sink and mounds of old papers spilling out of a cardboard box. The transit method of housekeeping, she thought, everything always on its way.

'Granny said to call in, 'bout half seven tomorrow morning. Says she'll cook you breakfast and got some bits and pieces for your new quarters.'

'Ta, I'll do that,' she said, her spirits lifting. At least someone wanted to give her a good sendoff. 'Will you miss me?' She blurted out the question as her father wiped the beer froth from his mouth with the back of his hand.

'What do you think?' he answered.

'I don't know,' she said, 'or I wouldn't be asking.'

''Course I shall, you bin the corner stone of this family.'

'What you mean?'

'"That which the builders rejected has become the corner-stone." Out of the Bible, that is.'

'When'd you last read the Bible?' she asked.

'In the navy from when I was a boy seaman. That's over twenty years, every Sunday, ashore and afloat. Not reading, of course, just having it spouted at us from the chaplain. Some of it was bound to stick.'

'What does it mean?'

'The most important brick in the building – holds all the rest together. Reckon me and Blyth'll gonna be strugglin' a while without ya. You're the top brick, always have been.'

'But will you miss me?' she persisted.

'Come to your old Dad,' he said, pushing his chair away from the table and holding out his arms. He hugged her to him, kissing the top of her head. 'What times we bin through, you and me,' he said.

Mary clung to him. Poor, poor Dad, how frail he was.

How he had raised her hopes and dashed them over the years. How she'd raged at him. 'Bin sink or swim,' she said, 'mostly sinking.'

He smiled at her. 'You looks done in. Sit down and have a read of the paper while I clears up.'

It was almost nine before Blyth came back from next door.

'Gotcha some toffees,' she said, handing him the bag.

'Thanks,' he said, snatching it from her. 'Off to bed, now.'

'Ain't you going to wish your sister luck afore she goes over to Gosport. Be snoring your head off when she sets off.'

'Be able to come over and have tea with me, when I'm straight,' said Mary, wanting him to kiss her.

''Bye,' He waved to her from the doorway before going up to bed.

'He'll come round,' said Dad. 'Grown out of kissing, he has. Frightened to have to do without ya, that's the top and bottom of it.'

Had she done the right thing? How would she and Jabez get on together? Would she get on with the other girls in the laundry? How would she manage to have the room halfway decent by the time Matthew came to see it? Her mouth was dry and heart racing as she tossed and turned praying for sleep. Everyone thought she was so tough, but inside she was terrified. At some time in the early hours she must have slept because she was startled awake by a tapping on the door.

'After seven, love,' said Dad, setting a cup on tea on the floor beside her mattress. 'Nice bowl of hot water out in the kitchen for yer wash.'

'Feels washed out before I've even started,' she mumbled, rubbing her eyes.

'Get the tea inside you,' he said, perching on the corner of the mattress.

'Anything I can be doing to help?'

'Can you make a bundle of the pillows, sheets and blanket,' she asked.

'What about the mattress?'

'Be too big. Only a little room.'

'I'll get young Blyth up off his later. He can sleep in the girls' room pro tem.'

'Don't want to set him off,' said Mary.

'Get yourself into the rig of the day and see Granny. Leave yer brother to me.'

'Morning Mary, big day for you,' said Granny. 'Come in and sit yourself down.'

The table was covered with a snowy-white cloth and before her was a plate heaped with sizzling bacon, egg and fried bread. Her mouth watered.

'That'll set you up for whatever the day takes out,' said the old woman sitting opposite her and taking up her fork. 'I've sorted out some bits and pieces you'll likely need. Look it over when you've finished.'

Mary ate slowly, relishing every bite. The anxiety of the night began to fade. She looked over at the heap of things in the corner, near the scullery. There was a card table, tin tray, a kettle; two cups, saucers and plates; some cutlery and a rag rug.

'What d'you think. Don't hang back. Take the lot, my dear, and welcome.'

'Thanks ever so much,' gasped Mary, beaming at Granny. 'I was worried about taking anything else from home.'

'Think nothing of it. Only what your mother would have done for you. Oh, and here's a cake tin. Made you a Victoria sponge and some jam tarts.' She took a round tobacco tin out of her apron pocket. 'Now here is a tin for your money. Hide it somewhere safe. There's ten bob to start you off. Inside I've put our phone number. Be useful in an emergency and you'll be able to keep track of your family.' She held out her arms. 'You take care of yourself, my duck, and let me know when I can come on a visit.'

Mary kissed Granny Pragnell and was saved from weeping by a loud rapping on the door.

'Likely it's your big brother with the handcart ready loaded. We'd best be quick and take these things out to him.'

'Ready?' asked Harry, standing in the road with Dad.

'I must say goodbye to Blyth,' said Mary, racing up the stairs. She opened the bedroom door and found him wound in a blanket in Dad's bed.

'Aint you gonna wish me luck?' she asked.

At the sight of her he rolled away, to the far side of the bed. 'Geroff,' he roared as she tried to kiss him. 'Hate you, hate you, hopes you drowns.'

'You don't mean it,' she gasped, stunned by the look on his face. 'You and me bin pals since you was a tiddler. Always loved you best, I have.'

'That was the olden days,' he scoffed. 'You're like a rat leavin' me and Dad in the sinkin' ship.'

'Oh, Blyth, don't let's fall out,' she begged.

'Go away,' he screamed.

Mary held him tight while he kicked and struggled.

'You coming or not?' yelled Harry from the stairs.

'Blyth, I loves ya,' she cried, managing to kiss the top of his head.

'Bleedin' liar,' he cried, throwing himself off the bed.

'It aint for good. You can come and see me, I promise.'

Blyth picked up his wooden pencil case and cracked her on the head. 'Bugger off,' he screamed. 'Bugger, bugger, bugger off.'

Mary fled down the stairs in tears.

'Off you go, love. Leave him to me,' said Dad, giving her a hasty kiss.

'If I'd known there'd be such a carry-on I'd've stayed in bed,' said Harry, hurrying ahead of her with the handcart.

Mary said nothing. It took her all her breath to hurry after him.

'Jesus Christ, is this it?' Harry said, as he set the handcart down outside Shore Cottage.

Mary nodded unable to speak. Blyth had quenched her courage. It was she who had cared for him since she was ten years old, she who had nursed him when he was ill. His first word was 'Mary'. It was to her he walked for the first time. When Mum had died it was Blyth she clung to. And, in his turn, he was her champion against the others. It only needed Harry to ask her to change her mind and she would be back across the ferry.

'What does Matthew reckon to this dosshouse?'

Pride forbade her to confess he hadn't seen it yet.

'Well, let's get it over with. I got a Sunday dinner and Dora waiting for me.'

Fortunately Jabez was out.

'Take no notice of downstairs,' she said, seeing his nose wrinkle with disgust.

Together they laboured up and down the steep stairs dumping her things in heaps on the newly scrubbed floor. As she knelt to fold a sheet over the mattress Blyth's smell, a mixture of old socks, sweat and biscuits, brought him sharply to mind. Mary gasped and bit her finger to stop herself cying in front of Harry.

'That's the last,' he said, setting down the rag rug. 'Gotta dash now, things to do.'

'I was gonna take you for a cup of tea,' said Mary, 'to thank you for helping me over.'

'Bloke at the lock-up wants the cart back by eleven.' He scratched his head. 'Wish you hadn't done it, just as I'm going on draft. Leaves everything down to Dora.'

'Since you ain't gonna wish me luck, you better bugger off to Dora,' she snapped, her temper rescuing her from tears.

'Suit yerself,' he said, and was down the stairs before she could call him back.

It took her no more than half an hour to make her bed, smooth out the rug and set her tea things in the corner on the tin tray. Then she was alone with only the view for company. Downstairs she realised that any cooking would be done over the fire in a witch's cauldron of a pot or an old black kettle. Washing was going to be another challenge. She took the last of the ammonia down to the outside privy and flung it around the cracked brown bowl, wedging the little window open with a pad of newspaper.

'So, you're taking over the place, are ya?' said Jabez, as she went back into the cottage. Dog bounded around her, yapping and barking.

'I've paid my way,' Mary snapped, refusing to be cowed by him.

'Don't intitle you to be down here ferretin' about. Get up to yer own quarters.'

'What about me cooking and washing and using the lav?' she demanded. 'Not room to swing a cat upstairs. Gotta come through here, 'less you wants me to fly out the window.'

'Never ast yer to come. Wanted a feller. He would've got his grub from the pub and done his dhobi-ing in a bucket.'

'Took me money quick enough.'

'You wants all these extras it'll be 'nother shilling each week. Take it or leave it.'

'They ain't extras, they're essentials.' Mary was nearly crying from weariness and disappointment but she knew that any sign of weakness would have her in Jabez's power.

'You get the money and I'll think about it. Now bugger off upstairs, I wants ter get me head down for the afternoon.'

Mary stormed back up the stairs. She sat on the mattress

and the walls seemed to close in on her. Even the view of the harbour, snatched between the prows of the yachts, failed to lift her spirits. She had rushed into living here and now she would have to make the best of it. It was so quiet with the boatyard empty. Mary picked up the old alarm clock that Granny Pragnell had wound up for her. It was two o'clock on Sunday afternoon and there were eighteen hours before she started work at the laundry and over three days until she saw Matthew. Panic-stricken she paced the room. Never had Mary been alone for so long. If she didn't get out of the room she would scream her head off.

As she crept down the stairs Jabez's snores rose to greet her. Dog wagged his tail, making it thump on the floor.

Mary saw his lead on a hook by the front door. Reaching up, she took it from the hook. The dog rushed across the room, nearly knocking her off her feet. 'Shh!' she whispered. 'Let's go.'

The dog slavered over her face, his tongue like sandpaper, as she fixed the lead to his collar. On the table was a dirty plate with half a crust of bread beside it. Mary snatched it up and put it in her pocket before creeping outside with Dog.

He pulled her down the road and she ran after him.

I'll survive this, she thought, gritting her teeth, ain't got no choice, 'ave I?

19

Cissie dried up the last of the Sunday dinner plates then peeped into the sitting room. Mrs Mowbray was sat there nodding over her embroidery frame. Patting the envelope hidden beneath her blouse, Cissie sneaked a couple of chocolate biscuits out of the barrel and hurried into the garden.

Oblivious to her approach, Ted Willow spaded the black earth up into hillocks ready for the asparagus plants, sat in the boxes, at his feet.

'Brought you some biscuits on account,' said Cissie, smiling at him.

'On account of what?' he asked, watching her undo her top buttons.

'On account of my letter.' She blushed. 'I ain't got the learning and I wants someone to read it for me. Someone as I can trust.'

Rubbing his hands on his trousers Ted tore open the envelope, then gasped. A flimsy white note fluttered between his fingers. 'Blimey! Don't zeem possible this bit of paper be worth five pounds.'

Cissie held it awestruck, then tucked it inside her blouse, noting Ted's eyes staring at her neck.

'My Dear Cissie,
  I am deeply sorry at having hurt you and most anxious to hear that you are recovering from your injuries. I shall never forgive myself for being so reckless. I hope the bullet

*has, by now, been safely removed and that you are out of
danger.*

She knew she was being ungrateful but she wished he
read better. It was hard having the Captain's words mangled
through Ted's halting Dorset tongue.

*'The police have forbidden me to visit you, and, in the light of my
action, I feel sure I am the last person you would wish to see.'*

Ted stared at her. 'Thought as how you'd fallen down zome
stairs,' he said, showering her with biscuit crumbs. 'This feller
could 'ave finished you off. By God, if I catch up with him
there'll be warm words.'

'It's a secret,' Cissie warned, alarmed at his fierceness. 'Was
an accident, weren't no one's fault.'

Ted Blushed. 'Sorry I blasted off like that, was caught
by surprise. Calmed meself, now I'll read it for you right
sober.'

*My sister, who is a kind woman, will look after you and see
that you have everything you need. I have enclosed money
for you to open a savings account, for yourself, and I will
happily write you a good reference when you are fit to work
again. If there is anything else I can do for you, write and let
me know, immediately.*

*Please accept my deepest apologies for the injuries that I
have caused.*

Yours most sincerely,

Charles Clements.

'My Lord, 'twas the Missis' brother what done it,' gasped
Ted, staring at her. 'Captain Clements, what were he doing
with a gun?'

Cissie snatched the letter from him. 'It was all a mix-up,'
she blustered, 'a bad mistake.' She slid the letter back beneath

her blouse, aware of Ted's fascinated gaze. 'He thought I was a burglar. Didn't mean me no harm, didn't never harm me.'

Ted looked at her, his eyes full of suspicion.

'Remember, I've trusted you,' Cissie snapped, regretting her earlier confidences.

'Only 'cos there was no one else,' he said, staring at the ground.

'What you want from me?' she asked.

'Nothing,' Ted sighed, returning to his planting.

Cissie bit her lip. 'Lots of people I could have give it to; doctor or parson or those biddies up at the church. I picked you.'

Ted beamed. His eager puppy-love weighed on her conscience. Whatever she did, Ted Willow was going to be hurt.

'Got to be on me own, now,' Cissie said, patting him on the shoulder then walking down the garden to the field beyond. She lifted the latch and shut the gate behind her. The sheep in the next field nibbled at the grass or bleated at one another as Cissie edged past them. Hawthorn blossom smothered the hedges and high up in the sky a bird she couldn't name was singing.

Sitting on a stile leading to the next field she took out the letter and ran her fingers over its swirling script. The word 'sorry' was somewhere on the page, Ted had said so. That was enough for her. The five pounds was a fortune, but the Captain's words held a value far beyond the money. They brought him to her mind with all his gentleness and courtesy. He had treated her as more than his servant. It had been important to him that she was happy, too. His letter had settled things. She was leaving.

Grinning to herself, she patted her dress and felt the satisfying crackle of the fiver hidden beneath. It had given her the power to change things. Tomorrow she would ask Ted to find out about trains to Portsmouth. The bees murmured in the hedgerow flowers and Cissie dozed.

Later she awoke feeling hot and thirsty and trudged back to the garden. Ted was gone. The asparagus plants were all in their beds and the boxes taken away. Not wanting to go inside yet and be drawn into kitchen tasks Cissie took a drink from the garden tap. Wiping her mouth on her sleeve Cissie walked down the sideway to the front of the cottage.

Parked behind Mrs Mowbray's motor was a shiny black car with a front shaped like a bulbous nose. Curious, she walked into the road and around to the back of the vehicle and peered through the window. On the seat was a knitted patchwork blanket. The colours were fading and the stitching coming loose between the squares. Cissie gasped in recognition. It was the one Mrs Mullins, the cook, had been making when she first went to work for the Clementses. She would know it anywhere. What did it mean? Keeping her head below the window Cissie crept round to the side away from the pavement. Then she knew for certain. There, hanging from the ignition key was the little brass elephant that Charlotte had given to her father one Christmas. It was Captain Clements' car. She tried the door behind the driver's seat and it swung open. 'Abracadabra!' Cissie slid herself onto the floor between the front and back seats and clicked the door shut. It was hot and dusty inside and smelt of petrol. She inched the blanket to the edge of the seat ready to haul it over her head when the time came. 'I'm going home, I'm going home.' Everything was falling into place. There was just one snag – she wanted the lav. Cissie blinked. Dare she dash down the garden to the privy? No, she couldn't risk being left behind. Still, hanging onto her water, all the way to Pompey, was a small price to pay.

Without warning, someone opened the driver's door and pulled the key out of the ignition and then slammed it shut. Cissie inched the blanket over her head with trembling fingers. The lid of the boot was opened and then shut. Whoever had opened the door was now going back to the house. Cripes! Captain Clements wasn't going to stay the night, was he? She counted to fifty then slipped from the blanket and wound the window down a crack. Almost immediately she crouched down again beneath her tent as footsteps approached the car.

'It's been lovely to see you, Charles,' gushed Mrs Mowbray. 'Thank you for Charlotte's drawings, she's a clever little girl. Don't worry about Cissie, she'll settle down. You wouldn't recognise her from that pathetic creature in the hospital. She's looking the picture of health.'

'I wish I had seen her, it would have put my conscience at rest,' said her brother. 'Anyway, darling, thanks for the tea. I shan't need to stop on the way now. 'Bye.'

There was the sound of kissing and then the driver's door swung open and he climbed inside, turned the key and the engine juddered into life.

Cissie breathed a sigh of relief. All she had to do now was keep out of sight.

Captain Clements wound down the front window. Gratefully she gulped some air. On and on they went up hill and down dale. From time to time the air changed from fresh to petrol soaked and worse. The stink that filled her nostrils later must surely have been from pigs. She was on the brink of dozing off when a bee buzzed into the back of the car. Cissie was terrified. Burrowing her head into the blanket she prayed for it to go away.

Captain Clements screeched to a halt, swung open the door and the bee buzzed off. Cissie heard his footsteps crunching off somewhere. Where were they? Throwing off the blanket, she looked out of the window. They were somewhere on a country road. She could see the back of the Captain's head as he crossed the stile into a field. Her limbs were cramped and her face was slippery with sweat but worse was the pain of holding her water. Judging him to be far enough away, she opened the door nearest the field and peed on the dusty verge. Stepping back over her puddle she got back into the car and kept watch out of the window. The Captain re-emerged from the field and drew nearer to the car. Out of uniform, in his sports coat and flannels, he looked much less grand. She mourned the gold epaulettes and naval sword.

The driver's door opened and he lit a cigarette before starting off again. The smell reminded her of Lancaster Terrace and the carved wooden box on the table in the sitting room. 'Balkan Sobranie,' that was the name. She wondered how many more miles there were before they reached home.

Would Mrs Clements be there? Cissie's stomach lurched at the thought? It was strange that no one ever mentioned her. Perhaps she was dead. She wouldn't exactly wish Lettice gone, but it would be much easier without her. Now that her arm was better and she'd picked up a bit of cooking and ironing from Mrs Willows, Cissie knew she could be a real help to the Captain. Only a few more miles and she would be back in her room with her box and all its treasures.

The car dipped as if they were going down a hill. There was the smell of petrol again and the sound of lots more traffic. And then, the car slowed to a halt. Captain Clements got out and slammed the door behind him. Cissie slipped back the blanket and prepared to follow him.

He ran up the steps and knocked on the door. Something was wrong. Why didn't he get out his key? The door opened and a man she had never seen before came out of the house and stood talking to his visitor, on the steps.

Alarmed, Cissie slid out onto the road.

'Charles, have you come for your mail? There's certainly a stack of it here.'

'I'm sorry, Jeffrey,' said the Captain, still standing on the doorstep. 'Thought I'd contacted everyone. Came round to bring the secateurs I promised you.'

Cissie blinked. She didn't understand. What was wrong? Why didn't he go into the house?

He took the letters from the man at the door and began to come back down the steps towards the car.

'Have you found a new place yet, Charles?'

What did he mean?

He shook his head. 'I'm still at the Pembroke Club.'

The man followed him down the steps. 'Not sorry you sold the place, are you, Charles?'

Sold! The word exploded in her head. No, it couldn't be true; she gasped as if she had been struck.

'Mixed feelings naturally, Jeffrey, but it's time for a fresh start.'

'*No, no, no, no,*' Cissie roared, rushing at him, hitting out wildly. 'Can't be sold, it can't.'

'Cissie! Good God, what are you doing? No, stop! Come back!'

She pushed them aside and rushed up the steps and into the house. She must get to the attic and shut the door. It was her room, hers and nobody else's. Wailing and gasping she hurried on. How, how could it be sold? Awake and asleep she had dreamed of it. Even when Mrs Mowbray had dragged her off to Simla Cottage she had not let go.

The footsteps were getting nearer. She opened her eyes and cast about for something to wedge against the door to buy her some time. The room had been stripped. Even the curtain wire had been removed and the corner cupboard ripped out. Now an even greater terror struck. 'My box,' she screamed.

'Cissie, please,' Captain Clements gasped. 'Let me talk to you.'

'Charles, whoever she is, she must leave. My wife will be home from church with the girls. I can't tolerate this invasion.' The man rapped on the door. 'Out this minute, or I'll call the police.'

She clung to the handle. 'I wants me box,' she demanded.

'Please, Jeffrey, give me time to talk to her. She's had a shock.'

'Charles, I can't have this sort of carry-on in my house.'

Erupting through the door she seized the astonished Jeffrey by the arm. 'You thievin', bloody bastard, give it back,' she roared, kicking him in the shins.

Captain Clements grabbed her from behind and marched her down the stairs.

'Spiteful little bitch. I'll have the law on you!' the owner yelled at her, running out of the house.

Cissie twisted, thrashed and fought all the way into the small room that had once belonged to Mrs Clements. 'I want my things,' she screamed, 'I want, I want . . .'

The Captain hit her hard across the face.

Gasping she sank down into a chair.

'Please, my dear child, you'll make yourself ill, whatever is the matter?' Captain Clements drew up a chair in front of her and held her arms firmly in his.

Cissie sobbed and sobbed. Everything was lost. She had nowhere and was no one. Without her box she was totally unconnected. It was as if she had never been. Who would believe she'd had a pretty mother without that photograph or a dad who'd been a sailor? How could she keep that memory of Christmas without the paper fan? And little Charlie's bonnet, she must find it, she must.

The Captain took out his handkerchief and pressed it into her hand. 'Cissie, I had no idea this place meant so much to you, no idea at all. I had to sell it. The children are at boarding school and Mrs Clements is abroad. We're divorced d'you see?'

Cissie didn't see anything. 'You promised,' she managed to gasp.

He turned away from her towards the door. 'Jeffrey,' he said sharply. 'You'd have been better off making some tea. Getting the police will solve nothing.'

'I will not be attacked in my own home,' the man protested from the doorway.

'Cissie, what did I promise?' he asked, sitting down again.

'My home,' she blubbered. 'Said – you said, "Cissie, this is your home."' There was a fresh burst of weeping and then she managed to gasp out, 'Didn't say "This is your home just so long as I feels like it."'

'Oh, Cissie,' he sighed. 'I'm so sorry. I thought you were well settled with my sister. I thought she would have explained. How did you get here?'

'In your car,' she gasped.

'Good Lord!' he said. 'I'd no idea.'

'Parcelled me off, you did,' she said, feeling her anger spluttering into life. 'Broke in and stole me life. Nobody asked me. Didn't care what I wanted.'

'Oh, Cissie,' he sighed, 'it wasn't like that at all. I was so ashamed. I wanted to visit you in hospital but the police forbade it. Didn't you get my letter?'

'Took me ages to get it read,' she muttered, unwilling to be pacified.

'How foolish of me, I didn't think. I wanted you to be settled before I put the house on the market. It's a wrench for me, too, you know. I was born in this house. But I can't afford to keep it on now, and there it is.'

'Wants me room back,' she persisted.

'Cissie, please,' he said, 'that's just not possible.'

'Hello, Cissie.'

She looked up to see Constable Perks standing in the doorway with the new owner.

'He's stole me box,' she raged.

'What box?' Perks asked. 'If you sit down and tell me. I'll see what I can do.'

'All me treasures was in a pink hat box in the cupboard in me room.'

'Chucked it all out in the yard last week, in a tea chest.'

'Why don't you and Cissie go and look for it?' said another policeman, who had been standing behind Perks.

'What about the assault?' demanded the owner.

'First things first, Sir,' the other constable said, quietly.

Cissie allowed Perks to take her arm as if she were an invalid. Together they went down the stairs and out to the yard. She stood there thinking of all the times she had turned the key and stepped inside. How safe she had felt once inside the yard. Later, up in her little room, she would rest and remake herself until, the next time, she had to back through the door again. Without the key she couldn't survive that way of life any more. As for the box . . . Cissie blinked.

'Tell me exactly what we're looking for?' the constable asked her, approaching a tea chest stuffed with rubbish.

'Round pink hat box tied up with string.'

'What we'll do is spread out this newspaper and get the stuff out a bit at a time, methodical like.'

Out came the old curtains a mildewed pillow and a couple of coat hangers and a battered suitcase.

'They're all wet,' she wailed.

'Don't worry,' said Perks. 'Rained a bit this morning but it's bin dry the rest of the week. Your box will probably be all right.'

Standing beside her, talking quietly, doing what she wanted, Perks calmed her.

'Lots of toffs' magazines here, *London Illustrated* and *Tatler*. Hang on, what's this?'

'My box,' gasped Cissie. She closed her eyes and held it tightly to her. The string was still intact.

'Anything else you need looking for?'

She shook her head.

He shoved everything else back in the tea chest along with the newspaper. 'D'you trust me, Cissie?' he asked.

She nodded, too moved to speak.

'If I was you I would go round and see that pal of yours in Lemon Street. Get her to put you up for the night. Have a good sleep and start again tomorrow.'

'What about the bloke in there?' she asked, doubtfully. 'Wants to summons me.'

'Have to find you first,' said Perks, sliding back the bolt on the back door.

'Won't you get into trouble letting me go?' she asked.

'I'll say as how you overpowered me,' he said, smiling at her.

Cissie wanted to smile back but she couldn't get her face to do it.

'I remember you at the hospital, looking all washed out,' he said. 'You've been through worse than this, Cissie. You know you have.'

'Don't feel like it,' she said, walking towards the alley.

20

The twins roared down the passage, into the kitchen, grabbed their father from his chair and danced him round the room.

At the sight of his daughters Fred felt his spirits soar like a balloon above the wretchedness of the past few months. 'My gals is home,' he blubbered, 'like Christmas and Easter rolled into one.'

'Dad, you're supposed to be happy, not bawling your eyes out,' said Faith, slipping her arm around his shoulders.

''Course I'm happy,' he coughed and spluttered, 'them's tears of joy. You don't know how much I've missed you.' Wiping his eyes on his sleeve he looked from one twin to the other. 'You just here for the week? Didn't see no posters down at the Coliseum or Hippodrome.'

'Home for good,' said Mercy, picking up the kettle and filling it. 'Had enough of tourin'. Them Debonnaires was slave drivers and the girls a load of spiteful cows.'

'We can stop, can't we, Dad?' asked Faith. 'You ain't gone and took no lodgers, have ya?'

'You're welcome as the flowers in May,' he said. 'Be good to have a bit of life round here. Can't abide silence. Here, give your old dad a hug. Can't get enough of ya.'

Faith flung her arms around him. 'It was horrible,' she sobbed. 'Landladies was right skinflints, had to pay for 'avin' a bath and the grub was 'orrible. We was always tired and hungry.'

'Wasn't that bad,' protested Mercy. 'Had some pretty frocks and our own spot in the programme.'

'Get the tea going,' Dad said, 'and then you can tell me the whole story, I'm all ears.'

After rinsing some cups and emptying the teapot the twins settled themselves at the table. The three of them sat there dipping broken biscuits into their tea as if they had never been apart.

'Tell us about your spot in the programme,' Dad said, spooning sugar into his tea.

'This Bunny Beaumont, the dance master, had us one each side of this mirror looking at our faces.'

'Ever so clever it was,' interrupted Faith.

'See, it gave the illusion of there being only one girl on the stage, and then, when they pulled the mirror away at the end, everyone saw as we was twins,' said Mercy.

'Cor! I'd love to have seen you. I'd have bin that proud,' said Dad. 'We bin short of things to celebrate round here.'

Faith laughed. 'Would have liked our last performance,' she giggled. 'One of the fellers threw a mouse onto the stage and I screamed the place down. Audience thought it was all part of the act. Laughed their heads off.'

Mercy joined in the laughter. 'Thought old Bunny would have a stroke.'

'Did they give you the sack?' asked Dad. 'That why you come home?'

'No,' said Faith. 'This Jeanette reckoned we'd stole her money. Kicked up such a stink she did. Could've been anyone. Then, once they told us they wasn't coming to Pompey no more we legged it home.'

'Who d'you think took the money, Merce?' asked Dad.

'Who cares?' she said, taking the last bourbon. 'Debonnaires is ancient 'istory.'

'Where is everyone?' asked Faith. 'Where's our Blyth?'

'Since you two bin kicking up your heels the whole family turned upside down. Only me and Blyth here now. We bin flat as pancakes without ya.'

'Go on, Dad, tell us; what's bin happenin'?' they asked.

'For a start, your brother Harry's in the West Indies for the next God knows how long. Poor little Dora's right cut up about it, coming round for tea later, she is.'

'We was lookin' forward to seeing Harry,' Mercy drained the teapot into her cup. 'He said we could have a go on the tandem now our legs is long enough. So where's Mary pushed off to?'

'She ain't ill or nothink, is she?' asked Faith.

'Working over in a laundry in Gosport. Living in a right dump according to Harry. He helped her move across. God know what her Dusty thinks of it all.'

'They back together then?' asked Mercy.

'Far as I know. Ain't seen her since she left with Harry, but that's her pride. Won't come back to us till she's made a success of it. As I said, Blyth's got her room now. Good lad he's bin to me. Helps up at the market, keeps us going with all his ducking and diving. You gals will be in the back bedroom, same as ever.'

'I'm gonna dig that Blyth out of 'is room, you'd have thought we would have woke him by now, all the noise we bin making,' said Mercy, pushing back her chair.

Fred laughed. 'Waste yer time, he's bin up for hours. Got a shoeshine stand. Reckons he's gonna make his fortune. Parks it outside that Pembroke Club where the officers goes.'

'What happened to mud-larking?' laughed Faith. 'Always good for a few bob.'

'Partickler is Blyth,' said Dad. 'Don't like getting mucky, specially when it's him as has to dhobi his clothes.' He shook his head. 'Things is bad, my gal, really bad – hundreds traipsing the streets fer work. Dockyard's laying off more blokes every week. I haven't had a sniff of work for ages. If it weren't fer me piddly pension, the market stall and Albert waiting for his rent we'd have bin in Queer Street.'

'We'll go round the brewery tomorrer and get our jobs back,' said Faith. 'We'll just stow our stuff upstairs, then I'll come down and give you a hand.'

Dad beamed. 'That'd be champion,' he said.

She sat on their old bed amid the litter of clothes. Coming home was not at all as she imagined it. There was no Harry, and she was surprised at how shaky she felt at the news of Mary's leaving. Her sister had nagged the pair of them half to death but they'd taken it for granted that she would be there, like always, holding things together. That wasn't the worst of it. While they'd been away Dad had got old and thin and . . . Her eyes filled with tears. 'He looks so small and tired, don't he?' she asked her sister.

Mercy was busy emptying her case. 'Weren't never big, was he? Don't look much different to me.'

'D'you reckon they'll come after us?' Faith dried her eyes on the corner of the sheet.

'Shouldn't think so, we wasn't exactly top of the bill.' Mercy painted a cupid's bow with her lipstick. 'Flippin' starving I am. Hope our Dora's coming round with some grub for tea. See ya downstairs,' she said.

Faith emptied her case and divided her clothes into two piles, the dirty and the clean, then looked around the room. There were no sheets on the bed and no curtains at the window. She would have to go through the house from top to bottom and pull it into shape. No good looking to her sister for help. Going over to the chest under the window, Faith saw Mercy's pink scarf half in half out of the drawer. Bending down to pull it out she saw, tucked beneath it, Jeanette's red leather purse.

*　　*　　*

Blyth had to run the gauntlet of the porter at the Pembroke for customers, but he had not done too badly. Three shillings made up from sixpences jingled in his pocket. It seemed strange that people would pay for his services when they could clean the shoes themselves, but that was toffs all over. Still, the one that gave him the shilling was quite a decent bloke. He seemed familiar but Blyth could not bring his name to mind. Most of his clients stood reading their newspapers while he got on with his task, but the shilling man talked to him.

'What are you interested in?' he had asked, smiling at him.

'All sorts,' Blyth had said, 'drawing, arithmetic and chess.'

'You surprise me,' he had said. 'In my experience, most boys want to be out on the football field rather than pore over their books.'

'I ain't most boys,' Blyth replied. 'Wants to make sommink of meself.'

'And what would that something be?'

'Planning out buildings or technical drawing. Likes measuring and calculations. Just comes easy to me.'

'Are you any good at drawing?'

'Got good eye-and-hand co-ordination. Least that's what my teacher said. Reckons I could be an architect, given the chance. Naval architecture, that's what I'm aiming for.'

'Well, very good luck to you,' the man had said, giving him the shilling. 'If you're here next Sunday I might give you a game of chess.'

'You'll have to be good,' he had said, putting away the polish and brushes.

Laughing, the man had disappeared into the club.

Blyth tucked his shoeshine stool under his arm and dawdled home. He had no expectations for Sunday dinner but pinned his hopes on Dora bringing round some treat or other for tea. Humming to himself he dragged the key through the letterbox.

As he went down the passage to the kitchen, he could hear Dad laughing.

'Surprise, surprise,' yelled the twins, nearly squeezing the life out of him.

'Geroff, geroff,' he growled, struggling out of their arms. 'When did you get here?'

'Bin waiting for ya all morning,' said Mercy, throwing him a bag of toffees

'Ta,' he said, not overly impressed. 'What we got for dinner?'

'Bubble and squeak and mushy peas,' said Dad, stood with the frying pan in his hand. 'There's some crisps from the pub, and Granny sent us over some pickled onions.'

Blyth sighed. He bet that bloke at the Pembroke Club was sitting down to a proper roast dinner.

He managed a smile. 'Where you two sleeping?' he asked. 'I'm not kipping back on the floor in Dad's room.'

'You can stay in Mary's room,' said Dad, 'seeing as she's not wanting it no more.'

His delight at having the downstairs room had been diluted by the loss of his sister. The only way he had been able to cope with Mary going was to scream out how much he hated her. It wasn't true. She had always been his champion. Up till he was seven he had shared her bed. When he was tired, she gave him piggy backs home from the market; when he was sick, it was Mary that made him drinks of hot lemon and honey; and when frightened his big sister held him tight until the nightmare faded away. Not even his brother Harry knew the secrets he and Mary shared together.

'Better than winning the pools, this is,' said Fred, later, looking around the crowded tea table. 'Only needs Mary and Harry to make it a full house.'

'You looks really grown up, now,' said Dora, smiling at the twins. Home for good, now, are you?'

Faith nodded, as she reached for the jug of custard.

'Any news of Mary?' Dora asked.

'Probbly fagged out,' said Fred. 'Working in a laundry's hard graft and she got her place to keep up to the mark. I 'spect she's out and about with Dusty in Gosport.'

'How was the market yesterday?'

'Quiet, ain't it, Blyth?' said Fred, getting up and settling himself in the chair by the fire. 'Hardly worth setting up. Blyth and me haven't got Mary's flair for selling. If it weren't for that Danny Sullivan giving us a hand and me promising Mary I'd keep it on for her, I'd jack it in.'

'You'll have to get the twinnies to help you,' Dora suggested. 'Pretty girls are always a draw.'

'Speaking of help,' said Dad, 'you two can make a start with the washing up.'

'What about Blyth?' moaned Mercy.

'He's done his share while you were away,' said Dora, knowing her way of sliding out of things. She was glad the twins were back. It would give Fred a well-needed boost and stop her worrying. It would be good to write some happy news to Harry.

'Someone at the door,' said Blyth.

'That boy got the ears of a bat,' laughed Dad, getting out his tickler tin.

'I'm a friend of Mary's,' said Cissie, when at last someone opened the door. 'There's been a bit of a mix-up and I got nowhere to stay. It's just for tonight,' she floundered. 'Tomorrer I get myself sorted with something else.'

A boy with blond hair stared at her. 'She don't live here no more. Better talk to Dad,' he said, holding open the door.

Clutching her box to her chest, Cissie followed him down

the passage to the kitchen. It seemed full of people staring at her.

'Friend of Mary's got nowhere to stay,' the boy told them. 'I said as we was full.'

The man in the armchair smiled at her. 'I'm sorry for your trouble, gal,' he said, 'but we ain't got nowhere to put you. Faith and Mercy have just come back home. Blyth's got Mary's room. She's gone off to Gosport, living in Shore Lane down by the ferry it is. Pity,' he sighed. 'Haven't even got a settee or nothing.'

The twins stared at her, identical in their red-haired prettiness. One of them began to smile shyly at her while her sister glared with eyes as hard as stones.

It was a girl called Dora who offered her a chair and put a cup of tea in her hand.

'Can I be excused?' Cissie whispered, feeling like an awkward schoolgirl.

'Down the end of the yard,' said the dad opening the back door.

She sat there with her box on her lap, not knowing what to do. Asking for the lavatory had been a way of buying herself time. Where was Mary? She needed her sharpness. She couldn't get her brain to move forward. It had stuck at the point when the car stopped.

'You gonna be much longer?' It was the pushy twin, she could tell by the voice.

'Won't be a minute,' she said, pulling the chain.

When she went back into the kitchen Cissie could tell that they'd had a confab about her. She stood there, stopping them enjoying themselves, she could tell. Once she left they would laugh and talk as if she'd never existed. 'Thanks for the tea,' she said, 'I'll get out of your way.'

'Hang on a minute,' said Dora. 'You can stop the night with me. My Harry's away and I'll be glad of the company.'

She smiled at her. 'Just let me get me hat and stuff and we'll be on our way.'

Dora took her arm and Cissie walked with her in a fog of tiredness.

'Here we are, love,' she said, at last. 'You sit down before you fall down. Ooh! you're so cold; here, put my cardigan on,' she said, helping Cissie's arms through the sleeves as if she were a child.

The warmth from her new friend seeped into her and loosened her defences. All her sorrows gathered themselves and swept her away.

Dora got a little stool and sat in front of her holding her hands. 'You have a good cry, love. No good holding on to your grief.'

Cissie sat and wept.

'Few years ago,' said Dora, 'I was so low I wanted to drown myself. Everythink got on top of me. Thought I would never be happy again. Felt I wasn't worth tuppence.'

'What d'you do?' gasped Cissie.

'Couldn't do nothing. I was wrung out. It was my friends what rescued me. Sat and listened, let me cry me heart out and let me rest. I had the pip good and proper.' Dora smiled at Cissie. 'You know what they say? A pip shared is a pip halved.' She drew a handkerchief out of her sleeve and gave it to her. 'What you need is some warm food a bit of company and a good night's sleep.'

Her kindness provoked fresh tears. While she dabbed her eyes and blew her nose, Dora pottered about the kitchen. It looked to Cissie hardly much bigger than a cupboard. She spread a cloth on the table and set two plates and spoons. 'It's banyan tonight,' she announced, coming in with a steaming saucepan.

'What's banyan?' asked Cissie, surprised at how hungry she felt.

'It's navy talk for leftovers. Tonight it's mashed spud, bacon bits and grated mousetrap. Cheese was like a bloomin' rock.'

'Smells good,' said Cissie, giving an experimental smile.

'Sit down, babes. Dig in!' Dora filled the plates to the brim. 'I loves banyan, nothing like it for flavour – bread and butter pudding, cottage pie, bubble and squeak.'

'Mary and me used to like the leftovers from parties when we was maids together.' She couldn't say, 'round at Lancaster Terrace', it would have made her cry again.

Dora chuckled. 'I knows Mary. We've had some run-ins, she and me. Jealous wasn't in it. When I got engaged to her brother Harry she was wicked to me. In the finish, I had to stand up to her, I still do.'

'We was pals,' said Cissie. 'Mind you, I knows what you mean. She used to answer back to Madam and Mrs Mullins, the cook. They used to come to blows. But she couldn't half make you laugh. Wish I had half her spirit.'

'She'll need you to cheer her up – probbly lonely in Gosport and dying for a friend.'

Cissie smiled. 'I don't think I'm ready for Mary just yet.'

Dora cleared the table. 'We'll have a cuppa and there'll be enough water for your wash. Have to share the bed with me. Don't snore but I may fart in me sleep, but what's that among friends!'

Cissie giggled, feeling welcomed and cared for. 'I got some money,' she said. 'Captain Clements give me a fiver for me savings.'

'Put it away,' said Dora. 'You can do some cleaning while I gets on with my sewing. The towel's on the hook with the nightie, and the soap's in the saucer.'

When Cissie returned, Dora smiled. 'Get yerself into bed, all seem better tomorrow.'

'Night, Dora, thanks ever so much,' Cissie muttered.

Dora shrugged. 'Glad of the company. It'll stop me talking to meself.'

The bedroom was minute. Dora's side of the bed was easy to spot, with a picture of Harry hung above her pillow. Putting her box safely under the bed, Cissie pulled back the covers and slid between the sheets. She lay staring at the sky through a gap in the curtain. Something inside her was broken like the spring of a clock. She didn't know how to mend herself. Didn't even know what she needed to set her ticking again. The only thing Cissie was sure of was that she couldn't do it on her own.

21

Mary joined the other women in the cloakroom, trying not to look too much the new girl. They shouted and laughed together as they flung their coats up on the hooks. Some had swollen ankles and bandaged legs, others red hands and burn scars on their arms.

'You just starting?' asked a girl with blonde hair tied back with a bootlace.

'Yes,' said Mary, grateful for her smile. 'In the sorting room, I think.'

'Name's Janey Scroggins,' said the girl, holding out her hand.

'Mary Vine. Pleased to meet ya.' Looking at her bitten fingernails Mary felt an instant sympathy. 'Where d'you work?' she asked.

'I'm a hand ironer,' Janey said. 'It's the top of the tree, where the money is. Needs it with all my kids. You wants to get out of the sortin' quick as you can.'

A whistle shrilled and there was a rush towards a rack of cards under a large clock.

'Ah, yes, Mary Vine, the new girl,' said the older woman with a caliper on her leg, consulting her list. 'Starting in the sorting room. I'll show you how to clock on, get you some footwear, and take you over there.'

'See you over the Vixen at dinner time,' said Janey, hurrying past.

Mary nodded, then concentrated on what the forewoman was saying.

'That's it. Check the time's been printed properly then put your card back in the rack, under your name. Now, for the clogs, you won't get a perfect fit but you got to wear them, for safety. They stops you slipping when the floor's wet or getting scalded or stuff dropping on you.'

Slocking about in the unfamiliar clogs, Mary followed her to the sorting room. A shrill hissing sound hit her ears as soon as she opened the door. The stench was overwhelming – a thick essence of all the possible body fluids. The workers, mostly young girls, were busy tossing soiled laundry into large wheeled-bins.

'Over there,' said the woman, 'with Midge, doing the hotel stuff. She'll show ya.'

'I'm Mary,' she shouted over the din. 'What we gotta do?'

Midge, a slight girl with a swathe of black hair caught up in a turban, nodded.

'Got diffrint bins for diffrint stuff,' she yelled. 'Them sheets is flat stuff, sheets, towels, napkins. That one's for shirts. Over there's the coloured's bin, then there's woollen stuff and silks, they're delicates. You put them in these net bags.'

Mary licked her lips and seemed to taste the fetid atmosphere. It stuck to her teeth. She held her hand to her mouth.

'Hold yer breath and suck on this mint,' said Midge, 'and get a move on.'

Slocking from one bin to another Mary understood why Janey urged her to move through the sorting room as quickly as possible. The others carried out shouted conversations with each other as they tossed the grimy laundry about, seeming oblivious to the heat and the stench.

'Water over there in the jug,' yelled Midge, stuffing a silk blouse into one of the nets. 'Dinner time, Floss collects the beer money. We puts in the kitty on Mondays.'

She pointed to a woman in a beret, her legs swathed in bandages.

Floss glared at her and Mary glared back. The water tasted furry. When she was almost fainting from the heat the whistle blew. Everyone hurried to the washroom.

'Coming over the pub?' asked Midge, handing her the soap.

Mary nodded. The women crossed the road with Janey in the lead.

''Ow d'ya get on?' she asked.

'It was 'orrible, just about stopped meself bein' sick or fainting,' Mary gasped.

Janey laughed. 'See you later. Best get Midge a drink. It's expected.'

Mary pushed her way through the crowd of girls and found her. 'What'll you have?' she asked, feeling in her pocket for the money she'd set aside for her dinner.

'Half a shandy,' Midge said, hardly pausing in her chat with the other girls.

Mary eyed the meat pies on the tray behind the bar but settled for a bag of crisps. She parted with her few coins, wondering whether her money would last out the fortnight. Perhaps Matthew could sub her for a few days. The thought of him cheered her, making all the toiling worth while.

'Here you are,' she said, handing Midge her drink.

The girl took the glass without a word.

Downing her own shandy, Mary made her way to the lavatory, in the back yard. She sat there eating her crisps, determined not to share with the unfriendly Midge.

'Here, hold up a mo,' called Janey Scroggins, as they walked back to work. 'Got sommat for yer.' She handed Mary a piece of pie wrapped in newspaper.

'Ta,' said Mary, munching gratefully, 'I was starving.'

'You got a feller?' Janey asked, putting her tobacco tin back into her pocket.'

'I'm engaged,' she said, proudly touching the chain round her neck where she kept his ring. He's on the *L75*, in *Dolphin*; don't know for how long he'll be there.'

'Snap,' said Janey. 'My bloke's out in Hong Kong on the *K13*. Make the most of being together. Sam's away so long sometimes, thinks I'll forget what shagging's all about.' Chuckling, she disappeared into the laundry.

Mary laughed. Matthew would hate the girl's coarseness, but she admired her grit.

The day dragged on, noisy, smelly and hot. Mary slid and slithered from one bin to the other, praying for clocking-off time. When she was almost dropping with exhaustion, the whistle sounded and there was a rush to the cloakroom.

Mary waved to Janey before making her way to Shore Cottage, her back aching and legs heavy with fatigue. From her window she could see Jabez and Dog out in the boat on their way across the harbour. Glad of some privacy, she took her washing things downstairs and poured some water from the kettle into a cracked bowl. It was barely warm but it would have to do. After stripping off her clothes, Mary began to lather her flannel with the lavender soap that Granny Pragnell had given her. Never had she appreciated cleanliness so much.

Once dressed she searched in her food box to see what could be had for supper. There was half a fruitcake, a lone jam tart, a couple of sausage rolls, and a can of baked beans. Opting for the beans she took out her tin-opener and saucepan, her stomach rumbling. Jabez's stew still festered in the pot on the fire and Mary spooned some beans into the congealed remains and stirred them round together. The thought of him unknowingly treating her to supper made Mary smile. She stood by the stove and ate her stew directly from the pot, stirring it about afterwards to disguise her theft. It was barely eight o'clock when she tottered up to bed.

The next two days and nights passed in a fog of weariness, and then it was Thursday and Matthew was coming. She prayed that Jabez and Dog wouldn't be around. It would be enough for him, on his first visit, to get to grips with the cottage without taking on old Churt, as well.

Matthew sprinkled the cod and chips with salt and vinegar before wrapping them in newspaper. He had sneaked some cake from *Dolphin* and a bottle of ginger beer. With all his goodies, he felt like Father Christmas. His desire to see Mary was tempered with caution. The waterfront, with its rough pubs, was a dangerous address, the last place he would have wanted for her. But he couldn't help admiring her courage. And then, outside a wreck of a cottage, he saw her. How defenceless she looked. He called her name and her face lit up with excitement. Swallowing down his doubts he smiled back.

'Hello, love, I bin waitin' ages for you,' Mary said, smiling up at him. 'Them chips smell good. Take no notice of downstairs, that's Jabez's quarters. Come up and see me room.'

'Can't wait,' he said, glancing at a collapsed armchair before mounting the stairs.

'I've spent ages cleaning it, just for you,' she said.

Matthew heard the appeal in her voice and prayed he could find something to praise.

The proof of her efforts stung his throat and made his eyes water. 'You've overdone the bleach, haven't you?' he gasped. The bareness of the room with only a mattress, card table and tea chest made *Dolphin* seem luxurious. He struggled for words.

'It's just the start,' Mary said, as if reading his mind. 'Lots of stuff to bring over from home yet, but that's not important. Look at the view – look, look.'

Obediently Matthew lifted the latch and poked his head out of the window.

'No, not the yard, look further.'

The harbour was spread out before him between the two yachts berthed in the yard. Black and yellow ferries crossed one another loaded up with dockyard-men and their bicycles. Fishing boats were returning to the Camber Dock, with seagulls following in their wake. And in the distance the masts of HMS *Victory* stabbed the sky. The reek of seaweed and raw fish competed with the remnants of the bleach. Matthew sighed. The view almost made up for the cottage – almost, but not quite.

Mary stood behind him her arms wound around his waist and face pressed against his back. 'I told you,' she whispered, 'our own window on the world. Might even be able to see your sub in Haslar Creek.

He laughed. 'You'd need a neck like a giraffe to twist round that far.'

'So? What d'ya think? Say you like it.'

'Let's have our supper first,' he temporised, setting the parcel of fish on table. 'Got any eating irons?'

'Couple of forks,' Mary said, 'and two cups.'

Matthew took off his cap and mac, stowing them in the corner behind the mattress before pouring out the ginger beer. They knelt either side of the table and began to eat their suppers out of the newspaper.

'How's the laundry?' he asked.

'It's bloomin' smelly,' she said, forking up a couple of chips. 'I have to sort all the dirty washing what comes in. Hand ironing that's what really pays. Trouble is, I gotta work a week in hand, down to me last few bob, with another ten days to go.'

Matthew smiled. 'Reckon I can let you have something at a price.'

'What price?' she asked, grinning back at him.

'A kiss,' he said, leaning across the table and taking her face in his hands. Her lips were soft and salty.

'I loves ya, ever so much,' she whispered. Her face was flushed and her eyes shining.

He reached into his pocket and slid two half-crowns onto the table.

'Five bob, that'll do me proud,' said Mary. 'That's worth lots of kisses. First, what d'ya think of me place? Say you like it. Bin working hard to get it nice.'

Matthew swallowed. The slightest lack of enthusiasm, and she'd flare up like a rocket, but he was determined not to give ground. 'I'll say what I think,' he warned.

Mary bridled. 'Well, I've taken it,' she said, 'so you can please yourself.'

'No,' he said, catching hold of her shoulders and turning her round to face him, 'I'm not having that; you sulking or having a tantrum every time I don't fall in with you.'

'I'm not,' she muttered, avoiding his eyes.

'It's so rough down here,' he said, 'anything could happen.'

'You don't like it,' she snapped. 'Got that po-faced look, like you trod in sommink. Might have known it wouldn't be good enough for his lordship.'

Matthew battened down his temper. 'What happens if you're ill, who will look after you? Come to that, who will even know that you're ill?'

'Get a message up to *Dolphin* I would or across to Dad.'

'I'm off day after tomorrow, to Scotland. Be gone a couple of months or more. Won't be much point phoning them.' He could see the tears shining in her eyes. 'Promise if it doesn't work you'll go home. I can't be worrying about you all the time.'

Her face was turned from him and she was struggling not to cry. 'I'll phone Granny Pragnell, if I need to.' She rolled up the chip paper, tossed it out of the window and folded the table, stowing it against the wall. 'Two months! Be July before you're back.'

Matthew sat on the mattress. 'Come here,' he said, holding out his arms.

'It's all bin for you,' she whispered, snuggling up to him. 'Somewhere of our own.'

'I know, love,' he said, drawing her to him.

They lay together face to face. Mary kissed his eyelids and then his lips. She stroked his beard and kissed him fiercely on the mouth, pressing herself against him.

Matthew felt his caution drain away as his body throbbed with wanting. He did love her, he did. Their kisses dizzied him. He stroked her neck and then her breasts.

'That's lovely,' she whispered, 'I feel like I'm melting.'

Matthew undid the buttons on her dress and she slid it down to her waist. How soft and white her skin was and how fragile she seemed. Her breasts were small with nipples like tight pink buds. He bent to kiss them and she shivered. Matthew felt stifled by his clothes and overwhelmed by the need to have Mary touch him as he was touching her. 'Help me off with my jumper,' he said, sitting up and beginning to pull it up from the waist.

Mary drew it over his head, untied his collar and put it with his jumper in a heap on the floor. She wrapped her arms around his neck. The feeling of her skin against his own was beyond words. Now! . . . now! . . . his body urged him.

'Mary,' he breathed against her neck.

'Loves you so much,' she whispered, 'do anythink for you, I would.'

He looked up at her. She seemed almost beautiful, her skin flushed and eyes shining, her narrow sharp-featured face rounded and softened by love. 'My Mary,' he whispered, pressing himself against her, his body taut with desire.

Crash! The sound of barking and something scrabbling against the door threw them into confusion.

He leapt up, his mind in chaos. 'What the hell's that?' he whispered, grabbing his clothes. 'Sounds like the blooming hound of the Baskervilles.'

Mary dragged on her dress. 'It's Jabez's dog, I could bloody kill him.'

The mood was gone.

Matthew was dazed. His only thought was escape. He couldn't look at her but concentrated on tying his collar tapes. 'I'd better get back,' he muttered.

'Will I see you before you goes off to Scotland?' she asked, her face pinched with disappointment. 'You can't just go off like this.'

'I promise you I will, love, now let me go.' It was his turn to plead.

Directly he opened the door a black retriever leapt up at him, trying to lick his face.

'Good evening,' he said to the old cove downstairs.

''Night sailor,' he said, eyeing Matthew with suspicion.

Matthew walked back to *Dolphin* in a ferment of frustration. Bugger that dog!

Tired and ratty the next morning, Mary trudged off to work. The day stretched endlessly before her, to be joined by all the other days without Matthew – empty of meaning or flavour. All Janey's joshing failed to raise a smile.

'Better cheer up tomorrer or you can drink on yer own,' she snapped.

Looking through her window she saw Jabez and Dog in the boat, setting off down the harbour towards Portchester. Why couldn't they have gone last night? she thought bitterly.

After washing herself and hanging her clothes outside the window to air, Mary put on her nightdress and wandered aimlessly about the cottage. It wasn't only the news of Matthew going away again that upset her but everything being left up in the air. What did he think of her? Had she been too free with him? What would have happened if Dog and Jabez hadn't interrupted them?

As she trailed back up the stairs to her room someone banged on the front door. Expecting one of Jabez's drinking cronies, she lifted the flap of the letterbox. 'He's gone off up the harbour, dunno when he'll be back,' she said.

'It's me. Can I come in?'

'Matthew!'

He was breathless and flushed as if he'd been running. 'Had to see you,' he gasped. 'Only got an hour. Bob's covering for me.'

'Thought I'd seen the last of you,' she said, angrily, 'rushing away like that.' She turned away as he tried to kiss her. 'Left me all mixed up,' She was close to tears. 'Made me feel cheap. Never gone that far with no one.' She began to cry.

'Come here,' he said, flinging down his cap and raincoat. 'Let me love you.' He held her close, kissing and whispering. 'I'm sorry. Here, take my hankie. It was a shock, I didn't know what to do. Been thinking about you all day.'

'Have you really?' she asked.

'Come here.' He drew her down onto the mattress. 'I was disappointed, too.'

Her anger died away. He did love her, she could see it in his eyes. The heat from his body next to hers and the beating of his heart excited her. They lay there kissing one another, sipping and tasting. She closed her eyes and felt herself opening to him as he ran his hands over her body. He stroked her breasts and slid his fingers down over her belly. Mary gasped as he slid her nightdress over her head.

Watching him looking at her was a new experience. She felt confused. The stroking and kissing whetted her appetite for more and more. 'I want to see you, too,' she whispered.

He fumbled his way out of his uniform and she helped him, seething with impatience, wanting to be swept away.

He turned towards her, covering his privates with his hand as if ashamed. Mary was curious and afraid. Matthew took her hand and pressed it to his chest. How strange and different his body was, like a foreign land. The curly hair on his body was like a fiery cross as it spread over his chest then formed a narrow path towards his belly. She stroked his ribs and kissed them one by one. Suddenly he took her hand and held it over his penis. She felt it throb beneath her fingers – for a moment she wanted everything to stop and for him just to hold her. It was all happening so fast.

'Please, please,' he whispered, kneeling across her and guiding himself inside her, thrusting and gasping. Mary cried out as he entered her, then the frenzy was over and he lay beside her spent and silent.

She was confused. There must be something more than this great rush of feeling that fizzled out before she was ready, leaving her sticky and dissatisfied.

'Are you all right,' he asked, not looking at her.

He's sorry, too, Mary thought, reaching for her nightdress.

'Never meant it to go so far,' he said, pulling on his clothes. 'Couldn't stop myself.'

'Thanks,' she said bitterly.

'Come here,' he said, holding out his arms. 'I just want you to be all right. You're not disappointed are you?'

Now it was her turn to look away.

22

⚬———⚬

Directly Dora had left the house the next morning, Cissie went back into the bedroom. She pulled the hat box out from under the bed and untied the string. Setting the lid beside her she began to take out her treasures. In a large brown envelope that Mary had pinched for her from Mrs Clements' desk were all the certificates. Cissie wished that she could read them. They recorded her parents' marriage and their deaths; her own birth and that of her baby. Worst of all was the one for little Charlie saying that he was dead.

She held the papers to her face inhaling the smell of Lancaster Terrace and the faintest whiff of Lettice's perfume. Finding the house sold had shocked Cissie. In the first terrifying impact she had not believed it and when her powerlessness to change things was borne in on her she demanded compensation. The least they could have done was take care of her box. Having it back proved her existence as the child of Luke and Martha Nugent and the mother of little Charlie.

She put the envelope inside the box lid while she revisited her other treasures. There in a paper bag from a sweet shop were the three photos. Her father, Luke Nugent, smiled shyly at her from beneath his straw sailor hat. Who was he smiling at? she wondered. Could it be her? And then Cissie smiled. There she was on her mother's lap in a tiny back garden. It was like looking at herself twice: once as the baby and a second time as the young mother. Cissie's blonde hair and way of looking up beneath her lashes were caught in that second of the camera's click. She couldn't remember her parents in any detail, just a fleeting warmth, a chuckle, someone whistling and a face leaning over her cot – a face shiny with joy. Looking at her mother in the yellowing snapshot she could feel a leap of connection. The last picture was of a ship's company formed up in tiers on the quarterdeck of a battleship, their faces no bigger than pinheads. Cissie was defeated in her efforts to try to find her father in that great mass of men and slipped the snapshots back in their bag.

She picked up the paper fan. It had meant so much to her when Father Christmas gave it to her. She had stood in the queue waiting to meet him with Miles and Charlotte. Cissie had pretended to herself that the children were her brother and sister and Captain Clements her dad. No, she didn't want it any more. All those foolish dreams had fled directly the car stopped yesterday outside Lancaster Terrace. She stuffed it in the pocket of her skirt, to be thrown away later.

The remaining items were a plate, an old rattle that had been hers as a baby and a brooch with 'Martha' inscribed on it – these, Cissie left untouched. It was a tiny bonnet that made her gasp. It had belonged to Charlie, the only thing that she had made for him. She had sewn every stitch. He had worn it for such a short time. Major Grice had asked if she wanted him to wear it for his burial. 'I want it to remind me,' she had said, refusing to have it washed and putting it straight into her box. Instead, she wrapped him in a piece of blanket, tucking it snugly round his head. Cissie rubbed the bonnet across her nose wanting there to be some lingering scent of her baby. 'I miss you, Charlie,' she whispered into the thin white cloth. 'I miss you so bad.' Slipping the bonnet beneath her blouse she felt comforted by the tenuous contact with her baby. Cissie sat on the bed, her hands pressed against her chest. Only yesterday she had treasured Captain Clements' letter and five-pound note, but little Charlie's bonnet was infinitely more precious.

Cissie sighed. She could not stay here doing nothing and feeling sad. After stripping and remaking the bed and washing the breakfast things she felt better. It was the least she could do after Dora's kindness to her. She found a heap of clothes folded ready for ironing in a basket and spread a blanket with scorch-marks on it over the table. Searching out the iron she set it on the stove to heat. By the time her friend had returned she had completed the ironing and the clothes were stacked in a pile on a chair.

'Hello, Cissie, how you feeling? You looks tons better,' said Dora, staggering in with two loaded bags. 'I'm done in,' she gasped. 'Stick the kettle on, there's a love.'

'Ta for letting me stop. Don't know what I've done without you,' Cissie said, filling the kettle and setting it on the gas stove. 'Feels brighter today.'

'White rabbits, white rabbits, white rabbits,' said Dora. 'March already. You wants to go out for a walk, Cissie. It's come in like a lamb; lovely day it is.'

'Might go down the Slum Post and see Major Grice. Good to me she was, lots of times.'

'Right ho, love, wrap up warm. Better borrow my coat, there's gloves in the pocket. Come back when you like. Make us something tonight, faggots and mash, most likely. It'll give me a good few hours to make a dent in this lot,' she said, unloading three naval uniform jackets from her bag. 'Benbow and Shanks got a rush job, this captain's sailing on Friday.' She smiled as Cissie set a cup of tea beside her. 'Ooh, ta, I was gasping! Thank you for clearing up and the ironing. You're spoiling me.'

''Bye, Dora, see you later,' Cissie said, pulling on the gloves. Once outside, she looked about her. It was good to be back. This was a neighbourhood she recognised, knowing every street name by heart. Passers-by were mostly sailors hurrying down to the dockyard or HMS *Vernon*, the barracks near Dora's house. Cissie felt quickened by the bustle and rush of Portsmouth after the quiet of Cerne Magna. Her mind skirted around the thoughts of Captain Clements and Lancaster Terrace. It was like inching a dressing away from a wound. She would think about it another day when she was stronger.

'Good morning, Cissie, and God bless you,' said Major Grice, looking up from her task of checking in the blankets brought back after being loaned out for the winter. 'You've just come at the right minute. Go in the kitchen and slice up some bread and give the soup a stir, will you? The children will be in for their dinner soon. I don't know where the morning goes. Slice up the three loaves and put out the mugs ready.'

Cissie did as she was told, falling into the old routine. It would be at least an hour before the Major would have time to talk with her.

All the consequences of the weekend turned up on the Sally Army's doorstep on a Monday morning. She heard the thin wail of a hungry baby and the rattling cough of a man in patched boots as she took up the bread knife and set to work.

'Walked to Southampton and back but there wasn't a sniff of a job,' the man gasped. In the corner the mother of the fretful baby unbuttoned her dress.

'Look, Rita, you must eat,' Captain Kellet was urging her. 'Baby won't thrive unless you look after yourself. Sit there for a bit and Cissie will fetch you some soup.'

'No, Lionel, I can't lend you anything today. Maybe I am a skinflint but hard words won't wash with me. Deeds are what we're looking for. You whitewash that kitchen in Hope Street and it might be another story.'

Grousing to himself the lad thrust his way through the

queue and out of the building. The next customer fared better. Major Grice opened her cash box and put half a crown into an old woman's hand. 'You send Frank up to the doctor's and tell him it's urgent, the Major said so. I'll be along to see your husband as soon as ever I can.'

And so the morning progressed.

Cissie was kept on the run: holding babies, pouring soup, and mopping up after a child with whooping cough had vomited on the floor. It was half past one before the queue abated.

Sitting between the Major and the Captain in the kitchen over the remains of the soup and bread she told them how she came to be back in Portsmouth.

'It was kind of Mrs Mowbray to take you in and no less than her Christian duty,' said Major Grice. 'But you're a city girl, Cissie. I thought the country would be a mite quiet for you. What are your plans now?'

'I'm lodging with Dora Vine down in Keats's Row while her husband's away in the navy. Ever so kind she is, but we has to share a bed and I feels I might be in the way.'

'I should think this Dora might be glad of your company,' said Captain Kellet. 'Being a sailor's wife can be a lonely business.' She got up and rinsed her soup plate in the sink. 'I'd best be off to sit with Mrs Kettle while her daughter sees to the children. Goodbye my dear, lovely to have you back with us.'

Cissie smiled. She was surprised at how much she had enjoyed herself. The morning had flown. Here she felt not only welcome but of real use. 'Don't know what me plans are. I was banking on going back to Lancaster Terrace. Always thought of it as me home.'

'This stay with your friend will be a breathing space for you. Give you some time to sort yourself out. I'm afraid work is scarce in Portsmouth and there is precious little accommodation of any kind.'

'Can I come here and help you?'

'We would welcome you with open arms but all we could offer in payment would be your food. It might suit you pro tem. Sometimes we get to hear of work but there are several girls in greater need.' She smiled at her. 'I would hardly have recognised you, Cissie, from the girl lying in that hospital bed. The Lord surely moves in a mysterious way.'

Cissie smiled. 'I got five pound to be put in the post office, but I would like to give some to Dora. How can I break it up?'

'At the post office they can give you five one-pound notes, and then you can decide how many to put in your account and how many you want to give to Dora. They'll give you a form to fill in,' said the Major.

There it was again – the blasted reading, thought Cissie.

'I'll give you a hand with the washing up and then we'll straighten the room up. It's the Home League this afternoon. Will you join us?'

'Be pleased to,' said Cissie, surprising herself.

Promptly at two, the women came in and settled themselves in chairs together. A blanket was put on the floor and some of the babies were set down, together with a few toys between them from a box in the corner. Toddlers sat beside their mothers and one bold curly-haired boy rushed up to the piano and plinked and plonked on the keys.

Major Grice gave them a talk about recognising different childhood illnesses and how to treat them. She led them in prayers and then wrested the piano from the little boy and got Cissie to hand out the songbooks before putting on the kettle.

'The mothers so enjoy meeting with one another, showing off their children and having a cup of tea and a singsong.'

Cissie smiled. She thought the promise of tea and biscuits was likely to be the biggest draw.

Standing in the kitchen she joined in the singing. It was one of her favourites.

Shall we gather by the river, where bright angel feet have trod
With each crystal tide forever, flowing by the throne of God.

She set the cup and saucers out on the top of the hatch leading into the meeting room. The women were in good voice, nodding and singing, jiggling their babies to the sound of the piano. The music was threaded through with coughs and sneezes, grizzles and whimpers.

Major Grice played and sang tirelessly, her homely face alight with joy.

'Yes, we'll gather at the river,' she sang, 'the beautiful, the beautiful river . . .'

Cissie began to sing too as she poured the milk into the cups and set the biscuits out on a plate. When was the last time she had felt not happy, exactly, but at peace with herself? She couldn't remember.

Once the Major had closed the piano the women swooped on the tea and biscuits. There was a buzz of talk between them, much nodding of heads, even laughter. The chubby toddler sat himself back on the stool and began more plinking and plonking.

She was intent on gathering in the cups and didn't hear Clive Perks until he was almost treading on her toes.

'Hello, Cissie, is there still some tea in the pot?'

'Should think so,' she said, taking off the lid and peering inside.

'Pour one for yourself,' said the Major. 'You've done well.'

She stood at the hatch pouring out the tea while Clive helped himself to a biscuit. The women gathered up their children and began to leave. Captain Kellet came in and was in hurried conversation with the Major.

'Why d'you come back here?' asked Clive, dipping his biscuit in his tea. 'Looked like you'd got yourself a good place with that Clements bloke's sister.'

'I was homesick,' she said, not looking at him. 'Only when I got here there weren't no home. It had all been in my head. Besides, it weren't as if Mrs Mowbray really wanted me. Just bothered about keeping her brother out of prison, I reckon. Still I've me bits and pieces with me now.' Cissie smiled. 'Got you to thank for that,' she said.

'Only doing my job,' he said. 'What sort of work do you want?'

Cissie looked at him. He had the dark eyes that always drew her to men, but none of the swagger. Most likely he didn't even know he was handsome. She had never been out with a man with good intentions. When she thought about it she had never been out at all. Her relations with men had all been back-alley deals – the use of her body for their loose change. Even Ted Garland had not wanted her for more than a bit of behind-the-scenes amusement, like stealing a cake when the baker isn't looking. 'Don't know what I could do 'cept housework. No good at book learning,' she said. 'I was too frightened of the teacher.'

'I could help you with that,' he said, 'unless you'd rather the Major worked with you,' he said. ''Course I got more time than she has. All depends if you're going to be staying around here.'

'I'll see what happens,' she said.

'Might bump into you again,' he said, turning and almost tripping over Captain Kellet in his haste.

Cissie busied herself with the washing up. It was a new experience for her to have a man wanting friendship. He is interested in me, she thought, not just what I look like. She puzzled over her own feelings in the matter. Clive did not excite her. There was no edge of danger to him, yet seeing him smile at her had given Cissie something. What it was she wasn't quite sure.

'I wonder if you could do me a great kindness?' asked Captain Kellet. 'I have a young woman recovering from pneumonia who needs a lot of care. Her family live away and her husband is at sea. I need to help at a confinement and the Major is busy here. Could you make her some tea and sit with her for a few hours?'

''Course I can,' she said, surprising herself, once more.

Captain Kellet's face creased into a smile. 'Cissie, you are a godsend, truly. I'll pack you up with some tea and bread and butter. There are a couple of eggs in the kitchen, could you scramble them for her?'

'No trouble.'

'I'll be along to stay the night at about ten o'clock. Here's the key, it's number seven.'

'I'm staying with my friend round there at eighteen. Be able to drop in and tell her where I am.'

'God Bless you, Cissie,' said the Captain. 'I'll see you later.'

Cissie walked down the street clutching the bag of food. Why did she say yes? What if she couldn't cope? What if the girl died? Her old anxiety at facing a new situation tugged at her new-found confidence. Cissie blinked. Well, she had done it now; whatever happened, she would have to manage.

23

They sat together on the sea wall in Rosyth, watching their floats rising and falling. It was well into April now and a warm Sunday afternoon for Scotland. Fishing suited Matthew. He could let his thoughts unravel and Bob was the ideal companion. Time drifted on without a word passing between them.

Matthew fretted about Mary. Since making love with her everything had changed between them. His feelings for her kept flickering from hope to despair. One moment he would remember her eagerness and warmth and long to hold her close, the next he would feel resentful as his freedom leaked away. He loved her – or he thought he did. Certainly he had wanted her that last time but it hadn't panned out as he'd hoped. His feelings had run ahead of him and it had all been over almost before it started. The look on her face had probably mirrored his – regret and disappointment. Had he been expecting too much? Matthew didn't know. Surely making love had to be more than that? Certainly Boggy Marsh's accounts of sex were little more than rutting. Matthew wished his brother were still around; it was the sort of thing they might have talked about.

It wasn't just the sex he found baffling. He never seemed to be in the same mind about Mary for two days together. Sometimes he admired her spirit and fearless way of going at things. At other times she seemed crude and insensitive, only looking out for herself. There were moments when he didn't like her at all. Of course, they could both change their minds about each other. Being engaged was not the same as being married. But having sex was a risky business.

'Got something on your mind?' asked Bob, handing over his line before taking out his tin and rolling them both a tickler.

'No more than usual.'

'Been off hooks ever since we sailed.'

'Yeah.'

'Tell me to pipe down, but if you wants to bend my ear I ain't going nowhere.'

'What d'you know about women?'

'Jesus,' said Bob, lighting two ticklers and passing one to Matthew. 'What I know could be put on the back of a postage stamp.'

'I don't know if I've made the right move in getting engaged.'

'How d'ya mean?'

'Well, we're so different.'

''Course you are,' laughed Bob,' 'you're a man and she's a woman!'

'It's more than that. Lot of the time we grate on each other's nerves, then just when I feel like jacking it in she'll turn loving and I want her again.'

'Sure it's not your dick talking?'

'Not sure at all.' Matthew laughed and some of his anxiety leaked away.

'I was engaged once,' said Bob, blowing smoke rings, 'didn't last, though.'

'Why was that?'

'Dunnow, really. Mad for her I was to start with, then it all fizzled out. She kept making plans for when we were married, what sort of curtains we'd have and who we'd invite to tea. It wasn't me she wanted, it was a house. Used to play me like a fish. If I lost interest she'd give me the green light and then when I was raring to go she'd come over all tight-lipped, saying as how if I loved her I'd wait. Get more honesty from a tart. Least with them you know what's on the counter.'

Matthew stared into the water. Mary was not one for games. He knew her loving and wanting him was genuine. It was how they were with one another when they weren't lovemaking that worried him.

''Course being engaged is something and nothing,' said Bob. 'You're not free to go off with another party yet you're not really together. Life's a risky business, mate, 'specially on boats. You got enough strife doing your job and risking not getting back to the surface. Last thing you wants is aggravation with your missis. Don't believe half of what Boggy says about marriage – keeps his brains in his dick. George Kendall's the one to ask. Bin married ten years. His missis is a gem. Quiet, hard-working little party, keeps their place trim and the kids are a credit to them – mannerly and well turned out.'

Matthew sighed. 'Mary hasn't had anyone to show her the ropes. Lost her mother when she was a kid and her dad was a bit of a boozer. Had to bring up five of them.'

'All credit to her,' said Bob. 'Reckon it's a bit like joining a new boat, settling into marriage. Takes a while to find out the strengths and weaknesses and to shake down together. You got to chew the fat a bit, say what you wants and what you can't hackle with. You ain't a saint, Dusty; moody bastard at times; faults are never all one way.'

Matthew laughed. 'Thanks for the reference,' he said.

They tossed their cigarette ends into the sea and settled back to the fishing.

Matthew's spirits lifted. He'd been crossing bridges that weren't yet there. Bob was right. He must talk to Mary when he got back. She might be as anxious as he was.

'You got a bite, Dusty; wake up, mate,' called Bob.

Matthew shook himself then reeled in his line. 'It's a conger, big one, too.' All talk was abandoned as they fought to land it. The eel thrashed and struggled against the line and Bob grabbed a piece of planking lying about and whacked it on the head. Bashed and bloody, it lay quivering in a silvery loop.

Bob cut the line from its mouth. 'We'll skin it in one here, then take it back to chef.'

They peeled it back from the neck and off the body in one long strip, then gutted it, throwing the head, skin and entrails into the water. Immediately a flock of seagulls dived after them.

Matthew took his paper from his pocket and shrouded the conger in The *Sunday Express*. His excitement was stained with regret.

'It'll make sweet eating,' Bob said; 'enough here for the whole mess.'

Matthew carried the eel while Bob took charge of the tackle. 'I reckon our time's bin well spent,' he said.

Matthew glanced at the gulls before following his oppo back to the boat. 'Well spent,' he agreed.

> *Dear Mary,*
> *Twinnies is home now and got their birthday Saturday.*
> *Come home Babes and make it a real family do. He*
> *don't say nothing but Blyth misses you. Come up the*
> *market and see how we're getting on. Needs you to set*
> *us right.*
> *Tata for now,*
> *Love Dad*

With her curiosity sharp as vinegar Mary set off on the ferry to see everyone. She was surprised at her own excitement at going home. It was the 29th of May and she had been gone six weeks. Striking out on her own had been a lonely business and she had needed every ounce of courage not to go snivelling home. But she had survived all that the laundry threw at her – and Jabez Churt's grouching.

Never had she worked so hard. Her pay when she got it felt like a trophy. Added to that was her friendship with Janey. She was a mine of information and salty wit.

'Teach you a few wrinkles about ironing,' she had said yesterday dinner time at the Vixen.

'Reckon wrinkles is the last thing you needs in your trade,' Mary had laughed.

'You wants ter move on to being a shaker. One of the women is leaving the end of the month. There'll be an opening for ya. Bring yer pay up another shilling.'

'What's shaking when it's at home?' she asked, taking a gulp of water.

'Gotta shake out the washing as it comes out of the drums and fold it for mangling.'

'Won't one of the girls in the sorting room want it? They bin there longer than me.'

Janey touched her nose and winked. 'Don't know about it yet,' she whispered. 'You get in with the forewoman, Daisy Fletcher. She's a real jewel. Her bloke's on the same boat as mine.'

Mary could do with a new forewoman after refusing Floss her dibs for the beer kitty. She stuck to water. It saved her money, allowing her to buy a meat pie now and then. 'Thanks, Janey,' she said. 'Like to meet this Daisy.'

Of course it had all been for Matthew. Being with him in her room had made up for everything. That one visit seemed so long ago. It had been over so quickly like the sex. She had wanted to be held and comforted and told that he still loved her. Afterwards they had not been able to look at one another. Why was that? she wondered. If she had known about the stickiness of loving she would have brought up a bowl of water and set out her towel and lavender soap. But she had not known it was going to happen or that it would be over so fast. And now he was away in Scotland. It had been much more than six weeks, more like half a lifetime. Of course, there had been letters assuring her of his love and Mary had written too, but she needed to see him face to face. Matthew was so gentle and mannerly, so much better than she deserved. If only she could keep a hold on her temper and be the girl he wanted. Sometimes she felt as if she could never measure up and resented having to try.

The ferry bumped against the jetty in Portsea and Mary raced up the pontoon. She wanted to go directly to the market and surprise everyone. Hurrying through Queen Street past the sailors out with their wives or girlfriends she soaked up the sounds and smells of home. There were the women with their prams loaded up with outwork from the naval tailors, seamen's collars at seven and six a dozen completed. The reek of Brickwoods' beer wafted out of the pub doorways and the smell of frying onions and beef gravy from the pie shop. Men in cheap suits littered the pavements wearing home-made sandwich boards announcing,

   '*Ex-serviceman, Hard worker. Anything considered.*'

There seemed to be more of these old soldiers and sailors about. But when had she last noticed them? They weren't really old. Some were perhaps in their early thirties. Thank God Matthew had been too young to serve in the war. At least he was in regular work in the navy, even if he was miles away.

Mary ran through Commercial Road down to the market in Charlotte Street. There down on the left, by the sweet stall, were the rest of the Vine family. She hid herself among the crowd wanting to watch them unseen.

Fred sat on an upturned orange box, coughing and smoking, his fingers nicotine yellow. The twins were laughing and chiaking the passing shoppers. Mary could see that they were an added attraction. Just as well, she thought, looking at the toys and books sat about in sorry heaps. Blyth stood at the other end of the stall examining a batch of crystal sets.

Mary grinned. In spite of everything her job-lot family had held together. She had missed them, for all their aggravations. As she began to shove towards them through the press of people she was grabbed and swung off her feet.

'Thought you was in Gosport making your fortune?'

'Danny Sullivan, I'll fetch you such a wallop,' she cried.

'Buy you a tea and a bacon sarney? Look like you could do with feeding up.'

Mary blushed, aware of the warmth of his fingers on her arm. Danny Sullivan was dangerous. 'How about standing the whole family to some grub? You're looking flush. What's your latest deal?'

He grinned. 'A bit of this and that, ducking and diving. Crystal sets is me latest scheme. Wireless is the thing of the future, you know.'

Mary laughed. He always drew her into his games, making her part of the fun of living life to Danny's pattern. 'Let's get the sarneys, your treat,' she insisted.

They stood at the café counter waiting for their food to be packed in a cardboard box, ready to take outside. 'Stall looks shoddy. Don't seem to be near enough stock.'

'Times are bad, darling,' said Danny, taking a heap of coins out of his money-belt and setting them on the counter-top. 'The stall's not earning enough to buy in new stuff. 'Course the General Strike beginning of the month didn't help. Tram men, builders and the railways, they were all out. None of their wives got money for toys.'

Mary stirred the sugar in her tea. She hadn't realised how closed in on her own concerns she had been. In all the time she'd been away Mary had not opened a newspaper and the talk at the laundry was either gossip or the work in hand. In the light of what Danny said, there had to be a rethink over the market. Certainly the stock needed jazzing up a bit. But the pricing was going to be tricky. Perhaps they would have to lower their prices for a while. Just make enough to pay the stall-rental for a while. She could see a notice forming, 'Hard Times, Easy Prices'.

'Come back, Mary,' said Danny, nudging her arm. 'Where were you? Dreaming about your sailor lad?'

Mary blushed. 'Must get this grub out to the family,' she said, picking up the box.

Danny followed behind with the mugs of tea on a tin lid.

'Wheyyy!' they cried as she threaded her way towards them.

Blyth beamed at her. 'Hello,' he said.

She was bursting to sweep him up in her arms, but nodded and smiled. 'Hello yourself,' she said, handing him a sandwich.

'Mary, ooh! It's good to see ya,' said Faith, giving her a fierce hug. 'We've missed yer, ain't we, Merce?'

'Cor! Bacon sarnies,' said Mercy, helping herself.

'You're a tonic,' said Dad, setting his fag-end on the edge of the stall before coming over to kiss her. 'Better than doctor's medicine, having you back with us.'

'Happy birthday, girls. I got sommink for ya.' Mary dipped into her bag and fetched out two newspaper packages. She had found the powder compacts on a stall months ago and set them aside. They were gold metal with one letter on each picked out in glass stones. She had cleaned them, set new mirrors inside and fresh powder puffs.

'Look, it got an F on it,' said Faith, delighted with her gift.

'Ta,' said Mercy, through a mouthful of bacon.

'You stoppin' the night?' asked Dad.

''Course I am,' said Mary, hugging him. 'Sit down and drink yer tea. I wants to have a sort-out here.' Trawling through the paint boxes, bags of marbles and tattered comics, she realised how much she had missed the market. 'Heard you'd packed in the dancing,' she said to the twins. 'What line of work you in now?'

Faith had the grace to look embarrassed. 'Dad lets us help on the stall.'

Mercy was busy flirting with Danny.

'There isn't enough work here to keep you all. Have to find something else. Can't live on fresh air. Mercy, you listening?' she snapped, nudging her sister.

'Didn't want us back at the brewery. I ain't doin' cleaning.'

'Who d'you think you are, Lady Bloody Hamilton?'

'Ain't up to you no more,' flashed Mercy.

'I could sell this stall to Danny, this moment.' Mary jabbed her in the chest with her finger. 'And you'd all be on the bones of your backside.'

'Jesus! What you gotta do to get served round here?' roared a sailor with a toddler riding on his shoulders.

'What can I get ya?' asked Mary, plastering a smile on her face.

'Couple of bags of marbles, ta, and one of them magic painting books.'

'Here you are, Sir, one shilling.'

It was as if she'd never been away. By five o'clock, with her price slashing, the stock was almost cleared. The twins sloped off early with Danny Sullivan who promised to return later to help them pack up. Seeing Mercy laughing up at him and Danny smiling back angered her. Why, she didn't understand.

Tired, but satisfied, at six o'clock Mary, Blyth and Dad

set off for home, leaving Danny to take the stall back to the lock-up.

It was a shock to find her room taken over by her brother. But he took such delight in showing her the changes he'd made that she couldn't spoil things.

The bed was made and all his books on shelves constructed from fruit crates resting on bricks. Nailed to the walls were detailed pencil drawings of ships and engines, and set out on a black-and-white board was a chess set.

'You done well, Blyth,' she said, sitting beside him on his bed. 'I'm proud of you. This is really shipshape. You still playing chess with Uncle Albert?'

'Sometimes,' he said, 'but I got a new partner. This bloke what lives in the Pembroke Club. Used to be a captain in the navy – school teacher now, reckons I'm best player he knows.'

Mary felt uneasy. Blyth was so precious to her and she couldn't bear it if any harm came to him. She had heard things about men taking a shine to young boys – especially boys as beautiful as Blyth. 'Where d'you play – in his room?' she asked, picking up one of the chess pieces and fiddling with it.

'In the library. Got an agreement – I cleans his shoes and then we gets to play chess. Some of the other men play too. Beat them all, I did. We haves tea together, Gentleman's Relish on toast. Fruit cake and lemon tea.'

Mary laughed. 'You're getting to be quite a toff. What's this captain's name?'

'Clements,' said Blyth. 'D'you reckon it's the same one what you worked for, that shot your Pal Cissie'

'Dunnow,' she said. 'What would he be doing livin' in the Pembroke when he's got that house in Lancaster Terrace?'

'Can't see him shootin' anyone. Sides he can't have done that Cissie in 'cos she was round here the other week lookin' for ya. Said she got nowhere to stay.'

'Where'd she go?' asked Mary, thoroughly alarmed. 'What happened, Blyth?'

'Staying with Dora, she is. Might be round tonight for the beano.'

It was strange being a guest at the twins' party without the responsibility of getting things ready. She sat next to Dad, like a parent watching them all.

'Wouldn't Mum have bin proud,' she said, grabbing a liver sausage sandwich and a pickled onion.

Dad laughed. 'Bin in her element – singing and dancing with them. But it's you what should be proud my gal. You was the one that kept us all together.'

Mary grinned. She had, hadn't she? Now they were all on their way. Perhaps now she could really get on with things.

The kitchen door opened and Dora came in carrying an iced birthday cake. There were hugs and cheers and Blyth helped her stick on the fifteen candles. Behind her was Cissie trying to be a shadow just like she did at Lancaster Terrace.

Mary rushed across the room and hugged her fiercely. 'Oh, Cissie, I'm so glad to see ya,' she cried.

'I missed you so much. All the time I thought, Mary'll know what to do.'

Mary sighed. What was it about her that drew the helpless and the weak? Didn't they know how much effort it took just to keep herself afloat without taking on passengers?

24

June 27th 1926

Dear Charles,

I am in London for a few months and hope that we can meet and put the past behind us. I know that our time in Singapore was painful for you. I am deeply sorry. If the thought of seeing me again is not too vile a prospect perhaps you could visit me here at my hotel.

I long to hear about the children. Being parted from Miles and Charlotte has been a cruel price to pay for my happiness with Lawrence. Even if you feel unable to see me could you please send me some recent photographs. My one desire is to make up to them for my past neglect.

By the way, what is all this about you and Cissie Nugent? A friend sent me a cutting from the paper some weeks ago. Honestly, Charles, I was astonished. You, with a revolver and that little waif wearing my nightdress – what a spectacle! Don't worry, I shall not breathe a word to the children's school. The last thing I want is for your behaviour to upset them or upset their stay in Chantry House.

I look forward to seeing you if you feel up to the ordeal.

Regards,
Lettice

Charles sank down onto his bed feeling as if he had been punched in the stomach. Reading the letter again he was possessed by rage. 'Aaaah!' he roared out of his bedroom window into the yard below, then tore the pages to shreds and flung them up into the air. They blew back in his face. Even on paper Lettice could reduce him to impotent fury. He felt sick. All his gains in the last few weeks were threatened by the sight of that spidery handwriting.

God Almighty! How was he going to stop her taking Miles and Charlotte away? His custody of the children and the threat of injunctions would be challenges that Lettice, with her powerful connections and acting abilities, could simply circumvent. Her timing had been impeccable.

Only minutes ago, he had returned from the estate agent's with the keys of his new house. Only an hour ago he had walked through the bedrooms assigning the small one to Charlotte and the one facing the garden to Giles. The children had written after the Easter holiday making plans for the summer. Miles wanted to learn to sail and Charlotte wanted a puppy. All the while the letter had been waiting for him like a primed grenade. No, he shouted – no, no, no!

In the last few weeks he had begun to enjoy his teaching. After their early diffidence the boys were now at ease with him. Charles had even started staying behind on a Thursday evening at the chess club he'd organised for the more promis-ing lads. None came close to the talent of the shoeshine boy he had met outside the Pembroke Club a few weeks ago. Never had he met a child with such powers of concentration or such facility with numbers. There he sat with the old fogeys in the club library, setting out the chess pieces, then snaring them with his quickness without the least conceit. Charles had been stunned to learn that he was Mary Vine's brother. Yet why? She had been full of artful dodges. Mary stood up to Lettice and gave as good as she got. If only he had half her pluck.

Even the misunderstanding with Cissie was beginning to fade. He had fretted over her. She was such an innocent, trusting creature. Her belief that he had promised her she could always to stay in Lancaster Terrace was insane. And yet it had haunted him for weeks. A meeting with Constable Perks had reassured him of her well-being.

Charles stared out of the window at the fragments of Lettice's letter still swirling about on the ground below. How clever she was, sucking him in like that with all the phoney regret at the beginning and then the veiled threat of what she could do if thwarted. Should he make a clean breast of the shooting to the staff at Chantry House? he wondered. The report had only been in the local newspaper and he and Lavinia had thought the incident mercifully closed. His sister had taken exception to Cissie's flight to Portsmouth, seeing it as gross ingratitude. The news that Lettice was in the country and likely to cause trouble would seem like the last straw.

Charles paced about the room. Christ! What a pathetic specimen he was. Unless he was able to stand up to his ex-wife his self-respect would be zero. If he couldn't fight for himself, at least he must make a stab at it for the children. It was ridiculous. He had commanded a crew of hundreds of sailors at Jutland with no difficulty, was known for his calmness under fire – yet his wife could reduce him to impotence. Christ! What a tangle it all was.

Mary and Cissie sat in the downstairs bedroom catching up with their news.

'Still can't understand why you wanted to come back,' said Mary, taking her slice of the twins' birthday cake from the plate on the bed between them. 'You had it good with old Clements' sister over in Dorset. Room of your own, clean clothes and good fresh grub – you should have stuck it out. Ain't nothing back here for ya.'

Cissie blinked. She had forgotten how blunt her friend could be. 'Missed me room and me stuff. I was bundled off with no chance to get nothing.'

'What stuff?'

'You know, me box where I kept little Charlie's bonnet and things,' she said, her eyes filling with tears. 'Never thought Captain Clements would sell up – so sure me room would be waiting for me. Said it was 'cos he and Lettice had got divorced and the nippers bin sent to boarding school.'

'Blimey!' gasped Mary. 'Divorced! Can't see him going off the rails; must of bin her. Where she gone to?'

'Married a bloke, a rubber planter, gone off to Malaya.'

Mary licked her lips. This was better than the *News of the World*. 'Proper cow, old Lettice. Like to have smacked me face, she would, 'cept she knew I'd hit her back. Bet that planter bloke don't know what hit him.'

'She was pretty, though, wasn't she?' said Cissie, biting into the cake. 'What about that black dress with all them beads on it?'

'And them pearls; cor, must have bin worth hundreds. D'you know our Blyth has palled up with him?'

'With who?' asked Cissie, losing the thread.

'Old Clements, of course. Goes round to the Pembroke Club and plays chess with him and the other officers – ever so clever he is.'

'You gotta lovely family,' said Cissie, wistfully.

Mary snorted. 'You ain't lived with them.' She looked at her friend. There was still the nervousness and the blinking, but apart from that she wouldn't have recognised her. Cissie had filled out and she'd got some colour in her cheeks. Out of maid's uniform she was really quite pretty. 'How'd you get back down here, then?' she asked.

'Crept into the back of the Captain's car and hid under Mrs Mullins' blanket.'

'Blimey, Cissie!' she gasped. 'Didn't think you had it in you.'

Cissie laughed. 'Just took me chance. 'Course, when I got home and found the place was sold I went mental. Kicked him in the shins and screamed me head off.'

'What! You kicked Captain Clements?'

''Course not,' snapped Cissie, looking horrified. 'The new bloke. He went and called the police. I said as how I wasn't going till I got my box. He'd chucked it out in the yard. But Clive helped me find it.'

'Who's Clive, when he's at home?' asked Cissie, enthralled.

'You met him. He was the policeman what sat with me when I was in hospital.'

'Oooh! Clive, is it? You're a dark horse! Not stepping out with him, are you?'

Cissie blushed. 'We're just friends. He found the box and told me to go round to your house and said as how he'd tell them, in the house, as I'd run away. When I got here you was full up but Dora took me in. I'm there still.' She smiled at Mary. 'Hear you got yerself a place in Gosport. S'pose you and your feller be getting married soon?'

'Probbly next year when I'm twenty-one,' said Mary, her stomach lurching.

'Hope you'll be ever so happy,' said Cissie.

'You gals taken root in there?' said Dad, standing at the door with a paper hat on his head. 'Come on out in the kitchen. We're having a singsong.'

On Sunday Mary sat up in the bow of the ferry going back to Gosport. The weekend had been such a mixture of things, like the bag of leftovers Dad had packed her up with. The joy of seeing Blyth and having him glad to see her was top of her list of pleasures. Mercy and Faith were another matter. Watching the family let the stall go to pot angered her, but she was determined to rescue the business. Then there was Danny Sullivan – a temptation she must not even think about. As for Cissie . . . ! Mary smiled. She was a bit of good news and had promised to come over and see her in Gosport.

She thought about what Dad had said to her as they were saying goodbye.

'Bin a real tonic, seeing you, gal,' he'd said, holding her close. 'Making something of your life, you are, I'm proud of you.'

Was she making something? Mary wondered. The laundry was a daily struggle and if it weren't for Janey she wouldn't have lasted five minutes. After her row with Floss the other girls, under the older woman's thumb, barely spoke to her. At the cottage, all her efforts had not shifted Jabez an inch in her favour. The only welcome back would likely to be from Dog. He barked joyfully at her each night, regardless of her mood.

The evening was warm and the ferry rippled through a calm sea. Above Gosport the sun was dipping beneath a sky streaked with red and gold. Mary looked over at Haslar Creek, hopefully scanning the conning towers of the submarines tied up there for the magic *L75*. It was not there. Was Matthew thinking of her? she wondered. The frenzy of the weekend had been welcome but it also underlined the loneliness of her daily living. She chewed her hand. This would be the pattern of her life with Matthew. Patches of time when he was home and they could do things together, like making love, sharing meals, laughing and talking. And then, like now, empty stretches with only herself for company. She glared at the couple in front of her: a sailor smiling down at his sweetheart. The girl was carrying a bunch of sweet peas. The pinks and mauves swam before Mary's tear-filled eyes. Everywhere couples out enjoying themselves.

The ferry bumped against the jetty and she dawdled up Shore Lane. Jabez was sat in his boat at the water's edge, fiddling about with some tackle, and Dog was rootling among the stones. Neither of them cast a glance in her direction. Mary grinned sourly to herself. She was even looking forward to the sorting room tomorrow, in spite of the stink and Floss's temper – at least there she'd be kept busy.

The cottage was, sat there, hovering on the right side of decay and inside, on the arm of Jabez's chair was a fry-up conjealing on its plate. Mary stood at the window, sipping tea out of her flask. The view with yachts drifting homeward increased her sadness. She hated the dying of the day when the light was overcome by the creeping darkness. Mary sank down onto her mattress feeling the walls closing in on her. She had yearned for a place of her own, for peace and quiet to think her own thoughts, but the silence went on and on making her panicky and afraid. Reaching under her pillow she took out Matthew's last letter. The sight of his handwriting brought him before her. Mary could imagine him sitting on his toolbox, shutting out all the noise of the boat as he concentrated his thoughts on her. She smoothed out the paper and searched for the passage she wanted.

We must be really careful, love. Getting married next year will be a struggle to make ends meet. I wish I was twenty-five instead of twenty-three, then we'd be entitled to the marriage allowance. I should be made acting Leading Hand soon, that will give us a few more bob to play with. I don't want us to marry too early because we've rushed things. I know you'll get all worked up at what I've said, but I love you and want us to have a happy life together. I am selfish and need you to myself. We will go places and do things before having a family. This means we must take care.

Hoping to be back for the next dance at Dolphin. I want to show off my girl to my mates.

I love you, love you, love you,
Your Matthew.

Mary shoved the letter back in its envelope. Thoughts that she had managed to hide from herself rose unwelcome now she was alone. Not since Blyth had been trapped in that burning house had she felt so powerless.

'Help, help, you got to get here.'

Footsteps thundered up the stairs, her door was bounced back on its hinges and Jabez stood there with tears striping his grimy face.

'What's up?' Mary cried, too startled to reproach him for bursting in.

'It's Dog, he's hurt bad,' the waterman gasped. 'You got to come.'

As she followed Churt below, Dog's howls increased. Mary chewed her nails. What would she find? The animal writhed in panic, his paw caught fast in a tin. Each time he struggled to free himself the pain increased.

'Ooh!' sobbed Jabez. 'He's hurt sommat cruel. Tried to get it off but I only makes it worse. Me fingers is too thick. Won't let me near him now.'

'Get your coat off,' said Mary. 'We'll roll him up in it to keep him still.'

Together they wrestled with the frenzied animal and managed to bundle him into submission. Still yelping, he fixed his eyes on her.

'Sit on him,' she commanded.

Jabez did as he was told.

'Be over soon,' Mary reassured Dog before taking hold of his imprisoned paw. Blood was oozing into his fur where the jagged edge of the tin-lid had bitten into his flesh. What was needed was for her to get her fingers between the paw and the lid and press it flat in order to release him. 'All right, boy! All right, boy! We'll sort it,' she whispered to him with more reassurance than belief.

Behind her Jabez, still crying, straddled Dog. His soggy

collapse amazed her. Never had he demonstrated the least affection for his pet, spending most of the time they were together kicking and swearing at him.

'Shuffle up his body closer to me,' she insisted. 'Keep hold of his paw, while I try to free it, and stop bellerrin', it's getting on me nerves.'

It was as if some unused part of herself were issuing commands and formulating plans. 'Now hold it tight.' Gritting her teeth, Mary pressed the paw away from the tin-lid and then attempted to slide two fingers of her other hand in the opposite direction. Dog howled and struggled but Jabez gripped him firmly with his knees.

Sweat trickled down her face. Her first attempt failed. She increased the pressure on his paw and managed to widen the gap by just enough to slide her fingers back against the lid. As it scraped away from his paw Dog yelped in panic. Blood spurted from an inch-long tear. Mary handed the tin to Jabez before gripping the paw and pressing her fingers against the wound. 'Chuck that in the boat for the time being. We better lug him inside and find something to bandage him up with.'

With amazing meekness Churt did as he was told. Gasping and slipping over the stones he and Mary made their way towards the cottage. She kept hold of Dog's paw while Jabez took most of his weight. By the time they got him indoors and onto the armchair the waterman was breathless.

'Got anything to wrap up his leg, anything clean?' she asked.

He shook his head.

'Keep yer fingers pressed, just there. We gotta stop the bleeding.' Mary searched the kitchen for a basin of some sort to fill with water to clean Dog's wound. The tin must have washed up and down the shoreline for days. It was without a label and orange with rust. Finally she settled on an empty, handleless saucepan that was the least dirty item she could find. After pouring water into the pan she shook in some salt and stirred it around. Leaving the water to cool she raced upstairs and opened her clothes box.

There at the bottom were some strips of towelling and safety-pins that she kept in readiness for her next period. Taking two pieces and some pins she hurried back to Dog. Cutting a piece off the end of one of the strips she dipped it into the saucepan and slid the remainder under his paw.

'Must be careful,' Mary said. 'Don't want to rub too hard or it'll bleed again.' The water turned red as she dipped the swabs in the saucepan. Cutting the other cloth into makeshift bandages, she fastened them around his paw with one of the safety-pins.

'I takes me hat off to ya,' mumbled Jabez. 'Fixed up Dog better than any sawbones.'

Mary smiled at the old curmudgeon as he staggered to his feet. 'You'd better go and wash your hands, looks as if you bin in a slaughterhouse or sommink.'

As he clattered out into the scullery with the saucepan and swabs she called after him, 'Reckon I deserves a cup of tea after all this.'

Jabez gave a wheezy laugh as if the muscles needed were woefully out of practice.

'Got a corner of rabbit pie and some cold spuds. Could stretch to two, I'm thinking.'

Mary sank onto the floor and rested her head against Dog who was slumped in the chair. 'Might even be a smidgen for you,' she said.

Whistling to himself, the old waterman clattered about the room. Mary closed her eyes. All the tension of the last half-hour caught up with her and she felt bone weary. When Jabez stuck a tin plate on the floor for her she was almost too tired to eat.

Dog roused himself and slid down from the chair and sat

beside her wolfing down the bits of supper that she shared with him. Afterwards he began to worry at his makeshift bandage.

'Have to find something to cover that or it'll fester,' said Jabez, pointing a full fork at him.

Mary saw an old glove, half caked with paint, lying on the floor under the corner cupboard. She went over and tugged it free. 'Reckon if we cut off a pair of these fingers, unpick and stitch them back as one it might just serve the purpose. You got any needles?'

'Thought that was something you'd have, Missie,' he said, before filling his mouth with a sizeable piece of pie. 'Work basket in bottom of the cupboard,' he mumbled, showering her with pastry crumbs.

'Who'd it belong to?' she asked. It was so clean and orderly it could hardly be the property of Jabez.

'Been there these last ten years, was my Ma's, God rest her.'

It was made of wicker, the inside lined with red satin. Among the collection of embroidery silks were needles in a screw of paper. Pins stabbed the quilted inside of the lid and she found a pair of small scissors wrapped in red flannel. 'Ain't much of a sewer,' Mary said, taking up the scissors and unpicking the glove.

'Don't reckon Dog puts much store in sewing,' muttered Jabez, licking his knife.

After much struggling Mary completed a rough bag-shaped article with a drawstring top. She slid it over Dog's bandage and tied it in place. 'I'm off to bed,' she said. 'You gonna wash the plates?'

'Still got some clean. Only fettles the pots when I've run out.' He got to his feet and Dog limped after him. 'Off up the Vixen. See you tomorrer.'

'Ta for the pie,' said Mary.

'You earned it, gal. I'm in yer debt.'

''Night,' she said as Jabez set his cap over his greasy grey curls.

Back in her room Mary settled into bed after a hasty wash and dropped into a sound sleep. In the morning she awoke with a sour, heaving stomach and barely made it to the outside lavatory before vomiting. As she got some clean knickers out of her box, she tucked the towelling strips underneath the rest of her meagre clothing. If her worst fears were realised, she would have no need of them for the next few months.

25

Cissie hurried along to Queen Street anxious not to be late. Every Sunday evening at six o'clock the Salvation Army band formed up there ready to march through the streets. Clive Perks had invited her to join them.

'I'd like you to come to the service,' he said. 'On Sundays we walk up from Portsea to the Citadel in Lake Road. I'm going to be doing a cornet solo.' He blushed. ''Course, if it's not the sort of thing you fancy . . .' His voice trailed away in embarrassment.

''Course I'll come,' she said and then it was her turn to blush. 'What's a cornet, Clive? I feel daft asking. Only one I knows is for eating ice cream out of.'

They both laughed.

'It's bigger than the bugle. I like it better; it's got a sweeter tone.'

'See you Sunday,' he said, shuffling out of the Slum Post.

Cissie smoothed down the jacket of the navy suit that she had bought from the second-hand stall at the market. Dora had unpicked and virtually remade it and lent her a straw hat with a matching ribbon.

'You looks lovely,' she said, waving her off from the front door. 'You go and sing yer heart out. Reckon that Clive won't be able to take his eyes off ya.'

Cissie couldn't believe how her life had changed. It was nearly three months since she had come back to Portsmouth, and she was beginning to find her feet. Living with Dora was cramped but cosy. They had become real pals. But Cissie knew that once Harry came home she would have to search elsewhere. Her mistake over Lancaster Terrace had cured her of taking anything for granted.

'One day at a time, Cissie,' Major Grice had said. 'Trust in the Lord. Leave tomorrow in His care.'

She didn't quite know what she thought about the Lord. It seemed He was still looking the other way. But she wasn't the only one He seemed to have forgotten. There at the Slum Post were people much worse off than her: nippers with no mum or dad, old folks dying alone and whole families living and sleeping in one room. Gradually she was making friends among them. It gave her such pleasure when they called, 'Hello, Cissie,' to her as she passed them in the street.

Through each day Major Grice and Captain Kellet went about their work cooking, cleaning, singing and saying prayers. 'What we have to have is grit,' the Major said. 'Soft soap is not an atom of good.' Once, she had horrified Cissie by fetching a drunken man a clout on his head with a broom handle. 'Out of here, Alfie, until you sober up,' she had told him. 'If I hear that you have hurt your missis or the children you'll get more of the same medicine.'

Yet she could be the gentlest of people when the situation required it. Even the most cast-down of the inhabitants of Portsea felt confident of being welcomed in by the Major.

She heard the band before she saw them tuning up outside the Sailors' Home Club. There were drums, trumpets, tambourines and even triangles. Clive was there in his Salvation Army uniform of red and black, busy practising with his cornet. He smiled shyly at her as she walked past to join the crowd forming up behind the musicians.

'Cissie, how good to see you,' called the Major, waving her tambourine, her bonnet strings fluttering in the breeze.

'Why don't you join the Captain over there, with Mrs Pitcher's boys.'

The Sergeant Major called for silence and then there was a short prayer before they moved off.

''Ello, Cissie,' said Mrs Pitcher. 'Budge up, Lionel, and you, Claude, make room for Cissie.'

The drums rolled and away they went marching to the tune of; 'Onward, Christian Soldiers'.

Cissie surprised herself at knowing all the words. She looked around her at the odd assortment of people following the band – the rag, tag and bobtail of Portsea. She recognised nearly all the people, and many she knew by name. Why were they marching? she wondered. Was it the Lord or was it the music that drew them?

As they strode along, some of the salvationists walked along the pavements with collecting boxes and onlookers tossed in their pennies and halfpennies. At the Citadel the band halted and then marched inside and took up their positions between the flags.

Cissie bent her head during the prayers and tried not to look at Clive too much. She sang the hymns, delighting in the shimmer of the tambourines and the roll of the drums, and then it was Clive's solo.

'"Trumpeter, what are you sounding now",' said Mrs Pitcher, 'I loves this.'

The music soared over the heads of the worshippers achingly sweet, and Cissie wanted to cry. It was followed by more prayers, and then an address by a man with a white beard, who reminded Cissie of Father Christmas. People were then invited to approach the Mercy Seat and repent of their sins while everyone else sang.

> *Is there a heart that is waiting*
> *Longing for pardon today*

Hear the glad message proclaiming
Jesus is passing this way.

After a penitent had knelt and requested forgiveness their name and address was taken and an officer sent to help them. Watching a young woman kneeling with tears rolling down her face, Cissie wondered what could have prompted her to come forward. What could have caused her such a need for repentance? Did you really feel cleansed, as the Salvation Army songbook said? What happened the next time you were tempted? Did you have extra strength to resist? Were Major Grice and Captain Kellet tempted, and if so what was it that led them astray? She was brought back from her questioning by the announcement of another hymn and got to her feet.

'Blessed assurance, Jesus is mine' everyone sang and she was once more caught up in the gladness. When the service ended people lingered talking outside on the pavement before walking back to their homes.

'That was ever so good,' Cissie said to Clive as he came up to join her.

'Thank you,' he said shyly, 'glad you enjoyed it.'

Gradually she became aware of a small woman beside him staring at her with a wintry expression.

'Oh sorry,' he muttered. 'Mother, this is Cissie Nugent, a friend of mine.'

'Is that so?' she said as if in disbelief that her son could possibly form a friendship with someone so unworthy.

'Pleased to see you,' said Cissie, stretching out her hand.

'That's as may be,' said Mrs Perks, turning her back. 'Clive, supper's waiting.'

'See you tomorrow,' he said, smiling apologetically before following his mother towards the bus stop.

Cissie felt all her new-won confidence ebbing away. She

walked back to Portsea with the Pitchers, glad of their chatter to drown out her disappointment.

'She's a mean old faggot, used to be my neighbour in Lemon Street,' said Mrs Pitcher. 'Leads poor Clive a hell of a dance. His dad was lost in the war. Lovely bloke he was. God knows how he got her in the family way,' she sniffed, 'must've used chloroform.' Mrs Pitcher laughed. 'Never make a salvationist out of me, I just goes for the music.'

Cissie smiled half-heartedly. It had been such a lovely evening and in one glance Clive's mother had quenched her joy.

'Don't you be so silly,' Dora said, when she told her of their meeting. 'You're as much deserving of Clive as anyone else is. If he's the man for you he'll tell the old boot to mind her own business. And, if he's not, you're well rid of him.'

The next day she had almost given up hope of seeing him when she looked up from a marathon washing-up session to find him talking to Captain Kellet.

'Hello, Cissie,' he said, smiling at her. 'Got a cup of tea in the pot?'

All the frustration of the day dissolved beneath his smile.

'I reckon we could squeeze you one out,' she said, staring at the counter, not wanting him to see how glad she was to see him.

'How you getting on with your reading?' he asked.

'Haven't got no one to help me yet,' she mumbled, embarrassed as always at any mention of her reading difficulties. 'I got my fiver changed, and I still got three pound I'm saving to put in the post office once I can do the writing.'

'How would you feel about me giving you a hand?' he asked. 'Haven't got anything else to do this evening.' He smiled shyly. 'Never know, you might enjoy it.'

'What? Round at Dora's?' she asked.

'If that's all right with her,' he said. 'I'll come round at seven and we'll start from there.'

She rushed home, her stomach pitching and tossing from excitement to alarm. Tonight Clive Perks was coming around to Keats's Row to give her a reading lesson and she was in a ferment of anxiety. What would Dora think?

'Cissie, sit down. You'll wear a hole in the lino and if you ask me once more if you're doing the right thing I'll smack you one,' her friend said, buttoning up her coat.

'He must think me a proper fool, not knowing how to read. Bet he wishes he'd never offered.'

'You'll start at the beginning, and if he didn't want to do it he could have left you to Major Grice. He likes you, Cissie, can't you see it in his eyes? Hark! That's him. Now, when you're settled I'll nip round to Mum's and leave you to it.'

'Hello, Clive,' Cissie said, looking up at him. 'Thank you for coming.' It was like being back at school. Her mouth was dry and she was so frightened of failing. Seeing him in shirt and flannels rather than in his uniform melted a bit of her nervousness.

'Hello, Cissie, you ready to begin?'

'Suppose so,' she said uncertainly.

'Right, you two, I'm off to Mum's. You know where the tea is,' said Dora. 'Don't let Clive here die of thirst.'

'Right,' said Clive, in a business-like voice. 'Let's start with what you know.'

Cissie blinked. 'I don't know nothing,' she mumbled.

Clive took out a notebook and wrote down four or five words. He passed the pad to her. 'Just point to the ones you know. Don't worry if you don't know any of them, I'm just guessing.'

She was too frightened to look.

'Come on, Cissie, they won't bite you. Look at them, just to please me,' he coaxed. 'I don't mind if you don't know them, I just mind if you don't try.'

Cissie looked at the page. She pointed to what she thought was her name and then she recognised another two words.

'That says Lancaster Terrace,' she said, in amazement, 'seen it hundreds of time.'

'Good, good!' Clive smiled at her. 'I'm going to put your first name and last name on another page, with some other words, and get you to pick them out. You've made a good start.'

Cissie stared at the words. She had seen them before lots of times but she could not make any connection. After a pause she managed to locate 'Cissie' and she made a stab at the longest word on the paper. 'I don't think that's my last name but I've seen it up high somewhere – like on the station. Is it Portsmouth?' She faltered.

'Yes, it is,' he said smiling at her. 'Over there is "Nugent" and the other word is "live". You're doing really well.'

Cissie laughed. 'Thought I was a proper fool. Teacher used to rap me fingers with a ruler. Was so frightened I used to get stuck. Frozen I'd be so I couldn't think or move and the slate what we was writing on would be a big black blur. Used to beg my Mum to let me stay home.'

'That was then, Cissie,' he said. 'This is a completely fresh start. It's just you and me with no shouting, no hitting with a ruler, just slow and steady progress.' He took out some greaseproof paper from the case he had with him and a pair of scissors. 'Before we finish tonight you are going to be able to read and write the words – "My name is Cissie Nugent and I live in Portsmouth".'

'Really?' she gasped. 'D'you really think I can do it?'

'All I want is for you to try. I believe you can, it's just getting you to believe it too.'

Cissie watched him cutting the paper into strips. Perhaps he does like me she allowed herself to think. He wrote out ten words. He told her what they were and made her repeat them. Clive mixed them up and then she had to pick them out in order.

'My name is Cissie Nugent and I live in Portsmouth,' she said. 'I've really done it,' she said. 'I've done it,' she laughed.

'Congratulations! Now you are going to put the greaseproof over the words and trace the letters with this pencil.'

Cissie stuck out her tongue and followed the track of the letters one by one.

'While I'm making the tea,' Clive said, 'you are going to write the words on this new sheet of paper, copying what you've done already.'

As he filled the kettle and spooned the tea into the pot, she shaped the letters with her pencil, feeling excitement bubbling up inside her. The result of her labours was a row of shaky letters, but she knew what they were. She turned round to Clive and beamed up at him. 'It's like you give me a hundred pounds,' she gasped. 'Don't know when I bin so pleased with myself.' She wanted to take him in her arms and dance around the kitchen.

Clive laughed. 'Let's drink a toast and pretend it's champagne.'

'D'you really think I'll be able to read? Like papers and stuff?'

He reached across and tapped her forehead. 'It's all in there, Cissie. Time, that's all we need.'

'I can't stop smiling,' she said. 'I suppose I shall need lots of lessons.'

'Heaps,' he said, smiling too. 'This is just the start.'

Cissie poured out the tea and passed a cup to Clive Perks. She would like to kiss him but she knew it would not be right. It would be like trespassing. It was not only reading that she needed to learn. Away from the pubs and alleys, men and women moved towards each other at a slower pace. They wanted to know about one another's thoughts and feelings before they moved to touching. Kissing was a big step forward. Kissing meant rings and promises.

'Have to draw up a programme,' Clive said. 'Lessons at least twice a week. Do you think it will be all right to meet here?' he asked. 'Only it's quiet here. Down at the Slum Post you can never guarantee five minutes' peace and quiet, let alone an hour.'

'I'm sure it will be fine,' said Cissie. 'Dora goes to see her mum most nights.'

'We can't make a regular night because of my work but I'm free next Thursday at seven. Are you happy with that?'

She nodded. 'Very suitable,' she said, trying to sound calm and serious.

Clive gathered up his pencils and paper and put them into his case. He held out his hand to her. 'Let's shake on it,' he said, smiling at her.

'Shake,' said Cissie, making the most of what he offered.

Later she danced around the kitchen. Clive was her friend. They had made an agreement. Twice a week they would sit here together. Who knew what could spring from those moments alone together? For the first time in ages Cissie had something to look forward to.

26

As he stood at the bar waiting for their drinks Matthew turned to smile at Mary. There was no response. She was staring out of the window and biting her fingernails. Something was wrong. Her joy at seeing him after eight weeks' separation was half-hearted to say the least. 'Fancy some crisps?' he asked, going over and tapping her on the arm.

'What's up?' she said, jumping in alarm.

'Crisps – would you like some?'

'Oh, no, ta,' she said, attempting a smile.

Matthew returned to the bar to pick up his drinks with a feeling of dread. How pale she looked and her eyes were puffy as if she'd been crying. What was up with her? Had she met someone else? No, that wasn't it. She would have told him already. Mary was no deceiver. 'Have you missed me?' he asked, giving her a glass of shandy.

''Course,' she muttered, 'bin bloomin' ages.' Still she wouldn't look at him but sat there twisting his ring round and round her finger.

The dread deepened. As he talked of the events of the last few weeks, of the men on board with him, Mary seemed hypnotised by a puddle of spilt beer on the table between them. Words dried in his mouth. In desperation, he took hold of her chin and turned her face towards him.

Mary was crying.

'Tell me,' he breathed. 'Whatever it is, just tell me.'

Still she stared at the beer puddle. 'I'm pregnant,' she whispered.

'Oh!' Matthew let his hand fall to his side feeling winded by her words. They changed everything. His world narrowed from one of possibilities to bare survival.

'That all you gotta say?' Mary said.

Now it was his turn to look away.

'Just been a bit of a shock,' he floundered. 'Are you sure? I mean, have you been to the doctor or anything?'

'Certain,' she mumbled. 'Missed two of me monthlies and I keep being sick.'

Matthew tried to swallow down his panic. He had stepped ashore that evening on top of the world – and now . . . ? 'This changes everything,' he said.

Mary rubbed her sleeve across her eyes. 'That all you got to say?' she challenged. Floundering, he pulled a handkerchief from his jacket pocket and handed it to her. 'Give me a chance to take it in,' he pleaded, unable to meet her eyes.

Leaving her shandy untasted, she stood up. 'Going up the park,' she said, flouncing out of the bar.

He sat there numb with shock. For a fleeting second he thought of sloping away back on board, even of volunteering for a foreign draft – anything to escape. It was more her fault than his, she was the one who took her clothes off, wanting to be like Adam and Eve, she led him on. Yes, he could do that, wriggle out of everything.

Another voice in his head reminded him that the child was his; spoke of his eagerness to follow where Mary led him. How could he live with himself if he abandoned his son? it said. What sort of chance would he have growing up without a father? Matthew thought of his own dad and how much he had missed him after his death at Gallipoli. But at least he had known him and had memories of his first twelve years with the tall genial man.

He imagined the response of Boggy Marsh, back on board, at his news. Could almost hear him laughing. 'Silly sod, getting caught. Should've used a dreadnought. What's up with ya? Bin keeping yer brains in your dick.'

It wasn't as if they weren't engaged already. It was only a matter of getting married earlier than they'd planned. Matthew stared into space. He, the meticulous planner, had cocked things up in more ways than one.

Still the Jack-the-Lad voice whispered at his elbow, urging him to wriggle out of things. As he sat there rolling a cigarette and wrestling with the competing voices, it occurred to him that he should go after Mary. Getting to his feet, frowning with distaste, he realised he had rested his arm in the spilt beer. What a mess!

Mary ran up the High Street towards Walpole Park, running until she got the stitch. All she could see was Matthew's face when she'd told him about the baby. There was panic there. He felt trapped by her. Bet he's sorry he ever met me, she thought.

I don't want it, I don't want it, the words drummed in her head. How could she turn things back to where they were before? At the laundry, there had been a girl with a big belly and face the colour of chalk. She had seen her having a confab with Floss. The woman had written something down and the girl was never seen again. Mary remembered asking Janey about her.

'Poor cow,' she had said. 'That Floss, I've a good mind to report her to the police, only I ain't got no proof of what she done.'

'Proof of what?'

'She's in thick with this woman what helps if you wants rid of a kid. All old Floss cares about is the money. Don't think about them poor frightened girls risking everythink.'

'What d'you mean?'

'Hope you never has to find out,' said Jane fiercely.

Mary's stomach lurched. Dare she go to some woman like that? She shuddered. Leaving aside the danger, where would she get the money? She walked on and until she reached the park and sank down on a bench. Her pride forbade her to look back to see if Matthew was following her. A cat jumped down from a wall and sprayed the side of the bench. Almost retching at the smell, Mary took out Matthew's handkerchief and blew her nose. What was she going to do? It was so unfair. There was Dora desperate for a child and here she was up the spout without even trying. She got up and began pacing around the paths.

'Why d'you rush off like that?' Matthew gasped, taking hold of her arm and leading her to a bench beside the pond.

She stared into the distance.

'Mary, please, we need to talk,' he said.

The early evening was warm and the sky still blue. Around them couples were strolling and groups of young sailors chiaked one another. If we were in a book, she thought, there would be rain lashing down and thunder cracking – or a snowstorm, like in *East Lynne*. In books, sunny evenings were for good news. She looked up at his face. It was pale and his freckles seemed almost painted on. 'You don't want it any more than I do,' she burst out.

'It's just taken me by surprise,' he said, his voice sounding sulky. 'Not as if we weren't planning to get married and have children later on.'

'Don't soft-soap me. You feels trapped and so do I. All your plans was gonna be next year. Nice church wedding, nice little rented home and a nice little wife, sitting knitting. 'Stead of that you got me.'

'We'll just have to move them forward that's all.' His tone was bleak.

'You could just bugger off overseas. Don't want you gritting yer teeth over it.'

'Mary, don't make it so hard for me. It was all a shock. You didn't give me a chance to take it in.'

'Weren't the only one with plans. None of them with kids in,' she said. 'Been caught up with them all me life – five years old when the twins was born. A nipper's the last thing I need.'

'Need or not,' he said, 'we must make the best of it.'

'That's not what you really wanted,' she challenged him.

'It's not what either of us wanted,' he said, taking hold of her hand. 'I could see us settled somewhere nice and having a good time. Getting to know each other. I wanted to spoil you. The last thing I wanted was for you to have a baby before you're ready.'

'I'm not ready,' she sobbed, 'not ready at all.'

Matthew put his arms around her and held her close. 'You're over the worst now, love,' he said. 'Least there's two of us now, we're in this together.'

'You sure?' she asked, looking up at him.

'It's my baby, too,' he said, giving her a fake smile. 'We're just going to be a family sooner than we thought. Have to make new plans, that's all.'

'Didn't think you could fall for a baby that quick, always thought you were safe the first time.'

'Like a free sample,' he said, reaching for his tobacco tin.

Mary gave a tentative smile. She wished they had taken more time and that she could remember more of how it felt. Looking back it had all been so rushed and, if she were honest, disappointing. She sighed. Matthew had said that the worst was over but she was not convinced. They be facing it together but ultimately it was she alone who would carry the child and give birth to it.

'You look tired, love,' he said, 'why don't we walk back to

your place and you tuck up for the night. I'm duty tomorrow so I'll see you on Thursday. Then we can make proper plans. Give you time to see the doctor and find out exactly when I'm going to be a dad.'

'You sure you'll be there, Thursday?' she asked, as they got to their feet and made their way towards the High Street.

'You sure you'll go to the doctors?' he countered.

'Bargain,' she said.

Matthew kissed her briefly at the door of Shore Cottage. 'We'll be all right, I promise,' he said, hurrying away without looking back.

Mary let herself in and climbed the stairs to her room. Barely had she undressed before there was the sound of scrabbling outside her door. Wearily she opened it and Dog bounded inside, settling himself on the mattress.

Mary curled up beside him, comforted by his undemanding affection. He turned and licked her face while she combed her fingers through his silky fur. 'What we gonna do?' she asked.

27

Beattie Pragnell picked up the receiver. 'Portsmouth 5432,' she said.

There was a pause and the sound of someone crying.

'This is Mrs Pragnell,' she said, struggling to keep calm. 'Who is it?'

'Mary,' the voice gasped and blubbered.

'Where are you, my duck?' she asked. 'Just blow your nose and start again.'

'In the box by the laundry.' There was more gasping and sobbing. 'Can you come over,' she pleaded.

Beattie sighed. She looked across at Albert, fast asleep in his armchair.

'What time d'you finish work?'

'Six o'clock. Please come, I'm desperate.'

'Meet you at the ferry, I'll bring a picnic.'

The line went dead.

Dear God, whatever could be the matter for Mary to ask for help?

Albert stirred. 'Where are we going?' he asked.

'I wasn't going to trouble you,' she said. 'It's Mary, she sounds in a real stew about something. Promised I'd go over with a picnic.'

He looked at the clock. 'We've got time to motor round, if you like. I can drop in on my chums at Ratsey and Lapthorne and have a yarn with them while you see your little waif.'

She bent to kiss him. 'You're a treasure,' she said.

'Aren't I just,' he chuckled.

Beattie ransacked her cupboards to put together a sizeable picnic and some items to boost Mary's store cupboard. It would be as well, she thought, to take a blanket so that they could sit out somewhere – there might be a spot along the shore. By all accounts the cottage she lived in was not much more than a hovel. From her earliest childhood, Mary had been special to her. Probably because she was so much in need of a woman's care. There had been something about her the afternoon of the twins' birthday that had caught her attention. But her own granddaughter Lily was visiting at the same time with baby Beatrice and Mary had slipped from her mind.

'You have a good chin-wag,' said Beattie, kissing her husband. 'I'll meet you back at the car as soon as I can.'

'Repair jobs can't be hurried,' he said, setting his Panama hat at a rakish angle. 'Give Mary my good wishes. If anyone can put new heart into her it will be you. 'Bye, my darling. Have a good picnic.'

Beattie sauntered up and down Shore Lane. It was a squalid waterside slum from what she could see, grown up around the boatyard, the sailmakers and the inevitable public house. She looked at Shore Cottage and her heart sank. It was the last place for a young girl on her own, still, there was not a lot she could do about that. The most she could achieve was to give the girl a happy couple of hours and a good picnic.

Beattie jumped at the shrill whistle from the laundry and stood watching the women pouring out of the gates. What a ragged bunch they were. Laughing, nudging and swearing they made their way home past her watchful eye. She made out Mary dawdling along with a woman rolling a cigarette. Beattie studied her erstwhile neighbour and her heart was moved to pity. How thin she had become. How beaten she looked.

'Mary. Mary, love,' she called.

'Gran,' she said, hurrying towards her.

Beattie would like to have gathered her up in her arms but instinct told her to wait. Mary would not want her workmates to see her cry. 'Fancy a picnic down by the water?'

''Bye, Janey, see you tomorrer,' she said to her friend, then smiled at Beattie. 'I'll get out of me work clothes first.'

'Going to show me your new home?'

Mary blushed. 'Bit of a tip, it is.'

'Another time. I'll go onto the beach and find us a spot. Fetch us a couple of cups, will you? I've brought some home-made lemonade.'

'Won't be long,' said Mary, fetching her key from a string around her neck.

Beattie stepped onto the stones on the meagre strip of beach, nodding to a grizzled waterman sat in the back of his boat sorting out his fishing tackle. She went along closer to the ferry and found a stretch of shingle near an upturned boat. Taking her blanket she spread it out on the beach beside her picnic basket. It was strange how much further away the ground became as one grew older, she mused. Being an old woman didn't suit her at all. Oh, for a body she could rely on. Gingerly Beattie lowered herself onto the shingle. Gratefully she leant against the upturned boat. To think she used to run across the stones in her bare feet – but that was half a century ago.

'Settle yourself down, my duck,' she said as Mary made her way towards her. 'What'll it be? Potted meat sandwich or cheese and piccalilli?'

'Cheese, please. The cups ain't up to much, but least they're clean.'

Beattie busied herself unstoppering the lemonade and pouring it into the cups. She studied Mary closely. The girl looked washed out. There were shadows under her eyes and her nails were bitten down to the quick.

'What's up?' she asked, passing her the lemonade.

Mary looked cornered. 'Just tired,' she said, looking away.

'It's more than that. We're old pals, you and me.' Mary had such prickly pride and she knew from past experience that care had to be taken not to offend her.

'I've made a muck of everythink,' she muttered.

Beattie laid her hand on her arm, intuitively knowing what was coming. 'Doubt if you mucked it up on your own,' she said, passing her another sandwich.

'Having a kid.' She blurted it out her face turned away.

'You must feel very frightened,' she said, 'and alone.'

Mary nodded. 'Told Matthew last night. He don't want it neither. Should've known he'd want to wriggle out of it.'

'Has he said as much?'

She shook her head. 'Looked like he was gonna be sick, when I told him. Said it would change everythink.'

'How long have you known about the baby?' Beattie asked.

''Bout a month now.'

'Well, you've had time to get used to the idea. What did you expect Matthew to say when you told him? Did you think he would be delighted?'

'Well, no,' Mary squirmed under Beattie's questioning. 'Just didn't reckon on him looking so down in the mouth about it all.'

'Has he said that he doesn't want to help you and your baby?'

'Said we'll have to get married earlier than he'd planned.'

'Didn't think by the look of him that he was a fly-by-night sort of chap.'

Mary stared at the stones. 'He was good really, considering.'

'Considering what?'

'Considering I was such a cow to him.'

'So you've put him to the test and he hasn't been found wanting. You're a lucky girl. Here, have another sandwich,' ordered Beattie. 'Sounds as if things are not as bad as I thought. What you need is a bit more support, a bit of feeding up and more rest. If you feel better everything can be managed. And you know, my duck, little babies bring their own love with them.'

'D'you think so?' asked Mary, doubtfully.

'I know so,' said the old woman, taking Mary's cup and refilling it. 'Look at your Blyth. Four children already and along he comes, number five, and gets showered with affection. Don't s'pose your mum was best pleased to know she was pregnant again, with your dad and Harry away in the war and not enough money to go round.'

Mary stared out at the water, saying nothing.

'Your Matthew, what I've seen of him, is a good lad. He's in work and that's a blessing at the moment. Hundreds of women having to have their babies in the workhouse and that's not a beginning I'd wish on anyone.'

'I was thinking of getting meself fixed up somewhere, finding a woman who would get rid of it.'

Beattie lunged forward and gripped Mary's arms, satisfied to see that she had frightened her. 'Now you listen to me,' she said. 'Don't you ever, ever think of such a thing. You could die. Matthew would never get over the shock. Even if you managed to lose the baby, what happens later when you're ready to start a family and you've damaged your insides beyond saving? This is a baby, not a disease. It's something you made together out of love. Matthew will support you and I will be with you all the way. And, what about your dad, how d'you think he'd feel if you died? Don't you think he's lost enough in his life?'

Mary started to cry and Beattie gathered her up in her

arms. 'You are my lionheart,' she whispered fiercely. 'You're a fighter and a survivor. With help you'll come through this, trust me. Have you been to the doctor?'

'Going tomorrer,' Mary muttered.

'Good girl,' said Beattie. 'Once you know that everything's all right and when his nibs is likely to arrive, you can get yourself organised. For instance, where do you think you'll live?'

'Dunnow. Managing all right with Jabez. Since I helped him with his dog he's been quite pally. Even said I could dish up the whole place long as I bought the stuff meself.'

Beattie looked sceptical. 'It'll do pro tem, I suppose, but it doesn't look exactly spacious. What will the old codger do when you and Matthew are there with a baby and all that that means?'

'Dunnow,' said Mary. 'I hadn't thought that far.'

'You could go back home.'

'Ain't going home again, be like I was going backwards,' she snapped with some of her old spirit.

Beattie laughed. 'That's my Mary,' she said. 'I shall help you all I can but you have to make me a promise.'

'What's that?' she mumbled.

'You will not go to some back-street crone with filthy hands and put your life in danger.'

Mary looked away.

'Are you listening to me?' demanded Beattie, gripping her arms, knowing she was hurting her.

'No, no, all right, I won't. Stop, you're pinching,' Mary cried, trying to wrench free of Beattie's grasp.

'You have got to promise me, or I will do nothing.'

'I promise,' Mary gasped, before bursting into tears.

While she sobbed against her shoulder Beattie looked out across the harbour. It was a beautiful late afternoon in June with the sun glinting on the water and the sky blue and cloudless. How cruel life is, she thought. We women are given such powerful urges, and then the moment we succumb to them the consequences hit us like a sledgehammer – five minutes of passion and a lifetime of regret. If I could have five minutes with the Almighty, she railed, I'd tell him a thing or two. She wanted to weep for the child lying unwelcome in the womb. Instead, she offered Mary a tea-cloth to dry her tears. 'Well this has been a queer picnic and no mistake,' Beattie said, smiling at her. 'You know, the sea air has given me an appetite. I don't know about you, but I could do with another sandwich.'

'You really think I'll manage?' asked Mary, after she had helped herself to a second piece of fruit cake.

'Certain of it,' said Beattie. 'Bit by bit you'll get there. Baby's not going to be here for quite a while yet. What you got to do is fix yourself up with a doctor and give that fiancé of yours a chance to get used to the idea. Now, help me on to my feet and I'll come and give your room the once over.'

'Good evening to you,' she said to the man sat outside with his dog. 'I am Mary's grandmother, and who might you be?'

'Name's Churt, Jabez Churt, waterman. We Churts bin watermen for centries.'

'Looking at your cottage I can believe it,' she said, frostily. 'I think your landlord has been most remiss to have let it get into such a state of dilapidation.'

'It's mine,' said Jabez, glaring at her. 'And I'll thank you to mind yer own business.'

'It is my business,' snapped Beattie, 'when my grand-daughter is living in such squalor. Does the council know that you are actually charging her rent?'

She had the satisfaction of seeing him squirm.

'You don't look like no grass to me,' he blustered.

'I shall have a look around,' she said, enjoying herself hugely, 'and see what needs to be done.'

She followed Mary up the stairs and tried not to look too dismayed at what she found. What a mean little room it was.

'What d'ya think?' Mary asked.

'Got to catch my breath first,' she gasped, wracking her brains for something encouraging to say. 'It's a real challenge,' she managed at last. 'A matter of making the most of the space you got.'

'What you mean?'

'Well, you've got very limited floor space and not much height. If you had a little bed, you could store things underneath. If Churt lets you keep your food and pots and pans downstairs, that'll release a bit of room. Then you could have a couple of fold-up chairs. Perhaps Matthew could put some hooks in the walls to hang things from. Those curtains need burning. I've got some nice yellow gingham ones that would cheer it up no end.' Already she could see Mary brightening.

'It sounds good,' she said, 'but I haven't got much saved yet.'

'This will be my gift as your adopted grandmother,' said Beattie, smiling at her. 'But we haven't finished yet. I must go downstairs and see what improvements I can scare Churt into there.'

The waterman glared at her. 'This is my quarters,' he announced.

'Doesn't it say on the legal rent book that tenants must have the use of washing, cooking and toilet facilities?' she said, making it up as she went along. 'My husband is a landlord and would be only too willing to step over and advise you,' she said sweetly.

'She could always find somewhere more suited,' he said. 'Didn't want her in the first place.'

'Glad enough of the rent, though,' she snapped. 'It's the

second of June. You must have just received a full month's rent.'

He nodded unwillingly.

'Here's what we'll do,' said Beattie. 'You fulfil my requirements and I think I might be able to restrain the rent officer.' While he was struggling not to hit her Beattie swooped down and took hold of the doormat and hefted it out into the lane. 'That's sweetened things up already,' she smiled. 'A few little imaginative touches are all that it takes to turn a hovel into a home.'

'Going out on the water,' he growled, 'come on, Dog.

'Can we say we have reached an agreement?' asked Beattie smiling graciously.

'Long as you gets out of me hair.'

'I shall be around tomorrow morning at ten with my list and a few pieces of furniture for my granddaughter. My husband will accompany me,' said Beattie. 'One visit will be sufficient, I think.'

'More than enough,' growled Jabez, pushing past her.

Mary laughed. 'You was wonderful!' she gasped. 'He was eating out of your hand.'

'I always think if you can't fight it's a good idea to wear a big hat.'

'Will you really be round tomorrow?'

'Certainly. I'll phone the laundry and say that you are sick. We'll visit the doctor and then you will know when his nibs is due. By the time you see Matthew tomorrow evening he will see a different girl entirely.' She gave Mary a hug. 'Two determined women can move mountains.'

Mary rewarded her with a smile. 'Dunnow what I'd do without you,' she said, flinging her arms around her.

'Well, you won't have to find out. I've appointed myself your grandmother so you will have to show me the proper respect.'

*   *   *

'How was your afternoon?' asked Albert, holding open the car door.

Beattie chuckled. 'I had a wonderful time, throwing my weight about, right left and centre. But the main success was leaving Mary smiling. Oh, by the way, we shall need to be over here tomorrow by ten o'clock sharp.'

'Right ho, Boadicea,' he said, drawing away from the kerb.

Beattie chuckled, but her heart wasn't in it. Poor Mary, she thought, it's going to take me all my energy and prayers to see her safely through.

28

Charles sat on the train to London on his way to meet Lettice. He viewed their meeting as if it were a naval engagement. Whatever it took in terms of humiliation he had got to keep the upper hand. Protection of the children was all that mattered. Or was it? Protection was part of it but the greater consideration was not losing their love to Lettice's extravagant treats and overwhelming charm. What if she found a way to take them away from him? Winning one of the opening skirmishes by refusing to meet her at Churchill's and lunching at a restaurant of his choosing was, he knew, a hollow victory. She would make him feel petty and provincial and wrong foot him from the start. Charles patted his inside pocket as if for luck. Inside were the children's most recent photographs. He slid them out of the envelope and stared at them trying to draw strength for the fight ahead.

There was Lottie with her friend Kate, in the school garden by the rabbit hutch. Both girls were holding up their pets to the camera. At almost eight Charlotte was tiny. She had Lettice's stature but as yet no inkling of her mother's beauty. Her straight blonde hair was blowing about her face and she was laughing. Dear, dear Lottie, he thought, so gentle and concerned. Was he being fair in excluding her mother from her life? he wondered.

'I want to be an animal doctor, Daddy,' she had said to him, on his last visit. 'Do you think I can?'

'Of course,' he had said, touched by her earnestness.

Charles slipped the photograph back into the envelope and studied the one of Miles in cricketing flannels. It was like studying a picture of himself, at eleven years old. There was the same earnest expression in his eyes and the same tight grip on the bat. Did he miss Lettice, he wondered. Like himself, Miles kept his hurts very much to himself.

Replacing the envelope in his pocket Charles stared out of the window as the fields, dappled in sunshine, gave way to the houses of Godalming. If only Lettice had been capable of compromise.

At last with much belching of steam the train arrived at Waterloo. Charles left his unread copy of *The Times* on his seat and strode onto the platform, glad of a chance to stretch his legs. He walked over Westminster Bridge and stood halfway across, staring down at the Thames swirling below him. It was alive with shipping: barges bringing coal from the north to heat the capital and drive her engines, naval frigates on courtesy visits and little pleasure steamers crammed with visitors to the city. Ahead of him the Houses of Parliament, their honey-coloured towers piercing the sky, delighted him every time he saw them. What perfection! Charles, the least jingoistic of men, allowed himself a small measure of patriotic pride. After an hour or so strolling around Westminster Abbey, feeling dwarfed and insignificant by the company of dead heroes and the damp smell of bones, he shivered and left by the west door.

Charles hailed a taxi to Chez Patrice a French restaurant he had eaten at before with a fellow captain and his wife. It was small and elegant and he felt fairly certain that it would be unfamiliar to Lettice. Meeting his ex-wife on her own territory would have given her an opening advantage. He had also to get there first so that he could see her first and gauge her mood.

He had finished his aperitif and was feeling hungry as he

watched the waiters bearing steaming plates past his table. Was she going to stand him up? No, it was her habit to keep people waiting and to make an entrance. As he studied the menu for the fifth time Charles became aware of a stir of interest among his fellow diners. Lettice swept in. It was a shock to see her after so much time apart. He had forgotten how beautiful she was. After smiling at the waiter and allowing him to take her coat, Lettice drifted towards him. She had on a tiny black hat, little more than a bow concocted from ribbon and feathers. Her hair was cut short and combed around her face like a golden helmet. She was all shimmer and glitter with long diamante earrings and a black satin jacket, trimmed with beads. Around him men were swivelling their heads in her direction. He remembered his own elation at having her on his arm in a different, distant lifetime.

You're batting for Miles and Charlotte, he reminded himself as he stood up and held back her chair.

'Hello, Lettice,' he said, holding out his hand. 'How are you?' he asked, trying to keep control of his voice.

'Darling,' she said, standing on tiptoe and kissing the air beside his cheek, 'lovely to see you. This is a rare treat.'

As she settled her green eyes on him in a slow seductive smile Charles felt everything tighten inside him. 'What will you have to drink?' he asked, struggling for composure.

'A Chablis, if you please. I've developed rather a taste for it.' Lettice looked around the room. 'What a dear little place – how clever of you to have found it.' She opened her handbag, took out a handkerchief and pressed it to her lips, leaving a trace of scarlet on the lace edging.

Charles watched her with reluctant fascination.

Lettice smiled. 'You know, darling,' she said, 'this is just like old times.'

Charles took refuge behind the menu.

'I hope you've brought the photos. I'm desperate to see them.'

Reluctantly he took the envelope from his pocket and placed it on the table between them.

Lettice took out the snapshots and studied them greedily. 'My babies, they're growing up so fast. Poor Lottie, what a dreadful haircut, she looks as if it was done with a knife and fork.' She took the picture in her hand and kissed it, tears glistening in her eyes. 'Miles looks terribly like you, Charles.' She smiled at her son and blinked away her tears. 'I can see he has your earnestness. I hope he will not be such a worrier.' She put the picture away without a kiss this time. 'These last two years has been a desperately sad time for me,' she said, fiddling with the strap on her slim, gold watch. 'I have missed them so much.'

'Your separation from them has not been my doing. At the time of our divorce you were only too eager to swan off with Lawrence Davenport, leaving Miles and Charlotte crying for you. I'm sure your husband has consoled you for your loss,' he said, bitterly.

'There is a streak of vindictiveness in you, Charles, which is most unattractive,' she snapped, her faced flushed and eyes sparkling with anger.

He bent his head. Whenever he attempted to challenge her she always turned his words against him. 'Lettice, please,' he sighed. 'I know you want to see the children. That's what this meeting is all about, isn't it?'

'It's Lottie,' she said quietly, studying her hands. 'Looking at the picture makes me ache to see her again.' And then she looked at him. 'You know, Charlie, little girls need their mummies.'

He was like a needle trying to oppose a magnet. 'You haven't mentioned Miles,' he said. 'Don't you want to see him, too?'

'I'm sure he is fully taken up with boys' things, now,' she said. 'It's Lottie who needs me.'

This was breathtaking.

'And how would I explain to him that his mother is in London and doesn't want to see him?'

'Have you decided yet?' asked the waiter, gliding up to them.

Charles forced his facial muscles into a smile. 'Why don't we have a truce while we eat. The food really is delicious. The spring lamb looks good, or perhaps the poussin? How about starting with asparagus and Hollandaise sauce. I seem to remember that was one of your favourites.'

'Why not?' she purred, smiling up at him beneath her lashes. 'I'm entirely in your hands, darling, and flattered that you haven't forgotten all my little foibles. All we need to do is smooth out a few wrinkles.'

Charles ordered their starter and a bottle of Chablis, to be followed by the lamb.

After the waiter had poured the wine he raised his glass. 'To the children,' he said.

'To Charlotte and Miles,' she said, clinking her glass against his. After the starter was finished she dabbed at her lips with the linen serviette, smiling at him all the while. 'Of course I should like to see Miles if Miles would like to see me. What is your difficulty, Charles?'

He struggled against becoming enmeshed again in the delicate threads of her seduction. How reasonable she sounded. 'They must be treated fairly, Lettice, and you must let me ask them what they would like to happen. Perhaps a day out in Dorchester or something like that,' he said guardedly.

'Pooh!' she scoffed. 'A day out. I was thinking of a week in London. We can hardly break the ice in a day trudging around Dorset. You'll be suggesting Lavinia comes as guard dog next.' She smiled spitefully. 'Or should it be guard bitch.'

Charles gulped down the urge to answer back. That would be too satisfying for Lettice, to see that she was getting under his skin. Instead he concentrated on eating the lamb. It was difficult to convey the impression of enjoying the meal with his stomach in turmoil. Swallowing down the food she had robbed of any flavour took all his concentration.

'Don't you trust me, Charles?' Lettice was flushed.

Again he tried to swivel his eyes away from her mesmeric stare.

'Lettice, it isn't about us. Miles and Charlotte have settled well at school and they are beginning to make friends. Coming back into their lives after all this time will be a shock to them. You will have to be patient and win their trust again – and mine,' he added.

'Surely we can be grown-up about this. Our falling out is all water under the bridge, now.'

'Grown-ups make compromises,' he said, putting down his knife and fork, the lamb barely touched, 'and don't take things for granted.'

'Well,' she sighed, 'if you are determined to be churlish, perhaps I could rent a house near the school and they could visit me there. They could bring their chums to stay.'

'I don't know, Lettice . . .' He felt himself floundering, like a fish on the end of her line. 'Provided I am convinced that that is what they would like to do,' he said grudgingly, wanting to kick himself for being outmanoeuvred.

'What shall we have for pudding?' she asked, changing tack. 'Oh, look, darling, they have your favourite *tarte tatin*. You're not the only one who remembers.' She smiled at him and he felt the pain of losing her tug at him afresh.

Remember the children, he prompted himself. After three glasses of Chablis and Lettice's scented closeness he was struggling to keep himself on course. How often intimate little lunches like this had ended in Lettice taking him to bed

– at least in the early days. 'Coffee?' he suggested. 'Afterwards I must go. I need to be back by six for the Chess Club.'

'Yes, please, darling,' she said. 'Now' – she leaned forward, confidentially – 'do tell, what really happened between you and little Cissie?'

'It was all a dreadful mistake,' he said, startled at the mention of her name but wary also. Lettice was incapable of the innocent remark. 'I took her to be an intruder. Do you know, the poor girl had been sleeping up in that attic in the cold and the dark for years? She was homeless and in such poor health.'

'I'd heard she was a common tart,' said Lettice, fitting a cigarette into an elegant tortoiseshell holder. 'Light, Charles, if you please.'

'She was certainly on the brink of destitution,' he said, very aware of Lettice's fingers resting on his arm. 'Prostitution was never mentioned as far as I know. She is working for the Salvation Army, so I believe, at the moment.'

As they sipped the coffee, Lettice smiled at him. 'I will be the soul of patience, Charlie, if you will only let me see them.'

'I will go down and talk to them this weekend,' he said. 'But I make no promises.'

'You realise I could have gone already,' she said, 'but I wanted to do things properly.'

Had she tried already? he wondered. The headmaster and his wife at Chantry House would surely have told him.

Lettice changed tack. 'We did have some good times, didn't we?' she said. 'Do you remember that weekend in France? I'm sure that was when Lottie was conceived.'

Charles blushed, furious with himself. There wasn't a trick she wouldn't try in order to get what she wanted.

Remember? – how could he possibly forget? Lettice had been totally abandoned, wandering naked through the little

flat they had rented in Normandy. She had tasted of the sea.
He looked up from his dessert and saw her smiling at him.

'Do you remember coating me with honey?' she asked.

Her calculated seduction wounded him. Of course he
wanted her. He always had. It was the look of utter boredom
in her eyes that had almost destroyed it. Hanging on to his
tattered self-respect he turned his head away. 'Waiter,' he
called, 'the bill.'

'I will await your phone call,' she said, sliding the handles
of her bag over her wrist, withering him with a contemptuous
smile. 'But remember they are my children every bit as much
as they are yours, more so in fact.'

All his attention was focused on not letting his hand tremble
as he wrote the cheque. He felt exhausted – wrung out by a
coil of twisting emotions. 'Shall I call you a taxi?' he asked,
as the waiter helped her into her coat.

'No need,' she said. 'My car is outside. Can I drop you at
the station? It's a long walk.'

Charles shook his head, and stared at his feet while Lettice
stood on tiptoe and treated him to another of her phan-
tom kisses. 'I shall wait to hear from you, darling. Please,
please, hurry.'

He nodded and she wafted away on her usual cloud of
L'Aimant. Feeling thoroughly wrong-footed he strode back
towards Westminster Bridge refusing to look at the little red
sports car parked outside Chez Patrice.

It was shaming to realise that however much he had come
to dislike Lettice, his desire for her was undiminished.

29

‘Come in the pair of you and welcome.’ Matthew’s friend, an older, stockier man, shook her hand and smiled at her. ‘I’m George. Pleased to meet you, Mary. I’ll call Mother, she’s upstairs with the baby.’

Mary looked about her. The little house smelt of lavender polish and was filled with pictures of children and submarines. A starched white cloth was on the table and six plates and cups and saucers. She stood shyly in the doorway not knowing what to do.

‘Mother, the love-birds are here,’ called George. ‘Sit down in the easy-chair, Dusty. Let’s be having your raincoat, I’ll stow it in the hall.’

Matthew stood in the hall talking to his friend while Mary took in the handmade rug and embroidered firescreen. On the mantelpiece was a picture of two boys in knitted jerseys playing football. She supposed them to be about seven and nine years old.

‘That’s my lads, Martin and Oliver. Grand boys, they’ll be home from Sunday school soon,’ said George, smiling proudly.

Mary cleared her throat, feeling that some comment was required. ‘They look like you,’ she said.

‘Wait till you see young Peter, the image of Mother, he is.’

‘What, your mother?’

‘No, Vi. Sorry,’ George laughed, ‘what with the children, I’ve got into the habit of calling her “mother”.’

Mary kept the smile pinned to her face. That was one thing she wouldn't have Matthew doing. The only people to call her mother would be the nippers.

'Hark! That's her coming down, now. I'll just stick the kettle on.'

'I'll give you a hand,' said Matthew disappearing into the kitchen.

The door opened and a neat little woman with glasses came in, carrying a chubby baby. 'Hello, Mary. Sorry I was busy, dear. Just hold baby, will you, and I'll bring in his pram, then we can settle to a nice chat.'

The baby gave her a long unblinking stare. He was rosy cheeked from sleep and smelled of milk and talcum powder. 'Hello, Peter,' she said, jiggling him awkwardly on her lap. His face crumpled and his blue eyes filled with tears.

'Never known him to do that before,' said Vi, bustling in and taking Peter from Mary's arms. She strapped him into a gleaming black-and-white pram, clucking and cooing at him all the while.

'He looks bonny,' Mary said, trying to sound enthusiastic.

'Light of my life,' said Vi, settling herself in the other arm-chair. 'Thought our baby days were over but, however much of a surprise, they bring their love with them, don't they?'

Mary was rescued from answering by a loud rapping on the front door.

'The boys. 'Scuse I,' said their mother, rushing to the door. 'Martin, Oliver, say hello to our visitor. Her name's Miss Nugent.'

They stood staring at her.

'I've got a brother about your age,' she said, to the older one, swallowing down her shyness. 'His name's Blyth.'

'Funny name,' he said, still staring.

'He's the only one I know. But it's because of a special thing that happened.'

'What did?' demanded the younger one.

'Well,' she said, smiling with relief as Matthew came back into the room, 'my Dad was shipwrecked in the war and we all thought he was drowned, but he was rescued by a lifeboat and taken to a place called Blyth in Northumberland. So when my brother was born we called him Blyth.'

'What's he like?' asked Martin, the big boy.

Matthew sat on the arm of her chair and Mary struggled on. The Kendall family were like no people she had ever met before. She felt smothered by all their woollies and their snugness. 'He's nearly ten but not as big as you, Martin. He loves drawrin' and chess and stuff. Wants to design battleships when he's older.'

'I'm going to be a footballer like Dixie Dean,' the boy said, looking up at Matthew.

'Gonna be a baker,' said Oliver. 'Get to eat all the cakes.'

Everyone laughed.

'Tea's ready, come to the table all of you,' said Vi, carrying in a tray from the kitchen, with plates piled with sandwiches.

Mary was just about to reach across the table when Matthew nudged her.

Everyone had their eyes closed.

'For what we are about to receive,' said George, his hands clasped together in prayer, 'may the Lord make us truly thankful. Amen.'

Everyone chorused, 'Amen.'

Flushing with embarrassment Mary sat with her hands on her lap.

'What would you like?' asked George. 'Cheese and tomato or egg and cress or fish-paste and cucumber. He smiled. 'Why not have one of each?'

She did as he suggested and passed the plate on. The boys sat there politely waiting their turn. What a difference to the carry-on at Lemon Street, Mary thought.

'Have you set the date for the wedding?' asked Vi later, slicing up a Victoria sponge.

'July the thirty-first,' said Matthew, 'at the Registry Office over here in Gosport.'

'Aren't you having a church wedding?' said Vi.

Mary blushed. 'I wasn't christened so it's got to be the registry.'

'You must be so disappointed,' said Vi. 'No white dress and no veil. If it were me I'd be heartbroken.'

'But it isn't,' said Mary, feeling her temper rising.

'Marrying the right girl is all that matters,' said Matthew, kicking her beneath the table. 'And Mary's the one for me.'

She gave him a grateful smile. His face was flushed with shyness and she knew it had taken courage to stand up for her. When, when could they escape?

The baby woke up and began to wail. 'Shall I pick him up?' said Mary, anxious to change the subject. She went across to the pram and undid the straps and lifted Peter into her arms. This time he rewarded her with a chuckle 'You're a big boy,' she gasped as she felt his full weight. Mary sat with him in the armchair while Vi refilled the teacups and handed round the cake.

'Are you having a little party after the wedding?' she asked. 'Only you could come here if there weren't too many. Of course, we couldn't agree to any drink but . . .'

'No need, thanks,' Mary plunged in. 'My grandmother has everything arranged.'

Matthew looked at her in surprise. 'I didn't know that?' he said accusingly.

'Only found out yesterday,' she lied. The thought of Dad and the rest of the family having to sit here praying and drinking lemonade didn't bear thinking about. However makeshift and second-best the wedding was likely to be, it was still her day.

'Well, I'm sure you'll be most welcome,' he said.

'Of course,' said Mary, trying to sound enthusiastic.

'Where you going to live?' asked Vi, not to be thrown off course.

'We've got rooms for the moment down in Shore Lane,' said Matthew, 'but we'll get somewhere else as soon as we can.'

'Bet you're counting the days to be done with that laundry,' Vi said. 'Those girls are such a rough lot.'

'Can we play Snakes and Ladders after tea?' asked Oliver.

'That would be a great idea,' said Matthew, choking off Mary's angry retort to Vi.

''Course you can, boy,' said his dad. 'Me and Matthew will give you a game while the ladies have a chat in the kitchen.'

'Rather play with you,' said Mary, smiling at the lad. 'You better take Peter,' she said to Vi. 'I think he needs changing.'

Matthew smoothed things over by helping in the kitchen while Mary had a noisy game with the boys. At seven o'clock they made their excuses and left.

'Why did you have to be so awkward?' he asked as they walked home over Haslar Bridge.

'They're your friends,' she said. 'Now don't get all sulky. I 'spect I'll get to like them in time but I wants Gran to give me a party. 'Course they can come if they want to. Felt all the time they was saying, "We're doing things proper and you just watch and learn." Made me mad.'

Matthew laughed. 'I wish you could have seen your face when Vi said it would be a teetotallers' party.'

The laughter blew away all the awkwardness of the afternoon and, linking arms, they strolled down to the High Street.

'You are wicked,' he chuckled. 'When you said you'd rather play Snakes and Ladders than wash up I thought Vi would throw a fit.'

'It was mean, I know,' she admitted, 'but I knew she wanted to worm out of me all about the baby and then be all sympathetic. Well, I want our nipper and I can do without her feeling sorry.'

'D'you mean that?' he asked. 'Really?'

Mary smiled. 'I think I do,' she said, surprising herself. 'Yes, yes, I really do.' She squeezed his hand. 'Race you to the ferry.' Running, laughing and gasping for breath they eventually arrived at Shore Lane to see an ambulance drawing away from Jabez's cottage.

A man came towards them with Dog beside him with a rope lead. 'You Mary Nugent?' he asked. 'Jabez wants you to look after the dog.'

'What's up with him?' she demanded. 'He ain't dead, is he?'

'Poor bugger slipped on the jetty over Pompey. I brought him back across but he was in agony. Wanted him to get sorted out over there, but he wouldn't wear it. "Get me home, the lass will care for me." Of course, he couldn't set foot out the boat. Landlord at the Vixen phoned the ambulance. He'll be took to the War Memorial Hospital. Reckon he might've broke his leg. I've moored up the boat and he asked me most partickler for you to have the key and look out for the mutt, here.'

''Course I will,' Mary said. 'I'll go and see him tomorrer, after work.'

Dog leapt up at Mary and began to lick her face and the waterman hung about expectantly.

Matthew took a couple of shillings from his pocket and handed it to him. 'Thank you for looking after him,' he said. 'We're obliged to you.'

'Thank you, sailor, much obliged,' he said, making his way towards the Vixen.

'Old scrounger,' said Mary.

'Ought to be grateful to him. You might have ended up with a crusty old invalid on your hands.'

She laughed. 'A two bob well spent. Wonder how long he'll be away? Might have the place to ourselves for a while – only three weeks to the wedding. How long do you think broken legs takes to mend?'

'At least six weeks,' said Matthew, grinning at her.

'Whatever time it is there's one thing I'm doing straight off.' Fishing in her pocket she took out the door key and turned it in the lock. Once inside she took up the stinking mat and dragged it into the lane. 'Tomorrer I'll get shot of that in a bin somewhere. Ooh! I'll scrub this place from top to bottom.' She turned and smiled at him. 'Old Vi Kendall will be able to eat her dinner off this floor by the time I'm done with it. But first we'll have a drop of shandy. Fancy some?' she asked.

They climbed the stairs closely followed by Dog.

'Beginning to look quite homey, now,' said Matthew, looking around at the new curtains and matching bedspread. 'Looks much bigger with all the boxes stowed under the bed. Where did you get those folding chairs?'

'Granny Pragnell sent them round. Been my fairy godmother, she has.'

'Even giving you a party,' he said; 'very generous.'

Mary blushed. 'All right, I made it up,' she confessed, 'but I'm sure she'll help me.'

'Did you make it up about being pleased about the baby?' he asked, drawing her towards him.

Mary kissed him. 'No,' she whispered against his neck. 'Something happened this morning that made me want him.'

'Tell me.'

'I was lying in bed and I had this funny feeling in me belly. Thought it was wind. Then I put me hand down there and it was like a flickering. It happened again.'

'What was it?'

'Called quickening,' she said. 'It's the baby beginning to move.'

'Really?' Matthew grinned in delight. 'D'you think if you lie down again it might move for me?'

'Let's try,' she said, grinning back at him.

He kissed her, then walked his fingers down the buttons on her dress. They waited expectantly for something to happen.

'Perhaps I need to get closer,' he suggested.

Mary slid out of her dress and lay in her petticoat with Matthew's hand on her belly.

'I can't feel anything,' he whispered.

'Why are you whispering,' she giggled, 'he can't hear you? Besides, he's not moving at the moment.'

'Because I'm so excited,' he said. 'How d'you know he's not moving?' he asked.

She burst out laughing. 'Because he's inside me, you daft 'aporth.'

Matthew began to kiss her neck. 'Four months old, I wonder what he looks like?'

Mary giggled.

He kissed her breasts and then her ribs. She closed her eyes, feeling drowsy with desire. Waves of feeling crept across her body. 'Ooh!' She murmured, 'that's lovely.'

Matthew sat up and began to take off his clothes. 'Perhaps he's sleeping in there. We might need to wake him up.'

Kissing and giggling she helped him out of his uniform. Dog stared reproachfully at her. 'Let's find you a treat,' she said, taking half a pork pie she had set aside for supper, out of her food box. 'Here,' she called, at the open door.

Dog followed eagerly as she threw the pie down the stairs. Closing the door quietly behind her she returned to the bed.

Mary lay down beside him. 'Let's take our time,' she said, slipping her arms around him. This was what she had needed

– this gradual unfolding. They lay together looking at one another, kissing and touching, trailing their fingers over each other's skin. 'Yes,' she sighed to herself. 'We are going to be happy.'

30

Matthew sat on a bollard blowing smoke rings and watching them float upwards in the still summer air. Below him the submarines lay tethered side by side. How ungainly they looked on the surface. Three boats along was the *L75* in for battery change. It was like a gutted fish with cables running like entrails between her and the dock side. This was the public face of submarines. Only he knew the grace and ease of them below the surface and the sense of brotherhood between the men.

It was seven o'clock on the last morning of July. In five hours he was getting married. In these moments alone he tried to tease out his thoughts before being overtaken by the day. He looked forward to having a home and someone to share his plans and dreams. In the last few weeks, since Jabez had been carted off to hospital, he and Mary had had the cottage to themselves and revelled in their privacy. Having more time together had helped draw them closer to one another. Alone with him Mary emerged from beneath her shell. How warm and loving she became – how easy to be with. Matthew had shared with her things he had never thought to share with anyone. Yesterday she had pressed his hand on her belly and he'd felt his son move beneath his fingers. He had wanted to cry at the wonder of it. Being a father, having a home to return to and a woman who loved him – nothing in his single life could compare with that sense of belonging.

How would the day go? he wondered. Would there be

last-minute hitches or unforeseen disasters? Mary had assured him there was little expected of him but to turn up on time and to make a speech. Matthew took a well-creased sheet of paper out of his trouser pocket. Yes, it was all there, thanks to Mary for saying yes, compliments to the bridesmaids and gratitude to his father-in-law for giving his permission for the wedding to take place. He laughed. In the face of his daughter's determination, Fred's refusal would count for nothing. He had even included a few nautical jokes but nothing too outrageous. He would leave that to Bob, his best man.

Matthew drew thoughtfully on his cigarette. Could he be all the things he wanted: husband, father and submariner? He looked across the harbour. There in Lemon Street, Mary would be sleeping, lying on her side, her thumb in her mouth, looking like a child. He turned back to *Dolphin* impatient for the five hours to pass.

Through a gap in the curtain the sun shone on her face and Mary climbed up to wakefulness. Minute by minute the knowledge of the day and what it would mean for her filled her thoughts. She stretched luxuriously. It was here. She had only to say, yes. At that word the ties to Lemon Street would be unloosed and she would step away from them. Matthew would stretch out his hand and she would take it.

Hanging from the picture rail was a blue suit and white blouse. Mary bit her lip. It was not the bridal outfit of her dreams. But she had never pictured herself as a pregnant bride getting married in a registry office. All her childhood games had involved a veil, a white dress and a triumphal procession to St George's Church, Portsea. She and the twins had made confetti from bus tickets and thrown it over each other. But today she must abandon her dreams. Matthew had said that marrying the right girl was all that mattered. She needed to cling to that to get her through the day.

Looking around her it was difficult to believe that this had once been her bedroom – a sanctuary from the demands of Dad and the nippers. Blyth had made it so much his own now, with all his drawings and models. It had been good of Gran to let her brother stay with them last night, for a treat. She needed these last moments to herself to say goodbye to her life in Lemon Street. Here she had fought her way out of childhood, dragging her brother and sisters behind her. To survive she had built herself a protective wall. Patiently, brick by brick, Matthew had helped her to take it down.

But it had not been completely demolished – simply lowered a few feet. Mary looked at the roses in the jam jar on the chest of drawers. She had got Blyth to pinch them from Victoria Park, so that her mother would be present at her wedding. It was there that Mummy used to take her when Harry was at school, before the twins came. She would make her daisy chains and sing to her. Those moments were the jewels in an otherwise stony childhood. 'Please let it be a happy day', she whispered.

Someone knocked on the door. 'Who is it?' she called.

'Mary, love, are you awake? Brought you some tea,' called Dad.

'Come in,' Mary said, sitting up in bed and smoothing a place for him to sit.

'Lovely morning, not a cloud in the sky. Be like a millpond going over the water today.' He settled a biscuit-tin lid on the bed between them. Set on top were two cups of tea and two fat bacon sandwiches, wrapped in newspaper napkins.

'Eat hearty, gal. It'll be a while till the party. Don't want yer faintin' or nothin'.'

'Hello, Dad,' she said, smiling into his faded blue eyes. 'How d'you know I was fancying bacon sarnies?'

''Cos I'm your dad,' he said, perching on the edge of the bed.

She chewed thoughtfully. 'This'll be the last time I'll be here as Mary Vine. Next time I'm over I'll be a married woman. Won't be your daughter no more.'

'What you talking about,' he snapped. 'You're me daughter fer life. Matthew's only yer husband from now on. I bin yer dad from the moment you opened your eyes till you closes mine. Through everythink, even when you wished I wasn't. Always, always I'll be your dad and proud of it.'

Mary caught her breath, feeling tears welling up. Her dad! How he had tried her patience, how she had raged at him and yet . . .

'Don't blubber,' he said, 'make the sarnies all wet.'

'I didn't mean to,' she gasped.

'Forget it, love. Just get on with yer breakfast. Got something for ya, nearly forgot.' He dragged a tissue paper package out of his pocket and dropped it into her hand. 'Bin in and out of the pawn shop more times than I can remember,' he said. 'Last time, Granny Pragnell had to redeem it for me, after the fire.'

Mary unfolded the paper. Nestling inside was her mother's locket that she had worn on her wedding day. Pressing her thumbnail against the catch she prised the sides apart and looked at the yellowing images of Dad and Mum.

Dolly Vine smiled out at her. A coronet of roses held her curly hair in check and around her neck was a high lace collar. How innocent and trusting she looked. Only rarely had Mary ever seen her look so happy. Dad was laughing with his head thrown back, looking as if he'd not a care in the world. He was wearing his straw sailor hat and his face was round and free of lines. Mary struggled to find any resemblance to the dad she knew. What were their hopes and dreams? she wondered.

'Let me fix it round your neck,' he said. 'It can serve as the something borrowed you brides worries about.'

'I'll treasure it,' she said, flinging her arms around his neck.

'Know you will, love,' he said. 'Earned it, you have.' As he fastened the clasp he said, 'You and young Dusty is miles readier for marriage than we was. Dolly and me was just a couple of kids. You two will make a much better fist of it.'

'D'you think so?' Mary asked.

'Know so, my duck,' he said, hugging her tight.

At eleven o'clock Mary surveyed herself in the mirror. Refusing to wear a hat she had fastened a blue velvet band behind her fringe and combed her hair in place before dabbing her face with a faint sprinkling of powder, and a touch of cherry lipstick.

'Ready,' she called through the open door.

'You looks a treat,' said Dad, fidgeting with his rosebud buttonhole, before kissing her cheek.

'Merce, don't she look pretty?' said Faith, giving her an enthusiastic hug.

'Not bad,' her sister muttered, grudgingly, more concerned with checking her own outfit. The twins had resurrected two matching scarlet Charleston dresses from their Debonnaire days.

'Smart,' nodded Blyth, bringing up the rear.

As she stepped out on the pavement Dad took her arm. They formed the head of a little procession made up of Blyth and the twins, Cissie and Dora and the Pragnells. The neighbours cheered as they made their way down the street to the harbour.

'Good luck, my babes.'

'May all your troubles be little ones.'

'All the nice girls love a sailor.'

Mary smiled at all their greetings. A few years ago they had sneered at the family and called her a guttersnipe.

Dad chuckled. 'Changed their tune,' he said. 'Fickle as the weather, is neighbours.'

'Eight returns to Gosport,' he said, at the ferry office. 'We're off to my daughter's wedding.'

Everyone laughed at his excitement. On the ferry they were the centre of attention, with Saturday shoppers smiling at them and sailors staring admiringly at the twins.

'This is my day,' she thought with a spurt of her old jealousy.

'Got a minute?' said Gran, taking her to one of the slatted wooden seats inside, out of the wind. Opening her handbag she took out a blue handkerchief. 'This belonged to Matron Sankey,' she said. 'You know, the woman that ran the orphanage I lived in. Better than a mother she was to me.' Gran folded it into Mary's hand. 'It's for you,' she said 'just to remind you, that you may have lost your mother but you've got me.'

'Ta,' Mary gasped, too overcome to say anything more, and gripping Gran's hand and smiling.

'You just enjoy your day and your life.'

Mary nodded and kissed her cheek.

'We're here,' yelled Dad, as the ferry bumped against the jetty. 'Stay together, everyone. Blyth, you got that confetti? Mary, take me arm.'

They walked up the High Street to the registry office laughing and talking to one another.

Mary, desperate for everything to start, paced about the anteroom in a fever of impatience. At last her family were taken into the registry room, leaving her and Dad alone together.

'Make up your mind to be happy, love,' said Dad, taking her hand and kissing it. 'Dusty's a good bloke. Don't nag him.

Count yer blessings. Remember not to take things too serious, and laugh; best glue fer marriage that is.'

Mary smiled. Poor Dad, how tired and makeshift he looked with his shiny suit and patched shoes. She hugged him. 'Let's not be adrift,' she said. 'I can hear me music.'

The pianist struck up the Wedding March on the piano and everyone turned towards the back of the room as the door opened.

Matthew stepped up to the Registrar's table, too nervous to turn round. And then she tapped his hand and he was able to look at her. All his nervousness dropped away. How beautiful she looked. There was a dignity about her that went beyond bridal prettiness. The pink lipstick brightened her pale face and her brown eyes shone. He smiled down at her and she smiled back, giving his hand an answering squeeze.

The Registrar, a thin man in gold wire glasses and a pinstriped suit sprinkled with dandruff, reminded everyone of the seriousness of the event. Then it was Matthew's turn to repeat the words he instructed him to say.

'"I do solemnly declare that I know not of any lawful impediment why I Matthew Vincent Miller may not be joined in matrimony to Mary Dorothy Vine."'

While he spoke Mary looked at him as if he were the only other person in the room. When she had said her words, he took the ring and slid it on her finger, making his vow to her. What little hands she had, like a child's. Her nails were short and unbitten, a real proof of her love.

She held tightly to his arm as she made her promise. '"I call upon these persons here present to witness that I Mary Dorothy Vine do take thee Matthew Vincent Miller to be my lawful wedded husband."'

Everyone cheered and clapped and he kissed her. 'Hello, Mrs Miller,' he whispered.

Mary smiled. 'I am, aren't I?' she said grinning at him.

The Registrar coughed. 'Will you be seated, Mr and Mrs Miller, while we sign the register? And your father, Mr and Mrs Pragnell and Mr Cowley, please.'

As soon as the ink was dry on the signatures the guests spilled onto the High Street, laughing and talking. The Registrar folded the Marriage Certificate and slotted it into an envelope and handed it to Mary. 'We're legal,' she whispered.

'Photographs now,' demanded Blyth, importantly, stepping forward with his Box Brownie camera. 'Bride and groom.'

A little crowd of Saturday shoppers gathered on the pavement opposite, shouting their good wishes.

Mary tugged her husband's arm. 'Look, there's Dog, with Jabez's friend. He's got a ribbon on his collar.'

'Bride and her family,' called Blyth, handing the camera to Matthew.

Matthew looked at them through the lens. How different they looked dressed in their finery. Fred eased the collar of his shirt away from his neck and squared his shoulders before smiling towards him. The twins in matching red outfits primped and preened. Mary put her arm around her father and grinned.

'Listen, you lot,' said Dad, stepping forward importantly, 'two bits of business. First there's bin a bit of a change of tack. Due to the kindness of Mr and Mrs Pragnell the happy couple will be riding around to their party in the car over there.' He pointed to a large, shiny black car with its bonnet festooned with white ribbon.

Mary and Matthew gasped.

'Second, we're having a do at the Ship Leopard and you're all to get yourselves across the water pronto.'

As she and Matthew crossed the street Blyth and the twins pelted them with confetti.

Mary had her handle on the door when someone tugged her

sleeve. It was a child clutching a silver horseshoe. 'Ratulations,' she sniffed thrusting it into her hand.

Behind her was Janey with two children wedged into an old pram between her shopping. 'Hello, babes,' she cried flinging her arms around Mary. 'Good luck to ya. Here's the present from the gals – see them over on the pavement. Give 'em a wave.' She rushed around the car and grabbed Matthew and kissed him on the cheek. 'You're a lucky bugger,' she yelled, in his face. 'She's a good'n. You look after her.'

Mary blushed and waved to the laundry girls while Matthew greeted his shipmates. And then they were whisked away. She turned to him and laughed. 'I feels like a balloon,' she whispered; 'if you don't hold me tight I'll fly away.'

'Happy to oblige,' he grinned.

'Let me look at you, didn't get a chance earlier.' She held him away from her and looked at his ginger hair slicked down with brilliantine and the white ribbon threaded through his lanyard. 'Don't look like my Matthew,' she said, 'you're too shiny.'

'I'll show you the real Matthew, later,' he promised.

They kissed, whispered and giggled all the way back through the country towns and onto Portsea Island. Once outside the pub, they were hurried upstairs to their guests.

'Hurrah! Hurrah!' the upper room erupted. Mary's Dad, beaming from ear to ear, led them to the top table. 'Speech, speech,' the guests roared.

Matthew stumbled through the words he had prepared, giving up halfway and kissing Mary before he sank back into his chair. Fred, well oiled by this time, entirely lost the thread and collapsed in tears. Bob Cowley had everyone bellowing and crying with laughter as he sliced nearer and nearer to the bone. He instructed the bridal pair to report their position at midnight and warned Mary of the wily bed snake.

'Drink up, everyone, and eat hearty,' yelled Fred, when the speeches were exhausted.

Mary looked about her. Granny Pragnell had done them proud. On each table were plates of cold meat, bowls of steaming potatoes, jars of pickles and crusty rolls of bread. She leant across the table and touched the old woman's arm. 'Thanks ever so much, Gran,' she shouted above the din. 'It looks lovely.'

'Wanted it to be a day you'd remember,' Gran said, blushing with pleasure.

'It is,' Mary breathed. 'Won't never forget it, not if I lives to a hundred.' She waved to Dora and Cissie, busy clearing the plates.

'You happy?' she asked Matthew.

'Best day of my life,' he whispered.

The tables were cleared and the girls returned with bowls of trifle. They were rapidly despatched and then Mary and Matthew were required to cut a large iced cake, tied around with a submariner's cap ribbon.

Once the guests had reached bursting point, the plates were removed and the tables pushed back to the sides of the room. Now was the moment for the twins to shine.

Someone had brought a gramophone and Blyth was in charge of winding it and putting on the records.

Faith and Mercy Charlestoned, black-bottomed and tapped away to their hearts' content. Dad performed a wobbly hornpipe and then it was the turn of the pub's famous Silent Band.

Three old men stepped onto the floor and mimed an elaborate tuning-up procedure. Judging from the bulging cheeks of one, the extended fingers of another and the vigorous wrist movements of the third their chosen instruments were a trumpet, mouth organ and drum set. Before each tune the trio mimed the title and the guests sang along, enjoying themselves hugely.

Mary smiled up at Mr Pragnell as he whispered in her ear. 'Give me the signal when you would like to be whisked away,' he whispered.

'When are we ready to go home?' she asked.

Matthew smiled. 'The sooner the better,' he said, kissing her neck.

31

Cissie opened her eyes. It was dark and stuffy in the hut and for the first few seconds she forgot where she was. Birdsong filled the air. Getting to her feet she crept past Captain Kellet's bed and opened the door. It was not yet dawn and the hopfields were shrouded in darkness. She stepped onto the grass, relishing the feel of the dew on her feet. In the distance a row of flickering lights climbed the hill.

When she had seen them on that first morning Cissie had been intrigued.

'It's old Ben's boys,' the Captain had said. 'He gets all the lads up before five and gives them each a jamjar with a string handle. It's filled with tea. When they've drunk it they stick a candle inside and it lights their way up to the hopfields for early picking.'

Even though she had been up in Walfords' Fields helping the Captain look after the babies for two weeks, now, she had not missed one of the jamjar processions.

Tomorrow was Saturday and Clive had written to say that he would be coming out on the bus to see her. It was the first letter she had ever received. I can read every word, she had told the Captain, excitedly. And now she knew them by heart.

Dear Cissie,
I hope you are well and getting Lots of sun and fresh air. On Saturday I will come up and see you.
  God Bless You
  Clive Perks.

She would have liked the word 'love' to be there but that was expecting too much. Had he missed her? Cissie wondered. Their reading lessons had become the highlight of her week and she had even opened her account at the post office at long last. Was it more than kindness that had prompted him to help her? There was something between them, Cissie was sure of it. It was so fragile, this new understanding, that she was afraid to do anything and waited for him to make the first move. Week after week they sat almost touching. Perhaps a day with her in the heat of the hopfields would bring Clive Perks to the boil.

The little hut she shared with Captain Kellet near the estate bungalow was luxurious compared to the hop-pickers' quarters. They had a camp bed each and a cookhouse and toilet set apart from the other pickers. Cissie remembered helping one of the hoppers' families to settle in. She had stood in the field outside the tin-roofed hut looking askance at the huge bale of straw, wondering what it could be for.

Mabel Haskins had spread it thickly across the concrete floor and covered it with bedding, leaving a clear path to the door and upending a tea chest as a makeshift table. 'Don't look much, now,' she said, 'but after a day's picking you'll think it paradise. Where you living?' she asked.

'Up with Captain Kellet, helping with the nippers.'

'You'll have yer hands full.'

'Mabel's right,' the Captain had said. 'A whole catalogue of misadventures. To name just a few: snake bites, sunburn, nettle rash and diarrhoea. They fall out of trees, into the river, fights break out. And there are always a few who try to eat the hops or rub the juice into their eyes. This will be an education to you, my dear.'

Over the two weeks, she had come to know more about Captain Kellet. She was quieter and less ready with a joke than Major Grice but there was a calmness and sureness in her actions that bolstered Cissie's own lack of confidence.

Each night before they settled to sleep she would say: 'Good night, my dear, and God bless you.'

It seemed to set the seal on each day and never had she slept so soundly.

The time flashed by filled with children. She and the Captain pushed them over the fields in two rickety old prams. They picked blackberries, played ball, sang songs; washed and fed them, sorted out their arguments and bandaged cut knees.

And tomorrow, she reminded herself, Clive would be here. Cissie smiled. What would he have made of her letter? she wondered. It had been written with no help at all with a blunt-ended pencil and fingers trembling with excitement. Again she smiled. Perhaps God had begun to look in her direction at last.

Soon it was light and after breakfast the hoppers came past the hut and dropped off the small children on their way up to the fields. They took sandwiches for the boys who had gone up earlier, wrapped in newspaper to keep the hop juice from the bread.

The morning was full of games and singing. At twelve o'clock Cissie spread blankets on the grass and everyone ate their picnic. Captain Kellet drew a piece of paper from her pocket and gave it to Cissie.

'Nesta Gibbons' daughter's had her baby. Little girl, six pounds and twelve ounces. Her husband phoned the farm. Will you give her the news? She'll be so relieved.'

''Course I will. Shall I take the Cattermoles with me?' Cissie asked, beckoning to the three liveliest children.

'Cissie, you're a gem,' laughed the Captain. 'Make sure the boys keep a tight hold of the pram handle, and strap little Maureen in tightly or she'll bounce out when you least expect it.'

As Cissie set out with the children, the fields seemed to simmer in the heat of the afternoon and, pervading everything, was the beery stink of hops. The pickers stood beside huge bins with the hop-bines heaped around them. Above them were the empty poles on which those hops had twined. She searched the rows to find Nesta Gibbons. Eventually she saw her steadily picking at the end of a row, with her distinctive black straw hat and flowered wrapover apron.

'Nesta, over here,' she called; 'got a message for ya.'

'Oh my God.' The new grandmother's freckled hands flew to her mouth. ''Tain't nothing wrong with my Ruby, is there?' Her eyes filled with tears.

'Had her baby, little girl,' smiled Cissie, delighted to be the bringer of good news. 'Six pounds and twelve ounces.'

She was hugged fiercely by the joyous Nesta and a cheer went up from the other pickers as the news spread along the rows. Even the Cattermole children got hugged and kissed.

'Sit down a mo,' said Cissie; 'have a drop of barley water. If you keep an eye on the nippers I'll do a bit of picking for you. Just tell me what I gotta do.'

Nesta pointed to the gold-coloured, feathery hops. 'Pull them off gentle and don't press them down in the bin. They're measured by space not weight.'

The sun beat down and Cissie's throat felt as if it would close up altogether in the dry dusty air. She bent over the hops picking and tossing them into the bin, while Nesta went up and down the rows sharing her good news.

As she stood up and rubbed her face with her handkerchief she saw a man approaching carrying a baby in his arms. He was tall with a graceful loping stride. As he got nearer she could see his straight dark hair brushing the collar of his shirt. Her belly knotted in fear as she recognised him.

To buy a few seconds to compose herself Cissie turned and pulled up the hood of the pram to shield the sleeping Maureen. The man approaching her was Ted Garland, her little Charlie's father. Cissie blinked. Seeing him with a child of his own was painful to her. What was she to do? Should she pretend that they were strangers or put on a bold front? They were trapped together. If she didn't speak to him now there would be another occasion later when they would bump into one another. The hopfields were a small, enclosed world.

As she stood there dithering his shadow fell across the pram, blotting out the sun.

'Can we set our bin here, on the end of you?' he asked. ''Aint no one else's place, is it?'

Cissie looked up at him, the little boy's arm curled round his neck. 'Hello, Ted,' she managed to gasp out. 'This your missis and baby?'

A red blush stained his cheeks. 'You got me wrong. The name's Eddy, Eddy Carver.' He turned to the young woman behind him and handed her the child. 'You go back to the hut, it's too hot out here for him,' he said, kissing her on the mouth.

She stared at Cissie before turning away and leaving the field. When she had gone Ted picked up the bin and moved to another row without a word.

'You all right, Cissie?' asked Nesta. 'I reckon the sun's got to you. Come and sit down under the tree here.'

She perched on the edge of the chair barely listening to Nesta babbling away to her, desperate to be gone. 'I best get back, Captain will be wanting to give them their tea,' she muttered, taking the break off the pram and calling the boys to join her. With head bent Cissie struggled back across the dusty rutted fields staring straight ahead of her.

'Sing, Cissie,' they demanded.

Cissie wanted to cry. All her little victories of the last few months counted for nothing. Ted had looked at her as if she were nothing. All her friendships, her reading and her good feeling about herself had been stolen in that one dismissive look.

'Come on, Cissie, sunbeam, sunbeam.'

She tried to sing but her throat was choked with tears. 'You sing for me,' she mumbled, staring at the ground.

> *A sunbeam, a sunbeam,*
> *Jesus wants me for a sunbeam.*

The two little boys tugged at the pram and shouted out the words. They scuffed the earth and dawdled until Cissie wanted to scream at them. She passed by the estate bungalow and Ted Garland's wife was sat outside nursing her child at the breast. She glimpsed the little round head covered in dark curls before turning away. Not, if he had taken a knife to her, could the pain have been more keen.

'Don't feel well, got a headache,' she gasped out, as the Captain came towards her.

'It's probably the heat, my dear. Here, have this glass of water and go and lie down for a while. You look exhausted.'

Cissie just about managed to shut the door before the tears came. She had thought herself well rid of Ted Garland and his casual cruelty, but seeing him walk towards her had stirred all her old longings. How she had wanted him. Lying in her little box room above the funeral parlour she had waited for him to join her, as soon as his wife had fallen asleep. He would lie on his side and trail his fingers over her body, slowly, teasingly, until she was mad for him to take her. Never, ever, did he say that he loved her but took her worship as his due. Did he know that she had had his child? she wondered. Would he have cared? Charlie would have been three years old now. Running about and talking. Why, why, just as she was feeling so hopeful, did he have to come and steal her joy?

Cissie pulled the sheet over her, trying to blot out the sounds filtering through the window. She heard the families coming back through the fields. Heard them calling out to the Captain. Heard the children running up to their mothers and still she didn't move. Soon she would smell the suppers cooking on the fire and it would be time to have her own. She knew the routine by heart. Once they had eaten, the Captain would go down to the hutments and see the women and listen to their concerns. On Friday night the children would be taken down to a house nearby where they would be given a bath and change their clothes. Tomorrow they would all be waiting for their menfolk to come up to Petersfield on the bus.

Clive would be coming. He would expect her to be pleased to see him. How could she pretend lightheartedness when her world had been turned upside down? She had told Dora about little Charlie, but it was something that she feared to speak of with Clive. Things were much too new and unsettled between them. 'Oh God,' she gasped. 'God, God, God.'

The hoppers' voices died away and the Captain came in and spoke to her. 'Cissie, my dear, what's wrong?'

'Can't tell you,' she muttered.

'Can I fetch you some supper or do you want to be left alone?'

'Dunnow.'

'Let me get you some water to bathe your face. I'll draw the curtain across, shall I? Would that be better?'

Cissie nodded. Almost anything would be better than the raw pain of seeing Ted Garland with his son.

'That's it, sit up and I'll hold the bowl. The sun has been very fierce today.'

She sat sunk in misery while the Captain handed her the towel. 'It's something more than a headache, isn't it?'

Cissie nodded.

'Is it serious enough for you to want to go home?'

'I don't know,' she answered.

'You have been such a help to me, Cissie. I don't know how I would have managed without you.' She sat on her bed and gave her a tired smile. 'There are another two weeks to go and more families arriving tomorrow. Think about it, my dear. If you're set on going I shall need to get someone to replace you.'

Cissie concentrated on drying her hands. What was she going to do? The two weeks in the hopfields with Captain Kellet had been some of the happiest in her life. Working with the children had eased her pain at losing Charlie. It had given her an outlet for all the love she would have lavished on him. Now Ted Garland had set her back to the beginning and she must start all over again.

The Captain got to her feet. 'I'm going to the hutments for an hour or so and then I'll get us some supper. By the time it's ready the heat will have gone from the day. We can sit out under the tree.'

Cissie paced about the hut trying to calm herself. If only she could see Dora before Clive came. Her friend's cheery warmth and common sense would put things back in perspective. Probably the Captain knew about her baby from Major Grice, but how could she explain about passion to that tidy little woman with the Bible beside her bed?

'That looks better,' said the Captain later, seeing Cissie in a clean blouse and with her hair tied back in a ribbon. 'I've got some lovely fresh runner beans and we've got the rest of that meat pie I brought back from Petersfield.'

Somehow she managed to get through the evening, letting the Captain do most of the talking: telling her about her childhood with her five brothers, on a farm in Kent. The sky darkened and at last it was time for bed.

'God bless you, Cissie. I shall keep you in my prayers,' said the Captain, before turning off her torch.

The next morning Cissie walked down through the fields to the farm gate to wait for Dora and Clive. She felt stained by her meeting with Ted Garland and struggled to clear him from her mind. As she walked past the place where his wife had been sitting nursing his child, she stared at the ground. The hutments seemed deserted. Everyone was either making the most of a Saturday lie-in or at the farm gate waiting for their family coming up from Portsmouth.

One of the hut doors was open and there was the sound of a baby crying. Fearful that she might run into Ted again if she went to investigate, Cissie walked on up the path. The crying grew louder and more desperate. She stood still. If in the next few moments the crying stopped she would carry on, if not . . . If not what? she asked herself. How long should she wait? In spite of herself, Cissie retraced her steps.

It was a natural concern to respond to the sound of a baby in distress. Of course it was. Nobody could blame her for showing concern.

She went up the steps of the hut and looked inside. Lying on the mattress was Ted's baby, flushed and crying. She judged him to be about six months old. At her approach he waved his arms and legs eager for her to pick him up. Cissie looked down at his brown eyes and dark hair plastered to his head with sweat. 'Oh,' she cooed bending down to him, 'come here, my little man.' She carried the child outside and walked about with him. He whimpered quietly, his head nestled against her neck. Cissie closed her eyes. Soon his mother would return and claim him and Ted would be with her. She couldn't bear him to look through her again as if she didn't exist. Her time with their baby would be a matter of moments. Not much less than she had had with Charlie. She told herself that once he fell asleep she would take him back and lay him on the mattress, where she had found him. Up and down she walked, singing softly to him.

> *'Little bird I have heard what a pretty song you sing.*
> *Sailing high in the sky on your tiny wing.'*

The baby nudged its head against her breasts as if in hunger. Cissie thought of her own brief nursing of Charlie. Slowly her stride lengthened and she found herself walking away from the hutments and up into the field. In the distance she could see a couple coming towards her. They drew nearer and she recognised them as Ted Garland and his wife.

Her grip around the baby tightened and she turned into the next field, walking rapidly in the opposite direction.

32

Clive Perks stared out of the bus window at the countryside flashing by and noticed nothing. In his pocket was the letter Cissie had sent. It was so precious to him. The first she had ever written. How fearful she had been when he first suggested helping her to read and write. And then, how joyful when she began to make sense of the words and to string them together. The terrified girl that had lain semi-conscious on the floor in Lancaster Terrace, with blood pouring from the gunshot wound, had gone forever. He had coaxed the new Cissie from her shell. He supposed that he had been falling in love with her for weeks but it was when he saw the envelope addressed to him in Cissie's shaky writing that he knew for certain. Today he was going to tell her how much she meant to him.

He walked up the path to the hopfields in a daze of happiness. At any moment he would see her and the fortnight's waiting would be over. Instead, it was Captain Kellet who met him first.

'Clive, good morning; I'm afraid I don't know where Cissie is.'

In an instant, the look on her face banished his well-being. Cissie hadn't just wandered off, there was something else – he knew it.

'Two things have happened and I pray that they're not connected,' she said, as she took him inside the hut for a glass of water.

'What are they?' Clive asked.

'Three things in fact, when I think back,' the Captain said. 'She took a message for me up to the hopfields, yesterday afternoon. When she came back I knew she'd been crying. Complained of a headache and put herself to bed. It was a boiling hot afternoon and I thought no more about it until later. She had set out so happily with the message and then came back a different girl.'

'Was it bad news?'

'Not at all – the reverse in fact. One of the women pickers had become a grandmother.'

'Did Cissie get on well with everyone? There couldn't have been a row at all?'

'You know Cissie,' said the Captain, smiling at him. 'She is the gentlest and kindest of girls. Thought a lot of her, they did. Trusted her with their children.'

'How was she this morning?'

'She was very quiet. Said she was walking up to the gate to meet you. All this week she had been so excited. Thrilled with your letter and so looking forward to seeing you. She has been gone a couple of hours now. Where can she have got to?'

'What was the other thing that worried you, Captain?' asked Clive. Although he was not in uniform he felt as if he were back in the station.

'A new couple came yesterday – a man with a young wife and baby. This morning the mother came to me distraught. They had been out for a walk together and when they got back the baby was gone.'

'Do you think the two things are connected?' asked Clive, knowing that they must be.

'She adores babies. I'm sure the explanation is quite simple. It's possible that Cissie passed by and found him crying. By now he may be back with his mother safe and sound. If he is not found quickly, we shall have to contact the police.'

'Can we go back a bit in time?' he asked. 'Could Cissie have met the couple in the fields, last night?'

'I suppose it's possible,' said the Captain, 'though why that would have upset her so much I have no idea.'

'Where are they?'

'I have persuaded the wife to go back to the hut and wait. The husband was beyond persuading. He's out in the fields with anyone else he can find, threatening all sorts of things. I was on the point of calling the police when I saw you, Clive, and thought I would seek your counsel.'

'How long has the baby been missing?' he asked, downing the rest of the water in one gulp.

'They came to me about an hour ago and so I should think it must be getting on for two, now.'

'Why don't you go and stay with the mother,' Clive said, walking to the door with her. 'Find someone to stay here and I will see if I can find Cissie and the baby or at least try and calm the man down, before he makes matters worse.'

'How long shall we leave it until we contact the local police?' asked the Captain. 'I want to protect Cissie but I don't want to get you into trouble.'

'If we haven't found them in an hour I'll call them myself,' said Clive, trying to sound calmer than he felt. If she had taken the baby Cissie could face a kidnap charge. Could even go to prison – and just as she seemed to be taking charge of her life.

When she had first seen the baby crying all she had wanted to do was pacify him. It was seeing Ted and his wife that changed things. Then, Cissie had wanted to hurt him, to make him feel just a little of her pain at the losing of Charlie. If he had just said hello to her yesterday she might have forgiven him, but his looking straight through her and lying had been so hurtful. No, he must be made to suffer. Let him feel just a tenth of her loss.

From her vantage point in a break in the hedge, in the next field, she could watch the hut where they were staying and judge the right moment to return the baby. Certainly she had no intention of keeping him overnight. He would need feeding soon and she did not want him to suffer in any way. She was going to give him back but – not yet, not yet, she breathed, bending to kiss his dimpled hand.

Off in the distance she could see a family having a picnic. It was Saturday, she remembered with a start. Clive would be here. Oh, Jesus! What had she done? If Ted called the police and she was found with the baby, whatever would Clive think of her? Stealing someone else's child was a terrible thing. What had started out as a simple, womanly response to a crying baby would, if she didn't act quickly, turn into a crime.

Was there still time for her to put him back without being seen? Cissie looked across the field to the hutments. There were people milling about all over the place. Sneaking the baby back would be an impossible task. Cissie blinked. And then she saw Captain Kellet coming out of the hut with her arm round the mother. The woman was weeping. She kept looking around and crying, 'Freddy, Freddy.'

Cissie burned with shame. It wasn't Ted she had hurt but another innocent woman. 'We gotta take you home, my lamb,' she said, kissing the sleeping child. Holding him close she left the hedge and stepped into the open. 'I got him safe,' she called. 'Missis, I got him safe.'

From the stile behind her Clive saw Cissie crossing the field. He leapt down and ran towards her, anxious to prevent any trouble. 'Cissie, Cissie, it's me,' he called, but he was too late.

Laughing and crying the mother had reached her and snatched the sleeping Freddy from her arms.

Cissie was smiling but only for an instant, for a tall man Clive took to be the father rushed forward and grabbed her by the hair.

'Gottcha! You thieving bitch,' he roared.

Clive rushed towards them, his heart pumping.

'Leave her alone,' shouted Captain Kellet, attempting to wrest the man's hand from Cissie's hair. 'Your child is safe. Mr Carver, leave her alone.'

Clive grabbed his arm, yanked it behind his back and twisted his wrist. 'Let go of her. I'll do you for assault,' he yelled.

Cissie twisted and turned to free herself, then kicked him in the shin. 'Leggo . . . leggo, you bastard,' she raged.

The man screamed in pain from the combined attacks and let go of Cissie. 'Bitch, you bitch, I'll have you,' he hissed.

Flushed and furious Cissie glared at him. 'You ain't got a leg to stand on, Ted Garland,' she roared. 'Scum, that's what you are. Your wife Sally had the right idea gettin' shot of you. What I ever seen in ya, must've bin mad.'

Clive was astonished. Cissie was flushed and magnificent. With her hair standing on end she looked every inch the avenging angel.

'What ya gonna tell?' gasped Ted.

'Your new missis – know about Mrs Garland, does she? Mister Carver!'

'Whose gonna take the word of a cheap tart like you?' Ted blustered.

'Constable Perks, here,' crowed Cissie. 'Be a good story in the *News of the World*.'

'Enough!' said Captain Kellet. 'The child is safe and that is all that matters.'

'You take back what you said about Cissie,' roared Clive. 'Take it back!'

'Yes, you tripe-hound,' Nesta Gibbons screeched from her ringside seat on the fence.

'Give it to him hot and strong, mate,' yelled her husband.

The hop-pickers crowded round, excited by the prospect of free entertainment.

'Mister Carver, I suggest you return to Portsmouth on the next bus with your family,' said Captain Kellet.

'I still think she . . .'

'Deserves an apology, you cheap-skate,' yelled Nesta.

'Eddie, shut up! said his wife. 'Freddy's fine. Let's get our things, never liked hoppin' anyway.'

'You two,' said Captain Kellet, 'are to come back with me. This has all been most irregular. I shall have to give Major Grice a full report. We can't have the army brought into disrepute.'

Clive smiled sheepishly at Cissie. 'Can't leave you alone five minutes,' he said.

Cissie laughed. 'Don't know about you,' she said, 'but I'm gasping for a cup of tea.'

Walking back to the Salvation Army hut, Cissie didn't know how she felt. It was a wild mixture of things: rage, sadness, triumph and joy at seeing Clive. She helped the others to carry the table out under the tree and put a salad meal together. Captain Kellet hardly touched her corned beef and tomato.

'I shall go to the telephone-box and contact the Major,' she said. 'I think you should be prepared, Cissie, to leave tonight.'

Cissie blinked. 'Right-ho,' she said, meekly. It was what she deserved after the rumpus she'd caused. Pinching the baby had mucked up everything. She sat fiddling with the edge of the tablecloth, feeling her earlier excitement trickling away.

'Talk to me, Cissie,' said Clive. 'There's so much I don't understand.'

Still fiddling with the cloth, she muttered, 'Don't think you'll make sense of it if I tells ya.'

'Please, Cissie, I promise to listen.'

'D'you promise not to look at me or think about me like I was on trial. You got that policeman look on yer face.'

'I'm your friend,' he said.

She wanted him to hold her hand, to give her courage, but he didn't and she had more pride than to ask him. 'Long time ago I knew Ted Garland. After I left the Clementses, when they shut up the house, I worked as a cleaner for his first missis and lived with them. Ever so green and trusting I was. He used to tell me how pretty I was. For a while I stopped being frightened.' Cissie looked up at Clive, but his face was unreadable. 'Began to kiss me, he did. Ain't bin kissed since I couldn't remember. Dad was always away and Mum was sickly. Old Aunt what looked after me wasn't one for petting kids or being soft. I thought I loved him.'

'But he was married, Cissie. Didn't you think about . . . ?'

'You wasn't me, Clive. You wasn't in my skin wanting a kind word or a look that told me I was something more than rubbish.'

'Sorry,' he mumbled.

'Long and short of it, he come into me room and Sally found out and slung me into the street. Begging, I was, when Major Grice found me. Was carrying Ted's baby. After I'd got over being frightened and feeling shamed, I wanted the child. Someone of my own to love; it was what I'd always dreamed of.' She looked up at him. 'You remember how I was so frantic to find me box?'

He nodded.

'In there was the bonnet what I made for my little Charlie.' She patted her frock. 'I keeps it all the time next to me, so I won't never forget him. Died he did. Only had him two days.'

'I'm sorry,' said Clive, not looking at her.

'After that, you know what my life's bin. In yer police records, I 'spect. After he was taken I didn't care no more, just drifted about like a bit of rubbish blowing in the wind.'

Clive said nothing.

Cissie's eyes filled with tears. 'You ain't making it easy for me, sitting there, all po-faced, like you was me judge and jury all rolled into one.'

Clive blushed. 'I'm trying to understand,' he said, still not meeting her eye.

'Last six months bin so happy for me, being with Dora and the Major and everyone. You've been so kind, helpin' me to read and everythink. I didn't mean to keep that baby,' she said, reaching across the table and touching Clive's arm. 'I picked him up because he was crying and just borrowed him a bit too long.'

He slid his hand from beneath hers and reached behind the chair for his jacket. 'I better get back, Cissie. I'm sure it'll be all right. There won't be any charges to answer.'

'Don't care about that,' she said. 'I want you to say something to me, Clive. Not just run away. You don't know how hard it was telling you. Least you could do is say something.'

'Cissie, please, let me go away and think about it all,' he said, staring down at his boots. 'I'll write to you.'

'Will we still have the reading when I gets back?' she asked.

'I'll have to see. Things are getting busy at the station.'

Cissie clutched at his sleeve. 'Don't you dare fob me off with busy,' she hissed at him. 'If I'm not fit to teach, you gotta have the guts to say so, Clive Perks.'

'I told you I'd write,' he said, getting to his feet.

'I shan't hold my breath waiting,' she said, hurrying into the hut and slamming the door.

33

Mary and Matthew walked up the street towards the War Memorial Hospital, hand in hand, with Dog lolloping behind. Jabez had summoned them.

'Wants to see you most partickler,' one of the watermen said.

They took him a pot of cockles, a Sunday newspaper and a slice of bread pudding.

'A bit of a surprise his sister turning up, wasn't it?' Mary laughed.

'Perhaps she's his big sister, who looked after him, like you and Blyth,' said Matthew.

'Our Blyth's got way past mothering,' Mary scoffed, 'what with all his schemes. Wonder what Jabez wants to tell us?'

'I expect he wants to move back in with his sister, just as we've got the place all shipshape,' said Matthew.

'Didn't think you would ever take to it,' Mary said. 'Remember your face that first time you saw it?'

'Well, you've got to admit, it did pong,' he laughed. 'Now there's bin a bit of air through the place, it's just the smell of Dog and diesel off my clothes.'

'It's lovely now the yachts have gone from the yard. You can see so much more. And the cottage is filled with light.'

'Those stocks won't be empty for long. Soon be another one being built for some other rich toff.'

'Wanted it to be our first home for littl'un',' said Mary.

'He's bound to be a sailor, looking out that window, hearing the sea and smelling the seaweed.'

'Certain it's a boy then?' Matthew teased her. 'S'pose we should call him Neptune. Shame we can't unbutton your stomach and take a peek at him.'

Mary turned and hugged him. After the false start of the engagement with its tears and uncertainties her marriage had been such a joy to her. The *L75* was in refit over in the dockyard and Matthew had been home almost every night. They shared everything together: cooking, cleaning and the care of Dog. She could feel herself calming down and daring to be happy. According to Nurse Boyden, her midwife, Mary was in good health and her baby was expected to arrive in early December. She hoped it would come on the seventh, Matthew's twenty-fourth birthday.

'I think you should prepare to have your baby down-stairs, Mary,' the midwife said. 'It's so cramped in that bedroom and crouching over that mattress will do my back no good at all.'

They were hoping to talk to Jabez about reorganising the cottage, but it all depended on what he had to tell them. As they approached the hospital garden they were on tenterhooks. 'He might be wanting to raise the rent,' thought Mary. They had been lucky it had stayed at three shillings for so long. Since starting work in the sorting room for nine and sixpence her wages had risen by one shilling.

She was now a shaker at the clean end of the laundry process, taking out the wet twisted sheets from the revolving drum. The untwisting bruised her hands and she had given up hope of growing her fingernails. The work was heavy; a monotonous bend, untwist, shake, bend, untwist, shake, endlessly repeated. Daisy, her new forewoman, was worlds different from the scheming Florrie from the sorting room. For a start there was no beer kitty and no favouritism. Daisy's second husband was a submariner on the same boat as Janey's fellow out in the Far East. But there the similarity ended. Where Janey was volatile and foul-mouthed Daisy was calm and steady. Mary valued both of them for different reasons.

Mary clutched his hand as they saw Jabez sat in his chair under the tree in deep conversation with his sister. 'You don't think he'll chuck us out, do ya?'

'We'll just have to wait and see,' Matthew said. 'It's out of our hands.'

Dog rushed up to his old master and licked his face.

Jabez's face split into a grin. 'It's the love-birds,' he twitted. 'Sit yourselves down along with Matty.'

'Got you the cockles,' said Mary, handing him the jar and the paper.

'Champion,' he said, immediately taking off the lid.

'How are you keeping?' Matthew asked him as he got out his tickler tin.

'They're turfin' me out next week,' he said, busy easing the cockles out of their shells with a pin. 'So I got to sort out me accommodation.'

Mary looked at Matthew. She hated the thought of their cosy twosome at Shore Cottage coming to an end. But they could hardly complain. The old waterman had been more than generous to them.

'Don't look so down in the mouth,' he said to her. 'Me and Matty, here, have chewed it all over and got a proposition to put to you both.

Mary took Matthew's hand and held it tight.

'I'm taking me brother to live alonga me in Gloucester,' said his sister, putting down her knitting. 'I bin lonely since my old boy passed on and Jabez and me'll be company for one another. So decision gotta be made 'bout the cottage and Dog.'

'He's a sea dog,' said Jabez; 'wouldn't be happy away from

the water. Taken to you, he has. So we'll have to do a bit of a sort out.'

They looked at one another, uncertain as to where the conversation was leading.

'Here's the plan,' said Jabez after a long draw on his cigarette. 'I'll go quiet up to Gloucester so long as you two takes care of me cottage and this old feller,' he said, rumpling Dog's ear.

''Course we will,' said Mary. 'No problem, Dog's part of the family now.'

'Matty's a widow woman, and between us we'll be hard-pressed to manage. Thought if you two could bring up the rent to five shillings and I gets a good price for me boat and tackle, that will see us right.'

Mary chewed her fingers. They could manage reasonably well at the moment but in December she would be leaving work for a while. Matthew was on to her to give it up for good. She had persuaded him to agree to her going back to the laundry later, provided she could get someone to look after the baby properly. The loss of her wages would be a big gap in their finances.

'What d'you think, Mary?'

'Let's take Dog for a walk round and chew it over,' she said.

'What's to think about?' he said, when they were walking back down the road. 'We would be settled, nothing would change.'

'It's just that I don't know how we'll cope when I'm not working and we've the nipper to clothe and feed.'

'I'll be a Leading Hand soon, that will be a rise of thirteen shillings. I shall be able to put up what I give you to well over a pound a week. The end of next year I'll be twenty-five and the navy will chip in with a marriage allowance. Compared to most couples we'll be quids in.' He took her face in his hands and kissed her. 'Let's have a bit of faith in the future. Why don't we make the most of it now?' he said. 'If we have to leave later on, well' – he shrugged – 'we'll find somewhere else.'

'You usually wants to play it safe,' Mary said, looking questioningly at him.

'Being with you makes me see things differently. I'm living for now for the first time in my life.'

'What d'you mean?'

'We haven't got any guarantees, love. Got to make the most of the moment, especially with the insecurity of boats.'

'Don't say that,' she said, letting go of his hand. 'Can't bear you talkin' like that.'

'Come on,' he coaxed. 'Let's take a gamble. We took a chance on each other and that's worked out. Now we'll go back to the old buzzard and nail our colours to the mast.'

Mary smiled. 'Ain't used to you being a chancer,' she said, kissing him on the cheek, 'but I likes it.'

When they returned, the brother and sister were deep in conversation.

'Thought you three'd deserted us,' said Matty, her knitting needles flashing.

Mary smiled at the old man. 'Yes, we'll shake on the deal,' she said, holding out her hand.

'And you, squire,' he said, looking at Matthew, 'you certain sure about it?'

Matthew took the old man's hand and shook it firmly. 'Sure as sure,' he said. 'Thank you both. It means a lot to us.'

'What about you, Dog?' Jabez asked, putting his head on one side and holding out a piece of cake.

Dog leapt at him, and once more licked his face.

'What does that mean?' laughed Mary. 'I think he's just a cupboard lover. Whoever feeds him gets his vote.'

'Right, you two, we'll be down next Saturday to sort out

what I wants taking and to get the boat sale sorted.' Jabez patted
Dog's head and seemed to dismiss them all from his attention.

That night, lying in Matthew's arms, with Dog asleep on
the floor beside them, Mary counted herself lucky. With her
hand resting on her pregnant belly she dropped down into a
contented sleep.

Friday October 15th 1926

Dear Mary,

   *Bet you're surprised to hear from your old Dad. This is
the way of it. Takings have been rock bottom on the stall and
we ain't hardly making the rent. Now the girls is working
at the pub it's just me and Blyth down the market. He says
he can make more with all his other little jobs than standin'
about in Charlotte Street.*

   *Danny Sullivan says as he will rent the stall from us and
put his own gear on it, till you decides what you wants done
permanent.*

   *Doctor says I gotta strained heart and must take things
easy. Now don't get in a panic. It's just a tired heart.*

   *Drop over when you can and we'll chew the whole
thing over.*

   Love to you and Dusty,
   Dad.

'Don't cry, love,' said Matthew, after she had handed him
the letter. 'Why don't you go over tonight. I'm duty at
Dolphin, you could stay till Saturday and sort things out with
this Danny.'

'Poor Dad, I should have helped more. God, you don't
think he's gonna die, do you?'

'Shh, shh,' he murmured, taking her in his arms. 'If he
was really bad the doctor would have put him in hospital.
It was lucky he went to see him when he did. You've go to

see this as a warning. Probably need to frighten the twinnies into doing more.'

She tried to make light of it, smiling at Matthew through her tears. 'How come you're always right?' she teased.

'I've got to go. Leave Dog with Jabez's old mate down the lane. I'll pick him up tomorrow morning and see you over there in the afternoon,' he said, kissing her and reaching for his raincoat before dashing through the door.

'Hello, my gal, cor you're a sight for sore eyes,' Dad said, looking up from his chair by the fire as she walked in that night. 'Look like you gonna drop that nipper any minute.'

Mary hugged him fiercely. 'You frightened the life out of me,' she whispered. 'Tell me exactly what the doc said.'

'On account of the rheumatic fever, what I had when I was a boy seaman – that and the shock of the fire. Strained the muscles of the heart. I just can't manage hauling the cart out every week and standing about in the cold.'

'What those girls up to letting you struggle like that. Wants a good smack, they do.'

'Calm down, love. Can't expect them to show an interest. It's your stall, when all's said and done. They're keeping themselves with their charring and that's all I ask.'

Mary chewed her hand. She had been so absorbed in her own affairs she had let him down. Poor Dad. 'You sit there and I'll make us a cup of tea, then I'll treat us all to fish and chips. Blyth can nip up Queen Street.'

'He's up North End at Captain Clements' place. Has tea with him every Friday night. His son is down for the weekend. Seemingly, he and yer brother have palled up and play chess and all sorts.'

'Getting' to be a regular toff,' she sneered. 'And where's Faith and Mercy?'

'God knows,' said Fred, throwing his cigarette end in the fire. 'Look, scrub round the fish and chips. Why don't you make your old Dad some scrambled egg? You makes it nice and fluffy. Last time I tried my hand it was all rubbery. Could've bounced it off the wall.'

As she pottered about, Mary's anxiety deepened. The place had gone to pot. There was dirty washing in a heap in a tin bath, a bundle of creased shirts and blouses shoved on a chair and what looked like several days' washing-up in the sink. By God those sisters of hers would get a tongue lashing when she got hold of them later.

'That's set me up good and proper,' Dad said, smiling at her as she took away his tray. He looked up at the clock. 'It's after eight. You best be making tracks. Dusty'll be waiting for you.'

'Staying the night,' she said, and was rewarded by Dad's smile. 'I'm going up the market tomorrow and I'll speak to Danny.'

'Best kip in Blyth's room. He can doss down with me.'

By the time she had cleared up the kitchen and done the ironing it was half past nine and Dad was nodding in his chair. 'You go on up,' she said, 'Blyth can kip on a couple of chairs just for one night.'

When the twins and Blyth returned Mary had stoked her anger to boiling point.

Hardly had they got their coats off than she was at them. 'Why didn't you let me know how bad he was?' she raged. 'You gonna just let him drop down dead 'fore you'd lift a finger?'

Faith burst into tears. 'He didn't never tell us about his heart,' she whimpered.

'I bin doin' lots of things,' said Blyth. 'I gives Dad five bob a week from all me schemes.'

'Why you getting on yer high horse,' snapped Mercy, glaring at her. 'You ain't troubled about us since you got married. When was the last time you was over?'

'I'm keeping myself and sending money over and you gets the takings on the stall. You,' she said, poking Mercy angrily in the chest, 'are one lazy cow.'

'Watch gonna do about it?' Mercy challenged.

The action was instinctive. She swung her arm and slapped her sister hard across the face.

Mercy screamed and put her hand to her flaming cheek before lunging at Mary. The two of them wrestled each other across the room with Faith trying to intervene.

'Shut up, shut up, shut up,' shouted Blyth, rushing sobbing into his bedroom.

The three girls drew apart, shocked by their brother's tears.

'You better say sorry,' hissed Mercy. 'Coming over here throwin' yer weight about, upsettin' everyone.'

'What ya want to go and do that for?' said Faith. 'We was going ter clear up tomorrer anyway. Belting Merce don't solve nothin'.'

The door opened and Dad stood there in his vest and pyjama bottoms.

'Jesus Christ! Can't a feller get a minute's sleep without you lot at each other's throats? Reckon I'd be better off in hospital. Least I'd getta bit of peace.'

'She hit me and our Blyth's gone off to bed crying his eyes out.'

Dad sank down into his chair. 'Blimey, Mary, thought you'd come over to give us a hand. 'Stead of that you starts a cat fight. Well, you better make yer peace so's we can all get to bed.'

Mary wanted to kick herself. Why did she and Mercy always rasp against each other? Why did her temper always get the better of her? Swallowing down her pride she stared at the floor. 'Sorry, Mercy,' she muttered.

'Didn't hear ya,' said her sister, with a satisfied smirk on her face.

'Mercy,' said Dad, 'you ain't the innocent party, not by a long chalk. I knows your game. Proper wind-up merchant you are. You gotta say sorry, too.'

Mercy glared at her elder sister. 'Sorry,' she mocked. 'Sorry, sorry, sorry.'

'Get up those stairs and out of my sight,' Dad demanded, 'the pair of you.' He turned to Mary. 'Go and see yer brother, then you can fetch us up a cup of hot milk. Be glad to see the back of today,' he said.

'Oh, Dad,' she whispered, hugging him. 'I could bite me tongue out.'

'Least said soonest mended,' he said. 'You go and calm Blyth down.'

Whether or not he was asleep, her brother had got into bed and pulled the covers up high around his head.

'Sorry, love,' she whispered into his ear.

He turned angrily away and burrowed even deeper under the clothes.

After taking Dad up some milk, Mary sorted herself a makeshift bed on the two wrecked armchairs by the kitchen fire. She tossed and turned, feeling like a juggler trying to keep all the different balls in the air. Nagging the twins was worse than useless. But she had not meant to upset Blyth; his angry turning away had hurt her. She would just have to do a repair job in the morning along with seeing Danny Sullivan and sorting out the stall. Her baby stirred in her belly. 'We'll be back home tomorrow,' she whispered to him, before putting out the light.

'It was all down to you,' Danny said the next morning when she stood with him at the stall. 'Your ideas and your drive, that's what kept it going. Customers knew they could get something just a little bit different at a fair price. Now it's a lot of tired old tat. You took yer eye off the ball and it's lost its bounce.'

Mary smarted under his ruthless assessment. He was right. 'Well,' she said, 'I'll just have to cut me losses. If you can take it on for the next six months and pay the rent we'll see where we go from there.'

'Will do. Like I said I'm willing to buy it off ya at a good price but in six months a lot can happen. There's your nipper in there, once you've got him the stall will be way down on your list of priorities.'

'"Bye, Danny, and thanks,' she said, shaking his hand.

'"Bye, Mary,' he said, holding onto her hand longer than was comfortable. 'Remember if ever you get fed up with your sailor I'll be in the front of the queue.'

'You'll have a long wait,' she snapped, tossing her head.

Back in Lemon Street she knocked on Granny Pragnell's door, needing a breathing space before tackling her family again.

'Mary, my dear girl, come in and welcome.' Gran hugged her soundly. 'You've timed your visit just right. Albert's out for the day so we can natter to our heart's content.'

They sat in Gran's cosy kitchen and Mary poured her troubles into her ready ear.

'Cutting your losses is all you can do my duck. Getting your Dad some help, that's the key. Those twins are as much support as a chocolate tea pot. Banging your head against a brick wall with them. D'you reckon he'd let Betty Frewin in to turn the place around?'

'We couldn't give her nothing,' said Mary.

'Let's just say I'll be calling in a favour. She's a widow on her own with the grandchildren miles away. Be glad of a couple of hours a day. See it as a challenge. After bringing up her nine your family will be chicken-feed. Those girls will knuckle down for Betty. I'll nip over and see her later and drop in on Fred. He wants to make those girls pay their way. Can't bring up a family on fresh air.' She leant forward and patted Mary's knee. 'Now we got that out the way, tell me about the baby.'

Mary relaxed and chattered away. It was getting on for half past one when she went next door to Dad and the family.

Her father looked more rested. He was sitting at the table with Matthew, eating fish and chips. The twins were knelt by the fire eating theirs out of the paper.

'Gran wants you all to go in for tea later on,' she said. 'Any grub for me?'

'You sit down, love, and put your feet up,' said Matthew. 'I'll get your plate out of the oven. Blyth and me are going to the football this afternoon see if Pompey can see off Everton.'

'Cheer them on for me,' she said, patting her brother on the shoulder as she reached across the table for the brown sauce.

Blyth rewarded her with a tentative smile.

'We're taking Dog fer a walk,' said the twins.

Mary bit her tongue. She looked around the room. There was evidence of a half-hearted clear-up.

'Looks better,' she said. 'Don't let him off the lead.' Later she and Dad snoozed away the afternoon either side of the kitchen fire.

It was gone six o'clock when she stood at the front door her arms round his skinny frame. 'You listen to Granny,' she said, 'and I'll be over again next week.'

''Bye, my babes,' he said. 'Take care of yourself and you, Dusty.'

On the ferry she clutched her husband's hand. They looked at the shoreline of Gosport getting closer. Dog nuzzled between their fingers.

'It'll be good to be home,' she said.

34

Chantry House School,
Cerne Magna
Dorset.
November 3rd 1926

Dear Captain Clements,

I write to you on a matter of great concern to us
both. Charlotte, who was settling in with us after an
uncertain start last year, now seems to have regressed. Her
housemistress reports that she has started to wet the bed
again and is biting her nails. This all seems to stem from her
mother's recent visits.

Mrs Clements has led us to believe that you fully support
her contact with the children. I would be grateful if you could
contact me and clarify the matter. It is important for us to
know the legal position on her access to her children.

Miles has been similarly unsettled. Not least because Mrs
Clements' visits to him have been less frequent.

If you could possibly spare the time to visit the school as
soon as possible or telephone me I would be most grateful.

Yours sincerely,

Harriet Finch

Charles could not keep still. He was possessed by rage and
paced back and forth, letter in his hand. How could she be
so unfeeling? Poor Charlotte! Poor Miles! He must, must
stop her.

Immediately, he telephoned the headmistress promising to visit on Friday and take both Miles and Charlotte home for the weekend. They would have a bonfire party. He was in the mood for fireworks.

'That is most reassuring,' she said. 'I shall be free on Friday, late morning. Perhaps you would like to have lunch with me, Captain. It will give us ample time to discuss the children before you take them home with you.'

His next call was to his own school to say that he would not be in until the next day. By eight o'clock he was on the train to Waterloo praying that he could get to Lettice's hotel before she went out for one of her lunches.

'The Churchill, please, and quickly,' he urged the taxi driver.

'Mrs Lawrence, please; tell her it is Captain Clements on a matter of urgency concerning the children.'

'Charles, what on earth's the matter?' she asked, standing in the doorway of her room still in her negligée. Her hand flew to her mouth. 'It isn't Lottie, is it?'

He pushed her aside and strode into the room, slamming the door behind him. 'What the hell have you been up to?' Charles yelled at her.

'If you are going to shout at me, I shall have you removed,' she said, reaching for the phone.

He knocked the receiver out of her hand. 'Listen to me,' he hissed. 'You are to leave the children alone. I will not have them upset.'

'Upset! Are you mad? I hardly recognised them. Pale and tongue-tied with no spirit. Upset! It's you that have upset them.'

'The headmistress tells me that Charlotte is wetting the bed again and biting her nails. All since you came back into her life.'

'That old crone. What does she know about children?

Naturally Lottie was upset. She had missed me so much it has taken her a while to believe that her Mummy is back in her life.'

'You just couldn't compromise, could you? Ease your way back into their lives, think about their feelings – no, not you. All or nothing and to hell with who gets hurt.'

'Always so bloody pedestrian,' she hissed. 'They were thrilled to see me, both of them.'

'Miles, too?' he asked.

Lettice hesitated. 'Poor fellow, he has become so solemn and righteous. Wanted to phone you and ask permission.'

'Don't you see what you've done? You swanned off, leaving them to come home to England without you. Barely gave them a thought, and now you come back and expect them to welcome you with open arms.' She was standing with her back to him, looking out of the window. Infuriated, he grabbed her by the shoulders, turning her to face him.

Lettice was crying.

No, he would not be sucked in by her trickery. 'They are not dolls. They have feelings – they are people. How long do you think it took them to stop crying for you? Blaming themselves for your going.'

'I hate you.' She spat out the words. 'You ruined my life.'

'That's over now,' he said. 'You can go back to Malaya and draw a line under it.'

'I want my children,' she demanded.

'No,' Charles said. 'No, they are staying with me.' He looked at Lettice, at her pale naked face, and realised that he had stopped loving her. She no longer had the power to seduce him. He was free. 'I shall be contacting my solicitor and visiting the school on Friday.'

'They won't be children forever,' she said, sinking down into a gilt chair beside the dressing table. 'Once they're grown they'll come and find me.'

'That's for them to decide,' he said. 'Goodbye, Lettice.'

'No kiss?' she asked mockingly, turning her face to him.

'It won't be the first time I've done without your kisses,' he said, striding to the door and slamming it behind him.

Lottie undid the latch on the pantry window and stood beside it in the dark. Mummy said she would be there beneath the window at half past six on Thursday, November the fourth. They had planned it all the last time she had come to see her, loaded down with toys and chocolate. She stood there in the dark, nervously switching her torch on and off. Beside her on the floor, in a cardboard box blanketed in straw, was Muriel her rabbit. Lottie wondered if it would be too hot for her in Malaya. She didn't want Muriel to be unhappy. She had been a present from Daddy. But, she absolutely couldn't go without her. Still fiddling with her torch she went into the kitchen and shone it on the face of the clock. It was half past five. Lottie knelt on the floor, opened the box and stroked Muriel. If only Mummy would hurry. Waiting made her worried. She knew that Daddy would be upset. When she said this to Mummy she had laughed in an ugly way.

'But darling, he has had you all to himself, he mustn't be greedy,' she had said.

Miles had told her last night that Daddy was coming tomorrow to take them both home to Portsmouth and there would be fireworks. She worried about him being disappointed and buying all those sparklers for nothing. Miles wanted rockets. It had been so hard fibbing to her brother. But he didn't love Mummy like she did.

'I hate her,' he said. 'She doesn't listen and she's always bringing me baby things and looking at her watch.'

She would miss Kate. They did everything together and she loved her giggly laugh. Once she had gone to stay with her at her home. Kate's Mummy was giggly too. She wasn't beautiful like her own Mummy but she made you feel comfortable inside.

Lottie looked at her watch. It was twenty past six. 'Nearly time, Muriel,' she whispered.

There was a sharp tap on the window.

Lottie's heart leapt. Yes, she was here! Quickly she stood on the chair and pushed open the window.

'Hurry, darling,' Mummy whispered. 'What's that?' she said, as Lottie pushed the box towards her.

'It's a surprise.'

'Hurry, hurry, pet. We don't want anyone to see us.'

Lottie almost fell into her mother's arms. Once her feet had touched the ground she picked up the box. In her hurry she couldn't have fastened it properly. Muriel jumped out onto the ground and bounded off into the hedge.

'Jesus!' Mummy gasped. 'What was that?'

'It's Muriel.'

'What the hell is Muriel?'

'My rabbit, I told you.'

'Well, it can't come with us. No, Lottie, it's out of the question. Take my hand, we'll have to run down the path to the car. It's hidden up by the tree.'

'I can't leave Muriel,' Lottie cried, pulling away.

'Don't be stupid, Lottie. Kate can have her.'

She began to cry. 'I must find her,' she insisted.

'Lottie,' her Mother snapped. 'This is your last chance. If you don't come this minute it's too late.'

From down by the lodge there was the sound of barking.

Lottie cried and Mummy hugged her fiercely.

'Oh Lottie,' she said, 'you silly, silly girl.'

And then she was gone, swallowed up by the early-morning gloom.

'What you doing out here, Miss?' asked the gardener, shining his torch in her face.

'I've lost Muriel,' she sobbed.

'You get back into bed,' he said, ''fore your teacher finds you. Reckon your rabbit will be down by the vegetable patch, safe and sound.'

The gardener lifted her up and helped her back through the window.

'You come down the garden later and I bet you I'll have her back in her hutch, right as ninepence.'

Lottie got back into bed and burrowed her head into the pillow to muffle her tears. If only Mummy had let her take Muriel. If only she had understood.

Lettice awoke suddenly, startled by the sound of a car hooting its horn as it passed by. She looked in the mirror at her tear-stained face. Her eyes were swollen, and her skin looked a ghastly yellow. Reaching into her coat pocket she took out her handkerchief and blew her nose. There was a yawning hole inside her. 'Lottie,' she gasped, 'oh Lottie.' She had gambled everything on snatching her child. If only she had had more time to think the plan through. But, the liner was sailing from Tilbury tomorrow. She laughed bitterly. All that work taking Lottie's photograph and forging Charles's handwriting in the letter she took to the Passport Office, saying that they had mislaid the old one – all wasted.

He had been boringly, predictably right. If only she had been prepared to compromise and share her daughter, working with Charles, gradually building trust. But that was not her way – all the cake or nothing. She had never been interested in crumbs. She took out a silver flask from her handbag and swallowed down a mouthful of whisky. Lettice supposed that part of her had known the plan couldn't possibly work. What she could not have imagined was the pain of failing.

Harriet Finch dabbed her mouth with her serviette and rang

for the maid to clear the dishes. It had been a most satisfactory meal. She smiled at Captain Clements: what a nice man he was, so concerned for his children. Now she was in possession of a letter from his solicitor clearly setting out the terms of the divorce. Yes, most satisfactory. 'More coffee?' she enquired.

'No, thank you, Miss Finch,' he said. 'I'm eager to see the children and be on our way.'

Again she tugged the bell-pull. 'Doris, will you get Miss Palmer to send Miles and Charlotte Clements to me, if you please?'

'Miles, Lottie,' he said, holding out his arms. 'How lovely to see you both. Are you ready for the off?'

They nodded, smiling up at him.

'Have you said goodbye to Muriel?' he asked his daughter.

Lottie shook her head.

'Better go and tell her that she can come later for her summer holidays. I don't think sparklers and rockets are quite her ticket.'

Lottie opened the door of the hutch and gave Muriel a quick hug. 'You wouldn't have liked Malaya,' she whispered into her fur.

35

For the first time Mary wished she were back in Lemon Street with Granny. Then she could ask her all the things she needed to know and not feel foolish at her ignorance. Her prickly pride got in the way with her midwife, Nurse Boyden. She was probably quite nice once she got to know her, but there was no one like Granny Pragnell.

Today was December the seventh, Matthew's birthday and supposedly that of their baby. What would start it off? Mary wondered. Was there some special signal that her body would make, like pressing a button or flicking a switch? Or was it something the baby did that set it off on its journey? She cudgelled her brain to remember any details of Blyth's birth when she was ten years old and the twins were five. It had been not long after the Battle of Jutland. A grey anxious time it was, with people crying in the street. The three sisters had come home from school, in the afternoon, and Granny had shooed them across the street to a neighbour's house for tea. At night-time they had been fetched back to see their new brother. Mum had been lying in clean sheets and a new nightdress with her hair tied back in a sat in ribbon, revelling in the rest in bed and all the attention. There had been no hint of what the birth entailed, then or ever. She chewed her hand. Last time she'd been with Gran their talk was all about Dad, with hardly a mention of her baby. Mary smiled, remembering her first sight of Blyth tucked in a knitted blanket. Oh! she had loved her brother from the start.

Often and often she looked at the tiny clothes she had made in readiness, trying to imagine the child who would wear them. Still it seemed unreal, in spite of the movements and the midwife listening to its heartbeat through a silver trumpet thing. Yet she refused to name her baby, superstitiously afraid of making a future for him only to have it snatched away by death.

From down the lane came an excited bark from Dog. Matthew was on his way. Mary pulled on her shapeless grey jumper and walked up the lane towards him.

'Hello love,' he called to her, shoving Dog aside. 'You get in the warm, it's freezing.'

Quickly she darted back into the cottage and took up the matches from the dresser and lit the candles, his candles. '"Happy birthday to you,"' she sang, the minute he stepped inside.

'Thank you,' he said, kissing her and smiling at the lopsided cake with its runny icing. 'You've got the place lovely. Let's pull up the drawbridge and shut out the world,' he said, closing the door behind him.

They took their tea sat on the bed together with Dog on the mat with a bone Matthew had brought home from the galley at *Dolphin*. He laughed. 'I remember watching all the married men going off home with their little bags of this and that for the missis. Now I'm a bundle-man, too.'

'I got a you a present,' Mary said, reaching under the bed and pulling up a lumpy pillowcase.

'It's not the baby, is it?' he teased.

''Course not.' She laughed, watching him unwrap the set of carpenter's chisels and mallet that she had bought secretly, week by week, and hidden upstairs.

A delighted grin spread across his face. 'They're beautiful,' he said, holding each piece and running his fingers over the blades and handles. 'What I shall be able to make with these,' he murmured. 'Thank you, my love, I'll treasure these and pass them on to our young lad. Where is he?' Mathew said, resting his hand on her belly. 'Thought he was going to pop out 'specially for my birthday.'

Mary burst into tears. 'I'm so frightened,' she wailed.

'Oh, come here,' he soothed, drawing her into his arms. 'I'll be with you and Nurse Boyden and Dog here. You're a strong healthy girl and having babies is what you're designed for.'

'What, like a submarine for going under water?'

Matthew laughed. 'You're prettier than any boat.' He took her hand. 'What bit frightens you?' he asked, holding her hand.

'All of it,' she whispered.

'Why don't you go and see the midwife tomorrow? Ask her to tell you what's likely to happen. How would that be?'

'Won't stop it hurting,' she said.

'Well, I think knowing what to expect might take away some of the fear. But I'm only a man.'

'You sure she'll let you stay with me?' Mary asked him.

'If I promise not to faint and keep boiling the water and making cups of tea,' he said, 'I'll be indispensable.'

By ten o'clock Matthew had taken Dog for his last walk and climbed into bed beside her. Mary lay tired but sleepless. She tossed and turned, unable to find a comfortable position. Matthew was sound asleep, his arm lying like lead across her stomach. From the mat came the regular sawing noise of Dog snoring. She wished she could wake up in the morning and find the baby magically arrived. Even she had to smile in the dark at her foolishness. At some point in the night she must have slept, for she woke to see Matthew getting ready for work.

'What's the time?' she asked.

'It's only half six. Got ages before I need to stir myself. Like a cuppa?'

'Dunnow, I feel funny.'

'Like how?' he said, coming and sitting beside her on the bed.

'Heavy and achey.'

'Achey where?'

'Down in my back.'

'What d'you want me to do?' he asked. 'Shall I go for Nurse Boyden?'

'Don't leave me,' Mary begged, 'don't feel safe.' She had always hated her own company and now the thought of having the baby alone terrified her. Everyone said that first babies took their time, but there was always an exception.

'Tell you what, I'll fetch you a bowl of water and you can have a wash and tiddly yourself up. We'll have a bit of breakfast and take it from there.'

Mary nodded, getting up and feeling under the bed for her slippers. As she came back from the lavatory a deep spasm of pain gripped her, making her cry out.

Matthew looked anxiously at her, making her more afraid.

'Come and sit on the bed,' he said, taking her arm. 'As soon as I see the women going off to the laundry I'll nab them to sit with you while I get help.'

'I – I thinks it's gone now,' she gasped, feeling foolish. 'Have me wash and you pour the tea.'

'I shall have to nip up to *Dolphin* and see the engineer officer about getting a day's leave, before eight o'clock, or I shall be in the rattle good and proper.'

'Never knew what that meant,' she said. 'Do you?'

'Ooh arr, lady,' he said, doing his Ancient Mariner voice, 'be lost in the mists of time. All I know is failure to turn up for duty could be stoppage of pay or leave. I'll borrow a bike from one of the blokes at the boatyard, but first I'll get the midwife.'

'Don't leave me on my own,' she begged.

''Course not,' he said, sitting beside her and taking up the hairbrush. 'Let's fix you up all tidy. That Janey of yours might stay with you.'

After washing and changing she felt better and even managed to sit in a chair with a cup of tea and eat some toast that Matthew brought her on a tray.

'It's half past seven,' he said. 'I'll let Dog out and catch your friend.'

'Here, Janey?' he called.

'Christ, it ain't started, has it?' she yelled, breaking away from her friends. 'Hello, Mary, how you getting on? Pains coming good and strong?'

'Matthew, you won't be long, will you?' Mary asked, chewing her hand.

'I'll ride like the wind.'

'Oh! Get on that bike,' Janey said to him. 'Don't need blokes cluttering up the place. You've done your bit poking it in. Her turn now to push it out.' Laughing, she took out her tobacco tin and rolled a cigarette.

'Be quick,' Mary begged, finding Janey's relentless cheerfulness hard to take.

He kissed her and sped away, with Dog bounding after him.

'That'll take some of that tyke's fat off, keepin' up with that bike,' Janey laughed, standing in the doorway.

'Shut the door,' she snapped. 'It's bloomin' freezing in here. And put out that fag, it's making me feel sick.'

'Narky mare,' laughed her friend. 'Be blooming ages yet. 'Might as well walk about a bit between pains.'

'Only had one. Now, I just feel heavy.'

'Well it's a start,' said Janey cheerfully. 'Let's get your stuff out and get the bed ready.'

They covered the mattress with a mackintosh and an old patched sheet she'd kept. Beside the bed was the box the midwife had asked her to have in readiness, with binders, safety-pins, a stack of old newspapers and a new nightdress.

'You got a cot for his nibs and baby clothes?'

'Cot's upstairs, no don't get it down,' she cried, 'not till he's here.'

'Calm down,' said Janey. 'You got ages yet, with lots of hard work ahead of ya. Them muscles got to stretch to buggery. Cor, I remembers my Frank, the first one, thought me back would break. Still, when you sees yer little one and takes him in yer arms, it's all forgot.'

Mary burst out crying. 'I think it's dead,' she sobbed.

''Course he ain't,' Janey said, putting her arms round her. 'Whatever's give you that idea, you daft mare?'

'Hasn't moved for ages,' she whimpered.

'Saving its strength,' she said. 'Means he's on his way. Didn't old Boyden say as his head was engaged last time she saw yer?'

Mary sighed with relief. Janey's rough humour could be grating at times but there was an underlying kindness and common sense that she valued. Especially today when she didn't know where she was or what having the head engaged meant.

'That's better. Now, you show me what you got fer the little feller, while we waits for Matthew to get back.'

There was a brisk rapping on the door and Janey sprang up and opened it to Nurse Boyden. 'Good morning, Mrs Miller,' she said, smiling at her. 'Your husband will be along later. He has gone to sort out some leave, I think. Right,' she said briskly, 'if you could just show me where I can wash me hands. I'll need a clean towel and a nail brush, if you please.'

'I better go and clock in,' said Janey. 'I'll call in tonight and see how you're faring?'

'See you later,' said Mary, 'thanks for dropping by.' She was glad of something to do and went up the stairs to the old bedroom to fetch a towel. Back in the kitchen she poured some water from the kettle into a basin and set it on the ledge by the stove.

'You have it very cosy here, Mrs Miller, very cosy indeed. Now, while I wash my hands you might as well refill the kettle. By the time I've examined you, your husband will be back and we can all have a cup of tea together.'

Mary began to feel calmer. Nurse Boyden was really quite nice. She asked her to lie on the bed and roll up her nightie while she gently probed inside her.

'You're barely dilated at all, my dear,' she said. 'Relax, you have a long way to go yet. For the next few hours do whatever suits you. Sleep, walk about, sit in a chair. I shall be checking up on my other patients.'

There was the sound of the key in the lock and Matthew rushed in. 'Got forty-eight hours,' he said. 'That should see us right. Oh, hello, Nurse,' he said, 'Glad you're here. Is everything all right?'

'Splendid, Mister Miller. You have come just in time to pour the tea.' She looked at her watch. 'Afraid I shan't have time for one now. I'll leave you a list of my visits and if the pains become frequent, you will be able to find me. I'll drop in again at one.' Picking up her case she nodded to Mary and hurried away.

She dozed for a while and was wakened by another dragging pain. At the next one she shouted at Matthew. 'Can't stand this. Gotta get the midwife. No, don't get her, stay with me. Don't look at me like that.' She knew she was being totally unreasonable but could not stop herself.

'Good job I love you,' he said ruefully, rubbing her back.

Mary burst into tears. 'I'm sorry,' she gasped, 'I'm rotten, don't deserve you at all.'

'I don't know who does,' he teased.

And then Nurse Boyden came back and took charge of both of them.

'Mrs Miller, have you got everything? Are the baby clothes ready? Where is the cot?'

'It's upstairs,' said Matthew. 'I'll go and get it.'

'Not yet,' cried Mary, 'just in case.'

'Oh! Stuff and nonsense,' said Nurse Boyden. 'It must be freezing up there. You'll need to put the bedding by the fire to warm. It's December, he's not an Eskimo.'

Her no-nonsense approach calmed Mary and she accepted Matthew being there with no qualms.

'As long as he doesn't faint and does as he's told we shall get along very well.'

The pains came closer and closer together. She pulled on a towel tied to the foot of the bed, her hair plastered to her head with sweat. Matthew rubbed her back and bathed her face and fetched her cups of water.

'Mary push, push, that's it, baby's coming. The head's here, stop now, I'm just turning the shoulders. Aah! It's a girl.'

Nurse Boyden smacked the baby briskly on the rump and it let out an indignant wail.

Mary burst into tears. 'Is she all right?' she gasped. 'Is she well?'

'She's perfect,' Nurse Boyden said.

Matthew was crying, too. 'I love both of you,' he said, kissing her face. 'Thank you; thank you, love.'

'Congratulations, the pair of you. Now, Mister Miller, if you could just hand me that thread and stand there with the scissors. I'll tie it just there, a couple of inches from baby and another one for her mother. That's it, I'll cut in between.'

'Let me see her, let me see her,' Mary gasped.

Matthew laid her in her arms.

'Oh! She's beautiful. Look at her face, it's so tiny – and those long eyelashes. Oh, I love her.' Mary could not stop looking at her baby. She uncurled her fingers and studied the tiny nails. She touched the soft blonde down on the edges of her ears. The baby opened its eyes which were a deep slatey blue. It poked out its tiny pointed tongue and Mary laughed delightedly.

'Mr Miller, I think we could all do with a cup of tea. Give baby to me and I'll weigh her and check her over.'

Reluctantly she let her go, but leant on her side, watching Nurse Boyden cleaning its eyes and nose and mouth. The midwife wrapped their daughter in a nappy and suspended her from a precarious looking hook and spring contraption.

'Seven pounds exactly, a nice weight,' she said.

'What shall we call her?' Matthew asked.

'Hope,' said Mary. 'Hope Elizabeth, for your mother.'

He wanted to cry again. Ever since he had settled to the news of the baby he had wanted his mother's name if it were a girl, but knew that it had to be Mary's choice. His thoughts were not allowed time to form themselves under Nurse Boyden's firm commands. He was kept busy, disposing of the afterbirth, fetching water to bathe mother and baby and setting the cottage pie in the oven.

'I'm starving,' Mary laughed.

There was an impatient rapping on the door and Janey stood there. 'What's happened?' she demanded.

'I'm a dad,' he cried. 'Hope Elizabeth. Come in, come in.'

'Ain't you the clever one,' she teased. 'Hello, Mary, you looks happier than when I last saw ya.' Janey lifted back the corner of the baby's blanket and smiled down into her face. 'I'n't she a little treasure?'

'Will you stay with them for a few minutes while I go and phone Gran?' asked Matthew, dragging on his raincoat.

''Course I will. Hey! Is that cottage pie going spare?'

'Mrs Miller,' said the midwife, 'I'll be back around nine to see you both again. You rest, now.'

'Thank you ever so much,' said Mary, her eyes shining. 'I couldn't have done it without you.'

'Think nothing of it. It's all down to nature. Once the birth begins, not even an earthquake will stop a baby being born.'

After she had closed the door, Matthew kissed Mary, called to Dog and set off for the phone box.

'Oh Matthew that's wonderful,' Granny cried. 'I'll nip in next door and give them the good news. If I know Fred he'll be like a dog with two tails.'

Matthew sat on the beach in a fog of happiness. He had no words to describe how he felt. He was a father. It was a wonder to him, a painful, sweating, toiling wonder. He had been by turns joyful, queasy and terrified. Matthew thought of his delight when Mary had given him his carpentry tools, only last night. Now that pleasure seemed as nothing compared to the bliss of holding his new daughter and watching her sleepy perfection. Mary had been so brave and fierce. Tears filled his eyes. For her to choose his mother's name had been such a loving thing to do. It completed things and joined the past to the future. 'Hope Elizabeth,' he whispered and it hung for a moment on his frosty breath.

Mary lay watching her daughter. Already she loved her, yet only yesterday she had hardly dared to believe in her existence. In the last twenty-four hours Mary knew she had grown up. Nothing would ever frighten her so much again. She had given birth not only to a baby but to a new family. Dad and her brothers and sisters were now the old one. At last she could let go of them. They were across the water and must look out for themselves. Even her market stall had lost its hold on her. She would sell it to Danny. If Dad and the nippers wanted it they would have to raise the money. Mary laughed. Perhaps if they owned it, they might stir themselves to make it a real success.

She thought of Matthew and wondered what he was feeling – exhaustion, most likely. He had been so good to her and taken all her fear and temper. She had surprised herself at choosing his mother's name for their baby and his delight had been a rich reward. Perhaps Hope Elizabeth had changed her fortune. Perhaps now she could dare to trust the future.

36

Dora burst through the door, grabbed Cissie and swung her round the room. 'It's come, it's come,' she cried. 'This calls for a drink. I haven't been so thrilled in ages.'

Cissie laughed, caught up in her friend's excitement. 'What's 'appened? Dora, sit down and tell me.'

'Mary's had her baby, a little girl, Hope Elizabeth. Last night at six o'clock. They're all in a ferment round there. Dad and Granny Pragnell are going over tomorrow. Ain't seen them so lit up in ages.'

Cissie watched her friend pouring the rum into their tea, chattering away, and thought how generous she was. Full of delight at the birth of her Mary's baby, while having so recently lost one of her own soon after Harry had sailed for the West Indies. A loss Dora had not shared with his family. It was only when Cissie had come back from the hopfields that she had told her. And even then it had been only after Cissie had poured out all her own distress.

They had sat talking half the night.

'I never ever meant to keep the baby, honest, Dora. I was on my way up to the gate ready to stand there and wait for Clive. Lovely morning it was. He'd written to me, first letter I ever had what I could read myself. But I heard the little mite crying and there weren't no one listening.'

'Saw him that week,' Dora said. 'He was so pleased with your letter and looking forward to seeing you. Think he was working himself up to tell you.'

'Tell me what?'

'As he loved ya.'

'Don't reckon he loves me, now,' Cissie had cried.

'What? On account of you taking the baby?'

'No,' she had sobbed, 'because of me knowing Ted before and what happened between us.'

'You lost me, now.'

'The bloke whose baby it was used to be called Ted Garland, my little Charlie's father.'

'Blimey! Poor Ciss, what a shock! So what's it to do with Clive?'

'When I give the baby back to his missis, Ted went for me and I called 'im a bastard and said something like, I wished I'd never known him.'

'Still in the dark,' Dora said.

'Later when all the shouting was over, Clive asked me how I knew Ted and it all come out. He sort of shrunk up inside – and couldn't hardly wait to leave. Said as how he'd let me know about the reading lessons.'

'Some bloody Christian, he is,' Dora had reared up. 'What's the good of blowing that bloomin' cornet and spoutin' the Bible when he dares to think he can judge you? Ooh! that makes me so wild,' she raged.

'It wasn't his fault, it was mine. I shouldn't never have took the baby, then it wouldn't have come out,' Cissie said, anxious to defend him.

'Just as well it did. Let's you know what a bleedin' hypocrite he is. He accepted about you bein' on the game, 'cos it was just words in an old police report. But once he saw a man, close up, what you'd slept with he couldn't take it. What's at the bottom of all this is jealousy.'

'He's bin ever so good to me, Dora. Helpin' me with the readin' and everythink.'

'That don't mean he don't fancy you. Just can't admit it to

himself. So he blames you and you let him.'

Cissie had burst out crying.

'That's it have a good beller,' Dora had said, putting her arm around her. 'Men are funny creatures. If I didn't know better I'd think they come from the moon.'

Cissie managed a watery smile.

'We've all done things we're sorry about after. Even Saint bloody Clive. But you loved this Ted and had his baby and would have made a lovely mum to him. You know you ain't the only one what's bin tempted. I was engaged to Harry and of course he was away, as per usual. And I met this bloke, out of the blue. Like a madness it was. Always sneaking off after him, I was. Knew he was rubbish but I couldn't stop meself. His missis turned up and socked me one,' Dora chuckled. 'Thought she'd bust me nose. Few months later I saw him in a café and couldn't understand what I ever saw in him. When Harry came back I told him. Carried on top ropes he did, nearly bust us up, but we got over it. He forgave me and I forgave meself. You mustn't feel bad about it, Cissie.' Dora gripped her hand. 'I wants you to be mad, mad as hell that he dared to judge you. You're kind and brave and worth ten of him any day of the week.' And then her eyes had filled with tears. 'You know, Cissie, you ain't the only one what's lost a baby. I've lost three – don't seem able to hold on to them. Last one was just after Harry sailed, not long before you come to stay. Even named the little mite Barney, after me brother.'

'You never said,' gasped Cissie.

'Well, I didn't want no one feeling sorry and I didn't want to talk about it. Harry and me we cried together and then had to get on with it. Last time was the worst, when he was away. It all had to be done by letter.' Dora blew her nose and smiled at Cissie. 'We just has to pick ourselves up and carry on, don't we?'

And now Cissie was doing just that. When she had gone

back to the Slum Post, Major Grice had been kindness
itself.

'Of course I want to see you and have you work here. I
value you, Cissie. It must have been very upsetting for you.
Coming back here is the wisest move. There will be gossip
in the fields about the baby. Things get embroidered and
suspicions aroused. Better for you to be here among your
friends. In a few days there will be something else for them
to talk about.'

'Was that the only reason you sent me home?'

'We have to protect the Army's good name – a name for
fairness in our dealings. Captain Kellet had sent the Carvers
home and it was only fair that you should go, too. And that
you should continue to work with us. Showing that we absolve
you from any wrongdoing.'

'So, I gotta work here to prove sommink.'

Major Grice smiled. 'You're here because I can depend on
you, Cissie, and because you have a gift for the work and the
people love you.'

'What about Clive? He don't want to know me any more.'

'That is your business, Cissie, yours and Clive's. That must
be dealt with outside the Slum Post. We are here for the
people of Portsea, to offer them support in their difficulties,
to show loving kindness and a way of Christian living that
they might wish to follow.' She smiled. 'That's quite enough
sermonising for one day. I want you to get the nit-comb and
the sassafras oil and deal with Winnie's children.'

Months she had been back and Clive had hardly shown his
face at the Slum Post. He still marched in the band and played
the cornet and sat beside his vinegary old mother, but Cissie
made no attempt to speak with him. She had too much pride
but not enough to stop her glancing over her songbooks at
him when she thought he wasn't looking.

Lately, she had felt an anger building up in her. It was a

new sensation. Something she had always been afraid of. But now she wanted to yell at him, to make him listen and wipe that frosty look from his face.

'Like to come with us on Sunday?' asked Dora, nudging her.

'Where?' said Cissie, miles away.

'Go and see the new baby and take her a present? Watcha think?'

''Course I'll come,' she said; 'be a novelty seeing Mary as a mum.'

They arranged through Granny Pragnell to go over Sunday morning, taking a meat pie, a bottle of gravy and a bag of vegetables. Matthew was going to be on duty until the next day.

'I've left you some bedding behind,' Granny said. 'You'll have to wedge up in the little bedroom. But you should be quite snug.'

It took a while for Mary to open the door to them and they were almost knocked over be her excitable dog.

'Lovely to see ya,' she said, smiling and hugging them both. 'In quick and slam the door.'

'Ain't you got it nice in here,' said Dora, looking around her.

Cissie took in the bed with its stripey knitted blanket and the polished dresser with its brass jug filled with holly. Near the fire was a wicker cot with a hood and a brightly coloured patchwork quilt tucked around the precious Hope Elizabeth.

After Dog had been let out and Dora had made them all a cup of tea they settled themselves to the real business of the day – admiring Mary's baby.

'Ain't she a little dolly,' cooed Dora, bending over the cot. 'Who does she favour, d'you reckon?'

'Think she's going to have Matthew's hair. There's ginger

nuts both sides of the family.' There was an indignant wail
from the cot and Mary said to them,' Why don't you two
have a hold of her while I goes out to the lav. Then I'll feed
her and you can see to the dinner.' She grinned at them. 'If
you haven't got Gran's pie you can push off back home.'

They all laughed.

'I think she's a bit like your Blyth, but with Dusty's colouring. She got his long fingers and neat little ears.'

Mary glowed. 'D'you think so? He was beautiful, still is
to me.' She smiled shyly at them. 'Ta ever so much for
coming, means a lot seeing everyone so happy for me. Wish
our Harry was here,' she said, 'that would round things off
a treat.'

'So do I,' said Dora. 'You two have a yarn, I'll see to the
veg. Ciss can do the washin' up later while I haves a hold
of her.'

'Poor Dora,' said Mary, picking up Hope and beginning to
nurse her. 'I was a real mean cow to her. Now I can't believe
what a rat-bag I used to be.'

Cissie laughed. 'Bet you will be again,' she teased.

Mary laughed. 'Remember the fly rounds we used to have
at old Clements' place?'

'Seems ages and ages ago,' smiled Cissie in surprise. How
important that house had been to her – what dreams she had
woven around it. Would she ever have a place of her own?
she wondered.

The day and night passed with Mary sleeping in snatches,
Cissie taking Dog for a walk and lots of time spent in
admiring Hope Elizabeth. The midwife called on her bicycle
and seemed well pleased with mother and baby.

'Didn't never think to see Mary so happy,' said Cissie as she
and Dora knelt together looking out of the bedroom window
at lights winking on the ships across the harbour and a sky
sprinkled with stars.

'Funny, I never thought of her as pretty, did you?' Dora asked. 'Probbly 'cos she was always frowning and in a rage.'

'Reckon being happy's the best beauty treatment,' Cissie yawned.

'Wakey, wakey, rise and shine,' Matthew called up to them the next morning. 'Tea down here, if you want it.'

Going back over the ferry, after seeing Mary and Matthew so settled together, Cissie felt her mood plunge. Always she seemed to be on the outside looking in. Even at the Slum Post she was the fly on the wall in other family's lives – never at the centre. She wrestled with a knot of jealousy in her stomach. If anyone deserved to be happy it was Mary.

'Feels a bit flat, now,' said Dora, echoing her feelings. 'Reckon I'll go round to Fred's and see the kids. Want to come?'

'No, I'll get home and sort out me ironing,' Cissie said, not in the mood for the Vines.

As she walked up towards Keats's Row from the harbour, she saw Clive Perks alone on the other side of the road. 'Hello, Clive,' she called.

He nodded and hurried on in the opposite direction.

His casual dismissal angered her. She crossed the road and hurried after him. 'I said hello,' she snapped, when she caught up with him at the corner of Queen Street.

He blushed. 'Sorry,' he mumbled, 'I was miles away.'

'Well, you better get back here and quick, 'cos I got a few things to say to you.'

'I'm on duty, Cissie,' he said, looking about him. 'Can't talk now.'

'Don't stop ya listening,' she challenged, 'and I got all afternoon.'

He bent his head and hurried on, with Cissie hurrying after.

'You owes me an apology,' she persisted, pushing past

some neighbours gossiping outside their front doors. 'Put me in the dock, you have. Bin, judge and jury.'

'Don't know what you mean,' he mumbled, staring at the pavement.

'Called deflamation of character.'

'It's defamnation,' he corrected.

'Oh thank you, teacher,' she mocked him.

The women stared at the pair of them and Clive marched on, his arms swinging. By now they had reached Victoria Park. It was cold and almost deserted. 'You scared of me?' she challenged. 'Frightened of sitting on this bench case I manhandles ya?'

Cissie sat down and Clive perched at the far end ready for flight. 'We was pals, more than pals,' she said quietly. 'You were really good to me. Showing me how to read opened up everythink. You can't know what it's like thinking you ain't worth teaching. All my life I bin afraid of everythink, settin' meself at the bottom of the heap.'

Although he didn't look at her she knew he was listening. He had sat further back on the bench and was staring at his polished boots.

'Thought as how you knew all about me, from when you used to sit with me in hospital; didn't think nothin' would shock ya,' Cissie said. 'All that you're weighing in the balance happened years before ever we was friends. You wrote to me, Clive. ''Spect you gets letters all the time. Only ever had one letter before yours. It was from Captain Clements. Took me over six weeks to find someone to read it for me. Yours was the first letter that I could keep private and read on my own. Treasured it, I did. And, d'you know what? You was the first person to get a letter off me.' She looked up and knew that he had been watching her, but directly she met his gaze he stared again at the ground.

'Was it me takin' the baby?' she asked. 'Or was it seeing

my old lover? Or knowing about our child?' She had talked out her anger and now she felt sad. If he couldn't even talk with her, what was the point?

Getting up, she turned to him and said, 'You must make up your own mind, Clive. One thing you ain't doin' is making me feel ashamed of meself. Sorry you feels we can't be friends no more. I won't never forget you teaching me readin', always be grateful. But I can find another teacher. Ain't the end of the world. Just a shame, that's all.'

Cissie got up and stalked away, her head held high.

Red-faced, he got to his feet and called after her, but Cissie continued walking until she was out of sight.

37

The twins stared at the two piles of clothes on their bed. On top of each was a bill. 'Laundry 6d Betty Frewin.'

'What she on about?' asked Mercy, tearing up the paper and throwing it on the floor. 'Comin' in our house and bossin' us about, who she think she is?'

'Said last week if we wasn't gonna do it ourself she was charging us,' said Faith, smoothing her hand over her clean folded blouse. 'They're ironed lovely.'

'Proper sniveller you are. We're gonna be skint by the end of the week. Just think, we was panting to get home and see Dad and everyone, now I'd even go back with the Debonnaires. I hates it working at that pub.'

'What else we gonna do? They don't want any girls at the brewery,' said Faith, 'and, what they pay at the Penny Bazaar ain't worth taking yer coat off. What we got at the market didn't amount to nothink, neither. Least we don't have to stand there in the freezin' cold no more.'

'Can't even afford the pictures,' Mercy wittered on. 'And now old Betty is after the little we got left. Reckon what we'll do next year is get a place with one of them concert parties, what does ends of the pier shows. Could go to the Isle of Wight.'

''Course if we'd got ourselfs organised we could have been in the panto at the Theatre Royal,' Faith said.

'If something don't turn up soon I'll go mental.'

'D'you hear what that bloke was saying to old Martha this

morning? You know, the one that runs that big hall over in Fratton – about a Charleston competition. Reckons the girl what can dance the longest time wins ten pounds.'

'Cripes! A tenner!' Mercy laughed triumphantly. 'We got it made.'

'How come? Might be girls there what's much better dancers than you or me.'

Mercy laughed scornfully. 'But they won't hold up against two of us. Blimey, Faith, it's tailor made.'

'What you mean?'

'Use yer loaf! We're identicals, only have to dance half as long as the others.'

'How we gonna fool them without no one smelling a rat?'

Mercy laid on the bed her eyes narrowed to two slits, a sure sign that she was on to something.

'Have to go up there and get a decco at the hall beforehand. I'll do that on me own. Can't have anyone seeing us together.'

Faith felt a familiar lurch of fear. Although they were fun at the time, most of her sister's schemes ended in disaster, with Mercy legging it away, leaving her to face the music. 'What about costumes?' she asked, hoping to have found a snag.

'We'll go down the Union Street market Friday morning, see what's around.'

'Be lucky to get two the same, whatever there is,' Faith said doubtfully.

There was a loud rapping on their bedroom door. 'You two, I wants me money,' shouted Betty.

'Private up here,' yelled Mercy.

The door opened and Betty swept in and gathered up the laundry. 'No money, no clothes.'

'You gotta cheek,' Mercy snapped, tugging at the bundle.

'No, my lady, it's you that's cheeky. Leaving your poor dad to flounder about while you two healthy young girls lounges around up here.' She glared about her. 'You might well say it's private. If I lived in this slummocky dive I'd want to keep it private.'

Faith reached into her purse and handed Betty a shilling.

'Here's yer change, my duck,' the old woman said, getting sixpence out of her apron pocket.

'That's for the two of us.'

'Don't work like that,' said Betty, holding out her hand to Mercy. 'Don't like passengers.'

Glaring at her, Mercy counted out six pennies from a jar on the dressing table.

Betty smiled triumphantly. 'There's bacon stew and dumplings downstairs. Don't forget to put some by for when your brother gets back.'

Blyth straightened his tie and cleaned the toes of his shoes on the back of his socks. He opened the door of the barber's shop on The Hard and the bell jingled loudly. Having satisfied themselves that he was beneath their interest, the customers went back to their talk. Getting up from a chair, the barber, Horry Jarrold, surveyed him with a critical eye.

'Get to the back of the queue, son,' he directed. 'Juveniles must wait their turn.'

'Haven't come for a haircut,' Blyth said, trying to look boldly up into his eyes. 'I've come about the position of lather boy.'

Horry looked down at him from the advantage of his six-foot frame. 'You look a bit young to suit my purpose, sonny. Need a ladder to reach the chins of my clients.'

Looking at the boy's reflection in the mirror the customers smiled.

'I've brought my shoeshine box,' said Blyth, carrying it across to a customer being prepared for shaving. 'See, I can reach him quite well,' he said, tapping the man on the cheek.

'How old are you?' asked the barber, fetching a shaving mug from a cupboard in the corner.

'The notice in the window doesn't specify age. I'm quick and a whizz at sums.'

The customers smiled to themselves.

'You'll have no need of sums, me lad. You'll not be required to handle money.'

'Lots of ways I could be useful,' said Blyth, determined not to leave until he had succeeded in his mission. 'I could go out and tell the taxi men when a chair is free, save them waiting about and losing trade. I can sweep up and clean the basins.'

The barber draped his customer's face in a hot towel. Blyth decided this was the moment to display his insider knowledge gained from Charlie Norman, his pal at school and neighbour to the barber's family. 'Horry used to get his son to run down with his dinner every Saturday, but now he's workin' somewhere else and his missis can't take it 'cos she's a cripple. You get him his grub and you could be quids in.' Blyth promised him a percentage of his first wage if he was taken on.

'Saturdays, I could run up to St Mary's road and fetch down your dinner, from yer missis. Even give ya a free shoe-shine.' He spread out his hands, 'Can't say fairer than that.'

'What's your name?'

'Blyth Vine. I only lives round the corner, be very handy for an early start.'

'Next thing you'll be saying as how you got references.'

Blyth smiled. Forward planning – it won out every time. 'How about Lieutenant Commander Pragnell, my next door neighbour, my headmaster Mr Frazer and Captain Clements. All gentlemen of my acquaintance.'

'Christ! With a pedigree like that you'll be wanting me to pay you for the priviledge,' smiled Horry.

'Regular little toff,' laughed a customer.

'It ain't the aristocracy I'm wanting but some lad as will jump to it when asked. You got way too much to say for yourself.'

'Give him a try, Horry,' laughed another man, further down the shop, being helped into his overcoat. 'I like his spirit.'

'Hours is half seven to half eight before school during the week and all day Saturday till six o'clock. Wages four and six.'

Blyth swallowed. He could make more at his shoe shining but it could never be relied on. One rainy evening and his takings were wiped out. Besides, the porter at the Pembroke Club said he was going to talk to the head steward and get him barred. He had his eye on a Meccano set in a shop window in Queen Street. It was a big set, enough to make a crane. Miles Clements had one he'd played with when he was up there the other Friday. Perhaps he could put half a crown deposit on it while he worked for the rest.

'I'll take it, sir,' said Blyth. 'Can I go and tell my Dad and have me dinner? I'll be back in a tick and give you this afternoon for nothing.'

'It'll be a month's trial.' The barber looked up at the clock above the soap-spattered mirror. 'It's half-twelve now, be back by ten to one. You got a high opinion of yourself, my lad. We'll have to see what I reckons to ya.' He swooped down and flicked him on the neck with a towel. 'Now, bugger off. I'll be watching the clock.'

'Thanks, Betty,' said Fred, taking the mug of steaming tea and setting the plate of fruit cake to rest on the floor beside him. 'Did ya get your money off the girls?'

The big woman chuckled as she sat herself down opposite him and stirred her cup. 'Not without a struggle, but I think I'm getting the upper hand. They forgets I reared three gals of my own. Up to all their tricks, I am.'

Fred laughed. 'I reckon you saved my life, Betty,' he said. 'You've turned this place round in no time.' He looked approvingly at the clean, ironed tablecloth and the new starched net curtain at the kitchen window. 'Wish I could give you a bit more money, don't seem fair.'

'Your girls will be making up the shortfall,' she laughed. 'Besides, it's a bit of company I was needing just as much as the money. Here, you said you had some snaps of your grandaughter come today.'

'Up there on the mantelshelf, Betty, in that envelope. Little darling she is. Our Mary is thrilled with her.'

Betty's brown eyes shone. 'She's lovely. Who d'ya reckon she favours?'

'Going to have red hair, she is, like her dad and the twinnies. We'll have ta wait and see.' He cleared his throat. 'Got sommink I wants to ask ya, Betty. Was wondrin' where you was going for Christmas? Ain't far off now.'

'Staying put as far as I can see,' she said, warily. 'What's your plans?'

'Be different this year. Mary and Dusty is staying put in Gosport and I 'spect Dora and Cissie might go round to her mother's place. Thought you might like to come over with us.'

Betty burst out laughing. 'I can read your mind, Fred Vine. It's a sprat to catch a mackerel. You wants me to cook the dinner. Thinks I came down with the last shower.'

He had the grace to blush.

''Course I will.' She smiled, patting him on the knee. 'I was wondering how I was going to get me feet under your table.'

Fred laughed. He wouldn't fancy homely old Betty in a hundred years but it was good to have a woman friend. A bit of a novelty for him, but one he could well get used to.

Their dance dresses hung from the picture rail in their bedroom: yellow petticoats, in reality, but eked out with yards of lampshade fringe all over the skirts. It had cost them a shilling each to get Betty to sew it on but it was worth every penny. The result was perfect. With a good brushing and steaming over the kettle their suede Cuban heeled shoes were as good as new. Betty had even sewn some sequins on a satin hair band for them at an extra threepence each.

It was cold and frosty when they hurried up Arundel Street on the Friday night, their shoes in paper bags and hearts knocking against their ribs.

'Reckon we'll get away with it?' asked Faith, hoping vainly for her sister to abandon ship.

'I've got it all planned out. All you gotta do is kick up yer legs and keep smilin'. Run through what I told ya.'

'Gotta go out in the yard, go through the door and near where the band plays there's a big Egyptian vase off to one side. Gotta get behind it and when you gives us a shove I gotta take over from you. I do five turns then comes back and it's your go again.'

'Got it,' said Mercy, triumphantly. 'What about when the competition's finished?'

'You legs it down the stairs behind the vase and out the door into the yard and over the wall into the next street.'

Standing behind the vase while the crowd whirled around her tested Faith's nerve severely. What if someone found her before they'd even started? All their plans for spending their winnings would be down the Swanee.

Faith almost jumped out of her skin as the band struck up. The heat, the cigarette smoke and the noise had her nerves in tatters. Suddenly the music stopped and someone began making an announcement.

'Ladies and Gentlemen, welcome to Friday night at the Crystal Lounge. It's time for the event that you have all been waiting for – the non-stop Charleston competition. Suzette, how much is the prize money, this week?' the Master of Ceremonies asked, his voice throbbing with fake excitement.

'Fifteen pounds, Johnnie,' the girl, announced.

'Are the dancers all in position?'

'Yes, Johnnie, all ten of them.'

'Very well, then – music, maestro, please.'

'Charleston, Charleston, dee dee deed deed dad da,' the band played and the dancers began to circle the floor. Faith tensed ready to spring out the moment Mercy gave her the signal.

'Out,' snapped her sister, giving her a shove.

For some reason old Bunny Beaumont's motto came to mind. 'Eyes and teeth, eyes and teeth,' Faith leapt into her performance waving her arms and kicking her legs for all she was worth. 'Out,' she snapped to her sister, as she completed her five circuits.

Mercy's excitement soared as two of the girls left the stage – only seven more to go. Round and round she went until her agreed distance had been passed. 'Out,' she whispered.

Now it was Faith's turn to gloat as another girl limped away. She was back sweating behind the urn when Mercy whispered again and off she went. By the time she was back to prompt her sister another two dancers had admitted defeat.

She crouched there sweating, keyed up for her next tour of the floor.

'Leg it to the yard,' Mercy snapped, just as Faith was poised to Charleston. She tried to crouch and step down the stairs at the same time and nearly fell at the bottom. Her hands were trembling as she pushed back the bar and found herself out in the yard, shivering in her thin dress. If only she'd thought to hide her coat out by the dustbin. She was perished.

Mercy was jubilant.

'That was stupendous,' said the oily Master of Ceremonies, kissing her on the cheek and pressing three crisp white fivers into her hand. Mercy bowed and smiled. Quickly she rushed to the cloakroom and picked up the two coats, one inside the other and made her way out to the yard.

'Thought I'd 'ave frostbite,' moaned Faith, her teeth chattering. 'Got the money?'

Mercy patted her coat pocket. 'Don't reckon I can walk home, me legs is burning,' she said, when they were safely over the wall and into the street.

'We can't catch a bus, someone'll see us; besides, I ain't got no change. If we could just make it up to Fratton station we might pick up a taxi.'

'Have ter be careful, don't want anyone rumbling us or we'll have to hand back the money.'

Suddenly Faith leapt into the road and held up her arm.

A taxicab came to a screeching halt. 'Where d'you want to go, my pretty?' asked the driver, leaning out of the window.

'Ain't yer pretty and there's two of us,' Mercy snapped. 'Down Lemon Street,' she said, opening the back door.

'Must be sisters,' he said, smiling into the driving mirror.

'Twins,' said Faith, yawning.

'Long way from Portsea. What you doing up here?'

'Just drive,' Mercy said. 'We ain't giving ya our life 'istry.'

They hugged each other and couldn't stop giggling.

'How much,' asked Faith, as the cab came to a halt at the top of Lemon Street.

'Five pounds,' said the driver, holding out his hand.

'Very funny,' laughed Mercy, sarcastically. 'You must be mental.'

'No it's you darling,' he sneered. 'Thought you'd got away with it, didn't ya?'

'You ain't havin' more than five bob and that's robbery?' Mercy blustered.

'Saw you at the dance place,' he said. 'Very nifty footwork the pair of ya.' He laughed. 'Only, old Johnnie Vernon can turn real nasty if he thinks anyone has pulled a fast one. Have to give back all that cash, could have yer faces in the paper.' He rolled his eyes in mock horror. 'Nasty, very nasty.'

'Oh give it him, Merce,' begged Faith, knowing her sister's temper and not trusting the greasy cabbie not to turn nasty.

'Bloody chiseller,' Mercy screamed, kicking out at the cab.

Faith grabbed her handbag and took out one of the five-pound notes and thrust it at the cabbie, just as he was about to step out onto the pavement. Before handing the bag back to her sister, she took her own percentage of the night's work. Long experience had taught her not to rely on Mercy's sense of fair play.

'Fancy a cocoa?' she asked, pulling the string through the letterbox and opening the front door.

38

Swathed in a blanket over her coat Mary stood on the shingle with Matthew listening to the ships' hooters bringing in the New Year. Nineteen twenty-seven it couldn't hope to be half as momentous as the year just gone. So much had happened: the move to Gosport, the job at the laundry, her marriage and the birth of Hope Elizabeth.

'Happy New Year, love,' Matthew said, kissing her soundly. 'And you, little one,' he said, kissing the top of his daughter's head were she lay tucked inside his coat. Dog stood at the water's edge barking defiantly at the hooters. From behind them came cheers and whistles as the crowd at the Vixen spilled out into the lane.

'Let's go and see the fun,' said Mary.

They joined hands with the merrymakers encircling the pub.

> *'Should auld acquaintance be forgot and never brought to mind, . . .*
> *We'll drink a cup of kindness yet for the sake of auld lang syne'*

Then joined up together in a snake, weaving up and down the road. 'Happy New Year, Happy New Year,' they called to one another.

Coldness drove them back inside their cottage and Matthew lit some candles and poured them each a glass of raisin wine, a present from Daisy. Mary sat on the bed, and pulled up her old jumper and began to feed her daughter. Hope Elizabeth sucked vigorously, her face flushed and eye seeming to focus more clearly.

'What d'you wish for?' he asked, leaning down and kissing her breast.

'Can't think of anything I haven't got already,' she said, smiling at him. 'Just you, me and babes, all of us well and happy. It's funny, I've spent me life wanting everything to change, battling on and feeling full of bitterness. Now it's as if I'm set free. When little Hope came she made us a new family, one we'd both chosen.'

'Wish I wasn't going away next week,' he said, dipping his finger in the glass and painting her lips with wine. 'Still, by the time I get back we shall be able to carry on where we left off.'

Mary giggled. 'Is that all you'll be missing,' she whispered, stroking his back and letting her hand slide down over his bottom.

'I shall miss little Hope,' he said, stroking her wispy blonde hair and circling Mary's breast as if by accident.

That night they held each other close, whispering far into the morning.

'It's gone too quick,' she cried the following week as he stood on the doorstep holding her tightly in his arms. In his pocket was a photo of all three of them taken at a studio in the High Street just before Christmas.

'Look after yourself, you two,' he said, setting his cap straight and hefting his steaming bag onto his shoulder.

Mary stood in the lane with Hope in her arms waving to him. Then he ran back and kissed her again almost savagely. 'I did tell you I loved you, didn't I?' he asked.

'Yes,' she said, returning the kiss. 'Over and over, I won't never forget.'

And then he was gone hurtling down the road and out of sight.

*   *   *

Matthew walked down to the boat, the next morning, with none of his usual excitement at going to sea. Half his mind was now back with Mary and his baby, Hope Elizabeth. Before her birth, his family had been his crew-mates and now he felt at a distance from them. Beginning a new family of his own had been an overwhelming experience and he was still coming to terms with it.

'Have to get my little black book out now we're going to Portland,' boasted Boggy, 'got a widow woman down there grateful as hell.'

'Her feller must have been dead a long time to find you worth shagging,' laughed Bob Cowley.

'Probbly that blind one that old Jumper told us about last time.'

'Just don't appreciate my sexual magnetism,' sneered Boggy.

'Where d'ya get that from,' somebody asked, 'electrician's manual?'

And so the chaff went back and forth.

Once on board and leaving harbour Matthew's thoughts became focused on the tasks needed to get the *L75* under way. He and Bob Cowley went through their usual routines and any thoughts of home were stowed away until later.

On arriving in Portland harbour they were called together on the depot ship to be given a talk about their forthcoming activities.

'The objectives of our exercises with the battle fleet are threefold: one, to get experience in receiving aircraft reports of enemy movements; two, attacking the Battle Fleet and three; exercising aerial reconnaissance.' The Commander paced about in front of them. 'There will be two forces,' he said. 'Red force comprises battleships, destroyers and submarines. We are to be the blue force. That is, the submarines of the *Dolphin* flotilla and aircraft from the tenth group of the RAF.'

Back on board the *L75* there was excited talk about the exercise the next day and its likely success. Matthew came off watch at eight that night and managed to write a few lines to Mary before settling to sleep.

My Dear Love,

How I miss my little family and look forward to seeing you both as soon as ever I can. Give Hope a kiss from me and tuck up warm. Will send you a longer letter when I've got more time.

Love you forever and always,

Your Matthew.

xxxxx

He slipped it inside his pay book ready to post with all the others when next he was ashore. Mary had often complained of the long stretches between letters and then getting a big batch of them all at once. 'Don't have letterboxes in the ocean,' he had laughed.

'Think I should have a pigeon,' she'd teased, 'with a little waterproof satchel.'

'Grey up on top,' said one of the deck watch to Matthew, as he passed him in the engine room. 'What with that and the spindrift, we'll be playing hide and seek with the rest of the fleet.'

As she steered towards the line of battle cruisers the *L75* rose slowly and levelled off at periscope depth.

The pipe, 'Stand by to surface', had Matthew busy carrying out the necessary engine-room routines when he heard the deafening noise of a battle cruiser bearing down on the submarine. Everything shook and the boat was plunged in darkness. The violence of the impact with its thrashing propellers and the rending of the hull plates was terrifying in its speed and finality. The *L75* and her crew were lost.

*   *   *

Mary slipped the letter into her bag then tucked Hope into her pram, fastening the apron across the hood. She shivered as the wind blew down the lane making her eyes water. Once she'd posted the letter she would get some shopping then wait outside the laundry for the girls to come out for their dinner break. Daisy was coming over for a sandwich and to see the baby.

Even though Hope Elizabeth was cocooned beneath the covers Mary chattered away to her as she walked up the High Street. 'I've written to Daddy and told him what a good girl you are,' she said as they reached the postbox. 'Bye-bye, letter, come home soon, Daddy.'

'She's a little treasure,' Daisy said, taking Hope onto her lap while Mary poured them both a cup of tea. 'You still want to come back to the laundry?' she asked, helping herself to corned-beef sandwich.

'Not so sure now,' Mary said, unbuttoning her blouse and beginning to feed her daughter. 'Reckon we can manage for a bit. Matthew's not at all keen on me leaving Hope with anyone yet. And to tell you the truth neither am I now. Funny, you've no idea how you're going to feel till afterwards.'

'Right enough,' said Daisy, helping herself to another sandwich.

When Hope was fed Mary slid her carefully back in the pram and saw Daisy off at the door. 'Come over again soon,' she said. 'Don't want to fall behind with the gossip.'

The next morning she went out to get a paper from the shop by the ferry. It wasn't a routine thing, but today she had a fancy for one.

As she came out of the lane with the pram she began to make sense of what the newsboy was shouting.

'Submarine missing off Portland, fears for the safety of the *L75* and her crew.'

The paper forgotten, Mary hurtled up the High Street

towards the submarine base, her stomach clenched in terror. 'Matthew, Matthew,' his name pulsed through her as she rushed on. At the entrance to HMS *Dolphin* she was joined by other women, looking equally distraught. They crowded round the notice fixed to the gate.

> *There is concern for the crew of HMS L75 who were on exercise with the fleet off Portland yesterday. The submarine failed to surface and a search is under way. Relatives will be informed immediately there is any further news.*

The women clung to each other in little distressed knots around the gate, some sobbing, others numb and dry-eyed. Mary did not want the comfort of strangers. It was too early. In the word 'concern' there was still a sliver of hope.

Beattie Pragnell read the stop press announcement in the paper that evening and got immediately to her feet. 'Albert, I must go to Mary. The *L75*, her Matthew's boat, is missing after colliding with a battle cruiser. I suppose there's no hope of survivors.'

'None at all, my love,' he said. 'Shall I drive you round there?'

'No, my dear, I need to get there quickly. I'll just gather a few things together and be on my way across on the ferry.'

At the door she turned and kissed him. 'Don't expect me back tonight,' she said.

'Let me in, love, I'm freezing,' Beattie called through the letter-box, 'It's Gran.'

Directly she had drawn back the bolt Mary launched herself into her arms.

'Say he's not dead,' she sobbed. 'Say it, Gran.'

39

It was the longest night of her life. Beattie held the sobbing girl in her arms until she thought she would drop with weariness.

'Say he's not gone,' she begged repeatedly.

'Mary,' she said, taking her firmly by the shoulders. 'I wish with all my heart I could say it to you. But I can't lie, it wouldn't help. There is really not a chance that he could be saved. Matthew's gone, my dear, and I'm so, so sorry.'

'No, no, no!' she screamed hysterically, setting Dog barking and the child crying.

She paced up and down the room and Beattie paced with her. In one of her calmer patches Mary fed little Hope and seemed to draw comfort from her daughter. By half past five she had sunk into a restless sleep.

Meanwhile Beattie splashed her face with water and combed her hair into some sort of order. She crept about the place trying to tidy up and search out something for breakfast. Heating a kettle of water she bathed Hope Elizabeth and changed her nappy, then walked her up and down trying to pacify her. The baby was hungry. Often, after such a shock, the mother's milk would fail and the child would have to be bottle-fed. She hoped it wouldn't happen to Mary. Nursing her child would give the girl a reason to keep going and the little one was barely a month old, still desperately in need of that special closeness. The feeding process would comfort both of them.

She looked down at Mary's pale tear-stained face; even in sleep she was whimpering. Hope began to scream and her mother's eyes flew open. She struggled to sit up and held out her arms. 'Don't say it,' she begged Beattie. 'I know it but can't bear to hear it.'

'My pet, you must have something to eat and drink to keep up your strength. Don't want your milk to go.'

'Dunnow what I want,' she whispered, tears trickling down her face, ''cept Matthew not to be dead.'

'I'll make you a bowl of bread and milk,' said Beattie, 'that'll slip down easy.'

'What we gonna do?' she heard Mary whisper to her baby.

By eleven o'clock Beattie had the place tidied and Hope Elizabeth settled to sleep in her pram. She had bullied Mary into having a wash and eating some breakfast. Now she lay on the bed in an exhausted sleep with an old shirt of Matthew's in her arms.

Beattie let Dog out of the door and saw Albert drive up the lane with Fred beside him. She put her finger to her lips and the two of them crept into the house.

Albert took down the lead from a hook on the wall. 'Why don't we take the animal for a walk while Fred sits a while with Mary?' he suggested.

Beattie got her coat and signalled to her old neighbour that there was tea in the pot on the table.

'My dear Beatrice you look exhausted,' said Albert, calling to Dog and fastening the lead to his collar. 'I must insist that you come home tonight. Fred is ready to stay as long as Mary wants him.'

She squeezed his arm, too weary and sad to say anything.

Mary woke to the sound of someone knocking on the door and the sight of Dad holding a telegram in his hand. She leapt to her feet. 'No, no,' she begged, 'I don't want it,' she cried, rushing upstairs and slamming the door behind her. Fred spoke to the boy and he cycled away. The house fell silent. Mary stared out of the window at the sea below. No, she couldn't bear to think of Matthew lying deep in the cold and wet miles and miles away. She wrapped her arms about her chest and paced about sobbing to herself. Somewhere in the distance Hope was crying. Mary's breasts were hard and full and she realised it was hours since her daughter had been fed.

Fred came up the stairs and tapped on the door. 'Come out please, love. Your little girl is crying for you.'

'Bring her up here,' she called.

Her father opened the door. 'Too cold, love, come downstairs. I've put the telegram on the mantelpiece; you read it when you're ready.'

Fred, his eyes red-rimmed from crying, was walking round the room with Hope Elizabeth in his arms. 'Granddad's princess, that's who you are, my pretty,' he whispered to her.

'Give her here,' said Mary.

'Make you a cuppa,' he said, going out into the kitchen.

She sat with her eyes closed while her daughter took her feed. All the time she was conscious of the telegram waiting like a ticking bomb. When Hope was satisfied, she changed her and handed her to Fred while she opened the envelope and forced herself to read its contents.

The Admiralty deeply regret that Acting Leading Stoker Matthew Miller of the submarine L75 is feared to have lost his life. A letter follows.

There was no possible way of misunderstanding the message. Matthew was dead.

'He's gone,' she said. 'He's really gone.'

'It would have been so quick, love,' he said. 'Wouldn't have suffered, the poor lad.'

'Hold me, Dad, hold me tight,' she cried, burrowing her face in his chest.

Dog barked and scrabbled at the front door and Dad got up to let him in along with Beattie and Albert.

'What d'you want me to do, Mary?' asked Granny. 'Your dad's staying tonight but I could come back tomorrow.'

Mary put her arms around her dearest friend.

'Dad'll ring you when I wants you,' she said. 'Till then, me and him will cope. Just one thing. Wants you and Uncle Albert to come and pick me up for the service, when they has one, in the dockyard church. Can't face the thought of crossing water.'

The week until the memorial service dragged by punctuated by walks with Dad and Dog and Hope Elizabeth. The letter of confirmation came from the Admiralty of Matthew's death and instructed her to send her various certificates to the Accountant General of the navy in order to assess the amount of her widow's pension. 'Widow' – what a hateful word it was – unchosen and foisted on her. The hand-written letter from HMS *Dolphin* comforted, especially as the sender, Lieutenant Commander Stevenson, had spoken to her and Matthew when they were out once in Gosport. He had leant into the pram and called the sleeping Hope Elizabeth 'A fine little chap.' How they had laughed. Tears filled her eyes. When would she feel like laughing now? she wondered.

Dear Mrs Miller,

On behalf of the officers and men of the submarine depot at Fort Blockhouse *I beg to offer my sincerest sympathy in the loss of your husband.*

I can assure you that the loss of so many of our friends and comrades has affected us more than I can say and I can only express our very deep sorrow and offer our heartfelt condolence.

Yours sincerely,

T.L. Stevenson

And then the day arrived. Mary havered about leaving Hope Elizabeth with Dora or Cissie but decided that she couldn't part with her. She needed to hold her and have her warmth to bear the cold reality of her husband's death. Today she would meet the other wives and see their faces as marked by grief as her own. She had hidden away with Dad and Gran but now she must expose herself to public sympathy.

A wreath had been delivered. Mary was taking it with her to the service and then out to the Naval War Memorial on the sea front. She remembered the other submarine disaster, the loss of the *M1* on the day she and Matthew got engaged. Both of them had walked later to the memorial and read the messages on the wreaths.

'I know it's a mournful place,' he'd said, 'but it's facing the water and I like the bit about having "no other grave but the sea," that would suit me well.'

Yes, that was the least she could do for him.

It was bitingly cold when she and Dad stepped out of Albert Pragnell's car near the dockyard and met up with the rest of the family. All of them hugged her but Mercy.

She gasped as she walked into St Anne's Church and saw that almost every seat was taken. Across the aisle she nodded to Vi Kendall, no longer the confident, bustling wife but a bewildered figure clinging to her little boys. Mary sat with Hope Elizabeth in her arms and flanked by Dad and Gran. Automatically she got up and sat down when required but was unable to steady her voice enough to sing any of the hymns. All around her were sailors with submarine cap ribbons, some of them known to Matthew perhaps, even mess-mates from other boats. Only they would know what he had felt in those last terrifying seconds.

The naval chaplain rose to read the lesson, much of it meaningless words to her. But then the last couple of verses caught her imagination.

'Then we which are alive and remain shall be caught up together with them in the clouds, to meet with the Lord in the air: and so shall we ever be with the Lord. Wherefore comfort one another with these words.'

How she wished she could believe that to be true.

After more hymns and the 'Funeral March' and 'Land of Hope and Glory' it was over.

At the gates of the dockyard she hugged Vi and promised to take Hope Elizabeth to see her one day.

'What you want to do, love?' Dad asked as they stood shivering together.

'I wants to take me wreath out to the Memorial on the front,' she said, 'and be on me own for a bit.'

'Let Albert drive you there and wait in the car for you,' said Granny. 'It's too cold for you and the babes to walk that far.'

'I'll come with ya,' said Blyth.

Mary kissed him and for once he didn't scrub it away with his hand.

'We'll all see you back home,' said Granny, gathering up Dad and her sisters.

She and Blyth stood looking up at the stone lions and Mary read the words she had written on her card.

*For Matthew Miller, husband, father and submariner
Very dearly loved by his wife Mary and daughter Hope
Elizabeth*

As if aware that she had been mentioned her daughter set up a howl of hunger as Mary laid the wreath of white chrysanthemums at the foot of the column.

'Thanks for coming,' she said to Blyth.

'Liked him,' he muttered, 'was a good bloke.'

They were getting into the car when a woman in a black

coat and beret hurried up to them. 'You relations of Matthew Miller?' she asked.

Mary looked at her. Hair the same colour as Matthew's was curling round the beret and there was even a faint sprinkling of freckles across her cheeks.

'Are you . . . ?' she asked.

'Auntie Peg, his dad's sister,' she said.

'I'm Mary, his wife,' she said, refusing to say the hated word, widow.

'Saw the bit in the paper and said to Fish that I had to come.'

'Who's Fish?' asked Blyth.

'Me husband, fisherman all his life. We lives in Whitstable. Matthew used to come and stay with us in the houseboat when he was a lad.'

'Will you come back with us and have something to eat?' asked Mary. 'Mr Pragnell there will give us a lift back to my dad's place. I gotta go, baby needs feeding.'

'Gladly,' said Auntie Peg, 'as long as I gets to the station by half past two. Don't like leaving Fish on his own too long on account of his chest. Hold up a mo, I got this bag I fetched up for you.' She went back to the memorial and picked up a large shopping bag bringing it with her into the car.

After feeding Hope Elizabeth, Mary laid her on Blyth's bed and went to join everyone in the kitchen. Auntie Peg had made herself at home and was talking to Gran as if they had been neighbours all their lives.

Mary felt like an invalid with everyone darting her sympathetic glances and wanting to feed her up. At a quarter to two she and Albert went with Auntie Peg to the station.

'Left me address in the bag,' she said. 'When you're yourself again, drop us a line and bring the young maid down to stay where her Daddy was so happy.'

'I'm pleased to meet you, Auntie Peg,' Mary said, kissing the old woman's leathery cheek.

'See you in Whitstable,' she cried. 'Come in the summer.'

Afterwards she lay on Blyth's bed and slept the afternoon away. Gran brought her a cup of tea and they sat together saying nothing for a while just watching Hope Elizabeth, asleep in her arms. And then Mary asked her: 'What did you do to get over it when your Joseph died?'

'I felt like I'd been wounded, struck deep in the heart,' Granny said. 'I just had to do whatever came to me at the time. I cried and screamed and raged. Sometimes I hid myself away all day in bed, escaping in sleep. Other times I paced about the house all night. Gradually the poor fragile creature that was me – minute by minute, hour by hour, then miraculously day by day – began to take hold of her life. But I think what saved me was having my son's children to look after.'

Mary hugged her fiercely. 'S'pose I'm over the first worst bit,' she said. 'It's just keeping on going on.'

'That's about it, my duck. Now what are you going to do tonight? You're most welcome to stop with Albert and me or I dare say you could squeeze in here with your family.'

Mary shook her head. 'No, ta, Gran, I want to be back home in Gosport. I still feel Matthew all around me there, and old Dog will be going mental. Could Albert drop me back, please? I know I've got to go back on the ferry one day, but not just yet.'

'You've forgotten Peg's bag,' she said, when Mary stepped back into the car.

She smiled. 'I'll open that tomorrow. It'll give me something to do.'

40

Why he had decided to do something about Cissie today, Clive wasn't really sure, except that it was his birthday and she was the only present he wanted. Having fiddled and faddled about for so long he didn't know how to approach her. He sat there at the breakfast table picking at his food while his mother went through her usual birthday routine.

'It's a miracle I'm here. Forty hours of agony I had birthing you. Ungrateful, that's what you are.'

As soon as he had washed up he dressed carefully in his best suit and made his way to Keats's Row. March the sixth was a Sunday and also his day off. He should have been at the morning prayer meeting and could now expect a telling off from the Sergeant Major but first he must put things right with Cissie. Clive had been a Sherlock Holmes in his observation of her. Promptly at ten o' clock, as expected, she opened the door and set off for the Mission Hall to help with the Sunday school. He had rehearsed over and over what he would say to her, and yet the sight of Cissie paralysed him. He stood behind the tree and watched her walk right past him. Savagely he kicked a stone into the gutter as she disappeared from sight.

'What you doing skulking about, Clive Perks?'

He flushed at the sound of Dora Vine's voice as she crept up behind him and tapped his shoulder.

'Nothing really,' he muttered, feeling foolish.

'Well, then, you've got time to peel me a few spuds.' She stood in the doorway challenging him to refuse her.

Resignedly he went inside with her and took a knife in one hand and a muddy potato in the other. After washing off the earth he began to remove the skin.

'Blimey, Clive, I wants potatoes not bloomin' marbles,' Dora said, scornfully. 'Don't cut chunks off them, pare the skin in thin strips. 'What was you really doing?' Dora asked, as she sliced up a cabbage. 'Or what was you planning to do?'

He felt ridiculous. 'I was going to talk to Cissie.'

'What went wrong?' she asked.

He tossed some peel into the muddy water and splashed his shirt. 'I was gutless,' he said.

'Just about sums you up,' said Dora, staring at him as if he were a stale bun or a limp lettuce. 'What ya goin' to do about it?'

He shook his head in defeat.

'You and Ciss was such pals. Blossomed, she did, with you being friends with her and helpin' her to read. And it wasn't just her. You was so thrilled with her letter, I know you was, told me in the street that day just before you went up to see her.'

'I mucked it up,' he said, 'I didn't give her time to explain and then I left it and left it and . . .' His voice trailed away.

'Well you're just going to have to make up your mind,' she snapped; 'from where I'm standing Cissie's worth ten of you. She's brave and kind and forgiving and she is beautiful. What you got going for you?' she asked.

'Nothing,' he mumbled.

'Well,' she said, piling the cabbage into a colander, 'least you got the grace to know you was at fault. What was you gonna say to her if you'd got your courage up?' Dora snorted at his peeling skills. 'No, Clive, sit down and stop mucking me spuds about.'

'I would've told her I was wrong and was sorry.'

'D'you love her?'

'Yes,' he mumbled.

'Were you going to tell her that you love her?'

'Eventually,' he gasped.

'Clive Perks I could shake you,' said Dora, pulling up the chair opposite and glaring across the table at him. 'Eventually's not bloody good enough. People get hurt, people get old and they die while waiting for eventually. You know Mary Vine what married that Dusty Miller the submariner? She was Cissie's friend.'

Clive nodded.

'He died when the *L75* was sunk last year. D'you know the last thing he did before he sailed?'

'No,' mumbled Clive.

'He went back down the lane to tell her that he loved her. So, the last words he ever said and the ones she will always remember are those words. Only twenty-five, he was, and gone' – she snapped her fingers – 'quick as that.' Dora looked at him and smiled. 'You see, Clive, eventually ain't an atom of good. While you're working yourself up to it some other bloke will snap her up and you'll be left standing.'

'Hopeless,' he whispered.

'Clive,' she said, 'you had all the cards in your hand and you threw them away. Cissie loved you and your sin of searching and judging and bloomin' Bible bashin' made her feel ashamed. Good job I knows some good practical Sally Army folk or I'd write you all off as tambourine rattlin' hypocrites. And d'you know what makes me want to give you a good slapping?'

Clive squirmed. Whatever it was he had no escape. Dora was going to tell him come hell or high water.

'None of the things that happened to Cissie were any of your damned business. All forgotten and forgiven by your Jesus, I don't doubt, way before she ever met you. Needs to look at yer own shortcomings and see if you measures up to what Cissie deserves.'

'I better be going,' he said, pushing the chair back under the table.

'Yes, you better,' said Dora. 'Gotta lot to think about.'

Cissie walked back down Queen Street humming to herself one of the songs that Captain Kellet had played for the children. She laughed to herself. What a wild, scruffy bunch of nippers they were: so full of life and mischief. Then she burst out laughing when she remembered what one of them had said to Captain Kellet after she told them about the Crucifixion.

'The soldiers nailed our Saviour to the cross, driving in the nails with big wooden hammers.'

There had been a dramatic pause and then little Frankie Horrabin had leapt to his feet. 'The bastards,' he'd shouted out.

She and the Captain had been hard pressed to control their faces.

Soon it would be Easter and a whole year since she'd been back in Portsea. Cissie felt as if she were a different girl entirely to the one that sneaked back in Captain Clements' car. She had set such store on that little bedroom in Lancaster Terrace and now it was of no account to her. Even the thought of leaving Dora's little place in Keats's Row no longer frightened her. She was braver now and more willing to take a chance. She'd given up looking back and regretting things, it wasn't an atom of good.

As she passed down the little side roads towards home, she could smell the Sunday dinners cooking. The meat would be eked out with suet pudding and lots of potatoes and what was left of the suet would be served up for afters with golden syrup.

'Hello, Ciss,' said Dora, her face flushed from cooking. 'You timed it just right.'

They chatted away as they tucked in to the breast of lamb and vegetables. Cissied laughed. 'What d'ya do with them potatoes, Dora? Like bloomin' marbles.'

'Must've bin wool-gatherin,' she laughed, 'didn't have me mind on the job.'

Cissie sat in her usual row in the Citadel that evening listening to the visiting officer preach. He had none of the rousing words of those she had heard before but spoke gently of Christ searching out the lost sheep.

'How valuable that one small creature is to Our Lord, how far and wide He searches for that lost sheep. And, then what rejoicing when he or she is found.'

He was an old man, with hair combed in strands across his balding head, not remarkable in any way. But his eyes smiled at Cissie and his words seemed meant only for her.

'Come back to Jesus all you who are lost and you will find a home in Him. Brothers, sisters whatever has caused you to stray, set it before Him and He will welcome you back into the fold. I invite you to come to the Mercy Seat and receive God's forgiveness as you begin your new life.'

Everyone stood to sing the next hymn, 'Just as I am, without one plea'.

Approaching the Mercy Seat was a weekly feature of the service and Cissie had watched in wonder at the people coming out of their seats, some smiling, others crying, all compelled to make the journey. Above the long bench in front of the raised platform were the words 'come with your sin.'

Now she was on her feet and walking up towards the preacher, who was holding out his hands. But there ahead of her was Clive. There must be some mistake. Clive had been a Salvationist from childhood. What had he to be sorry for?

The preacher continued directing the service from the stage and when Cissie knelt down it was Captain Kellet who stood beside her.

'I'm sorry for everythink and I wants a fresh start,' she whispered.

'Welcome home,' she said.

Cissie went back to her seat in a haze of happiness. She felt as if she were floating high above the congregation. All the pain and sorrow of her time on the streets had rolled away. All Ted's deceiving meant nothing. She could even be grateful for the brief time she'd had with little Charlie – nothing was wasted, nothing was lost.

After the service Major Grice came and kissed her. 'Welcome Cissie,' she said. 'I don't know when I've been so pleased.'

'Cissie, wait, Cissie stop a minute.' It was Clive.

'Hello,' she said, 'thought you wasn't talking to me.' How she had wept at his silent condemnation and how she had missed their reading lessons.

'Things I must say to you,' he mumbled, red-faced with embarrassment. 'But you must hear me out now, while my courage is up.'

Cissie stood outside the citadel with people milling about and Mrs Perks glaring at her from the other side of the road.

'I've been a fool,' he said, 'and a sinner and a hypocrite and a coward.'

Cissie wanted to laugh. He was certainly making a thorough job of his repentance.

'I was wrong very wrong, and I want you to forgive me and I know I don't deserve it but I love you.'

'Can you say that last bit again?' she asked him enjoying the chance to tease poor sobersides Clive.

'What, about not deserving forgiveness?'

Cissie laughed. ''Course you don't, Clive Perks,' she said, 'but I might make an exception in your case if you says them last three words again to me.'

Clive blushed and gasped them out once more, 'Cissie, I love you.'

'Does it mean the lessons is on again?' she asked, smiling at him. What a silly, serious, lovable fellow he was.

'If you think I'm worthy,' he said.

'Don't think worthiness comes into it.' She smiled. 'I just wants the reading. Anything else'll have to come later.'

Charles Clements and Lavinia strolled along the seafront in the June sunshine. Miles and Lottie ran ahead with their new dog, a lollopy black spaniel called Bones. Charles was not unhappy with how his life was going, in fact he felt a measure of contentment. The house in Battenburg Avenue was solidly built and plenty big enough for the three of them. Once Lottie had wanted to come and live with him Miles was quick to follow. He was now a day boy at Portsmouth Grammar School and Lottie was at the High School in Kent Road. Her rabbit Muriel had taken up residence in the garden.

'Miles, Miles over 'ere,'

His son turned to see Blyth Vine cycling towards them.

Miles ran over to him. 'You got it going then?' he said.

'Yeah, it's a bit of a mongrel, made it out of two old ones,' Blyth laughed. 'Don't look too clever, but it don't 'arf go.'

'Hello, Blyth,' said Charles, smiling at the lad. 'Have you met Mrs Mowbray, my sister?'

'Pleased to meet ya,' he said, gripping Lavinia's white-gloved hand with an oily hand. 'Good day to you,' said his sister, coolly.

'Hello,' Lottie smiled at him, but was prevented from further conversation by Bones suddenly taking off in the

opposite direction. '
running after him.

'Chase him up on
Miles, we'll have him

'Is he anything to
asked Lavinia, scowli
she was.'

'She's his sister,' C
killed in that submar
cottage in Gosport wi

'Great Heavens,' L

They turned away f
along the promenade t
that Bones had taken.
sailors and holidaymak
where a preacher was
and listen.

Charles and his siste
from where the Salvatic
waving of tambourines

'Charles, isn't that the
your house in Lancaster
at Cissie's bedside in ho
believe it. Look over th
Army bonnet.'

'Great Scot,' he excla
must speak to her.'

'No need, she's comir

'Hello Captain Cleme
held out her hand.

'Well, this is a pleasan
hand. 'You look splendic

'Feels splendid,' she s
Working for the Lord, no

'I hope He's a
Cissie laughed

Charles nodde

'Is that you, M
from the sun. 'F
thank you for all
ungrateful but, b
harm done.' She
a collecting box
build the kingdo

Speechless fo
dropped a half-c

Charles laugh
is quite, quite w
hurtled up to hi

'Can we have
one for Blyth ar

'Of course yo
I shall have one

When his so
'To Cissie,' he

better employer than me,' he teased her.

'Seems ages and ages ago now, don't it?'

and Lavinia scowled.

s Mowbray?' asked Cissie shading her eyes

ver so pleased to see you. I wants ter say

what you did for me. Must've seemed very

e Major Grice said, I'm a city girl and no

hook Lavinia's hand vigorously then waved

n her face. 'Mustn't miss an opportunity to

n.'

once, his sister dipped into her purse and

rown into the box.

d out loud when Cissie had gone. 'I think she

onderful,' he said. The children and Bones

n.

n ice-cream, Daddy?' Lottie asked him. 'And

d Bones.'

u may. Lavinia, what about you? No? Well,

' he said. 'Miles, you go and get them.'

handed him a cornet he raised it in the air.

ried.

41

Mary lay with her eyes closed trying to keep hold of a dream in which Matthew was still alive. He was smiling at her in that lopsided way he had and she lay there with tears leaking under her lashes. She had thought grieving would be a gradual process where each day the hurt would get less but her feelings lurched up and down between despair and a bored sort of misery.

It was the seventh of March 3 months since her baby's birth. If it weren't for Hope Elizabeth and old Dog she knew she would have gone under. Granny was right, having a baby to care for had kept her going. Mary surprised herself at how much she loved her daughter. Day by day she delighted in the changes in her. She searched Hope's face for any resemblances to Matthew and was thrilled to find the sun had brought a crop of freckles across her nose and her hair although a mass of curls, was the same rusty colour as her father's.

There were so many decisions to make and she felt incapable of deciding anything. Her only certainty was that she was done with Lemon Street. The thought of all the rows between the twins and the stale slummocky disorder of everything was too much to bear. Besides, Betty Frewin had waded in and sorted them out and she was welcome to it. Mary could see that the woman was smitten with Dad and angling to get her slippers under his bed. Poor old Fred was hardly much of a catch, but they were both lonely and good luck to them.

From the cot beside her bed the baby stirred and began a sort of chirruping noise. Mary sat up and took her into bed and began to feed her.

'Morning my precious,' she said, and was rewarded by a smile. 'Your Uncle Blyth's coming to see us tonight,' she said, 'and he wants faggots and peas for tea.'

Hope studied her face for a while and then concentrated on feeding. Mary was relieved that her milk had not gone in the shock of Matthew's death. She enjoyed the warmth and intimacy of nursing her child and was in no rush to wean her. Even if she went back to the laundry next week, as she had half decided, she'd make some sort of arrangement so that neither she nor Hope Elizabeth would lose out on their special time together.

On the chair by the window was the bag Auntie Peg had brought from Whitstable. Inside was the large photograph album that had once belonged to Matthew's mother.

'This is the Miller Family album begun on the 31st of August 1900 to celebrate Peter Nathaniel's first month of life,' Elizabeth Miller had written.

And there within the pages was Matthew's family: his father, mother and brother Peter living, from what she could see, a happy country life. There was her husband lovingly photographed from when he was not much older than his own daughter, Hope Elizabeth, up until only a few years ago, when he was snapped in uniform with his mother. There was a whole life: ordered, comfortable and secure. A family that did things together, went to church, had picnics and were organised enough to stick their photographs in a book and write the dates neatly under each picture.

When first she had opened it Mary had not been able to focus on the pictures for tears.

What a shock her lot in Lemon Street must have been to him, she'd thought. Her face had burned when she remembered the disastrous Christmas of the collapsing table. Why, why had he loved her? But he had and his last words were 'I love you'. Had he known something was going to happen? Was that why he had run back to her to reassure her of his love? She had put the book away upstairs, she was not yet ready to cope with it. But Blyth had asked to see it one evening, and together they had worked their way through from cover to cover.

She had been surprised at what a little woman Elizabeth Miller was and how immaculate.

'He looks like his dad,' Blyth had said, 'and his brother Peter. See these after nineteen eighteen when her husband and Peter was gone, his Mum's not smiling half as much.'

'P'raps it's a good thing she died before Matthew or she'd have had no one left,' she had said, feeling a sudden sympathy for the mother-in-law she had never met.

'Look!' Blyth had cried excitedly, 'that's that Peg woman and look at the houseboat. Cor! I'd like to see that, and that bloke with the big wellies and jumper must be Uncle Fish.'

Mary had been drawn to the picture because Matthew was there, laughing and holding up a rubbery strip of seaweed.

'We could write to them and go and see them. They're relations, she's Hope's Auntie.'

'Maybe next year,' Mary had said and the album had been put away and the subject dropped.

Since the disaster, she had not been able to travel, even across to Portsea, on the ferry. Water terrified her. She could not even go down to the Ferry Gardens and wait for any of her visitors. Even when taking Hope Elizabeth out in her pram she would turn sharply away from the waterfront. It was there that the newsboy's shouting had snatched her life away. She remembered the day she and Matthew had got engaged and she had run past the newsboy as he yelled about the loss of the *M1*.

Hope Elizabeth wriggled away from her breast and Mary made herself get up and get the breakfast. She must have the place straight for her brother's visit. She felt easy with him unlike some friends who were too kind and careful with her. Blyth said what was on his mind.

'This place is a tip. You can see Matthew isn't here no more.'

She had been furious with him, but it had stirred her to try to keep things going.

'We best get you bathed and get those faggots for your Uncle Blyth.'

They were laughing together as Mary bathed her daughter by the fire, and it was a while before Mary heard the impatient rapping on the door. She caught the baby up in a towel and hurried to open it.

'Thank God you're here,' Daisy gasped. 'Had a message from Mister Pragnell. Your Gran's took sick. Real bad she is and calling for ya.'

No, not Gran, she couldn't bear it. 'What'll I do?' she said, handing the baby to Daisy. 'I'm half dressed and I haven't got the money for the bus all the way round through Fareham.'

'I'm down to me last sixpence, too,' Daisy said. 'You'll just have to go over on the ferry. I'll look after babes here. Just get yerself over there.'

'I can't,' she said. 'I can't get on there, you know I can't.'

Daisy glared at her. 'I never took you for a selfish bitch, but you takes the biscuit.'

'But Daisy,' she protested, beginning to cry.

'But Daisy nothing. Who come over when your chap

died without even waiting to be asked? D'you wanna be too late?'

'I'll be back for her next feed or I'll send someone to fetch you.' She tried one last appeal. 'Couldn't you come with me?' she pleaded.

'I'll be more use over here getting this place straight. ''Sides if she's real bad you won't want a baby cluttering up the place.'

Mary dragged on her clothes and rushed to the ticket office, crying as she ran. She stood chewing her hand, her stomach lurching in fright. There was a press of passengers rushing down to the pontoon and the waiting ferry. She hid herself among them so that she was carried, unthinking, aboard. Mary faced away from the sea, her heart pounding. The engines churned and she was wedged between several women with shopping bags clutched tightly in their hands. Having steeled her courage to get on she was now at the most perilous part halfway across. 'Don't let me die, don't let me die,' Mary prayed. She must stay alive for Hope Elizabeth. She must conquer this. The engines slowed and the passengers prepared to leave. With a bump the ferry nudged against the jetty, the ropes were thrown and the crowd swarmed up the wooden pontoon, Mary included.

She ran all the way to Lemon Street and knocked on Gran's door with her heart thumping and a painful stitch in her side.

The door opened and there she stood, looking the picture of health, her cheeks flushed and arms open wide.

'You did it, Mary,' she cried. 'I knew you would.'

'Thought you was sick.' Mary gasped, beginning to feel her temper rising. 'I've left my baby half dressed and come over here on the ferry and . . .'

Gran was laughing. What the hell was going on?

'I was sick,' she said, 'sick of you funking it. Daisy and I cooked up this scheme and it's worked handsomely. And, now, my lady, you've mastered your fear and here you are just in time for a cup of tea and some fresh baked tarts.'

'I don't know what to say,' Mary said, feeling like a pricked balloon.

'Just get yourself sat down and I'll call yer dad, he'll be thrilled to see you.'

Mary sat down and caught her breath. Slowly the stitch eased away. Ooh! she could throttle Gran, frightening her like that, and Daisy. And then she began to laugh; good old Gran, what would she do without her? Yes, she had done it, frightened or not. Matthew would be proud of her.

'Hello, my gal,' said Dad, 'lovely to see you. You're looking bonny, got some roses in yer cheeks.'

'That's all down to this wicked woman here' she said, winking at Gran.

'I'm touched,' she said, patting her hand, 'that you would come over here to see me, fear or no fear, when you thought I was in need.'

''Course I did,' said Mary, beginning to feel proud of herself, 'it was the least I could do.'

The three of them sat laughing and talking and making short work of the plate of jam tarts.

Mary smiled at Dad. He looked better and more rested than she had seen him in ages. Well, that was one less thing to worry about.

'Got a letter for you from Danny Sullivan, wants you to make yer mind up about the market. Says he's bin waiting long enough.'

Mary took the letter out of the crumpled brown envelope and smoothed it flat on her lap. 'Let's see what he's got to say for himself,' she said.

Dear Mary,

Sorry about your chap being took at sea. It must be a sad old time for you.

I needs to know what you wants done with the stall, only I'm getting wed and need to straighten out my affairs.

Please let your Dad know what you decides. If you're selling I'll give you a fair price. My missis to be is a granddaughter of big Fred the butcher and knows the market trade like the back of her hand.

Regards

Danny.

Mary read the letter to Fred and Gran and they all chuckled at the thought of him 'straightening out his affairs.' 'What d'you reckon, Dad? Unless you wants it, I'm all for selling up. It served us well, but things are different now.'

'That's taken a load off me mind,' Dad said. 'We'll rub along all right. We always have. The twinnies is back at the brewery and I've got meself a quiet little number at the Captain Hardy, washing glasses of a Sunday. Betty found it for me. Her brother's the landlord.'

'This Betty seems to have you all well under control,' Mary teased.

Dad winked and put his finger to his nose. 'I'm saying nothin'. I leave the gossip to you two.' He got to his feet. 'I'll nip down and see Danny and see what he's offering. See you soon, love, good to see you over this side.'

When he had gone back over the wall, Gran poured her another cup of tea. 'You're looking better,' she said. 'Beginning to pick up the reins again by the looks of it.'

Mary smiled at her. 'Yes, I'm going back to the laundry next week. Vi Kendall's going to look after Hope along with her Peter. It'll give her a few bob. She's a good motherly sort and I need to be busy.'

'You're a star, Mary,' Gran said, giving her a hug. 'You just needed a shove in the right direction. It's a bumpy road you travel being a widow but I reckon you're over the worst. You've a lovely baby and she's got a mum to be proud of. Now, off you go, that Hope Elizabeth will be squawking for her dinner.'

''Bye, Gran,' said Mary, kissing her on the cheek, 'and don't give me no more frights.'

Standing on the pontoon waiting for the ferry back to Gosport she knew she was going home. It was where she and Matthew had been so happy together. It was where somehow she would be happy again.

Impatiently she waited for the engines to slow and the familiar bump as the boat hit the jetty. Then she rushed up to the Ferry Gardens where Daisy and Dog and Hope Elizabeth were waiting for her. Her baby chuckled and held out her arms to be picked up.

Mary laughed – she could never get enough of that gladness.